D0560087

# THE
# ISLES
## OF THE
# G◆DS

## ALSO BY AMIE KAUFMAN

The Starbound Trilogy
(with Meagan Spooner)

The Unearthed Duology
(with Meagan Spooner)

The Other Side of the Sky Duology
(with Meagan Spooner)

The Elementals Trilogy (for children)

The World Between Blinks Duology
(with Ryan Graudin, for children)

## ALSO BY AMIE KAUFMAN
## AND JAY KRISTOFF

*Aurora Rising* (Aurora Cycle_01)

*Aurora Burning* (Aurora Cycle_02)

*Aurora's End* (Aurora Cycle_03)

*Illuminae* (The Illuminae Files_01)

*Gemina* (The Illuminae Files_02)

*Obsidio* (The Illuminae Files_03)

*Memento* (The Illuminae Files_0.5)

# THE
# ISLES
## OF THE
# GODS

AMIE KAUFMAN

ALFRED A. KNOPF
NEW YORK

THIS IS A BORZOI BOOK PUBLISHED BY ALFRED A. KNOPF

This is a work of fiction. Names, characters, places, and incidents either are the product of the author's imagination or are used fictitiously. Any resemblance to actual persons, living or dead, events, or locales is entirely coincidental.

Text copyright © 2023 by LaRoux Industries Pty Ltd.
Jacket art copyright © 2023 by Aykut Aydoğdu
Map art copyright © 2023 by Virginia Allyn

All rights reserved. Published in the United States by Alfred A. Knopf, an imprint of Random House Children's Books, a division of Penguin Random House LLC, New York.

Knopf, Borzoi Books, and the colophon are registered trademarks of Penguin Random House LLC.

Visit us on the Web! GetUnderlined.com

Educators and librarians, for a variety of teaching tools, visit us at RHTeachersLibrarians.com

*Library of Congress Cataloging-in-Publication Data*
Names: Kaufman, Amie, author.
Title: The Isles of the Gods / Amie Kaufman.
Description: First edition. | New York : Alfred A. Knopf, [2023] | Series: The Isles of the Gods ; 1 | Audience: Ages 12 and up. | Summary: Selly's plans to follow her father to the north seas are dashed when a handsome stranger with tell-tale magician's marks on his arm boards her ship and presents her with a dangerous mission—to sail to the Isles of the Gods so he can complete a mysterious ritual.
Identifiers: LCCN 2022022287 (print) | LCCN 2022022288 (ebook) | ISBN 978-0-593-47928-5 (hardcover) | ISBN 978-0-593-47929-2 (library binding) | ISBN 978-0-593-47930-8 (ebook) | ISBN 978-0-593-70539-1 (intl. pbk.)
Subjects: LCSH: Magic—Juvenile fiction. | Secrecy—Juvenile fiction. | Sailors—Juvenile fiction. | Adventure stories. | CYAC: Magic—Fiction. | Secrets—Fiction. | Sailors—Fiction. | Interpersonal relations—Fiction. | Adventure and adventurers—Fiction. | Fantasy. | LCGFT: Fantasy fiction. | Action and adventure fiction.
Classification: LCC PZ7.K1642 Is 2023 (print) | LCC PZ7.K1642 (ebook) | DDC 823.92 [Fic]—dc23/eng/20220809

The text of this book is set in 11-point Calisto MT.
Interior design by Ken Crossland

Printed in the United States of America
10 9 8 7 6 5 4 3 2 1
First Edition

Random House Children's Books supports the First Amendment and celebrates the right to read.

Penguin Random House LLC supports copyright. Copyright fuels creativity, encourages diverse voices, promotes free speech, and creates a vibrant culture. Thank you for buying an authorized edition of this book and for complying with copyright laws by not reproducing, scanning, or distributing any part in any form without permission. You are supporting writers and allowing Penguin Random House to publish books for every reader.

For Eliza, Ellie, Kate, Lili, Liz, Nicole, Pete, and Skye

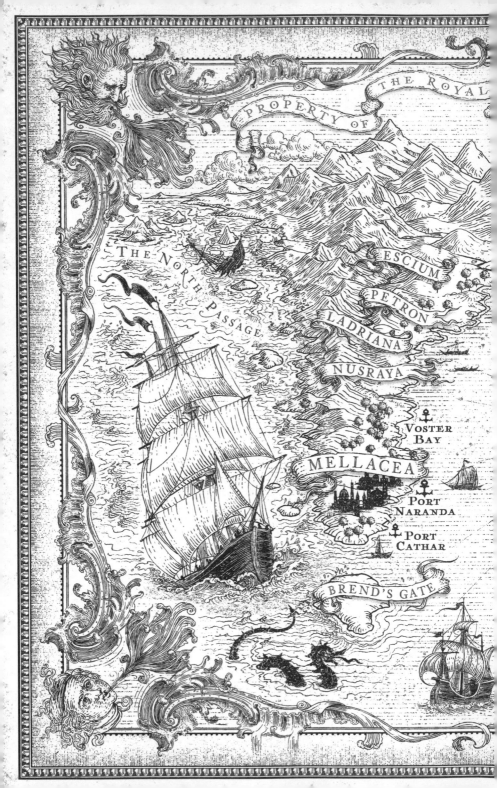

HOUSE OF ALINOR

TRALLIA

THE BARREN REACHES

Bibliotek

BEINHOF

FONTESQUE

LOFORTA

THE CRESCENT SEA

CASPIA

ALINOR

KIRKPOOL

KETHOS

The Isle
of the
Mother

The
ISLES
of the
GODS

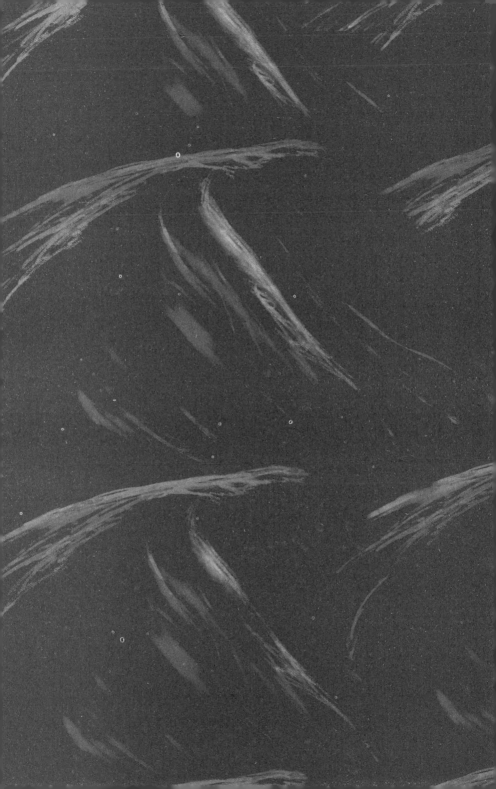

Five hundred and one years ago . . .

"It's not that I thought I'd live forever. I just didn't expect this kind of advance notice about when I was going to die."

"Seven hells, Anselm," mutters Galen, breaking off a piece of the hardtack the sailors gave us, then crushing it between his fingers. We watch the crumbs land on the mossy ground at our feet.

It feels strange for him to be doing something as mundane as eating, in a sacred place like this. Then again, maybe we've earned the right to do whatever we want.

The two of us are sitting outside the temple itself, the worn black stone at our backs. The clearing is hemmed in by jungle, thick and lush and as vibrantly green as the magician's marks that snake up my forearms. It's much warmer and wetter than our open fields at home.

We left the ship anchored down in the cove, and my best friend climbed to the peak of the island with me.

I wanted to see where it's going to happen tomorrow.

Barrica came too, though she didn't say why. Our goddess

stands on the far side of the glade, gazing at the sparkling blue sea below. She's a full head taller than me, and I'm the tallest man I know. The gods are built on a different scale. Larger than us, infinitely more beautiful, in that way you can't quite picture unless they're right in front of you.

I used to have trouble concentrating around her, her presence scattering my thoughts, but over the course of the war I've had a lot of practice in her company.

She stands like a statue, beautiful even in her sadness. I know she wishes with all her heart that she didn't have to ask this of me. Here we are, though. There's no other way. Not after what happened to Valus, and to Vostain.

I glance across at my friend next. Before all this, his priest's robes were plain, simply cut in Alinorish blue—but at some point during the war, our clergy shifted to wearing something close to a soldier's uniform, in deference to our warrior goddess.

His is open at the neck, unbuttoned as usual. He always had some part of his clothing askew when we were children, and that hasn't changed.

He's so familiar. His presence is a comfort.

*How did we two little boys ever grow up and find ourselves here?*

"I'm scared, Galen," I murmur.

"I know, my king." He lets out a slow breath. "Me too."

We're both silent for a time, the sun dropping lower in the sky through the tangle of green leaves. We didn't bring a lantern—we'll have to start our descent soon.

I'm the one who breaks the quiet eventually. "When we were young, and the priests told us tales about the heroes of old, they always seemed so noble. None of them were scared, or angry, or uncertain."

"They always seemed cleaner, too," Galen muses, glancing down at himself. "Smelled better."

I snort. "I used to wonder what they were thinking. Now we know, I suppose. When you tell those stories, make me a real person, all right?"

"I promise."

It's strange to imagine a future without me. It's strange to imagine tomorrow night without me, come to that. My sister will make a fine queen. I wish I could have seen it. But there's so much I'll miss.

One day soon, the cooks back in Kirkpool will make another batch of my favorite pastries, bursting with berries that stain your fingers pink. Everyone else will enjoy them, and I . . . won't be there.

Will they think of me?

"Oh, another thing," I say, picking up our conversation of the last few days. "There's a pair of blackbirds that make a nest outside my bedroom window every year. I don't want to insult them, but to be honest, they're not that bright. I usually lay out some kind of fluff along the windowsill so they've got something to line the nest with."

"I'll see to it," Galen says quietly, closing his eyes. I've been doing this ever since we boarded the ship, thinking of little jobs I'll need someone to take care of when I'm gone. He never hushes me, never tells me someone else will figure it out. He just takes note and makes that same promise.

"Galen, how did we get here?" I whisper, voicing the question that keeps presenting itself over and over.

He silently offers me a piece of his hardtack as he considers his reply. It's just flour and water and a little salt, baked until it's tough enough to break your teeth. It's sailors' food, and soldiers' food, and we've become both. But my interest in food has been waning, as if my body knows I'm not going to need it.

"Well, in the beginning there was the Mother," he replies, singsong, threatening to tell the whole story, trying to lighten the mood.

When he pauses, though, I pull in my knees and rest my chin on them. "Go on."

He blinks and glances at me, brows raised.

"I think I'd like to hear you speak the words one more time," I say quietly, closing my eyes to focus on his voice.

He softens, slipping effortlessly into the old tale. "The Mother made the world and watched it grow. The most annoying—but luckily for us, also the most entertaining—of her creatures began to demand more and more attention. So she did what all good leaders do."

"She delegated the problem."

"That she did. She created seven children: Barrica and Macean, the two eldest, born together and always jostling for leadership. Then Dylo, Kyion, Sutista, Oldite, and finally . . ." His voice catches, and then he pushes on. "And Valus, her youngest, always laughing."

I can still hear Valus's screams, some nights.

"Go on," I say quietly.

"They each took on the tribes that would become countries, and busied themselves with answering prayers, blessing crops, healing ills. All the usual godly business. It kept them out of trouble—for a while, anyway."

"But the gods spent too much time around us, and picked

up bad habits," I chime in, where ordinarily the children gathered around my friend would be calling out to show off how well they remember. He has a flicker of a smile for that.

"One way or another, they learned how to covet," he agrees, his words dying out. Now he's telling the story of our lives, and there are no old words to recite—there's no well-trodden path to follow to the end of the story.

It wasn't enough for Macean's people to come down from the mountains and carve him a new land by the sea. Barrica grew tired of her country's rolling green hills. Oldite was bored with her deep forests, Kyion with the high cliffs and rich soil of their kingdom, and Dylo with the azure waters of hers. Each of them had their own complaints.

It began as jostling and ended in a war.

As Valus was the god of merriment and tricks, so Macean is the god of risk, the Gambler—and take his risk he did, his armies reaching out to claim the lands of his siblings.

Our goddess, Barrica, is the Warrior, and we became her soldiers.

But for all the fighting and bleeding and dying we were capable of on our own, nothing we could do compared to the destruction the gods could bring to the battlefield.

I'm a royal magician—I command not one element but all four. I was like a child with my toys alongside my goddess and her siblings.

Armadas were destroyed, ships sent skipping across the sea like stones across a pond.

Armies died in fire.

And Macean's forces threatened to overtake Vostain, the

lands of his laughing, smiling youngest brother, Valus. His sister Barrica met him head-on in Vostain's defense, and . . .

And I will never forget that day.

The shock of their clash laid waste to the whole of Vostain, and every one of us heard Valus's screams as his lands were reduced to what we've already begun to call the Barren Reaches.

It feels like a lifetime ago.

It's only been a month.

Barrica held Valus in her arms, and she sent for me, the leader of her people. And we spoke. And slowly I saw what I had to do.

"I wish you'd come when we visited Vostain a few years ago," I say, startling Galen out of his thoughts. "I wish you'd had a chance to see it. I keep thinking of the people there."

"Who do you remember?" he asks. He likes to laugh, Galen—he would have made a beautiful priest of Valus had he been born somewhere, some*when* else—but he never shies away from what hurts. That's why he's here now, at my side when I need him most.

"The queen's cook made this fruitcake, and it had *something* in it—I could never figure out what, and I sent half a dozen different servants to bribe it out of her. I went down to the kitchens myself, but even my charm failed."

"Surely you jest," he snickers. "Who ever said no to you?"

"Well, today of all days, I confess it did happen once. Twice, if you count Lady Kerlion when we were fourteen."

"Who else did you meet?"

"There was a guard outside my quarters," I murmur. "He lent me his cloak so I could sneak out into the city, and I gave him wise advice on wooing his sweetheart. I hope he used it."

"I hope he did."

"I liked Queen Mirisal," I say quietly, glancing across at where Barrica still stands motionless. "She used to laugh with Valus—they teased each other endlessly. I wondered at the time if he made her so carefree, and Barrica made me a soldier, or if we just happened to be suited to our roles."

"I did not make you a warrior, Anselm."

I'm never able to describe Barrica's voice when I'm not in her presence. Sometimes I think it's musical, other times like a chorus speaking together. But neither of us is particularly surprised when she turns toward us and crosses the clearing. She can hear us whenever she wants. She only looks—sort of—like one of us. That doesn't mean she's like us.

Galen's never quite gotten accustomed to being in her presence, and he drops his gaze now, though I look up into the face of the goddess we both serve.

"No?"

"I am the frame upon which the vine may grow."

"Meaning you provided direction?"

"Yes. But there were many paths you might have taken."

She sinks to sit cross-legged before us, impossibly graceful. She moves like a predator, but I've never felt unsafe around her. My faith—the faith of all her people—is what strengthens her.

That's what tomorrow is about.

My sacrifice will strengthen my goddess, and she'll bind her brother Macean in sleep so he can never make war again. And then she and her other siblings will step back from our world, and no longer walk among us.

Barrica the Warrior will become the Sentinel. She'll leave

the door ajar and watch over her brother as he sleeps, to make sure he stays where he was bound. Make sure the god of risk's final gamble has truly failed. Perhaps sometimes she'll answer a prayer, or bless her people, but these times of easy conversation will be gone forever.

"FOREVER IS A LONG TIME, ANSELM," Barrica says, interrupting my thoughts. She's always been able to pull them from my mind, but it's never bothered me. I give her my faith, and she gives me a solid place to stand.

I can't imagine what it will be like for all of them when she's gone, but few know her as I do. They won't miss her as I would.

"True enough, Goddess."

"AND PERHAPS TOMORROW WILL NOT BE AS YOU IMAGINE."

I cast her a pleading look, and she drops the subject, inclining her head as she rises. She stands before me, as beautiful as ever. I've never been able to remember what color her eyes are when I look away, but now I see they're as blue as the sea around us.

She offers me her hand, and a shiver of her power runs through me as she pulls me to my feet.

Slowly, the three of us begin to pick our way down the jungle path to where the ship is moored, for our last meal. I doubt I'll sleep tonight, but it will be good to watch the stars. The skies are clear, here in the Isles.

I really hope Galen remembers to look after the blackbirds. They need someone to keep an eye on them.

Five hundred and *one* years later . . .

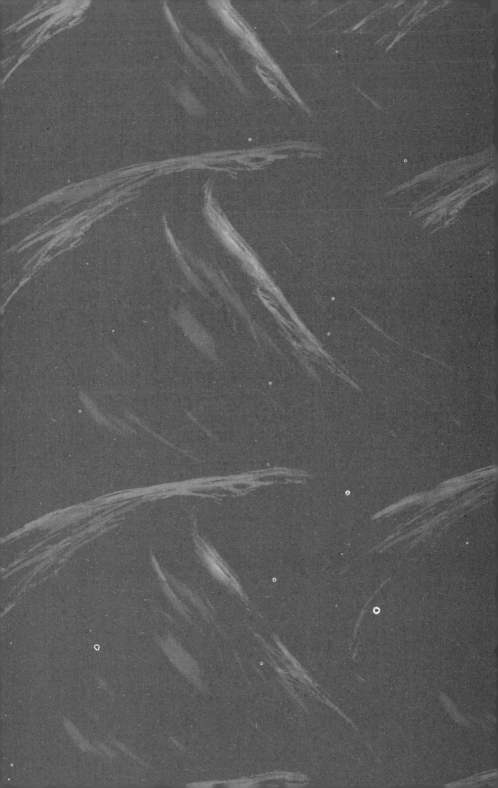

# PART ONE

## GLITTER AND GRIT

# SELLY

*Royal Hill*
*Kirkpool, Alinor*

The woman selling magicians' supplies is wandering around her little market stall like she's lost her map. It's as if every item she encounters, from the stacks of fat green candles to the bins of bright glass beads and stones, is somehow a new discovery.

"You said half a dozen candles?" She pauses to look over her shoulder and needlessly tighten her apron strings. She's dragging things out in the hope something extra will catch my eye, but although the grim, anxious buzz of the city has sunk into my bones, I am not going to lose my temper. I don't have time.

"Yes, please." I try to make my gritted teeth look like a smile, though I can tell from the woman's expression it doesn't work. But honestly, at this rate I should ask her name and how she likes her tea, because the two of us are going to grow old together.

If anything, she seems to slow down even more, lifting a newspaper and studying the crate beneath it. "Best in the city, these ones. Poured at the high temple, you know. Are they for you, young lady?"

My hands tighten into fists in my fingerless leather gloves, but I glance down anyway, automatically checking that they hide the green magician's marks on the backs of my hands. "They're for our first mate. Ship's magician." The words barely provoke their old, familiar ache. I've got other things on my mind today.

"Oh, indeed!" That catches the woman's attention, and *spirits save me,* now she stops altogether to study me with interest. "I should have seen you were a saltblood—look at those clothes. Where have you come from?"

Her gaze flickers back to the newspaper in her hand, and suddenly I see it: She's not vague. She's worried.

The questions have been the same at every stall I've been to so far today. There are strange shortages, and prices are shifting, and whispers are winding their way through the marketplace about new taxes and confiscations. About war.

When they see my sailor's clothes—the shirt, trousers, and boots setting me apart from the city girls in their tailored dresses—everybody asks where we've come from and what it was like there.

"We're just on a quick run down from Trallia," I tell the woman, digging into my pocket for a few crowns. "I'm actually in kind of a hurry. I need to get to the harbormaster's office before it closes, or my captain won't be happy."

Somewhere, Captain Rensa probably just lifted her head and sniffed the wind, smelling my lies from the deck of the *Lizabetta,* but the shopkeeper gives herself a shake, as if she's waking up.

"And here I am chatting away at you. We'd better—what

do you young people say? Something to do with autos." She finds a smile as she remembers, though now I can see the strain in it: "We'd better put our foot on the gas."

A minute later my candles are wrapped up and I'm on my way.

I leave behind the rough flapping of the spirit flags and the crowded market stalls at the top of Royal Hill, letting my momentum hurry me along as I jog past the magnificent façade of the temple to Barrica, my spirits lifting as I gather speed.

The priests and priestesses are out front in their soldiers' uniforms, brass gleaming as they call the faithful to the afternoon service, to prayers for peace. The stone steps of the temple aren't crowded with worshippers, though, and a sign pinned up by the entrance announces the meeting space next door will be hosting a dance-hall party tonight, with a live band. I didn't realize attendance was down *that* badly.

I drop a copper for the goddess into the offering bowl as I hurry by—we sailors always keep up our courtesies—and push on without catching the nearest priest's eye. *No time today, my friend.*

My captain gave me a long list of errands and not nearly enough time to complete them—her way of keeping me away from the harbormaster's office.

"You've been loitering there every day since we docked," she snapped this morning. "Today you can do some work for a change."

*For a change, Rensa? That's rich.*

For a year I've run every goddess-blessed errand my captain could dream up, working every inch of my own ship, from the bilges to the bowsprit. And finally it's over. It has to be—spirits save me if I have to spend one more moment under my tyrant of a captain. This *has* to be my last day.

Today at the harbormaster's office I'm going to see the news I've been waiting for up in chalk. The alternative is unbearable.

I cut through a narrow alleyway where the buildings crowd close together, the upper levels leaning in over the street, flowers spilling from their window boxes. Someone's playing a radio on the second floor, and I can hear the stern tones of a newscaster, but I can't make out her words.

Turning onto Queen's Boulevard, I pause as a brewer's wagon rumbles downhill, then lean out to inspect the approaching traffic, which comes in a constant stream. The city of Kirkpool wraps around the seaward side of a series of hills, golden sandstone buildings folded into the valleys between them. From the water you can see Queen's Boulevard running from the port at the base of Royal Hill all the way up to the palace at the top, straight as a mainmast rising from a deck.

Streets branch off it like spars, each home to clusters of shops and stalls—tailors, bakers, merchants hawking spices from far away. People from all over the world live and trade in Kirkpool, and the casual mix of cultures feels more like home than any other port.

A merchant's carriage rolls by, and without hesitating I grab the back railings and swing myself up like a footman for the bumpy ride downhill. I catch a glimpse of the merchant's eyes in the rearview mirror as she notices the change in weight and tries to shake me loose as we rattle across the cobblestones—but I'm used to a deck heaving beneath my feet, and I bend my knees and keep my place.

As we roll past the bakers' street, I'm hit with a gust of hot air and a memory just as strong. I used to come here with my da when I was small, every time we made port in Kirkpool. I'd take in the crowd from a perch on his shoulders, pretending I was up in the crow's nest, and he'd buy me a sticky bun.

They roll the dough up into a coil, a sugared glaze painted on top, mixed with spices that always stir up hazy memories of a voyage south when I was smaller still—small enough that my wobbly steps perfectly matched the rolling deck of the *Lizabetta*. I was steady on my feet at sea long before I ever was on land.

We round another corner, giving me a quick view of the water at the base of Royal Hill. My thoughts jump to the harbormaster's office again, and the message that *has* to be waiting for me. And from there my gaze slides to where my gloved hands grip tight to the carriage. I can't help imagining the leather gone, the unformed green marks on my skin uncovered. I grit my teeth and shove that thought aside.

It doesn't matter. He's coming. But we used to be simpler together, Da and I.

I bend my knees and brace as we wheel out to overtake a slower-moving cart, but up ahead the horses whinny a protest, and someone cries out, and that's my instant's warning before the carriage slews to a sudden halt, the wheels skidding sideways. My grip on the handles comes loose, and I feel myself start to tip—for one horrible second I'm suspended in midair, arms windmilling, then I hit the ground, pain shooting through my body. Hurriedly I push up to my hands and knees, scrambling for the gutter before another carriage sails through to flatten me.

"Never seen a sailor fly before," calls a woman leaning out her window, drawing laughter from most folks nearby. With my fair skin I know I give her a decent blush, and I scowl as I brush the dirt off my clothes.

Now I can see for myself what's causing the delay. A long line of sleek black autos snakes down the hill to the docks, crawling toward the water like a becalmed fleet—which is to say barely at all—because a horse and cart are plodding along in front of *them,* holding everything up.

"Who in seven hells is that?" I call up to the woman at the window, already half sure I know the answer.

"Prince Leander." She props her chin on her hand and stares dreamily at the autos, as if she can see straight through their tinted windows and admire the prince himself. "You'd think someone would move the horse out of his way."

"The horse?" I tilt a glance up toward her, raising an eyebrow. "The horse is the only one I can see doing an honest day's work. What exactly is His Highness contributing to society?"

She ignores me after that.

They say the prince throws parties all night and sleeps until lunch. That his wardrobe is the size of an apartment all by itself. That his private secretary sends out notes written on a gold-plated typewriter, declining the offers of marriage that arrive every day.

Everyone else hears the stories, and they say, *I want that.* All I can think is, *What's the point?*

I cut through a side street, pushing past rows of tailors and their rolls of fabrics from distant ports, until I can find a parallel way down Royal Hill toward the docks. Rensa will be expecting me back by now, and there'll be seven hells to pay if she figures out I disobeyed her orders.

The harbormaster's office is a tall, wide building in the

middle of the docks. On the upper floor is the office itself, with lookouts perched at telescopes, watching the mouth of the harbor. When they spot a ship arriving, they run downstairs to the giant chalkboards and record her arrival. But it's the lower level I want today.

It smells like sailors inside—cotton and canvas, salt and a faint hint of musty mildew—and usually I'd relax as I leave the city behind and return to my world. But I've been in here the last three days, ever since we made port, and every time, I've left wound still more tight.

"Looking for the *Fortune,* Selly?" It's Tarrant from the *Goddess Blessed,* another of my father's ships. His smile flashes against his dark brown skin as he holds up a finger. "No, wait! Seeking your *Fortune!* I knew there was a joke in there somewhere. She's cutting it fine, don't you think?"

"She'll be here," I say, clapping him on the shoulder as I push past to get closer to the boards. Then I remember and swing around. "Tarrant!"

He glances back, already heading for the door.

"You didn't see me here." I try to keep the plea out of my voice.

He winces. "Captain on your tail again?"

"When is she not?"

"Too crowded to see anyone, especially one scrawny little deckhand, all freckles anyway," he promises, and winks as he ducks away.

I return to pushing my way through the crowd toward the chalkboards.

My father has been away on the *Fortune* for a year now, and Tarrant's right—he *is* cutting it fine. He's been up north scouting new trading routes for the fleet, and these are the very last days of his return window. Soon the North Passage will be closed by winter storms and the deadly chunks of ice that come with them.

He left me with Rensa for the year when he went north. At first I thought it was disappointment that drove him to leave me behind, but the night before he left, he said otherwise.

"By the time I'm back, you'll be ready for a first mate's knot, my girl. It'll be a fresh start."

And that's what we need. After years of waiting for me to make something of my magic, we both need to accept I'll prove my worth as an ordinary sailor instead. We need to finally put the long years of my humiliating failures behind us and turn our minds to what I *can* do.

Except Rensa has taught me nothing—she's done nothing to prepare me for a mate's duties. Instead, I've spent my days in every dead-end job the ship has to offer, scrubbing and sewing and standing watch.

Sometime in the next few days, Da will ask me what I learned, and what can I possibly say? On the *Fortune* I'd have been with him at the wheel. On the *Lizabetta*—which was my home growing up and is the ship I mean to command myself one day—I've been treated like a new recruit.

Right now, though, I don't care. All I want is to see him. I've checked the boards religiously since we've arrived, every time certain I'm going to see the *Fortune*'s name up in chalk, and every day I've been disappointed.

I'm positive Rensa's going to keep me trapped aboard tomorrow, and the day after that we'll cast off, and I'll have missed Da altogether.

There are three boards fixed up on the wall, each covered in neat handwriting. Bare electric bulbs hang above them, one flickering on and off, like every moment might be its last—honestly, the windows are of more use when it comes to light to read by.

One board lists the ships that have departed today, another the arrivals, and the third ships that have been sighted—reports from other vessels newly docked, able to pass on word of who's on their way and how far out they might be.

The departures board is crammed full of ships ready to set sail for Trallia, for Fontesque, Beinhof, or the principalities—or even to make the now-risky run to Mellacea, despite the brewing war—with notes beside them to indicate whether they're taking passengers or looking for crew. There's a single ship heading to Holbard: the *Freya,* chancing the trip back north before the ice claims the passage.

I scan the arrivals board, my gut knotting tight as I reach the bottom with no sign of the *Fortune.* I push on to the sightings, running my gaze impatiently down the neatly chalked-up names. *Please, Da. Please.*

He's cutting it *so* fine, but he can handle it. No captain can run the North Passage better than Stanton Walker.

And he promised. It's been a year.

I read the board, then read it again, blinking, and then *again,* my heart slowly curling up inside my chest. There has to be at least a sighting. There *has* to be.

For the first time a new fear is prickling at the back of my mind. Could the winter storms have set in early? My father can sail a ship through anything, but there's a reason nobody braves the straits when the cold comes. They say there are waves halfway up the mast.

"Selly! Selly Walker! Over here, girl!" Someone's calling my name above the chatter of sailors, and I twist around to get my bearings. The voice is familiar, and I catch sight of a clerk working at the bank of counters down one side of the room. She's pointing at the mail wall, and I turn to set a course through the crowd, shoving now with a new urgency, shouldering past sailors who've stopped to greet old friends and exchange news. Everyone has something to say, with foreign ports changing their mood every day right now, but my eyes are fixed on my destination.

The mail wall is where sailors pin up letters we carry back for other ships. Ducking under a chatty bosun's arm, I find myself face to face with the board. I see the letter straightaway, and it's like my body knows before my brain does.

The air goes out of my lungs, and there's a sudden ache behind my eyes as I reach up to pull it from the pin jammed through it. There's another beside it, addressed to Captain Rensa of the *Lizabetta,* and like mine, it's far too thick to be a quick note telling us when to expect him in Kirkpool.

This isn't an arrival date. It's an excuse.

The crowd jostles me, squashing me in against a wall as I pull the letter open with shaking hands, nearly dropping the sheaf of paper inside. I unfold it, still hoping that somehow it's going to say—

*Dear Selly,*
    *I know this isn't the letter you were hoping for, but—*

*But*. My breath comes short and sharp as I scan the letter's contents.

*But* there's a fortune to be made up here.

*But* this will buy us another ship, perhaps one you'll like even better than the *Lizabetta.*

*But* there are some talented magicians here, and I can't pass up the chance to recruit them.

*But* I have to winter here, keep trading, keep working.

*But* it'll be another half a year before I'm home.

*But* I rest easy, knowing Rensa will teach you more than anyone, and Kyri is a talented ship's magician, so perhaps . . .

I crumple the letter in one fist and shove it into the bag with the candles, then grab Rensa's and cram it in as well.

This can't be happening.

Clenching my jaw so hard it hurts, I press a forearm over my mouth to muffle my scream of frustration. Suddenly the crowd around me is too loud, too close, and I'm searching frantically for a gap I can push through, a way to get out into the fresh air and sea breeze once more.

But then my gaze lands on the departures board, and I see it with new eyes.

The *Freya* is leaving on the dawn tide, the very last ship to slip up north until spring. And that means I have one more chance to fix this.

If Da won't come to me, I'll go to him.

One way or another, I'll be on board when the *Freya* departs.


I stumble out into the afternoon light, my pulse still drumming at my temples. The board says the *Freya* is across on the northern docks, and I duck and weave in that direction.

Kirkpool is one of the great harbor cities of the world and

Alinor's capital city—home port to my father's trading fleet. Her docks form a semicircle around her natural harbor, its mouth opening to the Crescent Sea to the west.

My *Lizabetta* is moored on the southern docks, so nobody will spot me making this visit, not all the way across the water.

The *Freya*'s captain won't say no to Stanton Walker's daughter, and getting their agreement instead of stowing away will make for an easier passage. Hells, if they let me aboard, I'll stay with them until they cast off. There's nothing on the *Lizabetta* I can't bear to leave behind.

Urgency drives me faster as I make my way past ships from every port, from Kethos to Escium to Port Naranda itself, all tied up side by side, the sea breeze whipping blond strands out of my braid and around my face.

That must be the *Freya* at the end, sandwiched in by two dirty steamships, her sturdy hull built to ply the North Passage. My pace quickens as I round the curve of the port toward her.

And I run straight into a barricade across the mouth of the dock.

Beyond it is the very fleet Prince Leander was heading for—a cluster of elegant schooners, their rigging hung with flags and wreathed with flowers. I've been watching them across the harbor for the last few days, but this is the first time I've been up close.

It's a hive of activity around them—sailors are hauling crates in teams, and above them rickety cranes hoist nets of cargo aboard, swinging them around to lower them to the deck. There's a truck backing up slowly to the edge of the dock, industriously waved in by three deckhands. Someone's playing a record on a gramophone down on the foredeck of the nearest ship. Girls in bright colors are dancing, throwing their arms up and shimmying to make the fringes on their dresses fan out, then dissolving into laughter as they try the steps again. They're ignoring the work going on around them, hordes of workers readying the fleet for departure.

*So much fuss for one spoiled boy.*

The queen is sending her brother off to charm the rulers of Alinor's neighbors, and he's gallivanting away like he's off to a fancy afternoon tea with dozens of his closest friends, oblivious to the tension in the air.

I'm sure the fleet won't be foolish enough to go as far as Mellacea, so the boats won't be searched and taxed as we sailors have been these past months. My father doesn't know about that change—one of many reasons he should have come back to us when he could. Still, I'll tell him when I arrive.

The barricade is overseen by a couple of Queensguard, shiny and pompous in their royal blue uniforms. The trouble begins straightaway.

"I have business with the captain of the *Freya*," I say, mustering as much courtesy as I know how.

The woman lofts one brow and makes a show of pulling a list out of her pocket. "Name?"

"Selly Walker, but it won't be on there."

"No?"

"No." I can't keep the irritation out of my tone, but I can already see how this is going to go. It's a familiar feeling— watching something unspool ahead of me, yet unable to bite my tongue and find a way to fix it before it happens.

"I'm sorry to say that if your name's not on the list, and you don't have a crew armband, then this is as far as you come," she informs me, not sounding even faintly sorry.

"Look, if one of you can tell the captain of the *Freya* that Selly Walker—Stanton Walker's daughter—is here, I'm sure—"

"Not here to run your errands, girl." She cuts me off, looking me up and down, and I lift one hand to smooth my wind-mussed hair back, then wish I hadn't. Her gaze lingers on the filthy knees of my trousers, a souvenir of my tumble off the carriage. Another thing I can thank His Highness for.

"Are you leaving," she asks, as her companion finally turns his gaze away from the girls dancing on deck and studies me thoughtfully, "or are we escorting you?"

I bite my tongue so hard I'm surprised I don't draw blood, sketch an elaborate bow worthy of the useless pieces of nobility up on deck, and turn away. If they won't let me through, I'll find another way.

As I walk down the dock, I check over my shoulder and find the Queensguard keeping a beady eye on me, but when I look back again, she's lost interest.

I duck out of sight behind a long stack of crates waiting to be loaded. If I can pause near the barricades when the Queensguard aren't looking, then with any luck I can slip past them and still reach the *Freya*. I need to get back closer to the barricade, though, so I'm ready to move.

I squash myself between two crates and pop out of the tiny space like a cork from a bottle, straight into something—someone—who stumbles back in turn and throws their arms around me to keep the pair of us upright. Our eyes lock as we steady ourselves, and I realize I've ended up in his embrace.

He's a boy about my age, with warm brown skin that matches the golden sandstone of Kirkpool, like he's a part of the city itself. Brown eyes dance beneath fashionably tousled black hair, and he has the sort of easy smile that says he knows just how handsome he is.

I hate that kind of smile.

"At last," he says cheerfully, apparently unconcerned about having a sailor crash into him without warning. "I thought you'd never get here."

I stare at him as I recover my breath, a little bit distracted by his face. He has unfairly long eyelashes.

His mouth twitches as if something's amusing him—me, presumably—and that's enough to snap me back to myself. I plant one hand on his chest and push him backward as I step out of his hold.

"I don't know who you are, but I don't have time for you," I mutter. "What the hells are you doing hiding behind a bunch of crates?"

"Well, I heard you were going to be here," the mystery boy replies without missing a beat, politely not pointing out that I am also hiding behind a bunch of crates.

I can't figure out what he is. He's dressed like he's from the docks—shirtsleeves rolled up to his elbows, black suspenders, and dark brown trousers—but his white shirt is far too clean, the fabric on those trousers too good, and he sounds too fancy. A palace servant, perhaps, trying to blend in down here?

I can't afford a delay, annoyingly handsome or otherwise, so with one last look at him, I shove past and reach for the top edge of the nearest crate. I grip, heave, and haul myself up on top of it, no doubt forcing him to dodge my kicks as I scrabble for purchase. I'll find out soon enough if he's going to raise the alarm.

This is a better place to watch the Queensguard. There are huge bunches of flowers set atop the crates, destined to decorate the rigging of the prince's fleet, and they make excellent camouflage. I nestle among them and set to waiting.

"What are we looking for?" asks a voice beside me, and I nearly fall off the crate.

The boy's climbed up too, and now he ducks my hand as it swings around to flail at thin air. He grabs me around the waist, steadying me and pulling me back into the nest of flowers, laughing at my scowl.

"What are you doing up here?" I demand.

"Couldn't stay away," he replies with a grin. "Also, I thought you heard me climbing up—sorry about that."

I'm only seeing now, as he withdraws his hand, that he's got emerald-green magician's marks down his forearms and across the backs of his hands, the jewel tone bright against the light brown of his skin. Something in my gut twists at the sight of them.

His marks are as intricate as I've ever seen, and so complex I can't even tell which element they signal—no wonder he's cocky. Though if I'm honest, the looks alone were enough.

I reach out with my own gloved hand to steady myself, resisting the urge to ask him what he's doing here, because he'll only ask me the same, and that doesn't end the way I want.

"That's Lady Violet Beresford," my companion says conversationally, and when I glance across to follow his gaze, he's looking at a girl in a dress the silvery blue color of the sea at dusk. She's leading the dancing, her head thrown back in laughter.

"Well, I'm glad someone's having a nice time."

"You're not?"

"Have you spent a minute in the city today?" I ask testily, easing forward to peek through the foliage at the two Queensguard, who seem a lot more dedicated to their duty than I'd like. As I watch, a third comes trotting along the dock from the direction of the city to talk to them.

"What about it?"

"Who out there is having fun, apart from nobles on boats? I'm only a few days ashore, but everyone I've spoken to is asking about foreign ports, about what they're saying around the Crescent Sea. About whether Mellacea's going to start a war with us. Now that I'm looking at this, I'm beginning to understand why they're so worried."

He leans forward alongside me to take a closer look at the ships, the warmth of his shoulder close against mine. Lady Violet is still dancing, urging her companions to join her as the music trips merrily over itself. "Why, what do you see?"

I snort. "You *don't* see it? His ships are covered in *flowers.*"

"You have to admit they look— What's wrong with flowers?"

Below, the Queensguard are now in heated conversation with the newcomer, and he's waving his arms. Dare I hope he's going to lure them away?

"I don't have any strong opinions on flowers," I say, aware that I sound a lot like I do.

"Just naturally cranky?"

"Listen." I remind myself it would be wrong to push him

off the crate. "Every trading ship at the docks knows how much trouble we're in, knows how tense things are at every new port we pull into. Alinor's in trouble. She's been taking a lazy nap in the afternoon sun, and over in Mellacea, let me tell you, they're up before dawn. And what's the queen doing about it?"

"Well, she's—"

"She's put the boy prince on the job. It's like she *wants* to fail."

"That's a bit harsh, don't you think?"

I snort. "We're talking about a boy who went through three different outfit changes at the solstice festival. In one evening!"

"I heard it was four, and he wore a gold-sequined coat for the ages."

"What part of that sentence do you think makes any of this better?" I splutter.

"I must say, you know a lot about him," he muses.

"I can't help it, he's all anyone talks about."

"Including you, and you don't even seem to like him."

"Liking has nothing to do with it," I snap back, making myself lower my voice. "He could keep every tailor on the Crescent Sea in business and I wouldn't care, if he was doing his job."

"Maybe he *is* doing his job," the boy suggests, though his tone concedes the evidence is on my side.

"Are you delusional? He's decided to decorate his flotilla with half the palace gardens—and we're on the doorstep of winter, so I can't think how many hothouses that sort of stupidity must have taken—then pack a Fontesquan chef and a bunch of his closest pals and waltz off along the coast to see if he can make friends with the neighbors."

"He shouldn't make friends with the neighbors?" the boy asks, frowning at the Queensguard, who are now watching a couple more of their number run along the docks.

"He should make *allies* of the neighbors," I shoot back. "But nobody's going to take him seriously. Who ever has?"

"Ouch," he mutters, and I turn my head to take a better look at him, crouching, framed by flowers.

Still handsome, but now I'm paying more attention to his voice. It sounds like money. *Does he know the prince?*

Suddenly I'm reminded of all the times Rensa told me to watch my tongue, especially around people I don't know. At least he doesn't know my name.

I know I'm taking all the frustration of my day, of my captain's endless orders, of my father's abandonment, of the blocked path to the *Freya,* and aiming it at him. And I know I shouldn't.

Then again, he's insisting on putting himself in my path.

Below us the Queensguard are still accumulating—there are a dozen of them now, and one's pointing in all directions, sending them running all over the place. Forget slipping past just a pair of them—they're swarming the dock.

I'll have to get past after dark and stow away, because I'm sure as hells not getting to the *Freya*'s captain now.

"I think it's about to get busy around here," the boy says, watching the growing swarm of guards thoughtfully. "Looks like they've lost something."

"Looks like," I mutter. It's fine. I'll get through to the *Freya* tonight. It'll be easier under cover of darkness, and she doesn't sail until dawn. I can hide aboard until they're well out at sea and it's too late for them to do anything about it.

For now, I should hustle back to the *Lizabetta* before Rensa realizes how long I've been gone and loses her temper.

"Hey, look," says the boy beside me suddenly, his voice rising, and I twist around urgently to follow his gaze.

"What? What do you see?"

He's pointing at the deck of the nearest ship, where the brightly colored young nobles are crowding in around a woman wheeling a fancy little handcart toward the bow. "They're bringing out refreshments. Bet you half a crown those are Fontesquan pastries."

I make a noise like a strangled growl, and he falls silent.

Yeah, he's definitely noble, not a palace servant. The rest of the city is humming with worry, we're in a port full of ships with everything to lose if war breaks out, and instead of thinking up ways to solve any of our problems, down on the progress fleet—which is what everyone's calling the ships embarking on this goodwill voyage—they're flocking to their afternoon tea like gulls in the wake of a fishing boat.

"First flowers, now you don't like pastries?" he asks, studying my frown. "What's next, kittens?"

"I . . . Will you just go away?"

He smirks. "I think you'll find I was here first. Come to that, when you arrived, you literally threw yourself into my arms."

I could push him out of our little nest and off the top of the packing crate, but that might be too subtle for him. Shooting him a too-sweet smile, I reach into the nest of flowers around us, plucking a delicate blossom in Alinor's royal sapphire blue. He watches me cautiously.

"There." I lean across to tuck it behind his ear. "Everything useless around here is beautifully decorated. I wouldn't want you to feel left out."

His wariness eases, and his lips twitch again to one of those small smiles. This boy looks like he knows all the mischief in the world, and invented half of it himself.

His brown eyes stay steady on mine, and as my fingertips brush his hair, my stomach gives the strangest flip-flop. Must be the sun.

We both hold still for a moment, gazing at each other.

"So you're not coming for a quick snack?" he murmurs, breaking the tension. I can't shake the feeling I just lost that exchange, and I don't know why.

"I've seen enough nobility for one day." I'm already shifting my weight, preparing to climb down with a speed that feels a little like running away, if I'm completely honest with myself.

"Let's hope there's more to our prince than you think," he counters.

"I doubt it," I reply—and before he has a chance to respond, I jump down into the gap between the crates, shoving my way back through it again.

I have the strongest urge to look over my shoulder, but I make myself keep my gaze dead ahead. I don't have time to think about him. There's only one thing on my mind that matters, and she's moored at the end of the northern dock.

Even if I have to swim across the harbor and climb up her side like a boarding pirate, by dawn I'll be sailing for the north aboard the *Freya*.

# JUDE

*Handsome Jack's Tavern*
*Port Naranda, Mellacea*

The crowd roars like a monster as I lash out, flicking up my wrist at the last instant so I land the punch with the heel of my hand instead of my knuckles.

It's a dirty move.

I don't care.

The other guy staggers back, spitting blood and calling foul, and the crowd-monster surges around us as I dance on the balls of my feet, taunting him.

The boxing ring is underground, the only light coming from lanterns swinging from the ceiling. My long shadow sways beside me as I wait for him to recover his balance, my breath coming quick. It's too soon to go in for the kill—the monster wants feeding first, and with my pulse pounding, skin slicked with sweat, I feel utterly alive. More than willing to provide the meal.

He wipes his mouth clear of blood with one bare hand, leaving a smear of crimson across his cheek, and raises his fists once again. This time he's sizing me up with more care, pale eyes flickering over me.

Half his size, sure. But twice as fast.

I rake my damp black hair back from my eyes, meeting his gaze square on. And he's the one who looks away.

Around us the crowd is a blur, but it's becoming *my* monster, just as it always does—roaring advice and protests, making bets and shouting for drinks. Light glints off glasses, acrid cigar smoke wafts through the ring, and I surge forward again.

The big man's fist swings around with terrifying speed, and I jerk down to avoid it, teeth clicking together and sending a sharp pain shooting up to my temples. I push back up before he recovers, taking advantage of that moment he's off balance to strike again, this time connecting above his eye, splitting the skin so the blood pours free, and the monster's roar grows deafening.

He shakes his head like a wet dog, trying to clear his view. I dance in after him, weaving past a clumsy punch to land a blow under his chin, his head snapping back.

Then hands are grabbing at my shoulders, pulling me away. I shout, trying to wrench free, but the fingers dig in tighter, and now I register the voice in my ear.

"Jude, stop! Stop, can you hear me? Take a break before you finish it!"

Slowly I lower my fists and let the landlord's men tug me backward, away from my staggering opponent.

A break, time for another round of bets—the larger the pot,

the more my cut will be—and then I can finish him off. He's stumbling to his own corner of the makeshift ring, swaying against the pairs of hands waiting for him.

"Try not to knock him down in the first ten seconds," the handler behind me growls in my ear, hands tight on my shoulders, as though I need to be held back from lunging forward, overtaken by bloodlust. The grip is mostly for show, for the gamblers, though I have no trouble keeping my scowl in place.

This is my persona, what they want from me. The cold-blooded killer. The private school boy dragged down into the gutter, proof the rich are no better than them.

"Did you hear me, Your Lordship?" the handler growls again.

"Don't call me that," I mutter. *That* part of it isn't true. Never was.

"Keep clear of him, drag it out," the man insists.

"I think I can resist him," I say, never taking my eyes off the man opposite us, though he refuses to look at me. Beaten already, and both of us know it. "I go for much prettier guys."

The man laughs in my ear, and someone offers me a towel to dry off my face. I let the roughness of the fabric on my skin block out the noise and light. Sometimes, if I'm tired enough, push my body hard enough, I can stop thinking, stop feeling, and just *be*. That moment's close now, and I want it with an ache that never leaves me.

But when I lift my head, Dasriel's mountainous figure is carving a path straight through the crowd, like he hasn't even noticed they're there. He has his shirtsleeves rolled up to his elbows, showing off the emerald-green magician's marks etched onto his skin, flames curling in on and consuming one another.

He shoves the spectators aside, leaving their indignation in his wake as he lumbers across the empty space of the ring—like he hasn't noticed there's a fight on either.

He halts directly in front of me to rumble his greeting, jeweled red pin sparkling at his lapel. "Ruby has a job for you."

"He hasn't finished," the handler protests, his hands tightening on my shoulders properly now.

"Ruby has a job," Dasriel repeats, like the other man hadn't spoken.

So I shake off the handler's grip and grab my shirt from behind the bar, leaving the howls behind me as I elbow my way through the press of bodies to the stairs. This place is always an escape for me. Now it's an escape for the crowd as well—they feel the tension on the street, sense the dark storm clouds of war looming—and I've just deprived them of their distraction. Too bad.

I don't bother trying to pull my shirt on until I'm on my way up to street level, the cold air outside chilling the sweat on my skin.

And I don't bother looking back as I follow Dasriel out into the lane, leaving one monster behind to head for another.

# SELLY

*The* Lizabetta
*Kirkpool, Alinor*

I plant one bare foot against the rough wood of the cross-trees, grabbing a line to hoist myself higher. The mast thins out toward the top, built to sway and give in strong winds, but here in the harbor there's nothing but a soft evening breeze.

Onshore, the city folk have left their day's work behind and turned to the taverns—dusk is falling, and most of the light and life I can see spills from open windows along the hills as the locals gather to eat, drink, and try to shake off the tension singing through the city.

There's always a jump in my belly when we make port and all the new shouts and smells and sights swarm up to greet me. But quick enough, my heart starts straining for the sea, my soul itching for the slap of water on wood.

Tonight I'm grateful we're not putting out to sea. It's time for me to retrieve the bag I stashed earlier and slip ashore. By dawn I'll be on my way to join Da, and Rensa will have no way to follow. By the time the *Freya*'s crew finds me, they'll be too far under way to do anything about it, and nobody's going to throw Stanton Walker's daughter overboard.

The view through my eyeglass tells me things have calmed down over on the northern docks—the nobles are on deck, the lazy drawl of a trumpet wafting across the water as someone plays the gramophone, but there's no sign of the swarm of guards. No sign of that boy, either—not that I'm looking for him in particular.

But like I've summoned him, I hear his voice all over again, see the smile in his brown eyes. *What's wrong with flowers?*

I snort. And then, of course, I hear him again: *Just naturally cranky?*

I mentally push him off the crate like I should have done today, watching his arms flail as he tumbles out of view. *That cranky enough for you?*

Then I realize I'm having an argument with an imaginary person, and turn back to surveying the harbor.

None of it—not the boy across the harbor on those boats, not the captain who thinks I'm currently confined to my cabin— none of it matters, because it's growing darker by the moment, and soon I'll be creeping over to the *Freya.*

I'll be sorry to leave my *Lizabetta,* though, and I peel off my fingerless leather gloves so I can curl one hand around the line hanging beside me, the rope rough against my skin. We have none of the decorations of the royal fleet, but our ship's a tried-and-true merchanter. A windjammer, built long and narrow, to run with a small crew and swallow up the leagues with a belly full of cargo. She carries more canvas than any other ship in harbor.

Of all my father's fleet, I love the *Lizabetta* the best. I grew up navigating the roll of her decks, squeezing into every corner of the hold to hide from his deckhands, falling asleep strapped into my bunk to start it all again the next day.

But this last year she's been my prison, and as I peer down, I see the reason standing amidships, her silhouette unmistakable. I haven't given Rensa my father's letter. She must suspect he's not coming by now, but if she knew *I* know, she'd be on the alert for something like my escape tonight.

Just now she's by the gangplank, watching it with a strange, almost suspicious intensity, like she's expecting it to stand up and dance away.

Nearly half the crew's ashore tonight. We don't usually wait in port as long as we have for the *Fortune* this time, and everyone's antsy. So straws were drawn, and Rensa sent the lucky few off to have some fun, and probably blow every last crown of their pay. I'm confined to the ship, after she tore pieces off me for getting back late this afternoon.

Why is Rensa so fixed on having her crew back? It's only just past dusk, and they'll be gone for hours yet, so why is she standing here waiting as if they're late coming home?

Perhaps she's finally sensed the tension in the city I've been sniffing for days now—the whispers of the city dwellers realizing what we saltbloods have known for months: the storm clouds are gathering.

Or wait—does she suspect I'm planning on using that gangplank myself? I really hope not—if she's going to stand there all night, I'm in for a very unpleasant swim.

As I'm trying not to think about the freezing cold waters of Kirkpool's harbor, something moves in the shadows near the bow—it's the scholar.

Where Rensa is short and solid, he's tall and gangly, like a collection of arms and legs all desperately trying to pretend they don't know each other. Her skin is a warm brown, made browner by decades at sea, and his is the kind of dazzling white you get from a whole life spent indoors. He came aboard this morning with trunks full of books too heavy for him to lift and took passage for Trallia, which is where the *Lizabetta*'s headed next.

When he first arrived, wrapped up in his heavy woolen peacoat, I thought he was my father's age. He has a scholar's stoop, his hair shaved close to his head—that boy does *not* have the skull shape for it—and it was only when Rensa made me carry the last of his bags down that I realized he was my age. I like him, even though he's a strange sort of creature. We only spoke for a few moments, but he seems like someone who gets to the point.

There's movement below on the dock, and at the same time a breeze ruffles the new spirit flags Kyri strung up this afternoon. I pull my gloves back on and ease silently down to the next crosstrees, my bare feet finding purchase in the rigging, then lean sideways, hanging out from the mast by one hand.

Rensa moves suddenly, walking down the gangplank to where an auto's pulling up with a low purr, the engine falling silent as it stops. It must be another passenger—cargo would have come in a truck, or on a horse-drawn wagon, and not at this hour—which means there's yet another thing Rensa didn't tell me.

We barely ever take passengers, and our one cabin's already full up with the scholar. Kyri and I haven't moved our things out of our little nook, but it's hard to imagine someone showing up in an auto like *that* and sleeping with the crew in hammocks.

As I creep down the mast, moving through the rigging as silent as a spirit, a chauffeur jumps out of the auto, tugging his white gloves straight as he jogs around to get the door, pulling it open and standing to one side.

A man steps out—or maybe a boy, it's hard to tell in the shadows. He's young, dark-haired, clad in a well-cut suit, a flash of his white shirt showing underneath. He turns in a slow circle, taking in the docks, the prince's fleet, the *Lizabetta*. And for a moment, I think he smiles.

He moves in an easy, loose-limbed way that's strangely familiar, nodding to the driver but making no move to help him unload luggage from the back of the auto. That's *way* too many bags for the class of passenger we take aboard a ship like ours. They don't arrive with servants, either.

What in seven hells is going on?

Another gust of breeze comes pushing past me, tugging stray blond wisps free of my braid and setting the rigging swinging around me.

Rensa steps forward to meet the stranger. The gramophone across the water mutes their voices, but her stance is unmistakable. She bobs her weight back and forth as though she isn't sure how to greet the new arrival.

Rensa's *nervous*.

In the past year I've seen Rensa every kind of thing—bellowing frustration, standing hard at the helm in battering seas, singing shamelessly off-key in the evenings, gritting her teeth at my latest complaint—but I've never, *ever* seen her lost for what to do next.

The new arrival solves the problem by offering her his hand. They exchange handshakes and a few murmured words, heads together. Then, with a cheerful wave, he sends the driver away.

I creep lower, fumbling inside my jacket pocket for my eyeglass. I raise it, twisting the little tube until he comes into focus. Rensa holds up a lantern, and I see him more clearly now in the circle of my magnified vision.

I see dancing brown eyes, and lips curving to a self-satisfied smile. He lifts one hand to push his fingers through tousled black hair, and I see the intricate magician's marks on the back of his hand.

*But what . . . ?*

Of all the people in Kirkpool who could have walked aboard, what's the boy from the docks doing *here*?

I climb hurriedly down the rigging, grasping at the cables as the lights of the prince's fleet twinkle through the darkness. The wind is picking up properly now, the spirit flags flapping around me, and where the strings of lights are reflected in the water, new ripples make them shimmer and dance.

I didn't think this kind of weather was due until morning— dawn is when Kirkpool's breeze usually makes an appearance— but it's as if the air around me is as off balance as I am.

Has the boy come to complain to Rensa, to report what I said about the prince and his friends? That seems impossible, and anyway, he's got luggage. But what could he possibly . . . ?

My bare feet find the deck damp with dew, and I ease my weight down slowly, trying to think what I should do. Rensa and the boy are nowhere in sight now. They must have gone belowdecks.

Should I leave straightaway, without slipping down to get

my bag? I'm still barefoot from climbing the mast, and it's one thing to leave my bag behind, but another to abandon my boots. And whatever reason brought the boy here, it's something out of the ordinary, which means I should carry that information to Da. The more I have to share, the less time his grumpiness will take to pass.

That, and I'll die of curiosity before the *Freya* rounds the southern tip of Mellacea.

I stay close to the mast as the scholar walks by, steps hurried as he makes for the companionway with his head down. He's cautious, holding on to the railing with both hands, as though the ship is some crafty, flighty creature who might take it into her head to buck him overboard, rather than a well-behaved lady moored at dock.

He meets Rensa, on her way back up from carrying the mystery boy's luggage downstairs—what was the *captain* doing playing porter?—and she pauses so he can squeeze past, holding tight to the railing. He manages to navigate his way to the bottom without falling down the stairs. So that's an improvement from this morning, at least.

The new arrival is nowhere in sight—he must have stayed wherever she stashed him belowdecks.

Rensa heads toward the stern, her stride purposeful, and I move quietly after her, ears practically flapping in the growing breeze. She stops just short of the wheel, and as I creep down the edge of the deck to flank her, the shrine comes into view. It's a sheltered spot set against the mizzenmast, almost like a fireplace but deeper. There are spirit flags strung across what would be the mantelpiece, and instead of a fire, you can usually find little gifts from the crew. I don't go anywhere near it if I can help it.

Our first mate and ship's magician, Kyri, is crouched by the shrine in the near dark, whispering as she lights the green candles I brought back from the city today, her face hidden by her sheet of red hair. As I watch, the candles start to vanish—not melting, but slowly disappearing into thin air from the top down as the spirits consume the offering.

So *that's* where the breeze came from. My own magic may be useless, but I still know how these things work. If Kyri's charming this many spirits on her own, that's a huge piece of work. It's one thing to encourage them to stir the breeze a little stronger, or ease it off, or tilt it the way we want it. It's another to get the air around us moving on a dead-still night. I didn't think Kyri was capable of something like this.

In fact, I'm sure she's not.

But a magician with powerful marks just came up the gang-plank.

"He's here?" Kyri asks Rensa, glancing up.

"Getting comfortable," Rensa says, hands on her hips. "He asked where the bell was, in case he needs anything, if you can believe it."

Kyri snorts, and I allow myself an eye roll in the darkness. Sounds like the boy I met today, for sure.

"This is going to be a story to tell," our first mate supposes. "The spirits are having a lot of fun, though. They love him."

"I'm told he has that effect," Rensa replies, dry.

Kyri looks past the captain, straight at me. "Selly, ready to cast off in a minute." Then her attention is back on the candles slowly disappearing in front of her, and the spirits she's charming.

I bite my lip against a curse. When they know each other well, magicians can often sense each other, and though my magician's marks are duds, hidden beneath my gloves, that gift has been getting me in trouble since I was toddling across these decks.

Rensa whips around, staring into the dark until she makes out my shape, and with a soft growl, she lifts one finger to beckon me out of the shadows.

There's no point pretending, so I step forward. "Captain, what—" And that's when Kyri's words hit me, and my eyes widen. "Did she say *cast off*? What in the seven—"

"We're leaving," Rensa says, voice low and tense as she cuts me off. "Take your station."

*"Leaving?"* The word's driven out of me like I've been punched in the gut, and as her gaze drifts over my shoulder, I whirl around to see what's left of the crew emerging onto the deck, spreading out silently to head for the mooring lines. "What's going on? Who is he?"

There are a thousand protests I want to make, but they die on my tongue. If we leave port tonight, I'll lose my last chance to get up north to Da. The *Freya* will be gone in the morning, and the storms will close the passage behind her.

I'll be stuck right here until spring, at least. The air goes out of my lungs, and it feels like someone's squeezing my ribs.

I can't do this any longer, not when it was supposed to be finished. *I can't.*

"Rensa, I—" My gaze leaps from one silhouette in the

darkness to the next as sails silently begin to unfurl above us. "No, I—"

"Not now, Selly," Rensa snaps, hurrying around to the wheel and running her hands over the smooth wood with a soft prayer under her breath.

"But I—"

"If you were ever wondering," she whispers, aiming the words at me like a weapon, "this moment is *exactly* why your father left you here to learn. I'm only sorry I haven't managed to teach you. We're leaving half the crew ashore to fend for themselves, we're creeping out of the harbor without a proper cargo to balance the books, and we're doing it under sail, no tugboat, no help, in the dark, without the harbormaster's clearance. And yet *your* first protest begins 'But I.' As if I didn't just give you a whole list of things you should have thought of before yourself."

I stare at her, wordless, but she's already looked away— she's watching the sails, her hands ready on the wheel.

"My father . . ." But I don't know how that sentence ends. She's just given me the list of reasons we can't be doing this. And yet we are.

"Your father would do *exactly* as I am," she growls softly, finally dropping her gaze to meet mine again. "And he left you to take my orders, so *take your place.*"

I'm frozen where I stand. I can't do it. The months stretch ahead of me—shut outside the captain's quarters, never knowing where we're going or what the next plan will be, treated like I'm fit for nothing but crawling around the bilges or mending sails.

Footsteps sound behind me, and I whirl to find the boy from the city sauntering up to kneel beside Kyri, setting down a candle of his own. He doesn't seem to notice Rensa and me as he rolls up his sleeves, revealing those magician's marks coiling and swooping across his skin, more intricate and complex than I've ever seen.

"Pleasure to make your acquaintance," he says cheerfully, offering Kyri his hand, his vowels rounded and expensive.

She stares at him like she has no idea how to respond, then blushes and reaches out to shake.

"Kyri," she stammers, and the pain in my jaw tells me I'm clenching it hard enough to nearly crack my teeth.

"I hope you won't mind showing me how it's done," he says easily, shooting her a dazzling grin, and then tilting his head back to look up at the silent sails.

The remains of the candles in the little shrine flare as the spirits respond to his touch.

"Selly, *now*," Rensa snaps, and for a wild moment I swing toward the dock. *Could I make a leap for it?* Could I leave them all—the boy from the city, the captain, my crew—behind?

But we're already drifting away, and whatever Rensa's doing to my *Lizabetta,* I can't just abandon the ship to her fate.

Da would forgive me for stowing away on the *Freya.* But he'd never forgive me for leaving the ship *now.* And by mentioning the risks in getting the *Lizabetta* out of port so quickly and at night, Rensa has managed to snare me with the one hook that could stop me from escaping.

Jaw clenched, eyes hot with an ache that wants to be tears, I break, pushing past my captain to get to the navigation lights.

Her hand lands on my shoulder. "We're running dark,"

she says quietly, almost inaudible over the spirit flags flapping above us.

A shard of ice slithers down my spine as I turn to face her. This is smugglers' talk. "They'll take away your master's license," I whisper. "What are you dragging us into? What are we doing?"

"Our duty," she replies, still soft. "And it'll pay well, besides. Your father would do the same, girl."

The crew are creeping back down the masts now, the sails unfurled, but reefed to keep them small—we don't need much power yet. We want to go slow and silent until we're in the open sea. Except my father's ships don't slink out like thieves in the night. They sail proud and fly the Walker standard—my family's crest—below the blue-and-white flag of Alinor.

"You have the best eyes," Rensa says. "Get up to the bow and have Conor run messages back to me. Get us out to sea, and we'll talk."

I'm left with no choice. The *Lizabetta* is moving beneath me, creeping along in the light breeze. The lights of the prince's fleet and the taverns ashore are slipping past, and one way or another, we're leaving Kirkpool.

The wood of the deck is slick with dew under my bare feet as I turn to run past Kyri and the boy from the city, past the companionway, past the masts. If we're going—and we are—I'll make damn sure we go safe.

The low, lazy wail of the gramophone aboard the prince's fleet echoes across the water as the *Lizabetta* leaves the rules behind, gliding toward the harbor's mouth, silent and dark.

# LASKIA

*The Gem Cutter*
*Port Naranda, Mellacea*

I leave behind the late-night bustle of the street for the alleyway, the air cooler as my footsteps click across the damp
cobblestones.

Behind me, the city's lit with a mix of gas and electricity.
The hum and honk of autos blends with the steady clop of
horses' hooves and the rumble of cart and carriage wheels.

In here it's darker and quieter—has been since I was a kid.
One thing has changed, though: these days there's a line of
patrons stretching toward New Street, the well-dressed huddled inside their coats as they wait for their turn to step inside
the club. They want to dance the night away, leave behind the
whispers and rumors and worries that walk the streets of Port
Naranda lately.

What light there is in the alleyway comes from the sign
outside the Gem Cutter. Most places have an electric bulb or
two, casting light and shadow across their painted names. But

not ours. Here, like everywhere else, it's like Ruby was trying to say, *See what I can do?*

A cascade of oversized jewels tumbles from Ruby's sign, made from dazzlingly cut crystal. They're clear, except for one tinted blood red, and each of them has its own electric bulb set behind it so it sparkles like it's alive.

*The Gem Cutter.* The name of the place delights the rich people who come here. The patrons have heard hints of who Ruby is, what she does. They whisper that the words aren't referring to an artisan with a magnifying glass and a set of tiny tools, but to the patroness of the club, Ruby herself. A gem with a very sharp knife. It makes them feel dangerous, to walk through these doors.

I nod to the two man-mountain bouncers as I slip past the folks waiting in line, and step inside my sister's domain.

The lights are dimmed, tables arrayed around a dance floor and a low stage, the bar running down the right-hand side of the room. Everything about this place is luxe—the Fontesquan chef, the gold threads woven through the fine linen of the white tablecloths, the polished wood inlaid into the walls. There's a woman crooning up on the stage, a few couples clinched on the polished dance floor, and the soft clink of glasses and silverware underneath it all.

The staff knows who I am, and they step out of my way as I head toward the far end of the bar. I can't pretend I don't like it, though really they're stepping out of Ruby's way—I'm just the little sister. But tonight is the night that starts to change, and I'm so, *so* hungry for the chance she's about to give me.

I fetch up against the bar, leaning on it and studying the room as I wait for the bartender to notice me. I know I look as good as anyone here—I've chosen my outfit carefully to-night. My dark gray suit is well cut, the waistcoat cinched in around my waist, my crisp white shirtsleeves rolled up. I stand out from the women in their sparkling dresses, and that's the way I like it.

I left the suit jacket off and fastened my ruby pin to my waistcoat—I want to look like I mean business. I saw the bar-ber today, and my curls are tight atop my head, the fuzz at the back of my neck soft. I look sharp. I feel sharp.

The bouncers get their suits the same place I do, but though mine fits to perfection, theirs always pull at the seams. Ruby's tailors could make them fit like a glove, but the whole point is to make the men look like they're just a little too big, too strong, to be confined by clothes like a regular person.

Like every other aspect of the business, no detail's too small to escape Ruby's notice, and she likes her toughs to look like what they are. A hint of the badness beneath all this beauty and class. That's our world—glitter and grit.

The bartender, a pretty girl with her black hair braided back tightly, skin the same warm brown as the rosewood along the front of the bar, smiles as she makes her way to me.

She's not the face I'm used to, though—Lorento's been be-hind the bar since the day Ruby opened, always ready with a barman's ear, polishing a glass while I talked out my problems. It's not like him to take a night off.

"I haven't seen you before," I greet her, leaning on the bar with one elbow and trying out a smile on her.

"I usually work at Ruby Red," she replies, reaching under the counter and producing an envelope, then sliding it across to me. "A girl left this for you." Our fingertips touch as I take it from her, and her gaze flickers up to meet mine and tell me it wasn't an accident. *All right, then.* Maybe when I get back.

"Lorento taking a night off for once?" I ask as I break the seal, pulling out the single sheet inside.

"I heard he retired," she replies casually, and I go still, my gaze flicking up to her. In our business, *retirement* doesn't mean a place on the porch with your grandchildren. But Lorento? After all these years? What could he possibly have done, and why, for Ruby to . . . ?

"Huh," I make myself say, glancing one more time at the bar, picturing him standing behind it in one of his embroidered waistcoats, telling me wild stories about the way the gangs ran when he was a kid. I let myself have that moment, that memory. Then I pack it away and turn my attention to the letter in my hand. I can't be distracted today.

It's a report from inside the Alinorish ambassador's office— confirmation the prince has kept to his plans. I tuck it into my waistcoat and lift my gaze to the girl behind the bar. I'm twisted up inside—anticipation fizzes alongside the knowledge that everything rides on this. I need to release a little of it, find a way to blunt the edge.

"You know," I say, "I think I'll have a glass of champagne before I head in."

She reaches under the counter once more, and produces a cut-crystal glass with a sugared rim, setting it in front of me. "Let me make you something new instead," she says, getting to work. "You'll love this."

"I'd love champagne more."

"I'm sorry, but Ruby . . ." She shoots me an awkward, apologetic glance as she mixes up something pink and full of bubbles.

Ruby said she doesn't want her little sister drinking booze, is what she means. And that's exactly why tonight matters so much. After I pull this off, I won't be anyone's little anything. For now, I pretend my cheeks aren't heating up, and I shrug like it doesn't matter much either way.

She slides the drink across. I take a sip, bubbles tingling on my tongue, and taste peaches, though it's not the season. I try to think about that luxury, instead of the petty humiliation of her embarrassed refusal.

*Never stop enjoying these things,* Ruby always says, and she's right.

She and I know what it's like to be hungry. We know what it's like to live on someone else's charity. It's been years, but no matter how I go to sleep, sprawled out with my arms and legs reaching for every corner of the bed, I still wake up in the morning exactly the same way. Every morning, crammed in against the wall, right over on one side of the mattress to make space for my mother and my sister in the same bed, even though nobody's been there for years.

Some things don't change. Even here in the club, inside, Ruby and I are still the girls who watched Mama leave to go up the coast, north to Nusraya.

*I'll send for you as soon as I've made a place,* she said, and Ruby had to peel me off her while I sobbed my tiny heart out. I think I knew already it was goodbye.

None of Ruby's people know where we came from, where we were before we worked our way up. That the very building this club occupies used to be a boardinghouse, and the two of us used to huddle in the cheapest room they had. We keep that between us, one of the thousand things that bind the pair of us together.

Sometimes it feels like I'll always be the girl who watched Ruby getting dressed to go out at night, braiding back her hair, slipping a knife up her sleeve.

*Stay home,* she'd tell me. *Stay quiet. Let me handle it.*

And I'd stay huddled in the dark, first in the dank room Mama rented for us when she left, and when the money ran out and she didn't come back, somewhere up on the top floor of this place.

Sometimes I'd creep to church and sit in the back few rows. Macean was a god bound by a fate he didn't choose, and the green sisters said he needed our faith to set himself free.

Now Ruby owns the building we used to hide in. But we both remember what it was like to be powerless, to jump at unexpected sounds and know everything could be taken from us, as it was so many times as we tried to climb.

And we will *never* be like that again.

Ruby's built her empire with a strength and focus most people can't even dream of, and she's never stopped, never wavered.

Thing is, I'm older now than she was when she got her start, and *still* she doesn't see me as an adult.

I'm like my god—I need faith too. It will strengthen me enough to throw off the bonds of always being the little sister, *her* little sister.

And finally I've brought her an idea that's made her pay attention. That's made her really look at me, see I'm ready.

Macean is the god of risk, and tonight I begin the biggest gamble of my life.

I sip my drink again, lick the sugar from my lips.

Tonight, my sister's going to let me in.

And I'm so hungry for it.


It's a half hour later when I see Jude standing by the door with the bouncers. He looks like Dasriel found him in a ditch, his black hair mussed, a smear of dark red blood across the light tan of his cheek. One of the suited man-mountains twists around to scan the club, and when he catches my eye, I shake my head a fraction. He pushes Jude back out the front door, and I only get a glimpse of his scowl before he's gone.

I duck under the divide and behind the bar, shooting the pretty bartender a grin of thanks as I set down my empty glass behind the counter, to make clear the champagne thing didn't matter. Then it's back through to the kitchens, the dimly lit, velvet-soft feeling of the club abruptly replaced with bright lights and the bang and clatter of pans, the shouts of the Fontesquan chef and his assistants.

By the time I reach the back door—which leads onto a nastier, dirtier alleyway—and slide the bolt across, Jude's waiting outside for me, arms crossed, glowering. Dasriel stands behind him, huge arms folded in just the way that shows off his magician's marks, scarred face as blank as ever. Sometimes I wonder what it would take to make Dasriel change his expression.

I make a point of looking Jude up and down—his clothes have seen much better days, and right now he's sweaty and bloodied—and step back to wordlessly invite him in. We haven't talked much, Jude and I, but I know a lot more about him than he thinks. He's part of my plan, after all.

Our footsteps are soft on the thick carpet lining the hallway to Ruby's rooms, and I hear his breath catch as he almost speaks. He wants to ask me what's happening, but he's too smart to admit he has no idea. Dasriel follows silently, probably daydreaming about breaking something.

"Good fight?" I ask Jude, glancing over my shoulder.

His hand goes immediately to his hair, raking it back from his face in a vain attempt to restore order. "Don't know." His crisp Alinorish accent rounds out his vowels, adding an air of class to his grumpiness. "Missed the end."

There's a black-clad woman with a ruby pin at her lapel waiting outside Ruby's door, and she silently opens it, then silently closes it behind the three of us. My sister's rooms are like an extension of the club—red velvet couches, thick carpet, wood-paneled walls, glimmers of gold on the chandeliers. She has half a dozen locations in the city, and they all have this in common, the red and gold.

I don't see Ruby at first, but Sister Beris is waiting on one of her sofas, clad as always in her neatly tailored robes, hands folded in her lap. Her black hair is pulled back into a no-nonsense and not particularly flattering plait at the back of her neck, skin as pale as ever.

Technically, our elected government runs life in Mellacea. It's possible there are even a few people who believe that. But most of us—including First Councilor Tariden and his advisers—know events are now being pushed along by other forces. One of those forces is Sister Beris and her decision to be here tonight, on this couch, having this conversation.

She looks hard-edged, but I know there's more to her than most ever see. I know that behind her reserve lies devotion, lies faith that has persisted when so many others have fallen away.

Sister Beris dresses no differently from an acolyte, but she's third in command within Macean's church. I listened to her speak at services for years before we ever talked, but over time she's taught me more than anyone but Ruby. And she was the first one I confided in when I cooked up this plan of mine.

I hadn't seen her smile until then.

"It's his time," she said quietly. "And it's yours, Laskia. Your faith is so strong, and it will raise up both of you." I know she's right—my act of faith will serve my god *and* yield the reward I want most.

Now she nods a solemn greeting, and in return I lift my hands, pressing my fingertips to my forehead and covering my eyes. *Our god's mind awaits us, though his eyes are closed,* the traditional greeting says.

A door on the far side of the room opens to reveal my sister, a wide, shallow glass of champagne in one hand. The stem is hollow, the bubbles zinging up and down inside it in an endless cycle.

Ruby's dark brown curls fall artfully around her face, and her golden headband—not that far from a crown—is studded with tiny red gems across her forehead. Her gold-sequined dress glows against her rich brown skin, rippling and shimmering with the smallest of movements.

"There you are," she says, lifting one hand to beckon us over as she crosses to the couch, her voice as warm as if Jude comes to call on her every day, and the two of them share all their secrets. "Come, sit."

Dasriel stays by the door, and I slow my breath as I walk over to take my place on the couch opposite Ruby and Sister Beris. *Calm body, calm head, calm voice. Ignore that drink. Soon enough you'll have one too.*

Jude takes his place next to me, perched on the very edge of the couch, back straight.

"It's good to see you, Jude," Ruby says, lifting her glass for a slow sip. I should have poured myself something before I sat. It would have kept my hands busy. "The doctor came by for your mother?"

Jude nods stiffly. "He did, thank you."

Ruby turns her head to address Sister Beris, all smiles and softness, all *we're all friends here.* "His Lordship's mother is sick— we're hoping there's something we can do for her."

"His Lordship?" Sister Beris asks as Jude shifts his weight a fraction, jaw tightening.

"No," he says, carefully controlled. "That was my father."

True indeed. And Jude, his son by his mistress, was left with nothing when his father died. So the mistress brought her son home to Port Naranda. And now, to keep the doctor coming for her, he wears a ruby pin at his lapel—though it's not there today—and when Ruby tells him to jump, he grits his teeth and asks how high.

"I'm sorry to hear your mother's unwell," Sister Beris says politely. "I will appeal to Macean on her behalf."

Jude nods warily, which she seems to interpret as thanks, though it's probably not. He was raised in Alinor, worshipping Barrica. He left his faith behind when his prayers went unanswered, but I haven't found any evidence he now asks Macean to help him and his mother. I think he learned after his father died that he can't afford to rely on anyone but himself. His eyes shift across to Ruby once more, looking for a cue. He's not usually addressed at meetings like these. He's not usually *at* meetings like these.

"So," Ruby says in response, and we all turn to her. "Jude, here is what I would like you to do. You're aware Alinor is sending Prince Leander on a progress to visit Trallia, Beinhof, and so on? You will have seen it in the newspapers, I'm sure."

"Yes, Ruby." All Jude's attention is on my sister now. He's gone still, like prey that's smelled a predator but isn't sure where it is.

"The queen wants to shore up Alinor's allies," Ruby says with a feline smile. "Mellacea's starting to flex her muscles, and they know it. If—when—it comes to war, they want to be sure of the support of their friends and neighbors."

I study Sister Beris, but she wouldn't lose a game of cards easy—her expression doesn't flicker even a touch, and there's no sign how much this means to her.

A few years ago, *she* wouldn't have been at a meeting like this any more than Jude. When I was growing up, church was something old ladies did to gossip with their friends on a rest day—I was always the youngest there by several decades. They say your prayers are amplified in a church, all the more powerful for being offered up in a place soaked in faith. I didn't think Macean could hear mine while he was asleep, but I figured it never hurt to try.

Then one day I met Sister Beris after a service. We talked. We understood each other. I learned that behind that stern façade is a woman who always has time to listen to me. Who believes in me.

More and more people have been at our services lately, and they say fewer and fewer are at the temples in Alinor.

They say if this war everyone's whispering about is truly coming, we'll be the ones with a god on our side.

"You went to boarding school with the prince," Ruby continues to Jude. "Yes?"

Jude's silent a long moment. He didn't tell Ruby that. He didn't tell *anyone* that, but I found it out for her.

I found out a lot about Jude. I know where he trains to win his fights at Handsome Jack's. I know he makes excuses for his bruises when he sees the boy he likes, the one who tends bar at Ruby Red, one of my sister's clubs. Hells, I know the drink he orders when he's finding a reason to hang around there.

"Yes?" prompts Ruby, one brow rising.

"Yes," Jude admits, holding very still. "The prince and I were at school together. We weren't close."

That's not true. They were friends. I think when Jude's father left him with nothing, he expected the prince to come to the rescue, and he was met with nothing but a blank stare. But I keep my mouth shut. No need to let him know how many cards I'm holding. Not yet.

"You could identify him?" Ruby asks.

Jude swallows. "Yes."

Ruby treats him to a smile that shines like a gold dollar. "That's good to hear, Jude. You're going to board a ship with Laskia tonight—there's a job I need you to do."

Jude's mouth falls open, his composure gone, and he tries and fails to muster a protest, ending up with "A ship?" in that aristocratic accent of his.

"Oh, don't you worry," Ruby says, leaning forward, all

smiles. "We'll take care of your mother while you're gone, Jude. We know she means everything to you."

Everyone's silent for a long moment, before Jude makes himself speak. "What is it you need me to do?"

Ruby turns that smile on me then, and I steady myself with a breath. I don't usually speak in these meetings, but I told her I wanted to step up. I brought her this plan. I convinced her she needed someone she could trust to carry this out and report back, and as her sister, I'm the only choice. This is mine, to win or lose.

"We're going to intercept the royal progress fleet," I say, my voice calm and even, not a bad imitation of Ruby's, though I can't do her purr. "You're going to confirm the prince is aboard, and we're going to sink it."

Jude pales, the bloodstain on his cheek standing out in stark relief as he turns sallow. "You're going to start a war," he whispers.

"Well," I say, "we're going to be dropping a few bodies in Mellacean navy uniforms into the debris, just to make clear who the enemy is. You can bet your last dollar we're starting a war."

"It's just business," Ruby says, lifting one shoulder in a *what can you do?* shrug. "Our business is in imports and exports, Jude. Think of it more as . . . an adjustment of the marketplace."

Sister Beris clears her throat, and Ruby rolls her eyes. The congregation might be coming back, but Ruby doesn't share my devotion, and she doesn't have to pretend it just yet. We all know who's who in this room. The fact that Sister Beris has come to Ruby for help tells the story.

It matters to Ruby to get this done, though. Her competitors have been pressing in lately. And when you know what it's like to come from nothing, you'll do anything—*anything*—to avoid going back. You can never afford to rest for a moment in our game.

If I were to guess, I'd say that's why Lorento was retired. After all these years, what he knew was worth paying for, and one of Ruby's rivals was prepared to front the cash. If so, it was a dumb move on Lorento's part—if he'd stuck with Ruby, she'd have covered his actual retirement. Now he doesn't get one.

Thing is, we can't know what he told whoever paid. You never know what's coming. If Ruby can pull off this alliance with the green sisters, she might well make herself untouchable.

"Aside from the business part," I say, because *I* would like to avoid annoying the green sister, even if I sold this to Ruby as a financial deal, "the first councilor is distressingly reluctant to do his patriotic duty and take on Alinor. Mellacea needs this too. Every day we edge closer to the fight that will free Macean, but without a spark, the fire will never start."

Finally Sister Beris speaks, in that soft voice of hers you can somehow always hear, even when there's noise around. "Alinor's royal family has forgotten its religious obligations. Barrica the Sentinel is forgotten by her worshippers, and Queen Augusta is sending her brother off to glad-hand and attend picnics. He should already have made his sacrifice in the Isles of the Gods and strengthened their goddess once more. In abandoning that duty, they have offered us an opening to slip past Barrica's guard and awaken Macean, and we must not pass it up."

"Exactly," I agree. "The church feels this is the moment, and our religious duty would also be profitable, so we find our interests aligned. If we work together, we have both the money and the means."

Jude shakes his head slowly, still struggling for words. "You're going to start a *war*. You're going to kill Leander?"

Ruby lazily lifts one brow. "Oh, you're on first-name terms with His Highness? I was under the impression you didn't get along." She casts an idle look at me, and my blood freezes in my veins. I'm *sure* they didn't. I confirmed it. The prince forgot about Jude. Nobody helped after his father died.

"We don't get on," Jude says, but his struggle is obvious. I guess it's still kind of a walk from not liking a guy to dumping him in the ocean.

"Listen," I say, waiting until he looks across at me. "This is happening, Jude. If you want to think about it this way, you're not causing it. You'll just be there. The parties involved would like verification he was aboard the ships."

Jude and I look at each other, and I keep my face calm as I study the blood on his cheekbone. Let him think. He's not stupid—he understands he'll die if he says no. So, not being stupid, eventually he nods.

"Can I say goodbye to my mother?" he asks softly.

"You won't be doing her any favors if you tell her where you're going."

"Understood."

Ruby sets her champagne glass on the low table beside her, and we both jump a fraction as it clicks against the wood. "Laskia, are your things already aboard?" she asks.

I nod, fighting to keep back my smile. Calm. Professional. Ready for this.

"Good," she says. "Take Jude home to see his mother and then to the ship." She turns to Sister Beris. "You will meet them aboard?"

"I am ready," she agrees, as calm as if we're off to the market to pick up fish for dinner.

I rise to my feet, and a beat later Jude does the same beside me.

"Have fun, you two," Ruby says. "And Laskia, don't forget to bring me home a souvenir."

I wink. "I'll get you something nice."

This is it. It's happening. Graduation day.

Jude doesn't say a word as we leave Ruby's rooms behind, heading along a quiet hallway. He doesn't speak until we're out in the alley once more and I'm shoving my hands into my pockets, silently wishing my coat wasn't already on the boat.

"Have you ever killed someone?" he asks quietly.

"First time for everything," I reply, making my voice stay even.

"It's not what you think it'll be, getting up close to blood. When it's actually happening, when it's all over you, when it's not just an idea anymore . . ."

"Maybe that was true for you. It won't be for me."

He shakes his head. "It won't get you what you want."

I snort. "I'm pretty sure his big sister's going to be upset, Jude."

"She will be. But *your* big sister knows there's only so much room at the top."

"You have no idea what you're talking about," I snap. Then I stop and force my voice into calmness again. Ruby rarely snaps, and never just because someone's needling her. "Ruby's my sister. It's a little different, I think, to your rich boarding school friends not having room at the top for the bastard."

"If you say so," he replies, eyes straight ahead.

"Shut up. Or we'll go directly to the boat, and your mother can wonder why you disappeared."

# JUDE

*The Tenements*
*Port Naranda, Mellacea*

E verything hurts, inside and out. The aches of the fight are
kicking in properly now, and my gut is clenching like I've
been punched again. I'm taking one step after another, driven
by this urge to get back to my mother—even though I know she
won't have any advice, any way out of this.

I just want to see her.

As we leave the club behind, we're hit by the full light and
noise of the city. Horns blare, horses stink, and the sidewalk is
packed with people pushing their way past, rushing home or
on their way to a fun night out, ready to dance and drink until
they forget their fears. I half close my eyes against the assault,
replaying the conversation in my head as I try to make myself
understand what just happened.

*Ruby wants me to murder Leander and everyone else on his fleet.*
*That could be half of my class from school.*

We cut away from New Street, leaving the noise and light

behind us once more as we make our way toward the tenements. It's like we're going a lot farther than six blocks, the world growing quieter, dirtier, darker. Battered shop fronts with their names painted in faded letters are closed up tight for the night. They use a lot of bars on the windows around here. There are no autos—they don't fit down the back alleys, and nobody here could afford one anyway. The air is cooler, to go with the quiet.

I look up when we pass the church, by far the grandest building in the slums, though I'm sure it was built here because the land was cheap. The building itself is painted black, to symbolize Macean's slumber. The usual statue of Macean himself, breaking the bonds laid on him by Barrica and awakening, is out front. Beside it stands a green sister, who nods to us politely as we pass by. Does she know who we are?

Ruby's little sister—no, Ruby's *younger* sister; I've made a mistake in underestimating her, and maybe a fatal one—drops a coin into the sister's bowl without a word. I know she goes to church regularly, though Ruby doesn't share her faith. She's smart, to have found a way to align Ruby's interests with the church's.

The question is what she'll do when the demands of her sister and the demands of her god begin to diverge.

For my part, I've never spoken to a green sister before today, and after meeting Sister Beris, I don't want to ever again. It's been years since I went to temple back in Alinor, but the fat, friendly priest at school in his mock military uniform was as different from her as it's possible to be.

We turn a corner, and I turn my thoughts to a more immediate issue. I'm going to have to bring Laskia upstairs with me when we arrive. Every part of me recoils from letting her inside our apartment—I don't want her anywhere near my mother, and the part of me that grew up across the sea doesn't want her to see how we live—but if I leave her standing in the street, in those nice clothes, there's an even-money chance someone will try to mug her while I'm gone. And however that ends won't be good for me.

"This the place?" Her voice surprises me, and I look up to realize we're here, sooner than I thought, or perhaps sooner than I wanted.

She solves my problem of what to do with her by holding the door open for me and just inviting herself to follow me up the stairs. She doesn't lose her breath, steadily climbing all six flights, and since leaving her in the hallway would provoke more gossip than leaving her in the street, I jerk my chin to beckon her in after me when I open the front door.

She stops just inside, pushes the door closed, and leans against it, shoving both hands into her pockets. She's a slim figure in her flawlessly cut suit, dark waistcoat over the crisp white shirt rolled up past her forearms. Everything about her is precise, and everything around her looks shabbier by comparison.

Our place is two rooms—this one holds a small table, a stove, and the sofa I sleep on. I leave Laskia and make my way through to the other room, where Mum lies in bed.

She's staring out the window at the dark night sky, but turns her head as I enter. Her golden skin is sallow, her eyes shadowed, and she looks smaller than I expect. She always does when I come back in from the city outside, so full of life.

I only hazily remember my grandmother, who we visited

here in Port Naranda when I was young. She was a tiny woman, made even smaller by age, who had made the long voyage from Cánh Dō in the south decades before, married a local, and stayed. She sat with the other grandmothers all day, issuing commands and criticisms with clear enjoyment. I always thought my mother would be the same one day. But though she's just as small as her own mother once was, instead she's fading away to nothing.

"You're bleeding," she says quietly, pausing to cough.

I wince, cursing myself for forgetting to wash my face, and sit on the edge of the bed. She coughs again, and I slide a hand behind her back to help her sit up. "It's nothing," I say when she's done.

"You can't fight the whole world, Jude," she says softly, settling back in against her pillows.

"Why not?" I murmur. "The world threw the first punch."

She gazes up at me, and I let her study my face. And I bite my tongue against all the reasons I have to fight—all the reasons I *want* to fight.

"What else should I do?" I ask her. "Just accept it? Let them do what they want to us?"

*Like you do.* The end of that sentence hangs between us, unspoken.

"Not everything can be blamed on someone else," she counters.

"How can you, of all people, say that?" I ask. "He abandoned you. He made promises, and when you needed him, what good was his word? Why shouldn't you blame him?"

She gazes up at me, silent, her breaths coming slowly and painfully. We both know we're not talking about my father, though only one of us knows why Leander's on my mind tonight.

When we left Alinor, Mum wanted it to be a clean break. She was desperate to leave her hurt and heartbreak behind, and to her, that meant fleeing to Port Naranda, the city of her birth. I lost count of how many times she said we had to look forward, not back.

I felt the opposite—I'd have done anything to hold on to my old life. My father had always paid my school fees, paid our rent, but he'd never had anything to do with us, no matter how often I dreamed of the day he'd show up at school, of the way he'd be amazed at my sporting trophies, my grades, the stupid little things that mean nothing now. A tiny part of me always foolishly believed he was going to accept me in the end.

But instead he died, and left us nothing. When we needed him most, he forgot us.

I was so sure Leander was better than him. That Leander would take care of me. A few weeks before, I'd been sitting beside him in class, lending him a pencil, tilting my test paper so he could see the answers to the equations that always baffled him.

I didn't believe he was coming to help me. I *knew* he was.

My mother told me over and over to let him go.

"Jude," she'd say quietly, "the two of you sat together in your classroom, yes, but you and he are not the same. A prince cannot reach down into the gutter for someone like you, not with all the world watching."

I refused to believe her, and she'd sigh softly.

"A clean break will be better," she'd insist.

And I'd keep waiting for Leander, like a fool. He was my

friend. It would have been nothing to him, to rescue me. It would have been so easy.

But he never showed up.

And I learned a lesson I've never forgotten.

"Jude?" My mother's weak, breathy voice draws me back to the present, and I take in her drawn features, the shadows beneath her eyes.

"I'm listening," I whisper.

"Everyone tells the same story different ways," she says quietly, and perhaps she, at least, *is* talking about herself and my father. There's no reason for her to think of Leander today. "And the only version we're the hero of is our own, Jude."

The unearned trust she gives everyone, her faith in everyone's better self—that's why we're here. Someone more worldly would have made sure my father provided for us instead of leaving us at his wife's mercy—and if he or his wife had different versions of that story, I can't bring myself to care.

But that faith my mother has in everyone is what I need to keep going, some days.

"I have to go away for a little while," I say, tilting my head toward the front door meaningfully. "Ruby has a job for me."

Her eyes flick after me, and I see her understand we're not alone.

"Ruby will send the doctor while I'm gone," I say, "and I'll be back quick as I can. There's some potatoes, and there's beans already soaking. When Mrs. Tevner comes by on her way to the market tomorrow, tell her I'll fix her stove as soon as I get back. She's been asking, so that should hold her attention for you while I'm gone."

"I'll tell her," Mum says, though we both know I have no

idea how to do it. I grew up in a neat house in Kirkpool with a cook and a maid, and they didn't teach repairs at boarding school.

The thought of school drags me back to what lies before me—the former friend whose body I'm supposed to identify—and I ease off the edge of the bed, digging underneath it for a bag. She's silent as I shove my spare clothes inside, as I fumble too many times, yanking the drawstring too hard.

"I'll be back as quick as I can," I say again, leaning down to kiss her cheek. Her skin is smooth, but her arm is so thin under my hand, the bones of her shoulder sharp. Something about her sickbed smells sweet, wrong. The tight ball of anger inside me threatens to push its way up my throat, but I force my features smooth, and I stand.

Is there anything else I should tell her, if war is coming? We don't have the money to stock up on food. Maybe what Ruby pays for this job will get us out of the city, though.

"Rest," I say. "Do what the doctor tells you."

"I love you, Jude," she says, reaching out with visible effort to squeeze my hand.

"You too, Mum." I want to say more, but Laskia's presence in the next room pushes the words back down my throat. So I give her a tight nod, and with another squeeze she lets me go.

I walk past Laskia, and as I head for the stairs, I don't look back.

# SELLY

*The* Lizabetta
*The Crescent Sea*

I t's only when the *Lizabetta* is under way that I realize just how small our crew is. She's bowling along in the starlight, her sails unfurled and full now, spirit flags flapping, the deck swaying beneath my feet. But for once, the smell of salt doesn't slow my racing heart.

That heart's tugging me back toward Kirkpool, to the *Freya* still moored at the docks. To my last chance to see Da before the winter storms block the way. When I picture the *Freya* unfurling her own sails in the morning, easing out of the harbor with no notion I was supposed to be aboard, not even a message from me, tears ache hot behind my eyes again.

And at the same time, my heart's beating like a drum in my chest for fear of what Rensa's done. Our captain's standing back at the wheel, and Kyri's near her, rising now from the shrine.

I'm still in the bow, looking out past the figurehead and the bowsprit, though I only know where the horizon is because the stars stop, giving way to inky black water. I curl my hands around the wood of the railing—my gloves cover the backs of my hands, but my fingers are mostly free—and the worn grain of the timber beneath my touch is a familiar anchor on a night when everything has gone wrong.

Besides Rensa, Kyri, and me, there are three more crew—so six in total, of what should be ten.

Abri will be up the mast, no doubt, and the twins have finished with the sails, though how they did it with just the pair of them I don't know.

I wonder what the four we left behind will do when, sometime before dawn, they find an empty space where their ship used to be. Rensa's words still sting—I *do* think of what it'll mean for them. What they'll do for pay, where they'll find to sleep.

I would have asked those questions myself, without her to remind me.

There's a flash of movement above as Abri comes climbing down, and I head to meet her as she reaches the deck, her face looming pale and white in the dark. Though she's not short on curves, and looks soft and round, she's as strong as any sailor. She always has a smile ready—but just now her features are drawn, worried.

"Not a light in sight except for Kirkpool disappearing," she reports. "We're on our own out here."

"Or whoever we're hiding from doesn't have lights either."

She grimaces, and without another word we make our way to the stern, to hear what Rensa has to say. To hear what this boy has to say—what excuse he has for whatever he's dragged us into. Jonlon and Conor drop almost soundlessly from their perches and fall into step with us.

Rensa's lighting a lantern, keeping the shield around it so the glow stays dim, but it's still enough to get a better view of him. And now he's ruined my last chance at happiness, I'm taking a much closer look at this boy.

My first thought is that it simply isn't fair for someone to look like this. He's about my age, but that's where our similarities end. I'm blond, fair-skinned, covered in freckles. He has black hair and strong brows, sandstone-brown skin, and an easy smile. His mouth is made for smirking, eyes ready to crease at the corners.

His breeding's in his face, and his fortune's in his clothes, though he's shed his fine peacoat, dumping it on the deck near the shrine and rolling up his sleeves to reveal those strong forearms and the intricate magician's marks I saw earlier.

I glance up from his lips and find he's watching me look him over. He lifts one brow, amused, and I instinctively narrow my eyes at him. He doesn't seem bothered.

Rensa's voice breaks the moment, and we both turn to where she stands by the lantern. "I thank you all for your quick work tonight. Let me say first, I know we've left four crew behind, and I'm sorry for it. Someone will be waiting for them when they make it back to the dock, and they'll be taken care of. We couldn't risk doing anything out of the ordinary, and keeping everyone aboard might have been noticed." She glances around at us. "Let me say second, we've come by this work because Stanton Walker's fleet has a reputation for keeping our bargains."

There's no *way* my father would have agreed to something

like this—he'd never have allowed us to be pulled into whatever mess we're now tangled up in. My jaw clenches, and I glance around the crew, but they're all staring at the newcomer.

"The *Lizabetta* is proud to uphold the Walker standard," Rensa continues. "As well as being reliable, she's fast, she's quiet, and she doesn't draw attention. All this is what caught the eye of Her Majesty."

"Her *Majesty*," Jonlon gasps, definitely speaking for all of us. I think Abri's mumbling a prayer. Conor flicks me a look that says he's no happier about this than I am.

"What does *he* have to do with the queen?" I burst out, and the fool boy grins at me like I've said something entertaining.

"No offense," Abri tacks on quickly, practically batting her lashes at him, and she winces when I scowl at her.

"*He* is the queen's brother, Prince Leander," Rensa replies simply.

For a moment there's not a sound, save the wind and the sea and my heartbeat in my ears. I'm trying to make myself understand what she's saying, but I keep coming up short.

I knew he wasn't just a servant, but the prince himself? Perhaps he's an impostor. If he's the prince, why was he skulking behind . . .

My mind chooses this moment to present me with a list of the various insults I leveled at him. Goddess, why can't I keep my mouth closed? Then again, I stand by what I said.

*Everything useless around here is beautifully decorated. I wouldn't want you to feel left out.*

And then I tucked a flower behind his ear.

*Spirits save me.*

"I received a message from the queen this afternoon, and

the decision was made quickly," Rensa is saying. "On short notice, to reduce the chance of word getting out. We've set a course for the Isles of the Gods. His Highness has business there."

*The Isles of the Gods.*

A group of islands not marked on any map, each home to a sacred temple to one of the gods, or to the Mother herself. It's forbidden to set foot on them—even if a ship's lookout spotted them, nobody would ever consider landing there.

"But we don't have a chart," I protest.

"His Highness has provided one," Rensa replies with a nod to him, which he returns, like they're equals of some sort.

"I—I thought— He's the *prince*?" Jonlon manages, wide-eyed, and his twin lays a hand on his arm to quiet him. Only their deep brown skin and matching smile lines even suggest Jonlon and Conor might be related, Jonlon tall and broad and calm, his brother short and wiry and usually not calm.

"Why our ship?" I ask, the words out before I think. "We're an honest merchant, not a single flower or garland or dancing girl in sight."

"The garlands are a good look for me," the boy agrees, drawing a snicker from Abri and a smile from Kyri. *Unbelievable.* Then he winks at me. "And I look great with a flower behind my ear."

Kyri immediately shoots me a *did he just wink at you we will discuss this later* glance, her eyes widening, and Rensa shoots me a *shut up or I will shut you up* glare.

"Alas, duty called," the prince continues, still grinning. "I'll make my family's traditional sacrifice when we reach the Isles and strengthen our goddess enough to maintain her watch over Macean. She'll ensure he stays bound in sleep, where he belongs—and so the Mellaceans will have to pack up their toys and wait to play war another day."

"A sacrifice?" Abri asks.

"Every twenty-five years," Prince Leander replies. "My family has been making the voyage for centuries."

I squint at him, trying to dredge up lessons from long ago—I'm not even sure this *was* a lesson as much as a story someone told of an evening to entertain the crew. Something about the twenty-five years sounds familiar.

"Sorry," I say slowly. "Just to confirm, we're on the verge of war, and instead of sending you to make sure our allies are on our side—already not a great plan—the queen is banking on the Mellaceans deciding not to play because they think their god is asleep?"

"Exactly right," he replies cheerfully.

I cannot believe I lost the chance to sail north for *this*.

"I don't even know where to start," I murmur. I know I should shut up, but I'm honestly beyond diplomacy.

"Enough, Selly," Rensa growls.

Prince Leander waves one hand in dismissal. "No, Captain, your crew aren't the only ones to think the royal family have been asleep on the job. But we know our duty. The danger of assassins means it's worth a misdirect, though, worth pretending our attention is somewhere else entirely."

"What's the progress fleet actually doing, then?" Conor asks, his tone much sharper than his brother's. At least one other person on this ship isn't gazing at the prince like they're smitten.

"The progress fleet will set off up the coast, nice and slowly, as though it's heading for the diplomatic visits I had planned," the prince replies. "They'll take their time, move out to sea first—the prince and his friends playing at making a real voyage. Meanwhile, nobody will track the *Lizabetta* as they would an Alinorish naval ship. She *is* beautiful, but unremarkable. Which means we can be down to the Isles and back up again before anyone knows what we're about."

He pauses, and looks around at each of us, lowering his voice and turning on the charm.

"My sister and I are grateful for your help," he continues, sounding like exactly what he is: a boy nobody's ever said no to in his life. "I'll do my best not to get in the way." He drops his voice further, and the whole crew leans in. "And when I was aboard the progress fleet today, I . . . borrowed a few supplies. We'll feast like—well, like princes, I suppose—for tomorrow morning's breakfast."

I snort, and I can tell Rensa hears me. But Leander's grin is so easy, so friendly, it makes co-conspirators of us all, like this is one giant prank instead of a mission so dangerous he has to complete it undercover.

Before any of us can reply, Kyri steps forward, raising her voice. "It'll be a quick trip down to the Isles, if all goes well—and it should, with His Highness charming the spirits beside me. Jonlon, Conor, you're on deck with me for now. Abri, take a look at what's in the galley and pull together something for us to eat. Selly, the prince will be sleeping in our room—I moved our things out an hour ago. You're off watch—grab a spare hammock in the crew quarters and get some rest."

And just like that, still gaping at her over the fact I've been thrown out of my own bed, I'm dismissed.

Leander steps in close to Rensa, they fall immediately into conversation, and spirits save me, he makes her smile in under ten seconds. I didn't know she knew how.

I don't even realize the scholar's on deck until he moves abruptly in the shadows, jerking his eyes away from the prince. I'm sure His Highness is used to being stared at—probably loves it—but all the same, something in the scholar's gaze makes me watch him as he rounds his shoulders and retreats belowdecks.

Kyri checks the shrine, then heads off with the twins to trim the sails.

Abri shoots me a look inviting me to come straight to the galley and gossip, and when I shake my head, she just links her arm through mine and hauls me along the deck with her.

"A *prince!*" she whisper-squeals, definitely not as softly as she thinks. "Don't look like that, Selly! We have the most eligible bachelor on the Crescent Sea aboard!"

"What, you think he's here to do some wooing?" I snap, and immediately regret it when her smile vanishes.

Kyri's voice sounds in my ear, and I jump. "Stow it, Selly. Can't you just enjoy the view?"

"I thought you were supposed to be trimming the sails," I mutter.

"Conor thinks he's handsome too," she replies, ignoring me.

"Then you three can talk about it," I reply, pulling my arm free of Abri's.

"He said his sister and he are grateful to us," Abri muses,

snapping back to her previous dreaminess like I never took the wind out of her sails. "That's *Queen Augusta* he's talking about. Grateful to *us!*"

"Queen Augusta doesn't know who you are," I point out, and Kyri jabs me in the ribs.

"I saw him wink at you," she says. "You're seriously saying you don't want to wink back?"

"I'm seriously saying . . ." But there I stop, because anything more will give away what I was planning. What's lost to me now.

I was *this close* to getting out from under Rensa's thumb. Instead, it'll be months before I have another chance to jump ship and head north.

And now the *Lizabetta* is sailing in the dark for a place nobody ever goes, searching for danger in a temple nobody's been to in years. All because of Prince Leander. It's like an adventure story. Does Rensa think this can work, or was there no way to refuse the queen?

Everyone knows Alinor and Mellacea are creeping closer to the edge of a cliff. Ships at both countries' ports are landed with new taxes, searches, and confiscations every day. Whispers are traveling on the wind about a coming war—and it's not the kind of thing a pilgrimage to an island temple in the middle of nowhere can save us from.

If the royal family thinks invoking a goddess is going to scare off Mellacea's navy, then everyone's in a lot more trouble than I thought, because that's not any prayer I've ever heard of.

There's something about this I'm not understanding . . . but I think I know who might.

# KEEGAN

*The* Lizabetta
*The Crescent Sea*

I force myself to breathe as I make my way along the narrow passageway. One of the sailors told me earlier to keep one hand on the wall once we were under way, in case the ship rolled unexpectedly, but that's hardly what I'm steadying myself against now.

The conversation on the deck broke up a few moments ago, and I've slipped back belowdecks unseen. I became adept at eavesdropping the last few weeks at my family's home, but though I've heard much unpleasant news, this moves to the top of the list by a comfortable margin.

I can see now why the captain tried so hard to convince me to take passage elsewhere this afternoon, only a few hours after welcoming me aboard. That must have been when she accepted this mission.

"I'm sorry for your trouble," she said, scowling at me as though I were the cause of her trouble, when she'd been polite enough as she showed me my cabin and watched me stow my things. "But our plans have changed, and we won't have the space for you after all."

"Captain," I replied, drawing myself up in imitation of my father, "you demonstrably *do* have space for me, as I am occupying it at this very moment."

There were no circumstances under which I was permitting her to deposit me back on the dock—I had only just reached Kirkpool ahead of my father's steward, and my one chance of staying that way was to hide belowdecks and hope he couldn't find my trail before the *Lizabetta* departed. Standing back on the dock with my trunks around me was the opposite of what I needed to do.

"Young man," she began, and as her tone firmed, I knew I could let her get no further. The longer this argument continued, the greater her chance of remembering she could simply assert her authority aboard her own ship.

"Captain Rensa," I replied, making myself sound just as stern. "Let me be clear. You have accepted my money, and you have taken me aboard. If you throw me off now, I will waste no time in telling all of Kirkpool you abandon your business partners for better offers."

Her steely gaze locked onto me, and I thought at the time I had hit a nerve.

Now I realize this would have drawn exactly the sort of attention she couldn't afford, if she'd just been recruited to a secret mission.

I only wish she'd stuck to her guns.

I'd prefer the prince's and my paths never crossed again, but I know he'll spot me eventually, and I'll have to talk to him, and gods, share a meal with him. Just now, even putting off that meeting by a few hours is desirable.

I need to calm myself, collect myself, and then hide in my room—my cabin, rather—and hope he forgets me as often as possible.

Of all the things to happen, and of all the *times* for it to happen, when I was *so* very close to making my escape.

I push the little wooden door open, slip inside, and wedge it firmly closed behind me. The space is small but sensibly constructed. A bunk is built into the wall, made up with a thick quilt that smells a little musty, though not unpleasant. A bracket is set into the floor beneath the porthole and provides a place for my trunk to sit without risk of sliding about. A small table and chair are nailed to the floor. The lamp, which I left lit, swings from a hook in the ceiling.

I assume the girl who went to investigate the galley—by the sound of the order given, she is not the ship's habitual cook—will arrive with food in due course. In the meantime, I'll do my best to distract myself.

I pull up the lid of my trunk, studying the titles nestled amid my few spare clothes. Reading always helps me push away worries, or worse. It helps me breathe. I pause as I spot Tajan's *Mythos and Temples*. I couldn't have brought better reading, it turns out, given our destination. Tajan is boring, often predictable, but he's nothing if not thorough.

A loud thump on the door startles me, and I narrowly escape slamming the trunk's lid shut on my fingers.

*Barrica, please let that be the girl with my meal, and not Leander.*

Holding the treatise carefully against my chest, I open the door and find myself face to face not with the girl who went to the galley, but the other one. She's distinctive—she marches everywhere, like she's bracing herself for battle.

We met this morning and exchanged a few words. She looked me up and down like she was measuring me, then nodded, which seemed to indicate I'd passed a test.

"I'm here to fix your porthole," she says abruptly, brandishing a bucket at me.

"Now?"

"We might hit rough seas overnight," she says, nodding at the Tajan I'm still holding against my chest, in a position I will admit is not unlike a shield. "Lots of paper in here. Hate to see it get soggy."

I'm in no position to argue with her, and I'm too rattled by recent events to resist, so I step back obediently and retreat to sit on the edge of the bed. She sets her bucket on my little table, and leans in to look at the seal on the window.

She's about my age, her blond hair pulled back into a messy braid, her suntanned skin heavily freckled. Her green eyes are narrowed, and she scowls at the porthole as if it's personally offended her. *Selly,* my mind supplies. That's what the captain called her.

"So, heading to the Isles," she says, retrieving a screwdriver from her bucket and beginning to remove the screws from around the brass edge of the porthole.

"Unexpectedly," I agree, and I'm sure I don't hide my grimace. I see now why she's here—she wants information, and she correctly suspects I'll have it.

She holds out the first screw, and I stare at it a beat too long before I understand what she wants. I push up from the bed to join her, holding out my hand so she can drop the screw into it.

We're both silent as she removes its fellows, dropping each of them into my palm, one after another.

She yanks the brass frame off the porthole with a grunt, sets it down on the table, and reaches into her bucket for a large jar, which she unscrews. Then she peels off the fingerless leather gloves she wears, revealing vivid green skin on the back of each of her hands.

I've never seen magician's marks like these on anyone but a child—rather than the intricate design that should indicate her affinity, they're simply a thick stripe, as if they've been painted on by a wide brush. I'm instantly curious, but as I draw a breath to ask, she follows my gaze and her face closes over. Cheeks flushing, she turns her hands over so the backs are hidden. And I keep my mouth shut.

Using her fingers, she scoops a generous dollop of black goo out of the jar, and I mentally implore Barrica to ensure she doesn't touch any of my books afterward.

"Does this make any more sense to you than it does to me?" she finally asks, dabbing the goo into the space she's made by removing the frame. "Because from where I'm watching, we're about to go to war—our ship is sinking—and instead of doing something useful, we're trying to bail it out with an invisible bucket, with a bedtime story."

"It's more than a story," I reply—not that I'm in any mood to defend Leander. "There's every reason to believe the prince can prevent a war if he makes a sacrifice at the Isles. It worked for King Anselm, and it should work now." It would have already worked if he wasn't running late, as usual.

She spins around to face me, eyes narrowing as she tries to decide whether I'm pulling her leg. "Are you serious?

King Anselm is a bedtime story too. That's what we're relying on?"

"King Anselm is much more than a bedtime story," I assure her. "He may have lived five centuries ago, but he was real."

"You're saying he truly ran around fighting a war with a goddess on his team?"

"Well, I think he was on *her* team, but yes."

"How can you possibly know what happened hundreds of years ago?"

"Books, mostly."

"You know they make up the stories in books, right? Especially the ones about magical kings?"

She sounds moderately concerned for my sanity, but finally I'm on solid ground. "Not all stories are made up, and in this case, there are multiple contemporaneous sources on the tale of King Anselm."

She eyes me sidelong, and I think *contemporaneous* might be the snag.

"There are plenty of written accounts of the original sacrifice," I say. "Many are by people who were alive at the time, rather than repeating something they'd heard. Also, they line up in the important details. That means it almost certainly happened the way they say it did."

She stops her work to properly study me, measuring my explanation. I find myself fighting the urge to shift my weight like a schoolboy found wanting, as if something depends on her accepting my words.

"If it's any comfort," I venture, "I'm also far from happy His Highness has chosen our boat with which to make the journey."

She snorts and retrieves a length of thin rope from her bucket, pressing it into place around the edge of the porthole, where it sticks to the mysterious goo. "All right. Let's hear the evidence, then."

I blink at her. "What?"

"You said there's plenty of it. That spoiled brat of a prince has cost me—well, enough. Too much. Convince me it wasn't for nothing. How's he going to stop a war?"

I back up a couple of steps to take a seat on the edge of my bunk again, cradling the screws carefully in my hand as I consider where to start.

"Well, the story begins about five hundred years ago. Or, to be more precise, five hundred and *one* years. And in this case, precision matters. Prince Leander's many-greats-uncle, Anselm, was king. And he was at war with Mellacea." I pause, to see if I've made this too basic—I don't know what sort of education girls who live on ships receive.

She nods, thumping the last section of the rope into place with her fist and retrieving a cloth from the bucket to clean off her hands. "Right, and in the stories, the gods were fighting too—I mean, literally running around like people, fighting each other. And in the end, Barrica the Sentinel made the king into a magic warrior, and together they put Macean the Gambler to sleep and defeated Mellacea, and then both vanished forever," she says. "Or something like that."

"Something like," I agree. "Though Anselm was turned into a Messenger—perhaps—not a magical warrior."

"What's a Messenger?"

"Well, his sacrifice comes first in the story. Religious and academic texts say the gods drew power from two sources: faith and sacrifice. The greater their number of worshippers, the stronger they were. That's the faith. The greater the sacrifices made in their name, again, the more powerful they were."

"Same as magic," she concludes. "Except spirits only need tiny sacrifices, like candles, or a bit of your lunch, and more like sweet-talking than faith, as best I can tell."

"Exactly," I agree, pausing as I notice her phrasing. *As best I can tell.* Odd, for someone with magician's marks.

"So his sacrifice was to help her bind Macean in sleep—this part I know. What did he sacrifice?"

"Well, you have to understand the stakes. The two gods had clashed so violently, the entire country of Vostain was destroyed. It lay in the place we now call the Barren Reaches."

Her brows rise. "Where the Bibliotek is?"

"Exactly. The Bibliotek is a neutral, independent place of learning—that's why they worship the Mother rather than any of the seven gods—and it was built in a place that reminds us of what happens when we allow conflict."

"I didn't know there used to be a country there," she admits. "So Barrica and Macean were fighting, and . . . and that had happened."

"Yes. And Macean was strong. And he was daring—there's a reason they call him the Gambler, the god of risk. Barrica used to be called the Warrior, and she knew she was the only one who could stop her brother. She saw what happened to the country of Vostain—and what happened to their youngest brother, Valus, who had lost all his worshippers in one instant—and she spoke to King Anselm. As king of Alinor, he was first among her followers."

"And she made him into a magical warrior."

"Not quite yet. She needed him to strengthen her first. So he did. King Anselm made the greatest sacrifice he had to offer. His own life."

She drops the rag she's using to clean her hands back into the bucket, turning to stare at me. "He killed himself?"

"The only way to save his people was with an overwhelming act of sacrifice and faith. One so great, it would strengthen Barrica beyond compare. It worked. She rose up and bound her brother Macean in sleep, where he has been ever since."

"And the king stayed dead?" she asks, frowning. "Barrica didn't bring him back, for her first miracle? When does the Messenger part happen?"

"There's . . . some debate. There are even older tales, from centuries before the War of the Gods, about the Age of Messengers. About beings imbued with the power of the gods, but themselves neither god nor human. They say there was a Messenger who created the flat plain Mellacea now stands on, another who diverted a whole river in Petron. The stories are so old, their origins are mostly lost."

"So maybe they never existed at all?"

"The most important thing a scholar must learn to say is *I don't know.* And I don't."

"What do you think?"

"Some say Anselm became a Messenger, centuries after the last of them were gone. But shortly after the battle he simply vanishes from history, and his sister is crowned, and her children after that. I think perhaps people wanted him to have survived, and they created stories to make it so."

"Grim," she concludes.

"It was a grim time. But it worked. With Macean bound in sleep and unable to assist them, the Mellacean forces were defeated, and Alinor prevailed."

"Simple as that."

"Except for King Anselm," I concede. "The royal burden is a heavy one. For some more than others."

"Doesn't seem to be weighing very heavily on the prince," she snorts.

I press my lips together, and allow my silence to make my reply for me.

"So tell me how this gets us on a boat now," she says, holding her hand out for the screws. "No, give them to me one at a time."

I hand her a screw. "Every twenty-five years, the sacrifice is renewed by one of the royal family."

She drops the screw and stares at me in open horror. "You're not saying the prince wants to sail to the Isles to die?"

I shake my head, and she drops to her knees to hunt for the lost screw. "The royal family doesn't share the details," I say, "but one of the king's descendants travels to the Isles of the Gods—to the Isle of Barrica in particular—and makes a sacrifice of their own. They always come back unharmed, so one assumes it will be something small—that the effort of the journey is an act of faith, and a sacrifice in itself."

"And it's been twenty-six years," she concludes, rising to her feet and returning to work. "So he's a year late for his appointment. They've been sailing there every twenty-five years for all this time?"

"Without fail. Discreetly, for obvious reasons."

"Nobody's ever tried to stop them?"

"They'd hardly talk about it if they did."

"And an extra year matters that much?"

"Not exactly," I say, passing another screw as she extends her hand. To my surprise, I'm almost . . . enjoying the conversation. Or the instructional element, in any case. I've daydreamed this sort of thing will happen all the time when I'm at the Bibliotek. When it's been hard, I've imagined myself lounging about in the library, debating issues of history and culture. "Tell me, are you religious?"

"I don't worship at temple," she says, closing one eye to focus on fitting the screwdriver into the head of the latest screw. "But who does? I've got a healthy respect, though."

I nod. "Faith is different in Alinor, compared to other places. The other gods withdrew from the world completely, and their religion has become more of a . . . formality, for want of a better word. But Barrica the Warrior remained to watch over the sleeping Macean. That's how she became Barrica the Sentinel instead. She left the door ajar, is the way the clergy often puts it. She no longer healed the sick, or performed great miracles, but she showed us she was present. The yearly filling of the wells, the way the flowers bloom in the temples no matter the season."

"The temple flowers don't do that anywhere else?" she asks, blinking. "How do they know their gods are real?"

"Well, they don't," I say. "They just hope, and believe, and not even very much of that these days. And in recent years faith has waned in Alinor, too. Most people are like you—they don't make it to temple very often. But in Mellacea, they say, the churches are full."

"Oh."

"Their green sisters say soon Macean will be strong enough to break free of his slumber. So in *that* context, with less and less faith empowering Barrica, and more and more empowering the sleeping Macean . . . an extra year might matter very much. A war between two countries is one thing. If he can shrug off her bonds and awaken, then war between two *gods* . . . We have only to look at the Barren Reaches to understand there's no telling how many would die, or what the world would look like afterward."

She shakes her head slowly. "You scholars really think they can come back and fight each other?"

"Personally, I'd prefer not to find out."

She considers this, reaching for another screw. "A war like that, they'd conscript ships like ours, wouldn't they? Do you think it'll happen? Is that why you took passage for Trallia?"

"No. I have no interest in being caught up in a religious war, but my motives were personal. I was going to travel from Trallia to the Bibliotek and take up a place as a student."

*And I was so, so close to making it there.*

"The war will be personal too," she points out. "Isn't your family in Alinor?"

"My family can defend themselves." My family are military through and through. They'd *love* an excuse to put their training to use.

We both hear the shift in my tone—the words arrive in a rush, too defensive. She turns her head, and I brace for a jab or a pointed question.

Instead, she takes the opportunity to shift to another topic I don't particularly want to discuss, correctly supposing I'll still choose it over the topic of my parents. "So, you know the prince? I saw how you looked at him, up on deck."

I grimace involuntarily. "I knew him at school," I settle on.

"What's he like?"

I don't particularly want to answer the question. This girl—Selly—is refreshingly blunt, and I don't want to lie to her face. I also don't want to say anything I'll regret later. "Prince Leander enjoys life," I say eventually. "And worries very little about anything."

"Huh." She drops the screwdriver back into the bucket and twists the lid onto the jar of goo. "That why he's running late for his sacrifice? He was too busy having fun?"

Again I say nothing, and she growls in the back of her throat.

"Well, he's cost you your trip to the Bibliotek, and he's cost me plenty as well. I guess I should hope he's not so late he costs a lot of people much more than that. Thanks for the lesson, Scholar."

I open my mouth to correct her, to give her my name, then close it again. "You're welcome."

She nods, hefting her bucket. "Let me know if you get any more water in through that porthole."

I stay on the bunk as she leaves, and it's only when the door closes behind her with a thump that I realize my hand is still resting on Tajan's *Mythos and Temples.* I fumble as I flip it open, and leaf through the pages in search of an interesting chapter to calm my thoughts.

I'd much rather study history than find myself a part of it.

# LEANDER

◆

*The* Lizabetta
*The Crescent Sea*

It turns out bunks on ships are narrower than you'd expect. I
nearly fell out of mine a couple of times overnight, when I
forgot where I was and tried to turn over, then had to scramble
to safety, tangled up in my covers.

I can make almost anything look good, but it's probably
not a bad thing the other bunk wasn't occupied. *At least try to
avoid witnesses,* my sisters always tell me, exchanging a look,
and sighing.

Someone packed a gold-threaded blanket in my luggage,
and I scoffed at it when I was hunting through my trunk to see
what was in there, then ate my words and cuddled up underneath it when I got a look at the quilt I was supposed to use.

Now, though, morning's here, and there's a glow around
the edges of the porthole's shutter.

Oh, and someone's knocking on the door. That must be
what woke me.

"Come in," I call, sitting up in bed, running one hand through my hair, then giving up as I feel it stand up in every direction. Whatever. I'm charming, I can make it work.

The door opens, and the girl from yesterday lets herself in with a tray and a wary expression. Then her gaze drops to my chest, and I realize a moment after she does that I'm not wearing a shirt.

The next ten seconds are chaos.

Her eyes widen, and an instant later she's juggling the breakfast tray. I start to move, ready to throw aside the blanket to help her, and then I *also* realize I'm not wearing a whole lot underneath the blanket. She guesses the same thing around the same time and yelps a "Don't you dare!"

I'm stuck under the blanket, praying she'll recover in time to save my meal, and we both breathe a sigh of relief when she dumps the tray on top of my legs.

"There, food," she mutters, already retreating toward the door.

"It's not the first time I've caused carnage by taking off my shirt," I reassure her. "There was this one time in— Actually, I'm not sure that's helpful."

She shoots me a look informing me my very existence isn't helpful and closes the door firmly behind her, leaving me with a very respectable, if simple, breakfast of eggs, sausages, buttered toast, and fruit.

That's the second time I've failed to make a good impression on her. Strange. I'm starting to wonder if she means it.

I turn my attention to my meal. Usually my own chefs take over when we're somewhere other than the palace, but though the decorative arrangements are missing, and someone's cut the apple into serviceable chunks instead of a flower shape or something, it's come together pretty well.

I decide, after brief consideration, not to call her back and ask about orange juice.

Half an hour later I'm fed, dressed, and ready to explore my new kingdom. I sling my satchel over my shoulder, feeling slightly foolish about it, but with my sister Augusta's voice in my ears: *Don't let it out of your sight.*

There's a tiny stone statue of Barrica in a hollow by the door, glued down, with a medal bearing the likeness of the Mother strung up beside her for good measure. I touch Barrica with one fingertip as I pass by, directing my thoughts her way for a moment. Her surface has been worn by all those who've done the same thing before me.

I know going to the temple is an obligation at the holidays for most people, but my family's bond to Barrica means my relationship to her has always been personal. I feel her presence clearly when I summon her, and it's like having a slightly scary, rather militaristic sister looking over my shoulder whenever I pray—and I'm not easily intimidated by those. After all, I live with Augusta.

This little statue's smoothed-out expression seems particularly disapproving, though. "Don't look at me like that," I mutter. "I'm on my way."

As I climb up the wooden steps, it's like emerging from a dimly lit, unsteady cave into a world of light and crisp, salty air. The deck is still wet with dew, the rigging creaking softly above me, the white sails full and round as the boat hurries along. It's earlier than I thought, and the sun is only just over the horizon.

That horizon is perfectly flat, stretching in every direction, and I turn in a slow circle to take it in, studying every aspect of the boat as I reach it. I can't help smiling. The sky is a clear, warm blue, the sea a wide blanket of white-tipped navy, and I feel the water spirits surging around the boat, following it with curiosity, the air spirits dancing across the sails. They're in a playful mood, and so am I.

One of the crew is heading for the nearest mast, and he nods a wary greeting at me before he sets his foot on a peg, reaching to haul himself up and start climbing. I follow his progress as he works his way up into the rigging, past the spirit flags, grabbing hold of the ropes with confident hands. The larger man the captain mentioned was his brother is already up there and greets him with a nod. Everything's quiet except the waves. It's not like anywhere I've ever been.

Turning farther, I find my new friend—or my new enemy, I suppose, but I have days to win her over—leaning against the railing, studying the sea. I was thinking about her yesterday afternoon, after we met at the dock.

I was wondering who she was, which ship was hers. I'm used to letting things go, though, and despite the strange tug I felt to find her, to find out more about her, to convince her I wasn't such a terrible person, I knew I had to let her go too.

It was hard to hear myself think about her over the chorus of lecturing Queensguard, anyway, once they found me and dragged me back home.

I walk over now to take a place a few feet along from her, leaning against the rail like she does and looking sideways at her, studying her more closely.

She's built like she uses her muscles for a living. Wisps of blond hair are loose from her braid, playing around her face, and she has tanned, freckled skin, full lips. They tighten when she looks sideways in return, and spots me there. Her eyes are a mossy green, and they immediately narrow, far from friendly.

"Morning," I offer, trying out a smile on her. It doesn't have the usual effect.

She grunts, turning around to rest her back against the railing and look up at the men in the rigging.

"What are they doing?" I try.

"Trimming the sails," she says, without taking her eyes off them. "The prevailing wind goes straight from Alinor to Mellacea. We need to sail across it, or we'll deliver you directly to your enemies."

If I'm honest, she doesn't sound like she thinks this would be such a bad idea. She's probably not a morning person.

I let the quiet stretch for a little, then try again, boosting the charm a notch or two. "Sorry, let me start over. May I ask your name?"

"Selly," she supplies grudgingly. "Selly Walker."

"And are you . . . Sorry, I don't know the names of the positions on the boat."

"*Ship,*" she corrects me. "I'm just a sailor. A deckhand." This, to judge by her scowl, is a sore spot.

We lapse into silence again, both looking up at the sails. I suppose she's assessing the way the men are trimming them. I let my focus shift until I can see the air spirits flowing around them, like golden motes of dust.

Then we both speak at once.

"Selly, if I've—"

"Listen, if you think for a minute—"

We both break off, and our eyes meet, and she flushes under her freckles. "What do you want?"

I shake my head. "Forget that. What was it you wanted me to listen to?" I risk a quick grin. "I'll be very attentive, I promise."

She fixes me with a flat look. "All right. I was going to say you can stop trying to make friends with me. You've got the captain, and I promise what I think won't make a drop of difference."

"It does to me," I protest. "And if you're Selly Walker, this is your family's fleet, so it sounds to me like you matter very much."

And beyond that . . . it just seems to matter. I choose to leave that unsaid, partly because it's confusing.

She snorts. "Look," she says, turning to face me and lowering her voice, her glare settling in for the long haul. "I have spent a year under Captain Rensa, running every thrice-damned errand she could dream up, and never to her satisfaction. I was *hours* away from heading back to my father's ship before you came aboard."

"Oh." I can't help my wince. "And now?"

"And now I'm half a year away from seeing him again, at best," she replies, in something like an actual growl. "Thanks to you. I *knew* you were . . ."

"Strikingly handsome? Destined to cross your path again?"

"Trouble," she shoots back.

An idea is starting to take hold, and I'm not sure what to do with it. "Selly, may I ask you a question?"

"Can I stop you?"

"Do you . . . do you *genuinely* not like me?" I can barely keep my tone serious, but as I take in the look in her eyes, my smile starts to die.

*She's put the boy prince on the job. It's like she* wants *to fail.*

*Nobody's going to take him seriously. Who ever has?*

I'm not sure what part of my brain thought it was necessary to memorize her insults yesterday, but now it wants to reproduce them for me at the least helpful time possible.

Selly's shaking her head. She switches tones, and I'm fairly sure her next words are an unflattering impression of me. "'I heard he wore a gold-sequined coat for the ages.' *Like* you, Prince? I don't even understand you. You take nothing seriously, and you have no idea what that means for everyone around you."

"Look, I'm very sorry about your father, but—"

"It's not your fault?" She drops into another impression of me. "Then I'm 'just naturally cranky,' I guess."

I open my mouth, then close it again. I can win over anyone, given enough time, but I'll admit I've made this difficult for myself.

"So you can stop trying to make friends," she continues, oblivious to my thoughts. "I'll be sailing the ship, and you'll be keeping out of the way." Her gaze slides sideways before I can reply, and her lips curve to a small, surprising smile. "You could try *him,* instead," she suggests.

I follow her gaze and find a stooped figure with very pale skin and dark hair shaved down to stubble coming up the wooden steps. He doesn't look like a sailor—he must be the passenger the captain mentioned last night. I owe him an apology for stranding him aboard my little expedition.

Then he lifts his head, and I start in recognition. "Wollesley? Keegan Wollesley?"

He freezes, then fixes me with a look like I've made a spelling mistake. "Good morning, Your Highness," he says, stiffly courteous. "I thought you would still be in bed." The implication is perfectly clear: *I wouldn't have come up on deck if I'd thought we'd run into each other.*

"What are you doing here?" I ask, trying to imagine what Keegan Wollesley, of all people, is doing aboard a merchant ship.

"It appears I'm sailing to the Isle of Barrica, same as you," he replies, all disapproval.

So, in the face of that disapproval, I do what I've been doing since we were eleven years old. I annoy him.

"Imagine what a research trip it'll be. There's no other way you'd ever be allowed to see the place. We're sailing to an island that's not even on a map, Wollesley. That doesn't interest you even a little? You could write a famous monograph on it."

"I'd rather read a monograph on it," he replies darkly.

"Lord Wollesley," I chide him. "If you keep your head buried in a book all your life, you'll miss all the fun."

"At least I've read a book," he shoots back. "And at least I will be doing what I choose. I will have set my own course, rather than simply drifting along, never striving for something that matters."

Beside me, Selly snorts, sounding suspiciously like she's amused.

Wollesley's flushed, caught somewhere between surprise and horror that the words in his head somehow made it to his mouth.

And I'm maintaining my easy grin, thanks to a lifetime of practice.

"Look at you, already dropping those nautical metaphors," I drawl. "It's like you've been at sea all your life. Tell me, where were you headed before you joined me on my way to the Isle of Barrica?" Something's prickling at the back of my mind, and I reach for half-remembered gossip. "I thought I saw your engagement announced in the papers?"

"I was supposed to be sailing for Trallia, then on to the Bibliotek," he replies icily.

"With your wife to follow?"

"We did not marry," he replies. "We found we did not suit each other."

"I didn't think any sort of romantic entanglement suited you, Wollesley."

"Correct."

"Better a book than a person?"

"A book rarely lets you down," he says crisply. "You will find friends in its pages when they are nowhere else."

"Come now, Wollesley, I—" I have no idea where I'm going with that sentence, because he and I were never friends at school, and it would be laughable to argue otherwise—or pretend we're talking about books at all.

"Please, Your Highness," he retorts. "Your friendship spans

wide but never deep. It didn't even reach the ones who thought they were assured of it, let alone someone like me."

"Hard to imagine why you could possibly have been excluded." I almost snap the words, and I regret them as soon as they're out. It's my role to be the generous one. It always is, when you have everything.

Wollesley levels a long stare at me, then takes the two steps backward determined by protocol—even if he and I are the only ones who recognize it—and turns away, to disappear below-decks once more.

I know what Wollesley was talking about when he said my friendship didn't reach the ones who thought they could rely on it—he meant Jude. If we were closer, he'd know what I tried after Jude disappeared. He'd know everything I tried, from the reasonable to the outright desperate. But I suppose for us to be closer, I'd have to . . . well, be a better friend.

This voyage is inducing a lot more self-examination than I anticipated, and I'd like it to stop.

I only remember Selly's beside me when she speaks, and I look across to see her studying the stairs speculatively. Then she turns her green-eyed gaze on me, and it's instantly ten percent less friendly.

"He did mention you knew each other," she says, studying me as if—and I didn't think this was possible—she's finding new flaws she hadn't seen before.

"We were in the same year at school," I reply. "He left a couple of years ago, though. His parents and the headmaster thought tutors would work better, as I understand it."

"What's that mean?"

"Too clever," I interpret, shoving away the mood he's left me in and reaching for a smile instead. "Drove the form masters mad with questions. And as you can see, he doesn't bring out anyone's best side."

"I like him," she says, eyeing me like she's issuing a dare.

"Oh, all right. I'll apologize later. But I'm *sure* Wollesley was engaged. Strange, to see him heading for the Bibliotek."

"He said it didn't work out," she says, shrugging.

"Mmmm." It's my turn to narrow my eyes now, thoughtful. "That sort of engagement is very carefully negotiated. It's not really about whether the happy couple are enthusiastic about it." Then the truth clicks into focus, and I grin.

"What?" She's scowling.

I ease in a touch closer, bowing my head to confide in her. "I'll give you any odds you like that the engagement wasn't called off properly. Or at all."

"What, you mean . . ." Her eyes widen, hostility momentarily forgotten.

"I promise you, Wollesley's not the sort to propose to anyone. I thought when I saw the announcement that his family must have bullied him into it. I'd say he's taken what he could, tried to disguise himself—that's the only reason shaving his head ever makes sense, it's *not* his look—and he's running for the hills. Or more accurately, the library. The Bibliotek is on neutral ground—so the knowledge inside it can never belong to any one country. His family could have wailed all they like, my sister never would have retrieved him for them."

Selly raises one brow. "Well, that's two of us who've had our plans ruined. We should form a club."

I'm about to shoot back a quick reply when she glances

away at the sails once more, and I get a better look at her face. There's a tension I hadn't noticed before in her jaw, and the shadows beneath her eyes are showing up like bruises on her fair skin.

And then I remember she usually bunks with the first mate, and it was probably her bed I was in last night, while she made do with a hammock.

"You know," I say slowly, "you're right."

She's all suspicion as she eyes me. "About?"

"I owe you an apology too," I say. "I mean it. I had no idea I was robbing you of your chance to see your father, but I'm truly sorry I did."

She glances away again, lips pressing together in a thin line, making me wonder if I've made a mistake in raising the subject of her father again. "Captain took the job," she says eventually, and I hate the tension that takes over her body with those words.

"On a ship that's a part of your family's fleet. I'm grateful. What we're doing right now, it will make a difference to a lot of people."

"Pretty sure it would have made even more difference if you were on time, a year ago," she points out. But the edge to her voice has faded. A little. I could still cut myself on it.

"Fair," I concede. "And I know it's a huge pain in the ass, having to haul me out to the middle of nowhere."

"Don't think taking responsibility will get you off the hook," she warns me.

I hold up my hands to protest my innocence. "What about a peace offering?"

She raises a brow, but it's not a no. I can work with that.

"Sailors like maps and charts, don't they? Want to see something you've never seen before?"

Her gaze, which had drifted out to the water, snaps back to me.

"You didn't give it to Rensa?"

"I gave her the official, royal charts. I've got something better." I open my satchel, reaching for the journal. It's inside a waxed cotton pouch—waterproof—for one extra level of protection.

"What is it?" She leans forward as I pull it free, unable to hide her anticipation, and I don't blame her. It's forbidden in every country to show the Isles of the Gods on any map. Clearly the lure of it is tantalizing enough that she's willing to put up with me for a few more minutes, against her better judgment.

"It's a map, and it's more than a map." I flip it open and riffle through the pages slowly. Generations of my family have written in this battered little book—most recently my father, and my grandmother before him, and this is just the latest in a long line of journals. The earliest, most faded pages of the first volume hold the thoughts of King Anselm himself, the night before he died.

My ancestors' handwriting crowds the dog-eared pages, interspersed with sketches, illustrations, and in the earlier days, marks where someone worked on the journal over a meal, I suspect.

It's the most valuable thing my family owns, and for all I dragged my feet on this voyage—at the time, the freedom of finishing school and the endless nights of celebration seemed far more fun—now that I'm out here at sea, I like the idea of adding my own thoughts. Of someone reading about *this* voyage, a century from now.

But once I've added my entry, made my sacrifice, I'll have fulfilled my entire purpose in life. All I'm needed for is this pilgrimage, unless they want me to do it again in another quarter century.

And people wonder why I like parties so much.

"Here are the Isles," I say, pushing that thought aside and flipping to an early page, which shows the map of the continent and the Crescent Sea we both know so well, but with one addition you don't find on a usual map.

I tap the Trallian city of Loforta, and trace a line straight down until I reach a circle of eight tiny islands, a long, long way from anywhere. They're joined by a faintly drawn line, and Selly leans in closer to take a look, her braid swinging over her shoulder, which presses in against mine for a moment—then she notices our close proximity and pulls back. Her eyes don't leave the little hand-drawn map, though.

"What's the circle the little islands are sitting on?"

"The Mother's Crown, it's called. A reef just beneath the surface, joining each of the Isles to its neighbors. Inside, it's flat as a mirror—the Still Waters, the journal calls it."

"That'll be something to see," she admits.

"Won't it? Here, the largest of the islands is the Isle of the Mother, and the other seven are each devoted to one of her children. We'll only visit Barrica's. It's here, next to the Mother's."

"I always say I've sailed every place that's on a map," she murmurs, still gazing at the sketch like it's gold-plated. "Now it'll really be true."

"Is that truly why sailors don't go there?" I ask. "It's not on the charts? I've wondered—I mean, who would know if you did?"

"Well, *we'd* know. First, most sailors are religious, so they won't go somewhere forbidden by the gods. And second, there are stories about what happens if you go there, don't you know?"

"No, what do they say?"

She grins. "They say if you go there, you get to find out what happens when you anger a god."

I raise my brows. "Lucky I'm sailing on the queen's orders, and I'm particularly charming."

She snorts. "You've been told that far too many times, Prince."

We gaze at each other, and I realize I'm reaching an unexpected conclusion: I like this girl. Even if she has no use for me.

Whatever happens on this voyage, we won't see each other again afterward. Unlike the people I meet in my normal life, she has nothing to gain, and it's refreshing.

Though it would be helpful if she were a *bit* more impressed by my title.

"Where's your favorite place on the boat?" I ask. And then, when her brow creases: "Ship, I mean."

"Why?"

I shrug. "This is your place. You know more about it than me. Teach me something?"

Her green eyes meet mine, and as she looks me up and down, I know she's measuring me up. Usually I'd try a smile about now, but I'm not sure that's going to work here. It's too much to hope she understands that showing her the journal, and the map inside, that meant something. I've never done that before.

Slowly she nods, and it's a bit concerning how much this pleases me.

"Come with me," she says, pushing off the railing. She just turns away, sure I'll follow. No *please,* no curtsy. It's great.

She leads me toward the front of the ship. The bow, she'd tell me to call it. We pass by a little boat turned upside down and lashed to the deck, its name painted on the back in neat gold letters: *Little Lizabetta.* Selly trails one hand along it in silent greeting.

"What's that one for?" I ask. I've seen lifeboats on big steamers, but this is far too small.

"Not every port is like Kirkpool," she replies over her shoulder. "Sometimes we anchor offshore and row in. Come on, right up forward."

Together we make our way farther forward, to where the railings from each side come in to meet in a point at the very front of the boat. The bowsprit juts out ahead of us, like an old knight's lance.

"Can you climb out onto that?" I ask, speculative. It would feel like flying.

"I have," she replies. "But if you fell off, you'd end up under the boat. I don't know what the punishment is for me if a prince gets himself knocked out cold and shredded by barnacles on my watch, but I'm guessing I won't like it." She pauses then, glancing up at the sharp point ahead of us.

"Go on," I say. "I'm curious, what are you showing me?"

Now that we're here, she hesitates, and I hold my breath, willing her not to change her mind. She looks back at me again, the wind tugging her hair free of its braid and sending it dancing around her face. I half expect the spirits to make a game of it, but they swirl past her and spin around me instead.

She just reaches up with one hand—she wears fingerless leather gloves, as protection against the ropes, I suppose—and brushes her hair back impatiently.

Then she takes the final step forward and beckons me to join her with a jerk of her head. We have to cram in hip to hip, shoulder to shoulder, and her glare warns me not to even notice how close we are, let alone say anything about it.

I follow her lead and lean out over the rail, and immediately I see what she wanted to show me.

There's a figurehead beneath us—a carved woman crowned with shells and seaweed—but lower still is the water. The front of the ship cuts through its surface like a tailor's neat scissors, and the white waves flare out to either side like lace. Rainbows glimmer where the light catches the spray, there and gone, there and gone.

"Oh, hello," I breathe. I felt them everywhere around us as soon as I came up on deck, but this is the place to greet the local water spirits, I can tell.

There are spirit flags flapping above us, but the first mate, Kyri, made the effort to string them up, so they won't do as my sacrifice. Instead, I reach into my pocket, pulling out the crusts of the toast I had for breakfast. I stowed them there by habit—you never know when you'll need something.

Anytime the spirits make magic, they need a sacrifice. Choose what you offer and they'll consume it—it just vanishes into nothing. That's why we Alinorish magicians like our candles so much—formed and blessed in temples to our goddess, they're rich enough that the spirits consume them slowly, rather than all at once. And no magician wants to be caught without an offering—if the spirits don't ignore you for the insult, they'll consume a piece of *you* instead. Magicians are good at having something in their pockets.

Crusts aren't much of an offering, but I don't need much for a hello. I toss them toward the water, and as they fizzle into nothingness, I reach out with my mind, opening myself up to see what I can find. It's like reaching out my hand in a dark room, knowing someone's there, waiting to see if they'll take it.

They leap for that connection in an instant, and I pour my friendship into the bond, my pleasure at their beauty. The waves around the bow flare in response, spray leaping up and catching the sun. The rainbows glint brighter, and I feel the spirits' willingness to do whatever I ask.

"Huh," Selly murmurs beside me, glancing at the emerald-green magician's marks coiling all over my forearms, vivid against my brown skin.

I follow her gaze. "What?"

"They're responding to you," she says slowly. "I can tell just by watching." There's something almost wistful in her voice, and some other note I can't define. "I've never seen a royal magician in action before."

Ordinary magicians can only charm one kind of spirit—earth, water, air, or fire. Magicians of the Royal House of Alinor have always been different. And even among them, *I'm* different. More powerful. I like to annoy my older sisters by telling them it's because I'm so very good at being charming. Despite the current evidence to the contrary.

"The water spirits love the *Lizabetta*," I say, as the waves build ahead of us, then come apart in swaths of foam.

As I anticipated, mention of her beloved ship diverts Selly. "Are they different from air spirits?" she asks, turning to study the water with me.

"Yes," I say, though I have to pause and think about how to explain that difference. "There's a sort of mischief to water spirits, more energy. It takes a lot of work to direct a breeze, and the way I communicate with air spirits is more solemn. It's a very polite *I respect you.*"

"And what do you say to the water spirits?" she asks.

I answer without hesitation. *"I love you, you beautiful thing."*

It's lucky I'm already getting used to that glare of hers, or my veins would turn to ice. "Hey," I point out. "You asked. And that's the answer. I flirt with them."

"I don't even know why I'm surprised," she mutters.

"At least it works on someone around here," I counter, and I swear, for a second I'm *this* close to coaxing a smile out of her. Pretty sure I'm going to be working every minute to the Isles for that—but the irritation is a little less.

"Was it always like this?" she asks, and then, seeing my confusion, clarifies: "You had both types of spirits early?"

"All four types, as long as I can remember," I say. "I know I started earlier than most."

You can tell a magician by their marks, which are on their arms when they're born: a thick green stripe on their skin, running down each forearm to the back of their hand. On a baby, it looks like someone's taken to you with green paint.

By the time they're five, a fire will flare when they pass, or wind chimes will gently sing, and a few years after that they'll manage to charm the spirits for the first time. In that moment the marks change, rearranging themselves into intricate designs that look like tattoos, reflecting the spirits with whom they share an affinity. It's a day of celebration, the magician's family throwing a party, inviting everyone they know to admire the new marks. For most people that's around age eight or nine, and it usually takes them until fifteen or so to truly master their gift.

I'm told I made my mobiles spin above my crib, and splashed my nursemaids with the bathwater before I knew how to walk. My marks were in place before my first birthday, curling and looping all over my chubby little toddler arms. I was apprenticed to the best magicians in Alinor before I could talk, in an attempt to stop me from wreaking havoc.

My sisters *love* telling the story of the time I nearly set our mother's hair on fire at a court reception when I was five. I'm eternally grateful they don't know that the earth tremor that left cracks in the palace a few years back was my first kiss. I've improved my control since then.

To Selly I say, "The spirits and I, we get along."

"It's only fair *someone* should like you," she allows generously, glancing away toward the horizon.

"Look, I think you're getting the wrong impression—people usually like me very much."

"Apart from the whole country of Mellacea, who want to kill you, right? Hence the secret voyage?"

"That doesn't count, it's not personal." When I follow her gaze, there's a steamship, a smudge of dark smoke rising from its funnels. It would be faster than a ship like this, but also a lot less discreet. We decided on a boat like the *Lizabetta* because they're so common, always on their way somewhere. The steamships are big, inelegant. No magicians needed to run them, no care or finesse.

"Do you think it'll work, what you're going to do at the Isles?" she asks, shifting the subject, and when I glance across again, her expression is serious. More serious than I'd have expected.

Although I said to the crew the royal family weren't asleep on the job, the truth is Mellacea's aggression crept up on us. My sister Augusta says she's been hearing worrying things from the sailors, and Selly's face makes me wonder what we *haven't* heard.

"I know it'll work," I say firmly. "It always has."

She hesitates, then: "You'll speak to the goddess herself?"

"I hope so," I reply, and I'm far too smart to make a joke about Barrica. "I know for most people religion isn't particularly personal. They know Barrica is watching, because they see the flowers in the temple bloom in winter, they see the wells refill themselves with fresh water at the spring festival. They see magicians use goddess-blessed candles as their offerings, though they probably don't realize no other country has them. Anyway, they drop a coin in the collection plate, they touch the statue of the goddess as they pass by, they hope it'll help them avoid bad luck. And that's it, for them. But the Sentinel goddess *knows* my family, and she's connected to us. She knows me. My sacrifice will mean enough."

"What *is* the sacrifice?"

"It's not much—the real sacrifice is the pilgrimage. A cut palm, a little blood, representing King Anselm's gift all those centuries ago. Renewing the royal bond with her."

"And it won't matter to the goddess that you're late?" she presses.

"I'm barely late," I assure her. "I was busy, was all."

The excuse sounds thin, and that's because it is. I can still see my sister, wearing her most Queen Augusta expression, glaring at me while her wife, Delphine, rubbed her shoulders and totally failed to calm her down.

We were arguing, and I was pushing all the harder because I knew in my heart I didn't have a lot behind me. It was the week before Mellacea abruptly accused an Alinorish captain of smuggling and confiscated her ship, imprisoning the crew.

That was when we realized things were worse than we'd thought. Back then, we thought we were having the same argument we always did, about me not living up to my responsibilities.

"I don't care if you said you'd be there," Augusta snapped. "You're going to skip a damn party and go do your duty."

"You could send Cousin Tastock," I countered. "He's looking peaky—a sea voyage would do him a world of good."

"I can't even tell if you're joking," she muttered. "I'm not sending a cousin."

"It just needs to be a royal magician," I pointed out.

"And it will be," she growled. "So help me, it will be the best one we have. This only happens once a quarter century, Leander. Don't you want to *do* something?"

"What is there for me to do?" I snapped. "You'll rule, Coria will be a good second daughter and produce a pile of babies so you'll have plenty of heirs, and what? Baby brother will come off the shelf every quarter century to be the family magician?"

"When have you ever wanted more?" she asked witheringly.

"Take on some real responsibility and it might get in the way of your social calendar."

"Augusta," Delphine murmured, leaning down to press a kiss to her cheek. She's from Fontesque's own royal family and doesn't mind a fiery debate, but she spends more time than I'm sure she ever expected refereeing fights among Alinor's.

Augusta took a breath. "You're so powerful," she said quietly. "You're the greatest magician our family has produced in generations. And you're charming. You get along with everyone. And yet all you care about is having fun. If you want to do great things, you have to risk failing at them. You could *be* something, Leander, if you weren't so busy proving to everyone that you don't care if you are."

"Hey, Prince?" It's Selly's voice, and I blink away the memory, shooting her a quick smile.

"My friends call me Leander," I tell her.

"That must be nice for them."

"You're a tough crowd," I inform her. "But I've got time on my side."

"Ha, good luck."

*"Selly!"* Her name's bellowed from somewhere down the back of the boat—Captain Rensa's voice. Surely we're hidden from her by the mast, but I go quiet anyway.

Selly rolls her eyes, though, and turns to hurry away in response to the summons.

I wait a minute before I follow. The skies are blue, the water stretches forever, and the spirits play gleefully around the bow of the boat.

When I make my way back, Selly's talking to Kyri at the

wheel, and the captain's heading for the steps that lead below. She pauses, though, and waits for me.

"Good morning, Your Highness."

"Good morning, Captain."

She sizes me up in a way that makes me feel like I'm back at school, but I know better than to squirm.

"Soon enough," she says eventually, "you'll be home to the palace."

"Yes."

"Selly'll be here," she says. "Where she's always been happy. Don't change that for her and leave her wishing life was different."

"Captain," I say, "I can assure you there's absolutely zero chance she'll be wishing that on my account."

# SELLY

*The* Lizabetta
*The Crescent Sea*

By afternoon, I've decided Prince Leander is the most annoying boy it's ever been my bad luck to meet. I didn't think he could beat the rumors about him, but here we are. Looking back to how I snickered when I imagined the scholar trying to dodge him on the voyage, now I'm wondering if I can harness our scholar's big brain to figure out a way to do it myself.

The only thing on my side is that I made the mistake of telling Abri I saw the prince without a shirt this morning, and she's volunteered to bring him all his meals from now on.

"You," she said firmly, "have lost your mind, Selly Walker. That is literally a *handsome prince* standing on the deck of our boat. If you don't want to talk to him, you can bet I will."

Every time I look at him, he's ready with a teasing smile. He knows what he looks like, and he thinks he can use it to make me fall all over myself for his attention. By far the most irritating part is that this morning he charmed me almost as well as he charms his spirits. By the time we were done talking, I'd half forgotten what he's stolen from me.

Then Rensa sent me below to clear away his breakfast plates and make his bunk—*my* bunk—up for him, and I remembered. There he was, up on deck, smiling and showing me secret maps and flirting with every spirit in sight, and now here I was, making *my own bed* for him to snuggle into tonight, while I'll be stuffing my ears full of cotton, trying to ignore Jonlon's snoring in a hammock in the crew quarters.

Prince Leander and his gold-threaded blanket are the reason I'm stuck with my captain for at least another six months. I won't be forgetting it again.

"I don't want you giving him any cheek," Rensa said sternly from the doorway, while I muttered under my breath, yanking his blanket straight. "I thought for a moment this morning you might have managed to see his good side, but clearly I was mistaken."

"What good side?" I shot back. "What are we doing here, Captain? This isn't who we are—we're a merchant ship."

"That's exactly why nobody will look our way twice, girl. As for what we're doing, we're playing our part. We're trying to make sure this ship and every other in the Walker fleet don't end up loaded past the waterline with Alinorish soldiers on their way to die on foreign ground."

"By giving a lift to a boy who should have been there last year?"

"By giving a lift," she replied. "Even small parts can be honorably played, Selly. Nobody will ever know what we're doing here, if all goes well. That won't mean it matters any less."

I bit my tongue, because there was no reply to that, and got on with making the prince's bed, trying not to think of what lay ahead.

Half a year of the worst watches, the messiest jobs, and being left out of every worthwhile conversation on the ship.

Right now he's standing in the stern with Kyri and Rensa, pretending to be interested in navigation but really being interested in Kyri, who's laughing and tossing her head and showing him exactly where to put his hands on the wheel. I'm sure he headed in that direction because he saw it was where I was heading, and he's figured out I'm not interested in another conversation. So he's trying to bait me.

I turn away. Retrieving the line I was working on splicing before my lunch, I glance around to check nobody's near, then peel off my gloves and unpick the end so I can braid it together with the new section.

Taking up a spot in the lee of the mast, I'm warm and sheltered. When I close my eyes, the sun shines red through my lids, and with the *Lizabetta* romping along, surging down the waves, I set to work forgetting the prince is there at all. Forgetting we're on this mad quest. Forgetting the *Freya,* already on her way up north to Holbard and taking with her my last chance at joining my father.

I'm not sure how long I've been working when there's a yell from the lookout. I can't make out the words, but there's something in Jonlon's voice that has me on my feet in an instant. I shove my knife into my belt as I crane my head back. The sun dazzles my eyes, tears streaming, as I blink him into focus.

His arm is stretched out northward, toward the horizon that hides the coast of Fontesque, or maybe Beinhof, and when

I duck around the mast, there's smoke astern. A dark, ugly smear a long way back, just starting to rise from the sea.

It can't be land, and it isn't a signal. It isn't a natural cloud, not in this clear blue sky.

It's a fire aboard a vessel.

My hand flies to my belt to check for my eyeglass, and then I'm throwing myself into the rigging before the thought's complete, the rope burning my palms. Grabbing at spars and lines, I heave myself up without a care for my hands. It's only when I reach the crosstrees that I stop, glancing down at Rensa at the helm.

With a wave of her arm, she urges me higher. Prince Leander isn't watching but standing at the railing, staring at the still-growing cloud.

A rope beside my head twitches, smacking me on the cheekbone, and I gasp against the sharp pain. Kyri's below me, her auburn braid swinging as she climbs with quick efficiency.

I don't wait but keep on ahead of her, scrambling over the rim of the crow's nest to join Jonlon, already pulling my eyeglass from my belt.

I've sailed with Jonlon my whole life—he's always been the big, quiet, comforting presence on my father's ships, the antidote to his twin brother Conor's sharp tongue and sharp wit.

Now his gaze is stricken, and without a word he slips behind me, taking hold of my shoulders and steadying me in place against the pitch of the ship. The roll of the waves is exaggerated up here, and I lean back against his broad chest as I search for the source of the smoke.

Kyri slithers over the rim and squeezes in beside us, taking

Jonlon's eyeglass with a grunt of thanks. She and I share more than a room—like Jonlon and Conor, she's the sweet to my sour, the one who hears my secrets in the dark. Even when things stretch and strain between us—when I remember that she's our ship's magician and my marks are useless, that she wears the first mate's knot and Rensa's made me into nothing—Kyri and I stick together.

Now she leans her shoulder in against mine to help her stay steady too. Braced against them, I scan the horizon until I find the telltale blur, twisting the halves of my eyeglass to bring it into focus.

It's a funeral pyre.

Flames leap for the sky from burning ships, and I flinch as something explodes on one of them, sending bodies and debris flying past the remnants of tattered sails. I sweep on to the next ship, searching desperately for some sign of what happened—some sign of life, or survivors.

The sick horror of it sits heavy in my gut, pushing up through my throat in a wave of nausea as I reach the third ship and finally, *finally,* I realize what I'm seeing.

This is the prince's decoy fleet. This wreckage is all that remains of the happy-go-lucky ships we left behind in Kirkpool, wreathed in lights and flowers, playing trumpet music on their gramophones as the young nobles danced on deck late at night.

Whoever did this wanted to kill Prince Leander.

The law of the sea is clear and unbreakable—you don't turn away from a ship in mortal peril. Not for profit, not out of fear. You turn toward them, and you render aid. But I know without a doubt there's nobody on those ships left to save.

"Barrica grant them rest," Jonlon murmurs behind me as I lower my eyeglass.

Kyri's shaking her head slowly, already pressing Jonlon's eyeglass back into the man's hand. "Pray later," is all she says, every ounce of her usual laughter gone. Mouth flattened to a grim line, our ship's magician points to the horizon.

At first I can't think what she's showing me that I haven't seen. Then I trace the line downward, and the breath goes out of me like a punch.

Between the dying decoy fleet and the *Lizabetta* is a huge ship. It has no mast, no sails—it's a steamship, the same gray as a stormy ocean. A hulking box of metal and rivets, spewing streams of smoke.

No merchant, this one.

It's a shark, and it's not done hunting.

I yank my gloves on, and without a word Kyri and I throw ourselves over the edge of the crow's nest. We half clamber, half fall to the deck below together. I stumble as I land and she catches me, shoving me toward the stern—she's only a step behind me as I race for the captain.

I can see it in Rensa's and the prince's faces before I speak— they know the black smear on the horizon is the progress fleet. Is the death of every soul aboard.

"They're sunk," I manage. "All of them. Not a one left alive."

Leander's brown skin has paled—he looks sallow and sick. "We have to go back," he says tightly. "We have to look for survivors. Those are my people."

"Your Highness," Kyri begins beside me, "they—"

"No!" he snaps. "Those are my *friends*!"

"They're coming for us next!" I break in, urgent. "We have to go!" I don't bother speaking to the prince. On the *Lizabetta,* he's not the one who gives the orders. Instead, I meet Rensa's eyes. "Captain," I say quietly, "there's a steamship coming straight for us. They're mopping up the witnesses."

Rensa's whisper is barely audible in the silence that follows, nearly drowned out by the slap of waves in our wake. "Gods preserve us all." She grips the wheel. "We're not killing ourselves to save those already gone. We pile on sail and we run from whoever did this."

Conor and Abri have come up from below now, crowding around us, and Jonlon lands on the deck with a thump, hurrying over to sling an arm around his twin, who's a full head shorter than him. The scholar hovers behind them, anxious. All eyes are on Rensa, and her gaze sweeps around, taking us in as if she's committing us to memory.

Then she snaps into action. "Go! More sail!" As the others scatter to their places—even the scholar runs to help—she casts me a wordless look, and I pull an already-protesting Leander out of her way as she braces at the wheel.

"We can't do this," he shouts, grabbing at my hand where I'm gripping his arm, trying to rip free of my grasp. "We can't just leave them to die in the water."

I saw a fire on a ship at dock in Escium once. The cargo was flammable, and there was nothing anyone could do but get their own boats clear of the explosions and wait for her to burn down to the waterline.

Then a man came running past us—so close he shouldered me out of his way—and he jumped from the dock straight onto the ship, straight into the flames. One of his crewmates was still aboard, someone said later. He was so out of his mind, he was willing to die trying to save him.

Leander's in that same place right now. It's all over his face—if he thought he could, he'd dive over the side and swim back. If he can find a way, he'll have Rensa turn us back.

"You didn't see what I saw," I say, gripping both his arms, lowering my voice. "They've already made sure there's nobody left in the water. I'm sorry, truly I am, but it's done. And your duty now isn't to your fleet, or to the dead. It's to your country."

"Selly, you have to understand—"

"I understand they'll kill you if they can." I cut him off, squeezing his arms again. "You don't think that was Mellacea back there, trying to start a war? How much worse do you think it gets if they kill the Alinorish prince?"

His brown eyes meet mine, laid bare. There's a depth in his gaze that he usually hides behind his smile. "You're saying I'm too precious for us to risk me." He speaks as if the words choke him.

It must be unbearable, to be held prisoner by his own rank when others are dead in our wake.

"I'm sorry, Leander," I whisper. It's the first time I've called him by his name to his face.

But he's not just Leander.

He's the prince of Alinor.

And we've got assassins on our tail.

# LASKIA

*The* Macean's Fist
*The Crescent Sea*

Two sailors heave the body across to dump it in front of us, one holding the arms, one holding the legs.

It's a boy about my age with dark hair, light brown skin that's gone paler from blood loss, and a nightmarish wound taking up half his torso, his clothes ripped open to reveal . . . meat, beneath. He lolls lifelessly as the sailors let go, unseeing eyes staring straight up at the sky.

I swallow hard, then make sure my voice is even, though it sounds thin and reedy to my own ears. "Well, is that him?"

Jude has one hand clamped over his mouth—he's already thrown up twice—and doesn't remove it or speak. When I glance across at him, he shakes his head.

*"What?"* I grab his arm, yanking him with me over to the railing and out of earshot of the crew, a bolt of pure panic turning my stomach. "Well, tell me where to look for him."

"I don't know," he whispers, wrapping his arms around himself miserably. He's a world away from the tough guy who lives in the boxing ring at Handsome Jack's now, and we both know it. "I didn't see him. How was I supposed to see him among all of . . . *that*?"

I glance over my shoulder, and though Dasriel looms farther up the deck, there's no sign of Sister Beris. "Look, it was his fleet," I hiss.

"Yes."

"So he was there."

"I'm sure he was," he replies, closing his eyes.

"And that's what you're going to tell Ruby?"

He holds still, the wind whipping his hair around his face, and bites his lip hard. But there's only one answer, and he gives it to me: "Yes."

He knows as well as I do how Ruby will take any news that isn't the news she wants to hear.

"Go," I snap, and he stumbles away.

Only once he's gone do I grip the railing, gazing out at the wreckage floating around us, keeping my gaze unfocused so I don't have to see.

The passengers on the prince's fleet waved to us as we approached. The ships were a sight to behold, streamers strung up and down the rigging, the sails decorated with bright designs, ribbons fluttering in the breeze.

Spirit flags danced gaily in the rigging, the blue-and-white standard of Alinor flying at the top of their masts.

They couldn't have made themselves more obvious.

No doubt their captains were wondering what we were

doing, flying no flag and steaming in so close—our ship, *Macean's Fist,* is a sleek, hungry wolf in iron gray, cutting through the waves with her engines thumping in her belly.

I was standing here at the railing rather than up on the bridge, but I had a clear line of sight to our captain. He gazed down at me through the glass panes surrounding him, waiting for my order.

I looked again at the three ships full of partygoers, most of them no older than me, dressed in their best and brightest. A girl standing at their railing blew me a kiss.

She was beautiful.

"It's time."

The voice came from behind me, and I jumped, then cursed myself for showing that Sister Beris had startled me.

She wore a padded green coat over her robes, her black hair braided back so tightly, not a single strand escaped. Her soft voice was somehow audible over the sounds around us.

"I know," I said, looking past her to check that Jude was on deck, ready to identify the prince. He looked like he wanted to be sick, both hands clenched around the railing.

They were still waving at us from the prince's fleet, and I turned my gaze away from them to look up at the captain on our bridge and nod.

Our cannons boomed, and a ragged hole appeared in the nearest ship. As our sailors streamed up from belowdecks, ready to hurl the grenades across the gap between us, the screaming began.

It didn't stop for nearly half an hour.

Their boats listed to one side shockingly quickly as we

ripped their sides out, and they tried to turn away and run, but they were far too big, far too cumbersome, to manage it in time.

We knew, and they knew from the start, that they had no way to outpace us.

We demolished them methodically, breaking their boats into pieces and pouring oil into the water, then setting it alight.

Bodies and flowers both burned.

I didn't expect them to scream for so long, to live long enough to try to swim away. To come close enough I could see their faces.

I hadn't thought about the fact they would be *people*. That they would look like people I know.

Sister Beris never left my side, never took her hand from my shoulder. I'm not sure even now if she was strengthening me, or stopping me from trying to back away from this horror, or something in between.

There was a lot more fire than I'd expected, and we've had to wait until it started to burn itself out before we can throw in the bodies we brought with us.

They were in the morgue at Port Naranda a couple of days ago. We picked a few that were past the point of stiffness, white-eyed and pliant, so we could stuff them into Mellacean navy uniforms.

Now I look up the deck as the sailors heave them overboard in a series of quiet splashes. They'll tangle with the wreckage and wait for whoever finds the ruins of the prince's progress fleet.

There'll be no question as to who should be blamed for his

death. No way out for our government, who should have been strong enough to fight for their god and to start this war themselves.

Then again, it's Barrica who was the Warrior. Macean is the god of risk, the Gambler, and I think he'd approve of the one we've just taken.

Sister Beris is walking toward me, and I squeeze the railing one more time and make myself straighten up to greet her with a nod.

"Shall we go downstairs, and find something to eat?" she asks quietly.

I think of what's waiting in the galley for tomorrow morning and close my eyes. But I make myself nod.

The plan has worked. I did what I promised I would.

Finally, Ruby will know I'm ready to step up.

So why do I feel like this?

"It had to be done," I say out loud, as if I'm answering myself.

"And you were the one to do it," Sister Beris says, squeezing my shoulder again and sending a trickle of warmth into the iciness of my body. "Your sister knows that. I've watched her attitude to you change since you brought her this plan. She sees you're ready to realize your potential, Laskia."

"You really think?"

"My child, I know it. You are doing great things, for your sister and for Macean. It's time for the Sentinel to loosen her grip on him. And to ensure that, we must see she is not strengthened. Macean *will* awaken, Laskia. He will rise, and so will you."

"Thank you," I whisper, and I'm not sure what I'm thanking

her for, but I'm keeping my gaze away from the dead boy on the deck, the carnage below, the blood and fire in the water. I'm keeping it focused on Sister Beris's pale blue eyes.

"If I have not said so before, let me say now," she murmurs. "I am grateful for you, Laskia. For your faith. I am grateful you came into our path, with the understanding of what must be done, and the will and the means to do it."

I blink at her, unsure whether it's the wind or her words making my eyes tear up.

*I am grateful for you.*

A sailor comes jogging toward us. "The captain says they've turned away, ma'am," he says to Sister Beris, pointing in the direction of the ship we spotted. "They know we're coming for them."

"Can we catch them?" she asks.

"Given enough time," he replies. "But it'll add at least a day."

"We can't have them telling anyone what they saw," she says, turning to me.

I gaze back at her, my heart pushing against my ribs.

Another ship. More death.

But I've come this far.

I've fought with everything I have, for Macean's rise and my own. And now both those things are within my grasp. My god and I are both so close to claiming the power that should be ours.

The memories flash before my eyes again—a girl swimming frantically away from fire, her dress weighing her down. A boy sprawling dead on the deck, staring at the sky.

My gut squirms with horror, and I close the door on what

I've seen, forcing those images away. It's done. I have to make it worth the cost.

I glance at the sailor, who's watching me with the wary respect they all have now. "Tell the captain to keep going," I say, my voice firming up, hardening as I speak. "Hunt them down."

# KEEGAN

*The* Lizabetta
*The Crescent Sea*

The crew is swarming up the rigging, releasing the ties on bundles of sails I hadn't even noticed before. The canvas thunders as it unrolls, cracking as it catches the wind.

The *Lizabetta* gathers herself for a moment, prancing on the spot in response to the increase in power, then surges down the next wave like a charging horse.

With a curse, Captain Rensa clings to the wheel, gesturing wildly to one side. "There, the ropes!" she shouts.

There are thick cords tied to the rail around the edge of the deck, and I lunge for one, pulling it toward her.

"Other side!" she bellows, and Leander appears and grabs at the second rope.

Selly's sprinting for the mast to help her crewmates as I haul on mine. The rope is rough on my palms, heavier than I expected, and I struggle to pull it across—then the first mate,

Kyri, arrives, auburn braid swinging as she grabs the cord from my hands and finishes the job.

The captain's spinning the ship's huge wheel, and Kyri loops the ropes onto it, to help keep the *Lizabetta* from veering off course as she surfs down the waves.

"Do we have any chance of outrunning a steamer?" Leander asks, panting.

"We're going to try," the captain replies with a grunt. "We're badly overpowered for this wind, carrying far too much sail, but it'll add speed. If the *Lizabetta* doesn't pull herself apart or nosedive through a wave, we might. She's fast."

"What happens if she nosedives through a wave?" I ask, my stomach clenching.

"She stops suddenly, and her masts keep going. Now get below and look through your clothes, Scholar. Find something plainer for the prince to wear. He can't look like that if we're boarded."

Leander hasn't taken his eyes off the black smoke on the horizon, an ugly smear against the clear blue of the sky. It doesn't look as though he's heard a word she said.

"Your Highness?" I prompt him, already mentally inventorying my shirts and trousers, my mind seizing on this one problem of a size I can solve.

"It should have been me," he says quietly. When he turns to face us, his expression is hollow. I saw him every day for years at school—laughing, or smiling, or teasing. I've never seen him look like this.

"Good news for everyone that it wasn't you," Rensa replies shortly.

He flinches. "They died for me."

"You haven't killed anyone," the first mate, Kyri, says, lifting a hand as if to comfort him, then halting the movement when she remembers he's royalty. She continues, though, fierce: "They did this. *They're* to blame."

Leander's gaze swings past her and lands on me. He wants to hear it from someone who doesn't like him. Not from one of the crew, awed to have a prince in their presence, dazzled by his rank.

I stare back at him, my chest tight with the anger and resentment of every time I saw him skip past his responsibilities, leave behind a mess for someone else to pick up. Because the truth is more complicated than Kyri makes it, and the prince and I both know it—if he had not delayed this trip, there never would have been a decoy fleet to *be* attacked.

He gazes at me as I struggle—and fail—to answer him, then turns to the captain. "Is the wheel secure?" he asks.

She lays a hand on one of the ropes. "Aye. Now help Kyri with the spirits, and you, boy"—she turns her gaze on me, and I straighten—"go and find those clothes."

I pause, though, as Leander pulls a ring from his finger and studies it in his palm. I know it well—it bears the royal crest, and I've always assumed it was inherited from his father. He wore it all our years at school.

Then, in one sudden movement, he draws his arm back and throws it as hard as he can.

The gold of the ring catches the sun as it arcs out over the water, and then it's gone, vanished into thin air, consumed by the spirits in the instant before it can be swallowed by a wave.

Wordlessly, he closes his eyes and spreads his arms as if in entreaty. He somehow stands steady on the deck, weight shifting and knees bending to keep him upright.

And the wind begins to build.

A wave picks up the *Lizabetta,* and every inch of the ship hums and strains as she surges forward, her sails nearly splitting at the seams as the air and water spirits do his bidding.

The whole world has changed around us in the blink of an eye—it's like a switch has been flicked, but that switch is just this boy I went to school with, who never seemed interested in using his magic for anything more than party tricks.

I've never seen a display of power like this in my life, and I can only stand and stare, my mouth open.

Kyri stares at him as well, then whirls away, dropping to her knees before the shrine by the mast, adding her efforts to his.

For a moment they're all still—Captain Rensa at the wheel, Leander and Kyri locked in concentration as they charm the spirits into speeding our passage along—and everything goes quiet around me. As if I could live in this moment forever, never facing what's coming for us on the horizon.

Then that breath goes rushing out of me, and I turn to hurry below, ricocheting off the walls of the passageway as the ship lurches and her timbers groan.

Stumbling into my cabin, I pull up the lid of my trunk, grabbing at the few clothes I brought with me, spare shirts and trousers in plain colors. Suitable for a scholar, and now a disguise for a prince.

The door flies open, and a burly sailor—one of the two I've assumed are brothers—pushes his way in. Without a word he shoulders past me, slamming the lid of my trunk and picking it up with a grunt of effort.

"What are you doing?" I protest. "I have the clothes—you don't need the whole thing."

"Anything not nailed down is going overboard. Captain's orders. Lightening the ship."

My whole body goes cold. "Wh-what?" I manage. "No, these are books—these are—you can't—" My throat is closing, my chest tightening.

"Think you're going to be reading them after they catch us?" he asks, hefting it in his arms.

I lunge for the chest, grabbing for the contents—my hands scrabble at the thin volumes inside. The Wilkinson fairy tales I read as a child, the worn leather covers as familiar as my own face. The Ameliad memoirs I couldn't bear to leave behind, my constant companions and allies against the world.

"Please," I say, as he yanks the trunk away and heads for the door. "Please—you don't understand."

The sailor doesn't look back as he disappears into the hallway.

I stand in the middle of the cabin, my eyes hot and aching, my breath coming too fast. This can't be happening. This can't be real.

I drop to a crouch, planting my hands against the swaying floor. My mind is numb, and I try to make it understand reality—like poking at the place where a tooth was, searching for the soreness.

*If they catch us, they'll kill us.*

*If they catch us, the prince won't make the sacrifice.*

*If they catch us and kill the prince, there'll be a war. A war we might well lose, without Barrica strengthened by sacrifice—but not until tens of thousands of people have died first. Not until whole countries have been scorched.*

*. . . And none of that will matter to me, because I will be dead.*

But though I can say it to myself, I can't make myself believe it.

Moving mechanically, I hurry over to my bedding before he can come back to claim it, and I reach underneath the pillow. I pull out the gold chains I hid there and slip both of them around my neck, inside my clothes. Some detached part of me understands I won't ever sell them, I won't need them to fund my first year at the Bibliotek, but after everything I did to get them . . .

There's a sliver in me that still hopes. That sliver lives in all of us—it's why we're fighting.

I wanted so badly to see the Bibliotek.

I've dreamed of it all my life.

I pick up the handfuls of clothes and leave the cabin behind, hurrying back up on deck. I collide with the girl from the galley, her cheerful face white with fear, and we push off each other and keep running.

I burst up onto the deck, unable to make myself turn my head to look for our pursuer. Then, steeling myself, I twist and scan the horizon. I see only the smoke, no sign of a boat.

I run for the back of the boat, where the captain still wrestles the wheel, barking orders up the deck to the crew. Selly has joined her, and they're working together without the need for speech.

"Are we gaining ground?" I call. "I can't see a steamship."

The captain shakes her head and my heart drops. "It's still too far to see. The world curves. While it's that far off, we'll only see it from the top of the mast."

A sailor rumbles past, the slighter of the two brothers on

the crew. He's rolling a barrel, which he heaves over the side of the boat—is that our water?

"What can I do?" I ask, making myself turn away from him.

It's Selly who answers me. She's leaning in on the wheel, holding it steady against a surging wave Leander's conjured. "We're barely armed," she says. "Does that big brain of yours have anything in it about makeshift weaponry?"

I consider the question, trying to slow my thoughts enough to scan my memory. "Yes," I say eventually. "If we have cooking oil aboard."

"Better go make sure the twins don't throw it overboard, then."

Time passes in a blur after that. It's easier to just do the next thing than grapple with what's happening. There's a strange, grim practicality to it all—you can't be terrified every moment. After a while your body just gets on with things, even if your mind is still screaming.

Leander stands like a statue as the hours go by, locked in communion with the spirits. He must be exhausted, but he shows no sign of wavering.

What I don't know anymore is what he's sacrificing to keep them on his side. He's the most powerful magician in Alinor, but what we're witnessing should be the work of dozens of magicians, not one boy. The spirits will demand more of him than his father's ring, however dear to him it was.

I have a horrible feeling what they're demanding is *him,* his very essence. I've never seen a magician overextend themselves, but the stories of their fates are brutal.

All around us, the sailors wrestle with the boat, barely managing to keep her together. I hear them praying to Barrica— presumably hoping our goddess won't notice we've got the boy who dragged his feet on her sacrifice aboard—and a couple of them go over her head, appealing straight to the Mother.

It's clear that in a wind this strong we should barely be carrying any sail, but instead we've hoisted everything we can find short of our undergarments. The *Lizabetta* sings and shudders but surges onward. Selly is up the mast once more as our lookout, and I dread the news she'll bring when she descends.

Descend she does, though, grabbing at ropes and spars to stop herself from being flung out into the sea. Her feet hit the deck, and she turns to meet the captain's eyes, her face a grim mask; she simply shakes her head and lifts her hands up until they face each other, palms inward. Then she slowly brings them closer together. They're gaining.

The bottom drops out of my stomach. This can't be happening.

This *can't* be happening.

But there's no more hiding from the truth: they're going to catch up with us.

"We have to fight," I say, hardly believing I'm saying the words out loud. I'm not supposed to be here. This can't be real. "We have to fight, no matter how slim the chance."

"I know," the captain answers, her eyes straight ahead. "Spirits save us. Nothing else will."

# SELLY

*The* Lizabetta
*The Crescent Sea*

The steamer appears over the horizon, and the taste of my fear turns sour in my mouth.

My mind's spent the past hours conjuring up pictures of the broken progress fleet, splintered timbers in the water, flowers and bodies floating among them. Trying to imagine that wreckage is the *Lizabetta,* and *we* lie still in the water—then shying away from that terrible picture.

I've always known there was a chance I'd end up on the bottom—every sailor does. But I've never *believed* it.

We've hoisted every inch of canvas we have, we've trimmed our sails, we've thrown everything we don't need and some things we do overboard to lighten the load, to eke a fraction more speed out of our groaning ship. When we left Kirkpool, I could barely believe we were sailing high in the water, without a cargo to pay our way. Now I'm desperately grateful our hold was empty.

And still they're going to catch us. Our pursuers are following the trail of debris we've left behind like it's a path we've laid out for them, our belongings and supplies disappearing beneath their bow.

Leander is starting to sway where he stands, and Kyri's on all fours by the shrine. Her candles are nearly down to stubs, the spirits consuming them far faster than I've ever seen before, but he hasn't taken anything from anyone in hours. I've had enough failed lessons to know what that means. He's paying the spirits with *himself.*

The ship surges forward on great white-tipped waves, but the steamer's fires are burning, and she's coming faster.

I stand at the gunwale near Rensa, my hair blowing around my face as I watch the big gray steamer eating up the distance between us, and soon enough I can make out individual figures on her deck, see the portholes along the side.

The last of the gap seems to disappear all at once—she looms above us as she comes up astern, and then big Jonlon's by my side, pressing a glass bottle into my hand. It's full of the captain's good booze and oil from the galley, a rag stuffed into the mouth.

"Don't throw too soon," he says, wrapping an arm around my shoulders for a quick squeeze, deathly tight. Big, strong, quiet Jonlon, a decade and a half in my father's service. He used to fish me out of the cargo hold, where I'd go to cry after a visit to a new magician in a new port. He'd hand me a boiled sweet and lead me off to something that needed doing, then silently remain until I was all right.

And we're about to die together.

The scholar's behind us, dragging a basket of bottles across the deck, and a brazier he's made out of one of the cook's big pots. His pale face is deathly white, his mouth set in a determined line.

He and the prince should be back at school, squabbling over homework like the rich boys they are. Not . . . not this.

But the steamer's drawing abeam, coming up beside us, and I can see their guns. Their cannons.

A wave from their bow surges out toward us, and the *Lizabetta* heels dangerously, shouts going up all along the deck.

"Now!" the scholar calls, dipping his first bottle into the coals. The wick catches alight, and he draws his arm back, narrowing his eyes. I can practically see the calculations allowing for crosswind and speeds of travel. Then he hurls it toward the enemy.

It arcs through the air, the flame drawn out long and thin behind it, and smashes into a sailor on the steamer. Fire engulfs him, and though the wind rips away his screams, I stare as he throws his arms up.

In two quick steps he's jumping over the side, and he vanishes beneath the water. One hand thrusts above the surface, but he's already in our wake, and an instant later I lose sight of him.

And then fire is flying through the air, and shots are ringing out, and everyone's shouting.

Keegan stands beside Jonlon, the two of them hurling their glass-bottle bombs, and my hand shakes as I lean down to dip the head of mine into the coals. It catches alight, and there's no time to hesitate—I draw my arm back and throw it as hard as I can, tracing its path all the way to the steamer's deck, where it lands between two sailors, showering them with sparks.

*BOOM!*

The whole deck beneath me shakes, and I whip around to see it broken and splintered, a hole gaping in the boards.

*The cannons.*

Keegan's climbing to his feet, and Jonlon's on his knees, holding his arm—he's bleeding, and there's a jagged piece of wood sticking out of it.

"Kyri!" The shout comes from Rensa, hoarse and urgent, wrenched out of her.

Kyri is lying sprawled by the shrine, arms outflung, red hair loose from her braid and whipping in the wind, and she stares up at the sky.

There's blood all over her, and the flames on her candles, which withstood a gale until now, have suddenly gone out.

She's not moving.

Leander snaps out of whatever trance he was in, and the wind and waves around us only grow worse, the spirits raging without his direction as he drops to his knees beside her, hands pressing helplessly at the wounds on her torso. Then he looks at her face, her staring, unseeing eyes, and he goes still.

A wave hits the *Lizabetta,* and the ship heels wildly, forcing us to grab for whatever's closest—the scholar grabs me as I nearly fall across the deck, and I climb back up him to hold on to the rail. I can't imagine that cannonball stopped on the way down—water must be pouring into the hull even now, swamping the bilges and filling the cargo holds.

*"Surrender, call off your magician, and you will not be harmed!"* The voice is tinny, coming from the steamer through a loud-hailer.

Then, apart from the wind and the water, everything goes

silent. No gunfire, no cannons. They're giving us time to consider.

As the ship steadies, Keegan, Jonlon, and I hurry toward Rensa. Abri and Conor emerge from belowdecks, where they were building more bottle bombs. Conor takes one look at his brother's arm and hurries over to him, pulling a rag from his pocket to try to stop the bleeding.

We gather around the captain and Leander, who still kneels beside Kyri's body. Her gray eyes stare up at the sky.

"Selly, Keegan, behind the mast," says Rensa immediately. "Out of sight."

"What?" I say as the scholar grabs my arm, hauling me into the lee of the mast without asking questions.

"I don't want them getting a count on us," Rensa says. "Conor and Abri were belowdecks before. Let them count them now and think we're fewer than we are."

"You're thinking of surrender?" Keegan asks slowly. "They're lying about our safety."

"Agreed," says Rensa. "But the prince can't keep this up forever, and one way or another, they're going to sink us if we don't stop running. If that happens, we'll die. So we have to try and see if we can't get some of us through it. Your Highness, time to stop the storm."

The prince, still by Kyri's side—his hand rests on hers, his skin bloodied—looks up at us as if he's only just registering the captain's words.

Then the wind begins to ease, and the waves sink to almost nothing. The wild gale and the huge seas are simply . . . gone. If any part of me doubted his magic created them, the quiet around us now reminds me how powerful this boy is.

The *Lizabetta* slows, the steamer pulling ahead of us, and the warmth of the late-afternoon sun reasserts itself. It doesn't help—I can't stop shivering.

"Conor, the wheel," Rensa says, leaving it and stepping forward to grab Leander by the arm, hauling him to his feet. "Selly, with me, before they slow too."

Already up ahead the steamer is losing speed, and soon she'll wheel around to head back toward us. But right now, Rensa is marching the prince along the deck, and I hurry after her—I don't understand what she's doing, can't make my mind slow down, make sense.

Rensa stops beside the *Little Lizabetta,* the shore boat we keep lashed on the foredeck. "Listen," she says quietly. "Stay down. Their count is two short. That gives us a chance to hide the two of you."

I open my mouth and close it again, unable to speak. It's like all the air's left my lungs. Like I'm underwater. Beside me, the prince makes a wordless sound, pressing one hand over his mouth.

"When we're gone," continues Rensa, "however we end up gone, maybe the ship'll still be afloat. That happens, young man, you listen to Selly. She's your best chance. You can try the shore boat if the cannon holes are too bad."

Her gaze swings around to me, and our eyes lock. I'm shaking.

"I've been trying to teach you to be a captain, girl, which means taking care of your people before yourself, seeing things through their eyes. It's why I've had you doing every job on the boat, and the worst ones most of all. To learn what you're asking others to do."

I try to speak, but she keeps me silent with a shake of her head. "I'm out of time to teach you the slow way, so you'll just have to listen: I don't walk the deck handing out hugs, but I'd die for my crew, and they know it. That's a lesson you need to learn this very minute, because you're about to become all the prince has in the world."

My breath's coming jaggedly, and I make myself nod, staring up at her.

"And if you see your father again," she says quietly, "you tell Stanton Walker I kept my promise, kept his daughter safe."

"Rensa," I protest, grabbing for words. "You can't—"

"Arguing to the end," she says. "The world's bigger than you, Selly Walker. Bigger than me. That's what I've been trying to teach you all this time. Keep the prince alive. Whatever happens—*whatever happens*—he has to survive."

Before I can reply, she's turning on her heel and striding back up the deck to Kyri's body, where Jonlon, Conor, Abri, and the scholar wait for her. He's white as a ghost, gazing at us without a word.

Numb, I force myself into action, dropping to crawl around behind the little shore boat, telling my arms and legs to move. But when I glance back, Leander's sitting on the deck, one hand pressed against the satchel that holds his family's journal, and I realize this isn't just fear and horror. He's spent, beyond exhausted by the magic he's worked to try and save us all.

I grab his arm, pulling, and slowly he shuffles around after me until I can position him in the gap between the *Little Lizabetta* and the railing. There, he leans back against the sun-warmed wood, his eyes closed, lifting the satchel to hug it against his chest.

The steamer sends out grappling hooks to pull us in against its metal side, and as a gangplank goes out between the two ships, I tuck myself away.

It's a dangerous run across the plank, which sways and moves as both ends rise and fall. The first one to board is a brown-skinned, short-haired girl in trousers, who leaps onto the deck as gracefully as a cat. Four others come after her, men and women with blank faces and big guns.

More of the steamer's crew lines their railing, weapons pointed in our direction. So many of them, so far above us.

Leander and I crouch together in silence as they move Rensa, Jonlon, Conor, Abri, and Keegan into line on the deck. The five of them stand there as the girl—she's clearly in charge, despite her age—surveys the ship.

"I thought there were more of you," she says, looking over the five of them, then turning her eyes to Kyri's body. There's something tight and contained about her movements, as though she's holding herself together and might fly into a thousand pieces at any moment.

None of the crew says a word—they stare straight ahead or at their feet. Rensa stares straight at the girl.

After a moment of silence, the girl walks over to Kyri. She crouches down, studying her, and picks up one of her arms to check her magician's marks. She takes her by the sleeve rather than touch her skin. When she lets go, Kyri's hand thumps back onto the deck, making her flinch. Then she straightens her shoulders, and when she pushes up to her feet, she's collected once more.

"One of you killed the magician," the girl tells her own

crew, her irritation obvious. "My sister wanted a souvenir—a magician would have been perfect. Especially one as powerful as this. Extraordinary. What a waste."

Her own crew looks almost as nervous as ours—none of them answers her either.

She dismisses them, walking up to the line of the *Lizabetta*'s crew and making her way along the row, examining each of them in turn. There's a pin at her lapel with a ruby on it, the crimson gem winking in the sun, and I can't take my eyes off it.

*Please,* I find myself praying, and I'm not sure if it's to Barrica or the girl on our deck. *Please, don't hurt them.*

Nobody speaks. It doesn't seem to bother her.

"I have a theory," she continues, "that you have something valuable on board. We saw the debris behind you, but we didn't see any big bales, any cargo. I *did* see a gold-embroidered blanket floating on the water, though, I'm sure of it. Not the sort of thing I'd expect to see on a ship like this. What else were you carrying, instead of cargo?"

Still nobody speaks.

"If one of you is a noble," she says slowly, "you can buy your way out of this. Don't miss your chance."

And still nobody speaks. Abri looks like she's going to be sick, her pale skin almost green. Jonlon's swaying on his feet, his wound oozing blood, Conor steadying him. The scholar is staring into space like he's performing calculations in his head.

The girl twists, looking back at her crew lined up along the steamer's railing, and I try to draw a line from her gaze, to see what she's looking at. The sun's setting behind them, and they're mostly silhouettes. Then one of them shifts, and I catch the color of her clothes.

There's a green sister aboard the ship. That's who this girl is looking at. Perhaps she's not in charge, despite the way the crew defer to her.

She walks along the line to Rensa, drawing a gun from her belt and lifting it slowly. "What are you hiding?" she asks, quiet and calm.

Rensa gazes steadily at her. I don't know what they see in each other's faces, but it holds them both still. "Please," Rensa says, calm and clear. "My crew will never speak of what they saw."

The girl's voice sharpens. "What are you hiding?"

"There's nothing to find here."

"I'm not a fool!" Her voice is rising in volume now, half commanding, half pleading. "You threw a lot of things overboard, but I didn't see any cargo. Where were you going? What were you doing? You must have something worth finding on this ship."

Slowly, Rensa simply shakes her head.

Then she reels backward, and an instant later a deafening *BANG!* is ringing in my ears, and Rensa's body is falling to the deck, and I'm trying to scream but Leander's hand is over my mouth.

I claw his fingers away and gasp for breath, but suddenly he's moving again, trying to climb to his feet. Now I grab for him, yanking him down beside me.

"What are you *doing*?" I whisper, pulling his ear down to my mouth.

"I have to stop her." He's trying frantically to untangle himself from my grip. "I'm the one she wants."

Out on the deck, the girl stands with the rest of my crew, her breath coming quick and sharp, still lowering her arm from firing the shot.

I can't move—I'm crouching, frozen, my arms locked around Leander.

This boy would give himself up to save a crew he barely knows. To save *my* crew.

"You can't." The words are out, barely a breath, before I know they're coming. But I know I'm right. My captain gave me my orders.

"Search the ship," the girl snaps, out on the deck. "The rest of you, who wants to save their life by telling me what I'm looking for?"

She's standing in front of big, gentle Jonlon.

He says nothing, gazing steadily at her as she lifts her gun again.

*Please, no.*

*Please . . .*

*BANG!*

Conor screams, dropping to his knees by his brother's body, curling over him with a high keening that drowns out everything else.

Beside me Leander's breath is jagged, his whole body taut—it's costing him everything to stay here and let them protect him. I hold him in place, and he wraps his arms around me in turn. He's warm and solid, and I turn in to him as he squeezes me tight, letting me bury my face against his chest. I can feel the way it heaves, the way he's fighting to steady himself—the way he's clinging to me as hard as I'm clinging to him.

But I can't hide my face, not now—I have to watch, be ready to move. I lift my head, forcing myself to take in the scene out on the deck.

And then time slows as Abri looks down at where Conor's cradling his twin, and at Kyri's body, and at Rensa's.

And then she looks back at the girl standing on our deck. The girl who's practically thrumming with tension, as charged as the air before a storm, ready to explode into thunder and lightning.

And I can see what comes next unfolding before it happens. Abri's going to lift her hand and point at the *Little Lizabetta*. She's going to say, *There, the prince is hiding, take him and spare me.*

But the next movement comes from the scholar, who suddenly throws his arms up, blustering in outrage, a million miles from the quiet, awkward boy I've been watching for the past day and a half. Have I really only known him that long?

"You can't do this!" he announces as every eye on deck turns toward him. "I'm Lord Wollesley's son, how dare you threaten me!"

That gets the girl's attention, and no mistake. She spins toward him. "You're what?"

"I'm what you're looking for," he replies, all puffed-up self-importance. "*I* am what was aboard this ship in place of cargo. I was undertaking an expedition on my way to the Bibliotek. I plan on making great contributions in the field of historical studies."

"Do you, now?" she asks, adjusting her grip on the gun. "Well, do you have something to offer me, Lord Wollesley's son?"

Keegan fumbles at his neck and draws a gold chain out from

beneath his shirt, yanking it over his head. "Here," he says, practically bursting with indignation. "Take it—it's yours. It's an heirloom, you know."

She steps forward, reaching out to take the necklace from him with two fingers, lifting it up to study it. Then she drapes it around her own neck, pulling it carefully past her curls. "That'll do," she agrees.

A hint of the tension leaves him, though mine is still singing through my veins. "You won't shoot me, I assume," he says, folding his arms across his chest. How can he be that gullible?

"No," says the girl, and gazes at him in silence. As if she's wrestling with something, or waiting for something. "No, I won't shoot you," she says eventually, softer.

She spins on her heel and nods to two of the sailors she brought with her. She doesn't look back as they move forward together, grabbing Keegan by one arm each and marching him toward the side of the ship.

He begins to realize what's going to happen halfway there, struggling wildly, feet kicking at the deck, body thrashing. They reach the rail, and with a quick heave, send him over.

I clap my own hands over my mouth this time, keeping myself silent. A detached part of me wonders if they know this is a crueler way to die. Most sailors deliberately never learn to swim—there's no way back from overboard, and they don't want the hours of waiting for what's coming. But a noble boy can probably swim well enough. Too well. Will I live to regret that I know how, too?

Leander stays quiet, but there's a trickle of sweat at his brow, and his jaw is clenched tighter than when he was conjuring the storm, as if he's conjuring spirits all over again. This time, though, it's the pain of being held prisoner by his own importance. And I can tell that it's killing him.

My whole body is taut with fear as I wait to see what the girl will do. If they search now, then Keegan sacrificed himself for nothing. There's no place to hide—we're crouched behind the shore boat, but it's sitting on the deck upside down and offers no real shelter.

The girl fingers the gold chain around her neck, turning in a slow circle, studying the ship that's been my home all my life. She moves slowly, cool and calm, but her gaze is shuttered, her movements just a little too controlled. She's not unaffected by what's just happened. The question is, what's she going to do about it?

She tilts her head back and looks up at the sky, closes her eyes. Takes a slow breath.

"Do it," she says quietly.

As she walks toward the gangplank, her sailors lift their weapons.

*BANG!*

Abri falls.

*BANG!*

Conor slumps over his brother's body.

The girl runs back along the gangplank, light as a cat, and her crew carries barrels of oil over to soak the deck.

They retreat, and I stare as burning torches come arcing through the air to land around us, the oil igniting with a soft *woof.*

A cannonball hits the *Lizabetta*'s hull, and another—the

wood splinters and the ship lurches as she burns, the flames leaping up the mast to catch the canvas sails. My home is alight.

She's already listing toward the steamer, and I brace myself against the *Little Lizabetta* to stop myself from sliding across the deck, holding tight to Leander, who's barely conscious, his exhaustion overtaking him now.

They don't stay to watch us burn—the steamer is already turning away toward the southwest, to begin the long haul home to Mellacea.

I can't wait much longer to risk it—I fumble with the ties lashing the shore boat to the deck, then realize I'm never going to need them again, so I pull the knife from my belt and slice through them instead. A sailor never cuts a rope—that lesson's always been drummed into me. Not unless it's life or death.

Almost immediately the *Little Lizabetta* starts to slide to starboard, downhill to where the edge of the deck is very nearly meeting the water. I grab at Leander, hauling him with me as I scramble after her in my own barely controlled slide.

The railing is broken and splintered, and I kick at it with one foot until it gives. Then I grab the gunwale of the shore boat, and with some last store of strength I didn't know I had left, I flip her right way up as I shove her through the gap in the railing and down into the water.

Keeping low, keeping tight hold of the prince, I jump into the water. And there I hide, one arm slung over the gunwale of the *Little Lizabetta* to keep us afloat, one arm around the semiconscious boy beside me. The shore boat's bigger than the rest of the debris in the water, but there's plenty of it, and if nobody looks closely, we'll be able to hide among it as the *Lizabetta* goes down.

For a moment I think I see a figure on the steamer looking back at us—a single person, outlined by the sunset. But if they're there at all, they don't see us.

The sun continues her journey toward the horizon, slowly bathing the water around me as golden as the flames above us, as everything I've ever loved is turned to ash.

# PART TWO

## THE CITY OF INVENTION

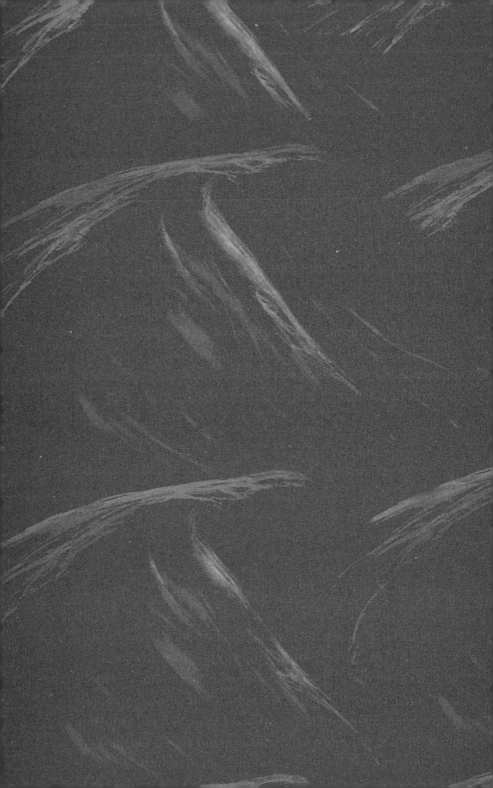

# KEEGAN

*The* Little Lizabetta
*The Crescent Sea*

I'm treading water with my eyes closed, trying to keep my back to the waves. I've discovered if I don't, each new one smacks me in the face, forcing salt water down my throat and up my nose.

"That way," calls the prince's voice suddenly, coming out of nowhere, rough with exhaustion.

My eyes snap open, and I nearly go under as I flail, twisting around to try and catch sight of him.

"I don't see anything," Selly's voice says, as I blink my salt-stung eyes to bring a small boat into focus. "Wait—I do, yes! Sit, before you fall overboard, you idiot."

The tiny ember of hope that lived inside me flickers, growing to a small but steady flame.

After I hit the water, it seemed as though it warmed around me, as though the current tugged me along after the *Lizabetta*. I truly couldn't decide whether it was wishful thinking or a sign that Alinor's most powerful magician was still alive aboard the ship, pulling off an outrageous feat of magic to keep me alive too.

The rowboat that was lashed to the *Lizabetta*'s deck is closing in on me, and Selly pulls the oars in as I give a few tired kicks to bring myself alongside. "Get over on the other side to counterweight him," she says, presumably to the prince, and in a tone he's surely unaccustomed to. The boat rocks, though I can't see him when he obeys.

I reach up to grab the little boat's edge, then Selly takes hold of my shirt and heaves, and I pull, give a kick, and somehow slither up and in, landing on the floor in a soaking pile and coughing up a lungful of seawater.

She clambers back to her oars and looks toward Leander, who's slumped against one of the benches spanning the little boat. There's a sick, pale tinge to his tan skin, his eyes shadowed by blue bruises of exhaustion. He's clinging to the bag holding his journal with one hand, the other steadying himself, as if he might slide over sideways.

"Wollesley," he says weakly, by way of greeting.

"Are the others . . . ?" My question dies on my lips as he slowly shakes his head.

With a sick feeling, I push up so I can sit, glancing at the *Lizabetta*. I had hoped that after killing me, the girl who boarded us would stop searching for anything else of value. A much smaller part of me had hoped she would leave the ship intact, the crew alive.

I couldn't see the ship from the water, but even with this small elevation, I have a better view. She's on fire, flames already climbing the masts and spreading across the sails.

I start to move to a bench but, at a look from Selly, stay where I am rather than rock the boat and make her work more difficult. The little boat is designed to hold a dozen people, sitting on the benches in rows of three—and it's definitely designed to be rowed by two people, not one. It's big enough that it's taking all her strength to move it, but in the vast ocean surrounding us, it's a tiny speck.

"That was quite a leap of faith on your part, Wollesley," the prince says quietly.

I blink at him, my eyes stinging with salt, my mind sluggishly trying to understand what he means. "Just a leap, I'm afraid."

He stares at me. "You mean you didn't know I could help you?"

I shake my head. "Turns out I don't think of everything. Your reputation as a magician is unparalleled, Your Highness, and clearly well earned, but I must admit the possibility didn't occur to me. In my defense, I was acting under pressure."

"So you thought . . . ?"

I shrug. I think my voice might shake if I speak.

Selly leans on her oars and studies me, her face unreadable. "You thought you were sacrificing your life to protect him," she says eventually. "And you didn't even like him at school."

Leander's gaze snaps across to her, and I think I flush, and for a moment neither of us speaks. He's the one with the social graces, though, and after a moment he finds something to say.

"I don't know if you're incredibly brave or completely insane, Wollesley. But thank you."

His tone irks me as much as it always did at school—the

mix of condescension and fascination—but I'm forced to pause and cough again before I can reply.

"I didn't do it for you," I say, and there's a strange satisfaction in seeing his eyes widen.

"Then why . . . ?"

"I did it for everyone who's relying on their prince to keep them from a war and save their lives. Our attackers couldn't afford to leave witnesses, which meant I was going to die anyway. I thought it might as well be in service of protecting you, giving you a small shot at preventing a war. It was the sensible choice, not a personal one."

"Sensible," Selly echoes, shooting me an incredulous look.

For a long moment there's no sound but the lapping of the waves around us.

"I did try to steer her toward the overboard bit," I admit. "Though I didn't have much of a plan for after that, apart from treading water. Still, it was a piece of luck they didn't shoot me."

Neither of them says anything.

Wordlessly, Selly sets to work with her oars, pushing at the one on the left to begin to turn us away from the wind, back toward the burning wreck.

"Can I help?" I ask, watching her square her jaw, knuckles white as she wrestles both oars at once.

"Do you know how to row?" she asks.

"Not really."

"Then we'll save the lesson for later. Right now we're in a hurry."

"Where are we going? We're in the middle of the ocean, and our ship's destroyed."

*And our crew is dead.* I see her lips press together, as if she's thinking the same thing.

"That's exactly why we have to hurry," she says, hardening her tone. "We won't last long in a shore boat like this—no food, no water, no shelter, no sail. We can use an oar for a mast—it's designed to fit into that bench in the center in an emergency—but we'll need to salvage a piece of the *Lizabetta*'s sails before they burn, and get some supplies from the ship."

Leander was staring at the horizon—now he looks at her, blinking slowly. "What?"

She shoots him the same look a thousand teachers did back at school. "What were you planning on doing?" she asks, exasperated. "Just floating around out here?" She jerks her chin toward the *Lizabetta*. The fire is growing quickly now, and the ship is listing hard to the right, her deck on a dangerous slope. "A ship like her won't usually sink, she'll just burn down to the waterline. The hull's too thick. But a bunch of cannonballs hit her, and if the masts fall to leeward, they could tug her over onto her side completely. I think she's going all the way under, so we need to get what we can first."

"And then?" Leander murmurs.

She leans on her oars, regarding us each in turn. "And then we follow my captain's last orders," she says simply. "We survive."

# LEANDER

*The* Little Lizabetta
*The Crescent Sea*

The ship towers above us as we draw in close, and I can feel the heat of the flames on my face.

Selly ships her oars as the gentle waves carry us up beside the *Lizabetta,* turning to regard her burning home. Her blond hair is plastered around her face in a wet curtain, and she's white as a sheet, even her freckles pale.

She's always had pink in her cheeks, the touch of the wind and sun, but just now she seems almost translucent. As if she could keep on fading, and simply disappear.

She hasn't stopped since we hit the water, green eyes narrowed in determination, moving ruthlessly to the next step of her plan, and then the next. But for an instant as she gazes up at the ship, I catch a glimpse of what's behind that purpose, behind her crisp orders. I see the way she presses her lips together hard, making sure they don't tremble.

"First things first, Prince," she says, her voice steady. "Can you help with that fire?"

I draw a shaky breath, and make myself nod. The truth is, I've already charmed more spirits today than I've ever come *close* to before, and most of it without anything to sacrifice. I'm not sure what part of myself I gave them in return for their help, but I felt something bleeding away. And I'm not sure how much I have left in me before I simply pass out, or worse. My arms and legs are shaky, my head aching.

But all of this is my fault, and whatever I have left, it's owed to others.

I dig in my pocket for something to sacrifice, and find a copper coin. Usually it would be nothing. Now I'm pretty sure it's all the money we have—and that means it's everything. That's what the spirits care about—how much *you* think it's worth.

My hand is cold, but I curl my fingers around it and draw back my arm, then send it arcing toward the deck, where it disappears midair, snapping out of existence somewhere above the flames as the spirits claim it.

Then I shift my focus until I can see the fire spirits dancing around the flames, playing with glee. Immediately they invite me in, and their presence is warm and tempting. Fire spirits are like the friend you know is a bad influence, but who's always a whole lot of fun—before you end up in a whole lot of trouble.

So I suppose fire spirits are to me what I am to other people.

They're the most dangerous of all the spirits, and around them I'm always half a bad idea away from letting them off the leash, to soar out and consume everything around us. They have a way of convincing you it would be a great time for everyone.

But I join their dangerous dance, and as I lay on the charm, they slowly part, leaving a clear way up onto the boat, the charred wood still smoking gently. Time for us to go aboard.

"Can you swim one more time?" Selly asks, sizing up Wollesley and me in turn. We each nod, no doubt both lying about how confident we are. He was treading water a long time and looks like a drowned noodle. I'm aching deep in my bones.

Together we all slip over the side, swimming and splashing the short distance to the ship. We use the broken and splintered wood from one of the cannonball wounds as a ladder, and as Selly climbs ahead of me, her soaking wet clothes stream water onto my head and cling to her body, weighing her down.

It's a sobering reminder that we're wet, and night is coming. The sky is already a velvety blue to the east, an angry orange to the west, toward Mellacea.

She scrambles over the railing, then turns to pull me up, and together we grip Wollesley's hands and haul him after us. He's been in the water longest of all, and he's shivering.

Up on the deck the light is brighter—the flames dance and flicker, lighting our way, though it's hard to see into the darkness beyond them. The ship herself is a wreck, tilting toward us. Farther along the deck I can see the crew's bodies, already alight.

Selly sees them too, and she stops in place, staring, lifting one hand to press it to her mouth. A shudder goes through her.

*I killed them.*

If they hadn't taken me aboard . . .

Selly tries to muffle the sound she makes, and tentatively I reach out to squeeze her shoulder. Silent witness is all I can offer her, and it's so desperately not enough. I'm not even sure

I should touch her—though I held her in my arms while they were shot, this feels different. But she lifts her hand and presses it over mine.

Then she draws a breath and turns away. "There should still be a couple of water barrels in the hold," she says, her voice breaking. "Leander, try to get down there and bring out one of the smaller ones, and float it back to the boat. Without drinking water, we're nowhere. Keegan, look for anything you can find to eat. There might be something we missed in the galley."

We nod, and without another word she turns to run for the mast closest to the back of the boat—the one least on fire, but nearest to poor Kyri's body—and scrambles up it with that quick ease of hers.

My eyes track her as she climbs, before I make myself turn for the stairs leading belowdecks. The oil has run down them and they're on fire. Beside me, Wollesley makes a noise of dismay.

I hold up a hand, watching the spirits where they play. There's no way to command fire spirits, or even to beguile them—you have to suggest they'll get the better end of the deal if they try your idea. So I show them how fun it would be to concentrate their efforts on one side of the stairs, to burn all the more brightly.

A part of me is grateful to have an excuse to shove the sharp horror of the last few hours away into a corner and put on a grin for the spirits. A part of me burns with guilt that it's even possible.

The fickle spirits shift their attention all too readily, and the flames gutter and go out down one side of the descent.

I take one careful step, Wollesley on my heels, and then

another, the heat rapidly drying out my clothes. Then, abruptly, the burned-out wood buckles beneath us.

I leap to the next step, then the next, half running and half falling to the darkened corridor below, my old classmate landing in a tangle of limbs beside me.

"Good luck," I call quietly as he turns for the galley, and I hurry along the hallway to where the captain pointed out the cargo hold the night I came aboard.

I hurry past the door to my cabin, and for a moment it's like I can see through the wall, see myself inside it, sitting up in bed sleepily. See Selly stumbling back, her eyes wide at the sight of my bare chest. I can see myself grinning. I can see the look the other girl—Abri—gave me as I headed up on deck this morning. Clearly, Selly had told her about our encounter, and just as clearly, she—

The shock hits me like a punch to the gut. *Abri's dead.* Her round-cheeked smile is gone. And there's no anger in me for the moment she wavered, for the moment she thought she could save her own life if she gave up mine. How can I blame her for not wanting to die? She never would have if she hadn't met me.

The light outside is fading quickly, and the cargo hold is almost dark, except for faint starlight coming in from the cannonball exit holes on the far side. The whole ship is listing badly toward me, and there's water all down her right-hand side. There's also a handful of small barrels that have rolled down the slope and are floating there.

I carefully slide toward them, splashing into the water. After the warmth of the stairs it's a shock all over again, and my lungs contract, breath stuttering as I force myself to drag the air in. Then I sling my arm around the smallest barrel. It's about the size of my torso, and judging by the weight, full. It's also about as heavy as I can lift, and I know I'm running out of time before weakness overtakes me completely.

I consider my options for getting it out and discard the idea of carrying it back up—the broken stairs would be impossible to navigate.

Instead, I scramble up the sloping floor, bracing myself against broken timbers and pushing the barrel ahead of me, until I reach the cannonball holes on the far side. A couple of quick kicks make one larger, and I shove the barrel through it, grabbing onto the smoothest part of the edge.

The little barrel scrapes and rolls along the wooden side of the boat, then splashes below, but when I stick my head out to see it bobbing in the water, my heart sinks. The underside of the ship is showing, and it's crusted with greenish-white barnacles. If I slide after the barrel, they'll shred me. I'll have to do it the hard way.

I wriggle out through the hole, trying not to snag and tear the clothes I borrowed from Wollesley, and look down at the dark waters below. No point hesitating, or my body will get the better of me.

I jump, and hang in the air forever before I hit the water, plunging underneath the freezing waves, all the air driven from my lungs. I kick hard, pushing up toward the surface, and find myself right next to my barrel. Coughing, eyes stinging, I begin a long, slow lap of the sinking ship, pushing our water supply in front of me.

When I round the back of the ship, the others are already aboard the *Little Lizabetta* and have gotten to work. Selly has one oar lashed over the back of the boat to steer with, and Wollesley is following her instructions to jury-rig the other oar as a mast. Together they pull first my barrel and then me back in.

I start to shiver once I'm out of the water, and I busy myself stowing the barrel.

"Here," Wollesley says softly, holding up a piece of sailcloth. "It's more or less windproof, should warm you up."

I nod my thanks, my limbs like lead as I wrap it around my shoulders and settle in the bottom of the little boat. Perhaps I should help them pin the rest of the sailcloth up to make our sail, but it's beyond me. I'm faintly aware of the spirits swirling around the boat in the air, on the water, but I don't have anything left in me to even try to reach out for them.

The sun's nearly down in the west now, the last of the glow fading. The sky is very big and very black above us, and a silvery swath of stars stretches across it, both moons coming into view. The sail flaps quietly, not yet pulled taut, and we drift with the waves. The *Lizabetta* is burning lower, mostly a red glow, and farther away than I'd have expected.

"We need to talk about what to do next," Selly says, producing a bag of apples that must have been part of Wollesley's haul. She passes one to each of us, and when I bite into the crisp, sweet fruit—the opposite of the salty water in my eyes and up my nose—it feels like I've barely eaten all day.

"We should sail for Kethos," I mumble. "Make our way up to Alinor by land."

Selly crunches into her apple and narrows one eye as she studies me. "New plan," she says. "We should talk about how sailing boats work, and *then* we should talk about what to do next."

"All right, teach us."

Selly chews her lip, considering how to manage the task, and then holds up her left hand, still clad in a fingerless leather glove that's slowly stiffening with salt. "Watch carefully," she says.

I lean in, and Wollesley twists so he can study her like there might be a test later. Though come to think of it, there will be. The only one we've ever taken that really matters.

"This is the continent." She makes an upside-down U with her left hand, fingers and thumb pointing down. "The end of my thumb is Mellacea. Then, working our way up and across the top, we've got the principalities, Trallia halfway, the Barren Reaches, Beinhof, and Fontesque. About halfway down my finger, we've got Alinor, and below it, at the end of my finger, Kethos." Next she stabs at the empty space in the middle of her U shape. "We're in here, obviously, the Crescent Sea. And the prevailing wind and currents . . ." She draws a line from Alinor on her finger over to Mellacea on her thumb.

"So we have to sail *into* the wind to get home," I say, my heart sinking. "There's no chance it's going to swing around and change direction?"

"No," she says, rueful. "Not unless we see a really serious storm, in which case we're done."

Wollesley exhales slowly. "And if we sail *with* the wind, we go straight to Mellacea. I assume we can't"—he reaches out to trace a path downward from that blank space in the middle, where we float—"say, sail down to the Isles?"

Selly shakes her head. "Sorry. We've got barely any food,

• 173 •

definitely not enough water. If the wind gets much stronger than this, we'll sink. I've also got no navigational instruments—the prince has a map in that journal of his, but without the right tools I can't get an exact fix on where we are. We could shoot right past the Isles without even knowing, especially if they came up at night. And even if we overcame all that, we'd end up trapped on the Isles with no boat capable of sailing home again."

The truth settles inside my chest, and I lay an arm along the edge of the boat, trying to stop myself from swaying with exhaustion. I'm suddenly aware all over again of how cold I am. "So we're going to Mellacea."

"That's our only option," Selly agrees. "Straight to Port Naranda. The coast everywhere else is cliffs—we can't be sure of hitting a village, but we'll see the city from a distance. We've got one thing on our side, at least: absolutely nobody in Mellacea is going to be expecting us."

"Indeed not," Wollesley agrees. "They will think the prince dead. Nobody will be looking for him."

"I'm not sure the Mellacean government thinks I'm dead," I say slowly. "The ship that caught us wasn't navy, and the girl who ran it wasn't in uniform."

"Private operators?" Wollesley murmurs. "That's . . ."

"A lot to unpack, politically speaking," I agree. "But not the first problem we need to solve."

"I think we could pull it off," Selly says thoughtfully. "Sailing to Mellacea. You're not going to look very princely when we arrive, so that'll help. If we can get to the port there, we have options."

"The ambassador," I say. "I have code words that will establish my identity to any ambassador on the continent or beyond. If we can get to Mellacea, and we can get to the Alinorish embassy, the ambassador will take over from there."

"Even before she finds a ship to get you home, she can send a message," Wollesley agrees. "The Mellaceans think they have succeeded in killing you, and whoever they are, there's no reason for them to keep that news to themselves. But it's worse than that: When word gets back to Alinor that the progress fleet is sunk, the queen will know you weren't aboard. She will believe we're still out here on the *Lizabetta,* sneaking to the Isles to make the sacrifice. She might even move *toward* war, believing you will strengthen Barrica and give her an unexpected advantage."

My stomach drops. He's right—Augusta is nothing if not a tactician.

"So not only will she start a war," Selly says slowly, "but it'll be one she has no way to win." She pinches the bridge of her nose, and I'm hit with a flash of sympathy. As foreign as prevailing winds and jury-rigging a sail are to Wollesley and me, this must be just as strange to her—and yet she can't escape it, any more than we can escape the *Little Lizabetta.*

Suddenly, whatever the three of us decide is liable to prevent a war or start one—and decide the winner.

"Mellacea, then," I say softly. "We just need to reach the ambassador, and she'll get word to my sister."

In Port Naranda we can find someone in charge, someone with resources. We'll escape from this nightmare, even if I'll never escape from the list of deaths that lie at my doorstep.

I can't believe that just a day ago I thought this was an adventure.

A shiver runs through me, and in the moonlight I see Selly grimace. "We don't have any way to dry our clothes until the sun comes up," she says. "We should start sailing now, though. At least the weather's good enough that we don't need your help with the spirits, Prince."

"I don't think I could raise a breeze if I tried right now," I admit.

She nods. "I'll sail the old-fashioned way, with what wind we've got, and the stars." She points first at Wollesley, then me. "Both of you lie down together, snuggle up under that piece of sailcloth—share body heat and try not to freeze."

"Your Highness," Wollesley begins.

"Under the circumstances," I say, "I think you'd both better start calling me Leander."

Wollesley considers this. "Perhaps, then," he ventures, "you might use my name as well. Wollesley is my father, or my older brother."

"Keegan," I say obediently.

"Bet you wish you hadn't shaved your head now, Keegan," Selly murmurs. "Think of all that lost warmth."

Wolles—no, *Keegan* and I lie between two of the benches, and I haul a piece of sailcloth over us, settling in to try and stop shivering and get some rest.

I can see Selly from where I lie, a pale shape in the moonlight. I can just make out her freckles, mirroring the constellations above.

She looks back over her shoulder as we leave the burning wreck of the *Lizabetta* in our wake—but only once. Then she turns her gaze ahead into the darkness, resolute.

# JUDE

*The* Macean's Fist
*The Crescent Sea*

I got to know one of the sailors on the way home.

The sun went down, and the stars came out one by one, the first few pinpricks of light appearing in the velvet blue sky as I watched, wishing the roiling in my gut would settle. Those first few stars were joined by more, and then more, until they were a stunning sweep across the heavens, more vivid here than anywhere I've ever seen. But my head was aching, and I'd thrown up everything I'd ever eaten by then, and the beauty was lost on me.

I was leaning against the rail, unable to bear the thought of shoving myself into the confines of my little bunk belowdecks—far too much like a coffin—and he came up to join me near the bow, looming out of the darkness.

His face was as white as the foam streaming beneath the ship, copper hair dulled in the dark. "Can't sleep?" he asked with a sympathetic grimace.

I shook my head.

"I'm Varon," he said, offering me his hand to shake. "Good to meet you."

"Jude," I managed. It made it worse that he was friendly and smiling. That he looked like the kind of guy I'd usually go out of my way to talk to. To flirt with.

*That* made me think of Tom, the boy I . . . well, I don't know what we are. He's a bartender at Ruby Red, one of Ruby's underground clubs, and though I suppose technically he works for a gang boss, the reality is he just likes mixing drinks, and he's good at it, and the club is where he happened to get a job.

Perhaps Varon is just really good at killing people.

It's so much harder, finding that they're normal people, the ones who did this, and I'd pass them in the street without imagining for a moment they were murderers.

"I *heard* you had an accent," he said, as if confirming it was some kind of personal triumph. "She was calling you 'His Lordship' before—you something fancy?"

I shook my head. "Couldn't be less fancy," I replied. "The accent's from Kirkpool, where I grew up. I'm from Port Naranda these days."

"What's Kirkpool like?" he asked, leaning against the rail and making himself comfortable. "Never made it that far, and I guess I won't be going there anytime soon, will I?"

I had just been beginning to relax, his smile unwinding something in me. But those flippant words pulled me back to earth with a thud, and I didn't reply.

He just absorbed my silence, giving up the view of the dark water below us and the bright stars above to study me instead.

When he spoke again, his tone was gentle. "You can't blame yourself, Jude. It would have happened with or without you."

"That doesn't matter," I replied, not knowing the words were coming until I spoke them. "It happened with me."

Because that's the truth of it.

I'm a part of this now. I participated in a slaughter, even if all I did was watch.

A part of me didn't believe she'd go through with it, but with the green sister at one shoulder and Ruby at the other, I think Laskia's as hemmed in as I am. The only difference is she put herself there.

Another piece of me wants to ask if there's something I could have done to stop it, and the rest of me knows I can't afford to wonder. They have my mother.

I'm positive that as we sailed away from that merchant ship, I saw a figure slide across the deck. I didn't say anything— I didn't want someone to kill them then and there—but now I keep wondering how long it took them to drown, or if they're still clinging to the wreckage, waiting to die. And if that's worse.

I keep thinking about Wollesley as well. It was like some kind of nightmare—as if wiping out a fleet carrying Leander and half our friends from school wasn't enough, then the witnesses we tracked down had another of our classmates?

The two of us never particularly got along at school—he had all the breeding to fit in but was still an outcast. I had none of it, but I made myself useful and managed to make friends. Leander never seemed to care I was lowborn, and since he didn't, nobody else did either. I can still see him, grinning like he knew a secret, holding out his hand and calling for me to join in his latest piece of madness.

That's another thing I'm not sure of—would it have been worse to see him die, or is it worse not to know how he died, which cannonball or grenade or falling mast ended him? Did he die before the friends we both had on that fleet, or after?

None of it matters now, though. My friends were never really my friends, and he's as dead as all the rest of them. And I'm standing with a sailor I don't know on the deck of this ship.

There'll be a purse in this for me, and I'm going to use it to get Mum as far from the city as I can.

"It gets easier," Varon said gently, drawing my attention back to the conversation. "Best thing to do is take your thoughts somewhere else for a little while." He pointed to a cluster of stars. "Every one of those constellations has a story. Maybe I've got one or two you haven't heard."

By the time the cliffs of the Mellacean coast loom on the horizon, I've spent most of the night here with Varon, swapping stories.

We're not bound for Port Naranda, where a ship like this one would draw attention. Instead, we'll land about an hour north of the city, at a place called Voster Bay.

It looks the same as much of the coastline—rocky, inhospitable cliffs rising from the sea—but there's enough of a dent that ships can shelter there. And the church has an outpost here, where apparently nobody is inclined to wonder what a warship is doing casually dropping anchor.

Varon ducks away to his duties, but I'm only left alone for a few minutes before I sense a presence beside me. The ghostly form of Sister Beris lingers near the railing, white face so pale it almost glows in the dark, body hidden by her forest-green robes.

"You didn't sleep, Jude," she observes, and hearing my name in her mouth gives me a twitch between my shoulder blades.

"No," I say, because there's no point in denying it, but I don't want to explain myself to this woman either.

"You're uneasy." Something in her tone catches my attention. When I glance across, she inclines her head. "So am I." Then, just as I'm wondering if I've misjudged her: "But we must subjugate our own discomfort for the greater good."

*Ah, there it is. The justification.*

"Can a war be for the greater good?" I ask despite myself.

She takes her time, giving the question more consideration than I'd expected. "I don't think an Alinorish boy—even an exile, even one who has lived your life of exclusion—can truly understand the experience of a people who have been cut off from their god," she says eventually. "For five hundred years we have reached out with our prayers, and they have been met with . . . nothing. They disappear into the great, muffling silence that is Macean's slumber."

She's right—I can't imagine that. Growing up, I always saw the flowers bloom in the temple, even through the dead of winter. The flame at the temple never went out and never needed fuel. I always *knew* Barrica watched over us, even if it was from afar.

"The green sisters have fought for our faith through those centuries," she says, in response to my silence. "Sometimes at great cost. Sometimes, we were the only ones. Sometimes— some years, some decades—we would maintain our churches ourselves, scrubbing away the dirt until our hands bled, knowing no faithful would come, knowing we must be the faithful ourselves. It has been a long, long road, Jude. The decisions we have made were not a whim, not made without the deepest understanding of the consequences."

"And now your people have come back to church," I observe.

"They have," she agrees. "We kept the embers alive, sometimes only barely, but when our people were hungry, *we* were the ones at their doors with food. When they were in need, it was the green sisters who gave of our own to support them. We kept the embers alive, and now the people of Mellacea return to the church to stoke the flame. Barrica's hold on Macean loosens. Soon our faith will swell his power enough to shake off his sleep, and he will return to us."

"And what will happen then?" I whisper.

"He will walk among us," she says simply, her eyes fixed on the horizon. "And he will lead."

"What about your government?"

"He is our *god,* Jude."

I let out a slow breath. There are stories about what it was like when the gods walked among us. Of their miracles, and their destruction.

"Last time they were here, we ended up with the Barren Wastes," I say softly. "A whole country, a whole people, gone. Destroyed in an instant. We learned about it at school." It feels impossible to believe, but I know it's not a matter of belief. Really, it's just impossible to *comprehend.*

"Perhaps there will be a war," she agrees, a touch regretful. "If Barrica returns to meet him once more."

"And that's what you want?"

"It is the only choice left to us," she replies. "We are not the ones who bound our god in sleep."

I don't know what to say—how to argue with the centuries of work she and the green sisters have put into this plan of theirs. How to make them see the horror of what they're doing, if they don't already.

"Do you pray to Barrica?" she asks after a pause.

I shake my head. "I did, growing up. I don't now."

"Do you wish to pray to Macean?"

I shake my head again. "I answer my own prayers, Sister Beris. Nobody else ever has."

I expect her to try and talk me around, but she simply nods. "Perhaps you are bound for the Mother," she says instead. "All her children are present in her temple."

"Perhaps," I say, suddenly desperate to get away from her, from the conversation. "I should see if Laskia needs anything, Sister. Please excuse me."

She glances at the ruby pin on my lapel and then nods, releasing me.

I force myself to keep to a walk as I retreat.

I keep out of the way as we reach Voster Bay, and Varon and the others get the ship squared away, dropping anchor and waiting as her great bulk swings around to face into the direction of the outgoing tide.

A signal is sent to the convent ashore—the sisters will send out a boat to collect Laskia, Sister Beris, and me before the ship heads on to its next destination. In the meantime, everyone troops below to the mess hall, to settle in at the long tables for a hot breakfast, though the sun's not up. Their work is done, after all.

There's no way I can eat without being sick, but before I can decline the invitation, Laskia catches my arm, wordlessly pulling me to stand in the doorway with her and Sister Beris.

There's a fixed look on her face—has been ever since we left the merchant ship in our wake. It says she's realized she has two choices now: either she can see what she's done and understand the horror of it—and get out—or she can go deeper.

I think her faith is real, and I think she truly believed she could have it all. That with one death she could provoke a war that would rally the faithful for Sister Beris. That would bring Ruby so much money, so much power, she would have no choice but to acknowledge her sister.

But Ruby will never see Laskia the way she wishes. Sister Beris serves her god—Laskia is no more than a tool to her. And Macean is bound in sleep and knows nothing of what she does.

Laskia, though? *She* knows what she's done. It's in the set of her jaw, in her fixed stare. She's like a girl trying to forget last night's bad dream but finding it behind her every time she looks over her shoulder. She has to keep moving and hope the nightmare doesn't catch up.

I stand at her side as the crew digs into porridge, which is ladled out from huge bowls, and a shout goes up when the chef brings out pots of honey to go with it.

He points at Laskia as he loads up his own bowl and thumps onto a bench a couple of places along from Varon.

"Consider it a bonus," Laskia calls out with a generous wave of one hand. "Thank you all for your hard work."

They cheer like big children with a treat and fight over the honey, passing it along the rows so they can spoon it onto their breakfast. A thank-you gift for dozens of murders.

Laskia turns to look back at Sister Beris, her expression unreadable, and the green sister lays a hand on her shoulder.

"Strength, Laskia," she murmurs. "And purpose."

My stomach is turning at the smell of the food, and I'm about to fade backward through the open door and escape to the upper decks when the talk around us dies away.

I look around at the crew for the cause, and I'm met with suddenly open mouths, bulging eyes. Their faces darken as they struggle for breath—Varon turns bright red as he meets my eyes, and I stare back at him in bewilderment.

"Laskia." I can't look away. "What did you do?"

"We're trying to frame our government for an assassination, Jude," she says quietly. "That's why we dressed those bodies in Mellacean navy uniforms and threw them into the wreckage. Witnesses are a liability."

As she speaks, Varon reaches out to me, fingers curling into claws. He's staring at me like I knew, like I betrayed him.

And I want to look away from what's happening, but something compels me to witness it.

All around him, the crew members slump, heads hitting

tables, or they push to their feet and collapse after a few staggering steps.

Laskia watches from the doorway, Sister Beris impassive beside her.

"Ruby's cleaners will tidy up the boat later," Laskia says as Varon falls from his bench, sprawling on the floor, motionless. Her jaw is set, her gaze distant. Whatever this is costing her, she's keeping it buried deep inside. "We can't afford to leave any mess behind."

# SELLY

*The* Little Lizabetta
*The Crescent Sea*

I'm at the helm when the sun climbs slowly behind me. The horizon lightens to a pale silver, and then the gold creeps in, lighting the way back to Alinor and safety. The first moon sets, the second lingering in the sky, then fading out as daybreak arrives.

A little while after, the chill of the night begins to leave my bones—my shirt starts to dry where it's stretched across my shoulders, the fabric hardening as the salt bakes in.

I slept a few hours in the night—Keegan woke, and I gave him the best lesson I could. He listened to me gravely, nodding from time to time. I'd figured he'd be snobbish about learning from someone who never set foot inside a school a day in her life, but he just kept on asking questions.

Our makeshift sail is fastened to the top of the mast and tacked down to the gunwales to port and starboard in a ragged triangle—it's about as rustic as it gets, and there's no way to adjust it in a hurry. It's fixed, and we have to handle the boat around it, rather than the reverse. We're vulnerable, liable to be picked up by a wave and spun around, tipped out into the sea as the boat lies over on her side—and I don't think we could get her up again.

So instead, we need to correct our course just as each wave reaches us from behind, picking us up to carry us along, surfing on top, almost weightless, before we gently slide down the back and wait for the next.

It's a quiet, lulling thing to do, and it's something to concentrate on. A way to escape my thoughts. My mind keeps tugging me back to the *Lizabetta*. To her crew. To the sight of their bodies burning.

We haven't woken Leander, and he didn't move a muscle as Keegan and I talked quietly through how to sail the shore boat.

"I've never seen a display of magic like it," Keegan said softly, gazing up at the stars to mark our direction. He was practicing what I'd just shown him, and our conversation had shifted to other things. "I was at school with him for years, and all I ever saw was idleness. They *said* he was powerful, but when was someone not flattering him? To conjure a wind like that, though, to speed the *Lizabetta* along for hours and hours, and then somehow still manage to keep me afloat and tame the fire? That's more than simply powerful. I didn't know it could be done."

"He's a royal magician," I murmured, watching Leander as he slept. It seems impossible that this boy who let me grouch at him, tuck a flower behind his ear, could be as powerful as he truly is.

"Even for a royal magician," Keegan replied. "Mustering

that much magic *with* a sufficient sacrifice would be extraordinary. Without . . ."

He paused and looked at me, a question in his eyes, and I remembered he'd caught a glimpse of my marks when I fixed his porthole. But I kept my gloves on, and my mouth shut. I wasn't in the mood for questions about magic, or to talk about all the teachers who failed to help me find my own magic.

So we let Leander rest, and once I was as sure as I could be that Keegan knew what he was doing, I took my turn at snatching a few hours of sleep as well.

Now the scholar is asleep once more, and I'm greeting the sun alone. Which means I'm watching when our prince finally yawns and rolls over onto his back. The morning light hits him full in the face, and I have a front-row view as he screws up those handsome features in irritation, tries to shift away, and encounters Keegan's damp back.

His eyes fly open, and I watch as it all comes back to him. What happened. Where he is. His jaw tightens, his eyes close again, squeezing tight against reality. And then he schools his features, relaxing them into the half smirk that must be instinct.

His black hair is stiff with salt, his eyes still shadowed with exhaustion, but he looks better than he did as the sun set.

In the plain blue shirt and dark brown trousers Keegan found for him, clothes that are well made but unadorned, he's nothing like a prince. I can't picture him in his tailored clothes, can't imagine him at his parties at the palace.

Instead, he just looks like a boy. Like someone I could know.

When he glances across, I flick my own gaze up to the sail, but I'm sure he knows I was watching him.

"Morning," he murmurs, pushing up on one elbow, then pausing to cough.

"Try an apple," I say quietly, nodding to the small pile sitting near him. "You should have some water, too, but the apple's better against the salt in your mouth."

He reaches across for one and shifts to sit as he takes a big bite. "Thank you."

We sit in almost companionable silence for a time.

"How long until we make land, do you think?" he asks eventually.

I puff out a breath. "If this keeps up? I don't have a fix on exactly where we were on the charts, and I don't know how fast we're going—we're just lucky we can use the sun for a rough direction. But if we keep up this pace, I'd say we'll sail all day today, overnight, and with any luck we'll make Port Naranda by nightfall tomorrow."

"Another day and a half. Did you sleep yet?"

I nod. "Keegan took over for a little. We let you rest."

"I could have sworn we never stopped snuggling." He glances back at the other boy with a hint of a smile. "He's all elbows."

"Well, those elbows let you sleep through the night," I point out. I meant it as a tease—something to draw out more of that smile, as a shield against the grief that keeps trying to push its way back up my throat. But it comes out sounding like a jab.

It's enough to silence Leander, and we crest a few more waves before he replies. "One more thing to add to my tab," he says quietly.

"Why doesn't he like you?" I ask. "I thought everyone did."

Leander snorts. "Well, not Wollesley. He had a miserable

time at school, and even if I didn't participate, we both know I could have stopped it." He climbs up to sit beside me in the stern, stretching with a wince. "I can't help but think—two days ago, he thought he'd escaped his fate. He thought he was on his way to the Bibliotek, where all his bookish dreams would come true. One day ago, he thought he'd been taken off course with a boy he didn't much like back at school. That he was delayed, that he'd miss the start of his semester. Survivable, still. And now here he is. He saved us from discovery. He's sailed your boat through the night, en route to a hostile port, and when he wakes up, he'll probably do something else extraordinary."

"What do you think makes him like that?" I ask, studying Keegan's angular features, the pale skin already turning pink in the sun. "He looks like someone who should fall to pieces if you leave him out in the rain. What is it that makes him strong?"

"I wish I knew," says Leander, almost wistful. "Maybe he's just someone who likes to be doing something. Who likes to be trying."

"What's the alternative?" I ask.

"Doing nothing," he says softly. "I'm good at that."

But neither of us can afford to do nothing right now. Not just because we need to keep the *Little Lizabetta* afloat—our tiny white speck of safety in the vast, choppy ocean—but because neither of us can afford to think too hard about how we came to be aboard her.

We're both quiet, me keeping my eyes on the sail and correcting our course with each new wave, him crunching on his apple.

"Copper for your thoughts?" he asks eventually.

"I thought you threw our last one to the fire spirits."

He tilts his head and studies me, letting the silence draw out as he takes another bite of his apple. They're not much of a meal, but Keegan didn't have a lot to choose from below—and even less when he discounted stuff that wouldn't survive being dragged through the water.

"I'm thinking about the apples," I say eventually, the ache welling up behind my eyes again.

"The apples?"

"I keep thinking about how when we threw all our ballast overboard, someone left these belowdecks, along with a couple of water barrels, in case we somehow survived. That no matter how brave my crew were when they stood up in front of that girl, no matter how sure it seemed they were going to die, one of them had hope. One of them clung to this tiny chance that they'd find a way out of this. It's so much worse, knowing they didn't want to die, and they weren't ready."

"Nobody was supposed to pay for this with their lives," he whispers, hoarse. "The progress fleet—those were my friends on those boats. I grew up with them. I *invited* half of them; they thought they were going on a trip with me. They'd have laughed when they realized I wasn't aboard. But they . . . they were my friends."

"I know," I say quietly, picturing the girl in the silver-sea dress dancing on the deck as Leander and I watched from among the packing crates and flowers. She was so full of life, full of joy, even if I begrudged her that happiness then. Now I'm desperately grateful she had it.

"If I'd thought for a moment they were in danger, I never would have—"

"I know." What did he say her name was? *Violet.*

"And your crew. Your ship was a cargo ship."

"I know," I murmur.

And then we're quiet again, the waves rushing in to fill the silence.

"I learned Kyri's name, and Rensa's," he says eventually. "And the other girl, Abri. What were the men called?"

"Jonlon," I whisper. "And Conor. They crewed for my father since I was a baby."

"I'm so, so sorry they died, Selly," he says softly. "I'd do anything to change it."

It feels impossible this boy beside me could ever be the reason something like that happened.

But my world has become so much larger than it ever was before, and my view has changed as surely as if I'd climbed up to the crow's nest.

I know how the continent looks on a map. I've traced out long routes across the Crescent Sea from one port to another with my finger on the paper, sailed them aboard my father's fleet. I've seen maps and charts of what's beyond, and when I was almost too small to remember, I even made a trip down to the southern islands aboard the *Lizabetta* herself.

But my world has always been confined to the deck of my ship, or a quick trip ashore for a few hours in a foreign port. I know the smell of timber and salt and tar, not the stink of backstabbing and blood.

Suddenly, far too late, I'm understanding why Rensa tried so hard to teach me about looking beyond myself. About seeing the size of the world. Because I tried staying in my own small part of it, and it didn't work at all.

But if I can see the ripples that will travel out into the world as a result of the *Lizabetta*'s loss, that's not the only thing my new view takes in.

"It wasn't your fault," I say quietly, my fingers tightening around the makeshift tiller, my gloves stiff.

His gaze snaps across to me. "It couldn't have been *more* my fault. If I hadn't been aboard—"

"They'd still have killed us as witnesses."

"Well then, if I'd made the sacrifice on time, the progress fleet wouldn't even have—"

"Leander, *stop*."

And he does, dark eyes on my face, lips pressed together against what he wants to say.

"Look," I say softly. "You should have made the sacrifice a year ago, yes. And believe me, I was furious when you came aboard the *Lizabetta*. You stopped me from getting to my father, who I haven't seen in a year. I missed catching a ship up the North Passage before it closed for winter."

He winces, but I hold up a hand to stop him, and he stays silent.

"What you *didn't do*," I continue, "was *kill people*."

"Selly, it was foreseeable that—" He cuts himself off when I glare at him, presses a hand over his mouth.

"There's plenty of blame to share here, plenty of justice deserved. But what *you* deserve is to be lectured, to be shoved in an uncomfortable hammock on a leaky ship to think about not living up to your responsibilities. Not to watch people murdered in your name."

"I—" Again he stops himself.

"You're really not used to letting other people get the last word, are you?"

"I have to admit, they don't usually try."

And perhaps another time, if we were talking about something else, we'd smile. But instead, the tension singing through both of us eases a touch. And that's not nothing.

A few days ago we were a world apart. But now he's just a boy, and a scared one.

"Can I ask . . ." When I look across, his dark eyes are on mine, and he crunches down on his apple to indicate he won't interrupt. So I ask my question softly. "Why *didn't* you go?"

He doesn't reply straightaway, chewing slowly, looking down at the journal tucked under the thwart next to Keegan, then up to the rigging.

"You don't have to answer," I say eventually. "It's not your fault, whatever the reason was."

He shakes his head, keeping his eyes on the sail as the ragged edges of it flicker and billow and slowly unknit themselves. "If you asked anyone at home, they'd say I was too busy having fun," he says quietly. "If you'd asked *me* at home, that's what I'd have said."

"What's the real reason?"

He's quiet a moment. "The journal. The journal's the real reason."

"What do you mean?"

Our eyes meet again. "My father died before my first birthday. Fell from a horse when it stumbled—no warning, no reason for him to think he wouldn't see tomorrow. My mother became regent until Augusta was old enough to take the throne. Both my sisters remember him, but I came years after, and I don't at all. He wrote in the journal, though, as my grandmother did, and all the generations before her. Whoever made the trip to the Isles. They wrote about what they saw, what it was like, left messages for whoever came after."

"Is there something in your father's entries . . . ?"

"I don't know," he admits. "I haven't read it all yet. It's like . . . when I do, that's the last part of him there is left. The last part I don't know. And I didn't want it to be over. That's the truth."

We're both quiet as the boat reaches the top of a wave, and I correct her course with my jury-rigged tiller, keeping her straight as she descends. It's a rhythm as familiar as my own heartbeat.

"I suppose, considering, it's a good thing my da stayed up north," I say eventually. "Safest place to be, if things go wrong."

"I wish you were there with him," he replies quietly. "How were you going to join him? I'd have thought the North Passage would be closed by now."

"There was one more ship due to make the run," I say. "The *Freya*. She was moored next to the progress fleet."

He pauses, and I see it click into place. "You were trying to get to her the day we met."

"Yes. And when that didn't work, I was going to sneak aboard that night. They'd have found me before we made Holbard, but it would have been too late to turn back."

His brows lift, and his mouth quirks to a half smile. "You were going to run away?"

"I'd have made it, too, if the dock hadn't been swarming

with Queensguard." And then I pause. "When you said, 'Looks like they've lost something' . . . it was you. The Queensguard were looking for *you*."

"But I was hiding on top of a stack of crates with a girl I'd just met, learning about all my personality flaws," he agrees, with another small smile. "They were furious when they finally found me."

"If I'd made it onto the *Freya,* Rensa would have been just as—" The words die in my throat as I remember all over again. It's like being punched in the stomach.

I've always liked conversations on the dawn watch. The world is quiet, the morning shiny and new, and it's so easy to feel like yours is the only ship in the world and you're the only two souls aboard her. Now I'd give anything for a loud, crowded harbor.

"What about your mother?" Leander asks, trying to divert me. "Is she up north with your father?"

"My mother's an actress from Trallia. She and my father were never together—they just . . . had fun, Da always said. When he was ashore. After I was born, she gave me to him, and he raised me aboard the *Lizabetta,* his first ship."

He lets out a slow, sympathetic breath for the home I left far in our wake. "My mother's more interested in parties than parenting—acting as regent took up everything she had—but at least she was mostly in the same palace as me. Your father's fleet is bigger now, I take it?"

"Yes, he's on his newest, the *Fortune.* He sailed up to negotiate new trade routes and decided to winter in Holbard, keep working on it. He has no idea any of this is happening—no idea Rensa accepted the commission. He left me with her for a year to learn the trade."

"And were you learning?"

"Not as much as I wish I had. Not as much as she was trying to teach me. We didn't get along, Rensa and I. But if she'd thought for a moment this job was dangerous, she'd have left me ashore." My throat threatens to close, and I breathe in through my nose, out through my mouth, settling myself. "That's what keeps coming back to me. She'd have left me behind if she'd thought there was any danger. But she didn't. She thought we were safe."

And then silence falls between us again.

"Will it work?" I ask, clearing my throat. "Can a goddess protect us? I know it's different in the old stories. Keegan told me some of them—he said it's true the gods were really here, back then. That they fought in wars, and created Messengers with special, magical powers. But that was centuries ago."

"Barrica is still here," he replies quietly. "Not like she used to be, not in a way that means she could sit in this boat with us. But she's more present than any of the others, because she stayed as Sentinel, to watch Macean. And I don't *believe* that, Selly. I *know* it. The journal I showed you is one in a long line, and they all hold accounts of my family's journeys to the Isles. They aren't old stories, they're *our* stories."

"And what's written in there says she's still keeping an eye on things?"

"Yes, but it's more than that. It's different for me when I pray. My family has a connection to her. We don't talk, not in words, but she's . . . she's there. She's present."

"How can you be sure?" I ask softly.

"Trust me, you can't miss it. She's . . ." He lowers his voice, as if that might keep our goddess from hearing. "She reminds me of my sister Augusta. Imposing."

"I can't imagine," I admit. "Knowing a goddess or a queen."

"I think both of them would like you," he says quietly. "Selly, I promise I'll do this. Get me to Port Naranda and I can find the ambassador. Nothing will stop me from making it to the Isles."

"Nothing will stop you," I agree, and I know from his face we're both thinking of the price that's been paid to get him even this far. "If I have to sail you there myself."

Silently, Leander rests one of his hands over mine where I grip the tiller. I realize my knuckles are aching—and that his touch is easing that sensation as the warmth of his skin leaches into mine.

Our eyes meet, and he holds my gaze, something shimmering in the air between us. I feel my cheeks heat, but I can't look away, or don't want to. Then one corner of his mouth tugs up in a hint of a smile, and my instincts kick in.

"I'm only letting you do that because my hands are cold," I mutter.

"Of course," he agrees, soft.

But he leaves his hand there even as the pain in my knuckles slowly fades away and my fingers grow warm beneath his.

And as the sun continues to climb toward her zenith, I let him.

"Teach me to steer the boat," he says, perhaps an hour later. "If Keegan already had his lesson, we can manage it together while you get a few more hours of sleep. How are you using that thing?"

"The tiller," I correct him automatically.

"The tiller," he agrees. "I won't be as good as you, but I can ask the water spirits to keep us on a straight course, ask the air spirits for a gentle enough wind that the sail's easier to manage."

I want to disagree, but the truth is I do need to sleep. So I let him rest his hand on the oar beside mine and show him how the boat turns when he pushes it away or pulls it toward him. He's distractingly close, and I'm paying far more attention than I wish I was to the places we touch at hand and knee, turned slightly toward each other. It's as if having noticed, I now can't tear my attention away from him.

"Every movement should be small," I warn him, making myself sound businesslike. "Subtle. Anything big, you risk tipping us. So just go against your instincts at every stage, and we should be fine."

He snickers, and I carefully ease my hand free to let him try it on his own. The air's chill against my skin when I pull away. He laughs at me when I twitch, ready to grab the tiller from him at the first sign of trouble, and it's mostly to keep my hands occupied, and because my skin is itching with dried salt, that I start peeling off my gloves.

The moment he sees the backs of my hands, I realize I've made a mistake.

"Selly! What's—" He tries to grab for my wrist, and I lunge for the tiller, and suddenly he's dizzyingly close and I'm shoving him back onto his side of the boat with far too much force.

"You want to tip us?"

"But those are magician's marks!" He's not interested in helming the boat anymore, leaning in to get a better look at my hand, and I can't pull it away since I'm the one holding the tiller now. He bends his head over my hand like he's reading a map. "I've never seen them like that. Not on an adult. How does your magic work?"

"It doesn't," I reply heavily, that new, different connection between us gone in an instant. "I'm not a magician. I just have the marks."

"That's impossible."

"And yet here I am. This is my least favorite topic, Leander. Pick another one."

"Did you ever apprentice?" he presses. "With Kyri, or someone else?"

"No point," I grit out. "She tried to explain it, but I don't have an affinity. She always says—"

My voice dies in my throat.

She always *said*. Not *says*.

For a moment, impatient, I forgot that . . . I forgot.

The smallest details keep hitting me, keep washing over me like waves that want to drag me under.

Kyri will never light another candle with her sure hands. Her spirit flags are burned to ashes. Last week she was mending her best dress for a night out when she got shore leave. Now she'll never wear it. It's underwater somewhere, or ashes. Even her possessions are gone. Nobody alive but me knows that dress existed.

I keep hitting these small, new realizations and repeating them to myself, trying to find a way to understand. But it just doesn't seem possible she's gone forever.

I realize I'm gripping the tiller so hard my knuckles are turning white, and when I lift my gaze, Leander's dark eyes are waiting for me again. Solemn now. Kinder than I'd have expected. Sad.

He has to clear his throat before he can speak again—he keeps his voice low, out of deference to Keegan, who's somehow managing to sleep through all this in his spot behind the mast.

"I've never heard of someone who couldn't use their magic before." He pushes up his own sleeve to study the intricate designs there—by far the most complicated I've ever seen. Nothing could highlight more clearly the thick, lifeless strips of emerald green visible on the backs of my hands.

"Do you want to steer the boat or not?" I ask, trying to divert him.

"Not," he replies promptly. "Can you think of a reason you would have suppressed your magic? Something that might have made you afraid to use it, even if you don't feel that way on the surface?"

I shake my head. I've thought about this myself, more than once. "I didn't have an early traumatic experience with a gust of wind or anything."

"Air," he murmurs. "That's what's in the family line? Who did you inherit it from?"

"My mother," I say. "She has air magic. Or had it, I don't know. It's been a long time since my father and I heard from her."

Deep down, a part of me has wondered for years if I somehow rejected my own magic, in response to the magician mother who rejected me. But the world is full of people with fault lines in their hearts, and they all manage to keep going—plenty of them are magicians, even.

"You never talked to her about her magic?"

"No. I told you before, she handed me over when I was born. That makes two parents who can do without me, given my father's recent choices. Any questions?"

My tone is deliberately sharp, and I expect him to wince, but he just rests his hand on the tiller over mine, his fingers warm.

I yank my gaze away to study the sail, to hide the effect it has on me. Without my gloves to cover the backs of my hands, it feels impossibly intimate. I have to stop reacting this way whenever he touches me, it's ridiculous.

"Tell me about your magic," he says gently. "What it's been like, what you've tried so far."

There's a knot inside my gut at the very idea, but there's nothing but encouragement on his face when I look across at him—that and exhaustion. It's the tiredness in his eyes that softens me again.

"It's always been like this," I say quietly. "I was born with marks, like everyone else, but nothing ever came of them. Da tried so hard to help me. Having an air magician in the fleet would have been worth a lot. He always said if I could be as good a magician as I was a sailor, I'd be unstoppable."

"I'd say you're pretty unstoppable now," Leander counters.

"Well, he took me to magicians in every port when I was young. They all tried to teach me." My cheeks heat as I recall that shameful parade of failures. *But what is she? How can this be?* They made me feel like a freak and a failure, but I listened to them all, desperate for someone to help me.

"Did any of them have a theory?" he asks.

"Every one of them was so sure they could help, from the lady in the big house in Petron to the man in the hut in Kethos. And in the end, every one of them was just . . . angry. As if it might be contagious. One woman said the spirits didn't *want* to talk to me. Another said it was like they couldn't see me at all." My voice catches, my throat thickening, and I fall silent, biting down hard on the inside of my cheek.

I can still see my father's face, over those years—he always started out so determined, and faded to frustrated defeat every time.

"They were wrong to blame you for their own failings," Leander says, his fingers tightening over mine.

"Well, my father didn't give up on me, not for a long time. Every time he came back from a trip, it was the first thing he'd ask." As much as I looked forward to his return, I always dreaded that question. Dreaded the answer I'd have to give.

Leander's expression is difficult to read as I press on.

"Anyway, eventually even he couldn't pretend it was coming. So he bought me gloves instead."

"And I've noticed you never take them off," Leander says quietly. "Selly, I know he was trying to help, but for him to have a daughter capable of"—he raises his free hand, gesturing at the jury-rigged boat coasting along the waves—"of *this,* and to make you feel anything less than—"

"It was a kindness." I cut him off. "He tried everything."

I could never find a way to explain the mixture of shame and gratitude that washed through me when he handed the gloves over. When he accepted that whatever the fault was in me, it wasn't something we could mend.

It was why I was desperate to learn from Rensa while he was away. My magic was such a disappointment to him—if I could have shown him I was ready to step up and take my first mate's knot, young as I am, that would have helped me claw back some part of his good opinion. Would have given him something to be proud of.

Leander opens his mouth, closes it again, and I can tell he's choosing his words carefully when he continues. "Well, those magicians who tried to teach you—I'm sure they were doing their best, but every one of them was wrong. Your lessons should have been here, on the sea. This is your home. This is who you are. This is where your magic will be."

I look across at him then, meeting his brown eyes, searching for words. He's wrong about the magic, but he understands the way I belong to the sea—that much I can tell. I didn't expect a boy from a palace to see me so clearly.

"Look," he says. "I'll shut up if you want. I know I come off as arrogant, but I really *am* different to everyone who's tried to teach you before. I'm stronger. And I didn't learn this once, I learned it four times, for the four elements. I apprenticed with the best magicians in Alinor. Let me teach you once—just once—and if it doesn't work, I'll never mention it again."

I let myself close my eyes. Behind my eyelids, I can see the parade of failed teachers—their scowls, their frowns, the way they studied me like some sort of insect. Is it worth the humiliation of reaching for the spirits in front of a magician like Leander and finding nothing, to never have to discuss this with him again?

*Probably, yes.*

When I lift my lashes to glare at him, he has a gentle smile waiting. Does anyone ever say no to him?

"None of this is making me like you more," I mutter.

"I can hear you being surly at me, but I'm very good at ignoring what I don't want to notice," he says with a grin. "Let me take the tiller so you can concentrate. Now, there's a reason we refer to it as *charming* the spirits. You're appealing to them, you're not ordering them around. You're convincing them to do what you want by getting them on your side."

He says it like it's simple. Like it makes no difference he's a prince known for charm above all else, and I'm . . . not known for my charm. "Tell me how you do it, then," I say, already mentally pulling back.

Leander considers the question. "Most magicians have just one affinity, so I've only been able to ask a few of my family about this," he admits. "In my experience, the different types of spirits have different personalities. It's like I said when we were up on the bow of the *Lizabetta*. Water spirits are playful—to charm them, you invite them into a game with you. Air spirits are haughtier. You compliment them, then you politely leave space for the thing you'd like them to do."

"I can't even connect with them," I reply, "let alone figure out my tone of voice for talking to them."

"We'll get to that," he says. "The charm is only one half of it. The other you've seen plenty of times: a sacrifice, just like with the gods, but in this case much smaller. They're simpler creatures—mostly they want a material thing worth something to you. So far on this trip I've given them my father's ring, then my last copper coin, which was a lot smaller, but worth a lot to me right now, and the spirits sense that."

"And what did you give them when we were running in the *Lizabetta*?" I ask the question in a whisper, and his face clouds over.

"I truly don't know. Time, maybe. Luck. Strength. Whatever it was, I feel the lack of it. But let's keep our eyes on you. It's a lovely view."

"It's a bedraggled view," I mutter. But I can still see the shadow in his gaze, so to keep it at bay, I do as he asks. "Which are the spirit flags?" I watched Kyri string them hundreds of times, but I never thought to ask. "Charm or sacrifice?"

"Charm," he replies, finding his smile again. "I suppose there's a little sacrifice, a little effort in stringing them up. But mostly they're flattery: *Look how important you are—I'm showing off that I know you.*"

The boat plunges down the back of a wave, and we each reach out to steady ourselves with a hand—they land side by side, his larger than mine, his skin browner, nails neater, his marks swirling and looping beside my thick green line.

"The spirits know I'm talking about them," he murmurs. "Let me show you how to do this. I know you've tried before, but this time they're everywhere. They . . . tend to show up where I am."

"That's an understatement, isn't it?"

"A little. What have you got to sacrifice? Anything'll do, if it means something to you."

I look down at myself—I have the clothes I'm wearing, crusted in salt, and precious little else. I can't afford to waste my knife on a failed attempt—a sailor never gives up her knife. "An apple?" I ask, wincing at the suggestion. We have so few, and a full night and a day left—my belly's already gnawing on itself, demanding another.

"What about a lock of your hair?"

I blink at him. "My hair?"

"It's beautiful," he says. "But it doesn't matter what I think. You must like it, or you'd cut it just short enough to braid, instead of having it most of the way down your back. Must be a pain to wash it when it's that long, and there wasn't a shower aboard your ship—not that I saw, anyway."

We look at each other for a long moment. I'm realizing he's been paying more attention to me than I thought, and he's realizing he's admitted that.

And I'm also wondering if he's thought about me washing my hair. His poker face is promising me he hasn't.

Wordlessly I pull my knife from my pocket, flick out the blade, and use it to cut off the tip of my braid, careful to keep my leather band tight around the end. Lifting the pinch of hair, I rub finger and thumb together, and like snippets of golden thread, the scraps of hair are whipped away on the breeze. I try to see whether they vanish, like a magician's would, but they're too fine for me to tell.

"Good," says Leander simply. He tilts his head, looking at nothing in particular, and frowns. "Huh, interesting. It's like they can't even see you. Like you're invisible to them."

My jaw aches, and I realize I'm clenching my teeth. "Great."

"I've truly never seen anything like it. You're unique, Selly—it's fascinating. I'm going to point them at you. If you think you see any, make a respectful request."

"How will I see them?" I ask.

He grins. "You see them by closing your eyes."

"You what?" This is new advice.

"Focus on the sounds around you," Leander says softly. "The waves, the water breaking against the boat. The sail flapping. Whatever that clicking noise is."

"It's the oar against the stern," I supply.

"Doesn't matter, just notice it. This is your place. Be a part of it. Hear your own breath and focus on sounds, nothing else."

"Do you do this every time?" I ask quietly, trying to ignore the way the dried salt on my skin is suddenly itching, the way my lashes want to lift so I can check everything's as I left it, check if he's looking at me.

"No," he murmurs, and I hear his smile. "But I'm exceptional, didn't you know? Focus on the sounds, sailor."

So I do, and after a few moments I'm surprised by how many more of them there are than I'd noticed. How many layers there are to all the noises around me. I thought it was silent out here, but it's as complex and many-voiced as the bands I heard on the gramophone across the water, just a couple of nights ago.

"Now, without opening your eyes," Leander says quietly, "push your mind out. You know what's there without looking. The shape of my body sitting next to you, the shape of the boat. The planks under you. The mast up ahead, the curve of the sail, Keegan in the bow."

I try to imagine these things, sketching them into the darkness around me, the sunlight playing across my eyelids. I don't picture them in color, but rather as white lines roughly drawn in chalk. The sounds almost bring them to life.

"And now," says Leander, so soft I can barely hear him, "don't pay too much attention, and try to just . . . *notice* the spaces between things. Don't focus, just observe them out the corner of your eye."

I almost blink my eyes open to protest—but the hoarse edge to his voice pulls me up short. He needs this. So instead I turn my mind to the sounds around me once more, sinking into the swish of the water, the flap of the sail.

"I'm asking the spirits to look out for you, too," he murmurs. "They're curious—they'll do it."

And then . . . *what was that?*

A shimmer.

A flicker.

Something not quite there, but not quite . . . not.

"Leander," I breathe, worrying I'll scare them away. "There's something in the air."

"Like fireflies?" he whispers.

"Almost. They don't glow, but they do sort of shine sometimes. Like they're reflecting the light. They keep moving."

"You're not alone," he says, a smile in his tired voice. "Where are they most concentrated?"

Carefully I turn my head, and I know I'm not seeing anything, not with my eyes closed, but I'm definitely *sensing* something. "Around the sail," I breathe, elation washing over me. "And around you. There are thousands of them in the air around you."

After all these years, I'm a *magician.* Leander was right—here on the sea is where my magic makes sense to me, and with a royal magician beside me . . . it's finally happening. I have to tell—

Not Kyri.

My father. I'll tell Da when we get out of this.

"Air spirits," says Leander. "Greet them gently."

I'm trembling, my breath sticking in my throat, and for a moment I feel like the *Little Lizabetta,* poised on top of a wave and ready to slide down it. But I hold myself in check, instead pushing my mind out toward the spirits slowly, showing myself to them as gently as I know how.

There's a swirl and a flurry in the shimmering, flickering mass of spirits—they whirl in a quick eddy, and the sail flaps and strains as the gust hits it. The fabric of its rough triangle bulges, trying to pull away from its bonds.

"Hey, careful!" Leander says from somewhere very far away, and I'm not sure if he's talking to me or the spirits, but I have to keep all my focus on them.

My hair blows around my face, strands pulling free of my braid as if the spirits are inspecting it, confirming the sacrifice came from me—others pluck at my clothes and whirl around me in the excitement of discovery.

*Over there,* I try to tell them, directing them back to the sail. I try to show them where they need to be—to picture in my mind and show them how the air should flow over the sail, how the boat should glide forward.

They're not interested, and they abandon the sail, leaving it shivering and deflated, swerving toward me once more. The *Little Lizabetta* slews dangerously as her sail empties, leaning precariously to windward, and I reach out in a panic to push the spirits straight back to the sail.

*No, there! Go there!*

The wind gusts wildly as they rebel against the order, whirls and flurries tugging us in every direction at once, and my eyes snap open as the sail rips away from one side of the boat.

The *Little Lizabetta* tries to round up into the wind, and Leander fights the tiller because he doesn't know any better, trying to wrestle us back on course.

The oar catches like a lever stuck into the sea, and the whole boat starts to tip back toward me. He curses, scrambling to act as a counterweight as the barrel of water comes flying at me. It catches me square in the gut, paralyzing me and leaving me gasping for air and trying to grab at the barrel, some part of my brain screaming that we can't lose our water—but it bounces away and jams against the gunwale as seawater begins to spill in, washing around me where I sprawl on the low side of the boat.

Keegan's nearly tipped straight into the sea, and I catch a glimpse of his white, terrified face as he wakes to find himself falling. The apples go flying past him, and he clambers up toward the high side as the sail flaps in his face.

"The water barrel!" Leander shouts, but the boat's still listing, and if she goes over, the three of us won't weigh enough to get her back upright, not with a bellyful of seawater.

"Keegan," I shout, and his quick brain does what I need: he looks around, makes the calculation, and lets go of his side of the boat to thump down beside me. He catches the barrel before it escapes, pinning it to the boards with one leg, then uses both hands to shove me up to Leander's waiting arms.

The boat is nearly over, and we both throw ourselves against the gunwale to lean out as hard as we can.

"Leander, cut the wind," I gasp, and he shoots me a wild-eyed *are you serious?* look, then closes his eyes, presumably reaching for some sort of calm, some sort of control.

An instant later the wind drops, and I climb over him so I can get to the oar, which—thank Barrica—is still lashed in place. I only have a moment to register the smell of salt and sweat, the brush of his hair against my cheek, and then I'm past him and grabbing for the oar handle.

The boat levels off abruptly, and we slide inside. I wrestle the oar with both hands, guiding us back into our path before the waves—and suddenly, with the wind behind us, the boat traveling at the same speed as the breeze, everything's quiet and calm.

Keegan's still clinging to the water barrel. The sight of him reminds me of the apples, and I twist around, but they're long gone in our wake.

Nobody speaks—Leander's chest is heaving, and slowly, as everything returns to normal, his eyes open.

"What did you *do*?" he asks weakly.

"Me?" I protest. "Nothing!"

"Is Selly," Keegan gasps, "a magician after all?"

"No," I snap.

"Yes," Leander says at the same time. He squints at me with reddened, salt-sore eyes. "They're haughty, air spirits. Did you ask them nicely?"

Cold trickles down my spine. In my excitement at connecting with them, in my hurry to react to their excitement, I forgot. I can hear Rensa's voice in my head. *Thinking about yourself again, lass?*

I was. About *my* excitement. *My* relief. *My* orders.

Because I'm exactly who she always said I was, however much I deny it.

I won't lie to Leander, so I say nothing—and he has his answer.

"We'll try again later," he says. "I'm going to leave them alone for a little, let them settle."

I nod, wordless.

"Why don't you get some sleep? Keegan's awake now; he can help me with the boat."

I can't believe I did it—Leander was right. All it took was a royal magician the spirits adore, a lesson out on the sea itself . . . and if I'm honest, a teacher I feel a connection to. A connection I can't seem to shake.

And I can't believe I finally, *finally* found my magic, and I couldn't follow the one instruction I was given. I'm not an asker, and I never have been. I've always taken.

But I nearly cost us everything.

Our water, our boat.

Our lives.

All because I couldn't meet the spirits halfway.

I can now see clearly what my mind knew all along when it was blocking my gift: I wasn't made for magic.

# LASKIA

*The Gem Cutter*
*Port Naranda, Mellacea*

I get cleaned up before I head downstairs to the Gem Cutter. My room's on the top floor of our building, with Ruby's below and the club itself on the ground floor.

It's an extra set of stairs to climb, but I love being up high. The view out my windows takes in the jagged rooftops of our neighbors, and past them the tall buildings of New Street, their windows gleaming back at me when the sun rises.

We made our way down the coast to Port Naranda by auto before dawn, and the first light appeared an hour ago, hints of silver painting the city lighter in color as it stretches out before me. I can make out the curved roof of the church from here, still a shadow in a matte black.

I'll attend a service this afternoon, after I've checked in on how my various pots simmered on the stove in my absence. Already I'm looking forward to the familiar chants, the soft scent of the incense in the air, the patterns of rising to stand, sinking to kneel.

Sometimes I wonder if it's different in Alinor, where their goddess is present in their temple. What it will be like in ours, when Macean awakens.

Still, the ritual always soothes me, centers me, and there's a tension in my core, a burning in my gut that won't go away. I need to settle myself.

I haven't slept yet, apart from a short doze in the rattling auto, and my eyes are aching with tiredness. But I couldn't now if I tried. So instead I duck into the shower, tipping my head back as the hot water hits my face, and taking my time as I methodically scrub myself from head to toe.

I press my fingers into my skin, smooth away sore muscles, and watch the soap swirl away down the drain as I think. I need my report to Ruby to be detailed but concise. I need to keep emotion out of it.

The sequence of events has to be clear—what happened, and when? What time? How many? I need to assure her everything was done, just as I promised. That Jude confirmed it.

Most of the work was in the doing of the deed, but now I need to bring it across the finish line—to show her how well I handled it.

I sent Jude home to his mother—he wasn't going to put up a reassuring front for Ruby. His Lordship doesn't have what it takes, however hard he punches in his bare-knuckled boxing rings. It was perfectly safe to keep him from joining the others for breakfast, though—he's bound to us by what he's done now, as much as by the doctor Ruby sends to his mother. And he might have useful information on the Alinorish, still.

Ruby says nothing worth having ever comes clean. That if the good stuff was easy, everyone would claim it. So it doesn't matter if you find it hard, doing what's necessary. *That* isn't what makes you weak.

You're only weak if you turn away from the hard parts.

I will *not* be weak.

An image of a girl floats up in my mind, like a body surfacing after it's been dragged underwater. All I can see is the instant she jumped off her burning ship, her colorful dress trailing through the air behind her, and splashed into the water. She surfaced, hair plastered to her face, and looked around desperately, realizing there was no safe place to swim.

Then the water around her, covered in oil, caught fire.

And so did she.

I square my jaw and shove the image away, beneath the waves.

*What's done is done.*

I step out of the shower and wipe the mist from the mirror with my palm, the surface cold beneath my skin. I look tired, disheveled, but stronger than I was before. I didn't turn away.

I reach for a towel and keep rehearsing my report as I get dressed: a tailored suit, polished shoes. I fasten my ruby pin to my lapel. Carefully I dry my hair, then rub wax between my palms to warm it before I see to my curls. They need to look as sharp as they ever have, because this is it.

This is my moment.

I'm about to deliver everything Ruby could ever want, and I'll be the one who made it happen for her.

She'll have her power—she'll see off her rivals. And even if she doesn't come to church, she'll know her sister did what it took to awaken a *god*.

I take one last look around the room and walk over to twitch the bedcovers straight, smoothing them down. Then I let myself out, locking the door behind me, and slip the key into my pocket.

The wooden stairs creak beneath my feet as I start down them, mouthing my report to myself. This meeting is going to kick off so many big things for me, and I'm ready for them all.

When the war begins, we'll expand our weapons import arm. There'll be demand, and we've already got supply lined up. I know Ruby's stockpiled other things that will become scarce as well, from food to fabric. There's a constant jostle among the gangs of Port Naranda for the kind of influence that comes with owning a part of the market, and Ruby and I both know what it's like when you don't have it.

This moment—being there with what's needed when nobody else is—it'll seal her place at the top. And aligning herself with the green sisters while she does it? She'll be invincible. She'll be a playmaker.

Ruby saw this war coming a long way back. But *I'm* the one who figured out how to bring it forward, and now I've pulled off exactly what I promised. I've earned a bigger part in her operations, and it couldn't come at a better time—the war I'm giving her will mean more work than she can do alone.

Between everything Ruby will need from me and all the work that lies before Sister Beris—work I'll be there to help with, ready for the day when Macean awakens and witnesses our faith—it'll be a long time now before I rest.

So after I talk to her this morning, I'm going to get a few

hours of sleep—then I've got work to do before church. I need to check in on what I missed while I was gone. I have contacts all over the city, kids like I once was, who know to bring me what they learn for a coin.

And I have more than that—more than even Ruby knows. A junior staffer at the Alinorish ambassador's residence, for a start. A girl with bright eyes and dimples, who made the mistake of taking a few dollars for pieces of inconsequential gossip inside the embassy. Who then took a few more. Who now has no choice but to take more, and tell me more each time.

Later I'll check in with her and see if there are any whispers of trouble yet. It's taken me two years to cultivate her, but the way Ruby's brows will go up when I casually drop *that* detail . . . why shouldn't I enjoy the anticipation? I earned it.

*The girl jumps off the boat, her colorful dress trailing out behind her as she plummets toward the water.*

*No.*

I earned it.


I make my way through the back hallways on the ground floor, past the kitchens—her expensive Fontesquan chef is deep in discussion with one of her fire magicians, probably talking about roasting something in some new way.

I pause outside the door, push my shoulders back, and knock, rapping out the rhythm we've been using since we were kids.

"Come," she calls, in that same drawl as always, and I walk into her den of gold and dark, polished wood and red velvet, the same at every hour of the day.

I make it to my second step before I stop.

Sister Beris, whom I dropped off at the church not long ago, is already sitting on the couch with Ruby. She turns, unhurried, and stares at me with her pale eyes.

"Laskia," Ruby says with one of her easy smiles. "Good morning. Sister Beris has been filling me in on your adventures."

"Oh," I say stupidly, blinking. She's giving *my* report. How dare she— But I pull myself together and forward. "Well, I can take care of that now, and—"

Ruby holds up a hand to stop me. "I have all the details that matter," she says. "Well done. I asked the cook to fix you a proper breakfast. You must be hungry."

I stare at her, unable to move, unable to speak, my words caught in my throat.

I'm not stupid. I know what this is. I know that tone.

I'm being dismissed.

Ruby never outright tells you to go away—you're just supposed to understand. But I can't do that. I need to report to her. I *earned* this.

"I should catch you up on the specifics," I try. "We had to—"

She raises the hand again. "I've got enough for now. You should be pleased with your work, Laskia. The honey was effective?"

*Effective.*

I open my mouth, then close it again, something hot building up inside me. She mentions it to take credit for it—as if giving me the honey was the hard part, not standing in place as the crew cheered and poured it onto their breakfast.

As if the *idea* was the thing, instead of the deed.

*I'm* the one who left a ship of corpses anchored off the coast.

"Ruby," I try again, my voice rising, "I want to stay and—"

She shakes her head, just a fraction. The smallest movement. "We'll talk soon, Laskia. The sister and I need to talk about our next steps."

I stare at her in frozen disbelief. *The sister and I,* while I'm sent to breakfast.

I swing my gaze across to Sister Beris, my throat thick, my words stuck there. She brought me into the church, she told me what *I* was doing would matter, that Macean needed *me.* And now she's staring back at me, impassive, waiting for me to leave.

I've finally worked out what she reminds me of.

A kid I used to know had a pet snake. It never blinked, just stared. And then it tried to eat you.

*Her dress was golden, the girl who jumped into the water. Covered in sequins and fringes, it was like fire already as she arced through the air, legs kicking, arms flung wide.*

*And then she landed and disappeared with a splash, and broke the surface, gasping for air.*

My gut twists, bile rising in my throat.

I *cannot* have done all of this to find it's for nothing. I've gone too far, too deep, for it to be for nothing. How can I have done such a thing, gambled everything for the god of risk himself, to come back here to a pat on the head?

If Ruby isn't willing to let me in yet, then I'll find a way to show her she *must.*

And if I'm going to leave this room right now with nothing but my dignity, I'm sure as hells not giving them that.

I'll bring back something from the ambassador. Something new. I'll make them see how much I can do, and then Ruby will wish she'd had me here since this morning.

"You're right," I say with a smile on my face. A mask. "I'll go. I'm *very* hungry."

# LEANDER

*The Docks*
*Port Naranda, Mellacea*

We spot the towers of Port Naranda as the second evening falls, outlined against the sunset like jagged teeth. We're salt-crusted, sunburned, aching, and exhausted. But we've made it.

"There she is," Selly breathes from her place at the helm. She's gazing at the coastline with her lips parted, perfectly still, as if she can't quite believe it.

I didn't realize, until this moment, how unlikely she thought it was that we'd make it here at all. Now, as I study her in the dying light, my gut twists with that realization.

"You did it, Selly," I murmur.

"Not yet I didn't," she corrects me straightaway, and I duck my head to hide my smile. Nobody treats me like she does. It's great.

"What'll we do when we land?" she asks. She's been business-like since the disaster with her magic, and I recognize survival when I see it. She doesn't want to think about it, can't let herself, and I understand that. For now, at least. I can't let the mystery of her magic go, but I can pick my time.

"It's getting late," Keegan says, frowning up at the setting sun.

"Straight to the embassy?" Selly suggests. "The word ship to ship has been that the mood's getting uglier in Port Naranda. And if they don't like your average Alinorish sailor, they're not going to love you, Leander."

"Impossible to believe."

"Is it, though?"

"It seems to me we have two choices." Keegan interrupts our squabbling in that thoughtful tone that makes me extra sorry he's not tucked away safely at the Bibliotek, where he really does belong.

"And what are those?"

"We can go about this slowly and meticulously. Make every move in a carefully considered fashion, minimize every risk. It will be safer, but take much longer—and the longer we take, the more we risk opening ourselves up to other, unforeseen dangers. Alternatively, we can move swiftly and decisively, and hope that by the time we attract attention, we will have found safety."

I bite my lip, trying to work my way through the possibilities. Someone else has always made these decisions for me. Now the consequences that loom if we get this wrong . . .

"We don't have time to go slow," Selly says. "I'd prefer it, but we're on a clock—someone's going to see the smoke from the progress fleet, probably already has. And they'll go to look for survivors, and they'll figure out which ships they are. And no doubt they'll blame Mellacea. If we want to avoid word getting out that the prince is dead, we have to get to the embassy straightaway."

"First thing in the morning is probably as early as we can manage," I reply.

"The embassy closes?" Selly asks, her brows shooting up. "What if there's some kind of international emergency? Like, you know, a *war starting*?"

"Then somebody wakes up the ambassador at her residence, I suppose. But her residence will be under surveillance, always. There's going quickly, and then there's marching straight into trouble," I say. "We're ragged and sunburned. Some lackey might decide not to let us in, might not pass along my code words to her. And then we'll have been seen trying to get into the embassy."

*Is that right? Am I being smart, or am I scared?*

"I agree, first thing in the morning is the best we can do," Keegan says. "Right now we have one great advantage: we've seen the girl who wants to kill you, but she's only had a brief look at me, and she hasn't seen you two at all."

"So we know who we're watching out for, but she doesn't," Selly concludes. "Or even that she *should* watch out for us."

"Exactly. There's no reason anybody should expect to see the prince in Port Naranda, or recognize him out of context. We can sell the boat, and use the money to get a change of clothes and somewhere to stay tonight. Something to eat. We . . ." He trails off—Selly's staring at him.

"Sell the boat?" she echoes, almost inaudible. The sun has

slipped below the horizon, and the moons are rising close to-gether, casting pale light across the water, outlining every wave and ripple in silver. I can pick out her lashes in the moonlight, the firm line of her mouth.

"You said yourself she cannot be sailed to Alinor," Keegan points out. "Possessions can be replaced, and we need the money now."

"Is that what you said when my crew threw your books overboard?" she asks, close to a snap. "Possessions can be re-placed?"

Keegan just blinks at her, processing this idea, and I ease into the gap.

"Of course not," I say. "Because neither the boat nor the books are just *things*. They're who you are, both of you. But if it's anyone's fault you're losing them, it's mine. I'm sorry."

Selly glances across at me. "It's fine," she replies immedi-ately, batting away the offering. "I can manage losing a boat if you can both manage losing your luggage. Have you ever been without a change of clothes in your life?"

"Not really," I reply cheerfully, more than willing to take the hit if it'll help, though I wonder if a fight would settle her nerves better. "I'm spoiled rotten, haven't you noticed?"

"I have another necklace," Keegan says suddenly, before she can reply. "We should sell it. The boat is all you have, Selly."

Slowly, regretfully, she shakes her head. "An abandoned boat will draw attention in a day or two," she says quietly. "And we have no use for it. Wherever I go from here, I can't take the *Little Lizabetta* with me."

I add another boulder of guilt to the pile already sitting on my chest. This has cost her everything.

"So we'll sell the boat, find a room at an inn to hole up in, and try for the ambassador in the morning," I say. "She'll be able to get me on a ship home, and she'll arrange for both of you to go wherever you choose—to the Bibliotek, to another boat from your father's fleet, Selly."

She shakes her head, and something strange takes hold in my chest.

"You don't want to go back to your father's fleet?"

"No, of course I do," she replies, and I push away . . . disappointment? Surely not. "I was just trying to imagine what I can possibly tell them about what happened."

I'm left searching for something, *anything,* to say to that.

Keegan rescues me. "We will find a suitable explanation," he says.

"All we have to do first is survive this city that wants to kill His Princeliness," she agrees.

"Have you been to Port Naranda before?"

"Barely." She turns her attention to checking on the sail, then glances ahead at the looming city. "I've crewed on ships that have put in here, but I've never left the docks. It's a big city, different from Kirkpool. Louder, taller. Kirkpool's all golden stone, and the city folds in around the hills like a blanket on a bunk. Port Naranda, it's like they smoothed out the ground and plunked a city on top of it."

"You're a poet," I murmur, reaching for a smile for her. "You know that's more or less what they did, to make Port Naranda."

"How do you mean?"

"The land's no good for farming—it's rocky, and mostly steep, all along the peninsula. Alinor's been a nation for over a thousand years, but Mellacea only showed up about six hundred years ago. There were little fishing villages before that, made up of hardy souls from all over."

"What changed? What made them build a city here?"

"Depends who you ask. They say a Messenger created by Macean was powerful enough to flatten out the site of Port Naranda just enough that if they built tall, they could fit in the people it takes to make a city."

"A Messenger like King Anselm?" she asks, glancing toward Keegan, who inclines his head.

"If King Anselm was transformed into one at all, then yes," he says. "The records from the time of the gods are vague on the subject—presumably it was well enough understood that it didn't require much detail when they were recording it. The Messengers tend to vanish from history after only a few mentions, which casts some doubt on whether they really existed."

"It could just have been a group of talented earth magicians," I add. "One way or another, the land was flattened out, and Mellacea, a new nation, was born."

"Huh. I guess you do learn something in those fancy schools."

"Less than they'd have liked, in my case, but something," I agree. "It's also the story of how the first War of the Gods happened, five centuries ago. The Mellaceans were hungry for farmland, and they'd had a few generations to work out how hard it was to import everything, so they tried for more territory. If there's one thing Alinor has plenty of, it's rolling green hills, and many of the settlers were from Alinor—that's why we share a language. Settlers often leave for a reason, so they probably weren't short on grudges, and between one thing and another, they set their gaze on our farmland."

"And started a war."

"Which they lost—the god of risk took a gamble that didn't pay off."

I catch Keegan glancing at me, maybe on the verge of pointing out the only thing that saved us then was the willingness of my many-greats-uncle Anselm to give up his life for the cause. He and I don't compare that favorably right now.

"Anyway," I press on, "Macean was bound in sleep, with Barrica the Sentinel to watch over him, and since then his people have become a nation of traders, of inventors. Mellacea is a fascinating place. Under other circumstances."

"I'm sure it is, but I'll settle for a brief visit," Selly says, dry. "And we'll have to see the sights another time. I remember the wharves here stretch out from the harbor square in every direction, like the crosstrees off a mast. We should be able to pull in at the outermost end, where there'll be fewer people to see us, and leave the boat before any of the officials come to find us, if we're lucky. We can sell the boat in the dockside square. For less than we'd get another time, but it'll do us for somewhere to stay tonight."

We're closer to shore now, and all three of us are watching the land as it looms larger in the dark. I can see the piers she described—from the sky, this place would look like one giant tree. Huge limbs stretch out within the shelter of the harbor walls, smaller ones branching off, each of them lined with dozens of boats from all over the world.

The city itself is a crammed-together collection of tall, square buildings, jostling for space on the only flat ground for miles. I've always wanted to visit. I wanted to see what was the same as home, what was different. I wanted to see the bright lights—they say it's like a rainbow come nightfall—and walk the streets between their towering buildings, and go to their dance halls. I wanted to have an adventure, and to be anonymous.

Now my life depends on that anonymity. Selly was right. This place wants to kill me.

"We'll moor as far out as we can go," Selly says, pointing to the end of a smaller branch. "Keegan, get the sail down. Leander, can you have the water spirits guide us in?"

"We need to stop using his name," Keegan says quietly, rising to his feet and reaching out to take her pocketknife so he can saw through the rope where the sail's lashed to the top of the mast.

"What should I call him, then?" Selly asks.

"Maxim," I volunteer. "It's my favorite middle name."

She lifts a brow. "How many do you have?"

"Leander Darelion Anselm Maxim Sam—" I begin to recite before she cuts me off.

"Maxim it is."

"Or nothing," Keegan says. "Ignore him. If we pay attention to him, it draws attention to him. He's just a sailor— a nobody."

"You've been waiting years to say that," I tell him, forcing a quick grin, shoving down the fear that wants to rise up in my chest at the thought of being noticed. "Not sure it's a workable plan, though. Who's going to believe it? I mean, look at me. This level of handsome can't be ignored."

"I don't find it difficult at all," Selly replies blandly, and Keegan actually snorts.

He gets through the rope holding up the sail, sitting with a startled thump as the ragged sailcloth comes away from the mast, and the whole boat rocks with the impact.

We glide slowly through the water, the masts of the ships around us stretching toward the stars, their hulls crammed in side by side like animals in a pen, watching us in the dark.

I pull the lowest button off my shirt and drop it into the silent waters as my offering. Then I close my eyes, reaching out to the water spirits to show them where I'd like the boat to go. It's almost impossible to find the playful touch I need for them—the fear and the guilt beating through me in time with my heart are making me sick.

Every part of this—every soul killed at sea, the risk the two who are with me now are taking, the risk of war itself, and everything that will cost the world—lies squarely on my shoulders. If I'd made the sacrifice when I should have, Mellacea never would have dreamed of war. Alinor would have been too strong.

All for the lack of me boarding a boat to visit a temple, cut my palm, and spill a little blood. It would have taken no time at all.

"Take this," I hear Selly say quietly, and then she's pushing past me up to the bow. A minute later we bump softly against one of the rough wooden pillars supporting the pier. She reaches up for a big loop of rope secured to the pier itself and ties it to something in the bow of the *Little Lizabetta*.

Slowly, our boat drifts the few feet out to the end of her line, and there she stays, held in place by the tide that's gently flowing out of the harbor.

For a long moment nobody speaks.

We've done it—we've sailed an impossible distance in a too-small boat, and hit our target. We've survived the death and destruction we left behind, the burning ship sinking into the sea, and with only half a dozen apples and a shore boat, we've made it to Mellacea.

But though it should feel like a triumph, I'm realizing our plan was mostly academic. I never imagined what it would be like when we found ourselves in the port of an enemy city, in a place where the churches are filling up every day with worshippers of a god who'd like to dismantle ours. We're hungry, thirsty, exhausted, salty and filthy, and flat broke.

And we still have a long way to go.

We climb up onto the wooden pier on wobbly legs, and Keegan and I trail along behind Selly like a pair of ducklings as we approach the dock itself. It's immediately obvious that though we in Alinor might have been sleeping on the possibility of an approaching war, nobody in Mellacea will be caught by surprise.

As we make our way along the pier toward the dockside square, Selly slows her pace and falls in behind a gaggle of sailors from Beinhof, to judge by their clothes and conversation. Glancing past her, I see what she saw—a squad of city guards marching along the narrow pier toward us.

The captain leading the group of sailors pulls a piece of

paper from an inside pocket and holds it up, and they wave him past—it's a permit of some sort, and without breaking stride, Keegan and I slide in behind Selly, heads down as we tag along like we're part of the crew.

I don't exhale until we reach the big, paved harborside square, where the captain stops to argue about taxes with a group of officials, and we can meld silently with the crowd. It's bustling with people even in the dark—at home, city magicians would be lighting the lamps, but here, the bright Mellacean lights buzz and glow, flashing in garish colors as they advertise the businesses all around us. They love everything new, in the city of invention.

The square is lined on the eastern edge by the water, a big row of cranes standing ready to lift cargo up off waiting ships. There are tax agents everywhere I look, and animated conversations that verge on fights taking place by the cargo cranes. This isn't friendly haggling, either—there's an edge to their voices, an aggression to their gestures, and it's not the captains who have the upper hand.

On the other three sides of the square are tall, thin buildings crammed in together. Most of them are about three stories high, windows staring down on the square like eyes.

I see a church devoted to Macean, the statues and stonework that decorate its edifice painted black, representing the Gambler's slumber.

Two silent green sisters stand vigil outside the open door, and passing members of the crowd drop coins into their collection plates as they pass. There are plenty of them, and plenty of worshippers walking in and out of the church as well, despite the hour. I have an uneasy feeling I wouldn't count the same numbers at home, at the temple of Barrica.

"That's the harbormaster's office," Selly says, jerking me back to the present and pointing at a bustling building, "and the rest are buyers' agents, who'll bargain for the cargoes that arrive each day, or inns for any sailors who can afford a night in a room that doesn't rock."

"We can stay here on the square?" I ask, a little of the tension leaving my chest. We're closer than I thought to shelter.

"Soon as I sell the boat," she says without turning her head, pointing to a spot beside one of the cranes, where there's shelter from the crowd. "Wait, and keep your heads down."

She disappears into the crowd, and I lose sight of her blond braid. It's a strange sensation, standing here in plain sight as people flow around us like water. I don't know why I'm worrying about her—she's more competent in this place than I am—but I'm twitching with the urge to follow her.

She's back in less than ten minutes, though, freckles standing out against paled skin, her mouth a thin line. "It's done," she says simply. "And I got the name of a place we can afford—the Salthouse Inn."

She turns away again, and once more we follow her, buffeted and bumped by the sailors and traders around us. I grip the strap of my satchel too tightly as a tattooed sailor pushes past me, and I press one hand against my journal, where it's wrapped up inside.

Everywhere, voices are rising as the moons make their way higher into the sky, the energy of the square changing as traders grasp for the last few deals of the day and turn their minds toward the evening's revelry.

When we reach the square's edge, Selly ducks down a foul-smelling alley between two buildings that's barely wider than my shoulders. I draw them in to avoid touching the sludge-covered walls, and I hold my breath until we emerge into the alley running behind the row of buildings.

The glow from the windows above us only makes the shadows darker, and the metal ladders reaching down the backs of the buildings are like unnatural vines that could come to life at any moment and snatch us off our feet.

"You should wait here," she says to Keegan. "You're the only one with a face anyone's seen. We're going to get a room in this inn we're behind, and you can climb in through the fire escape. Two's easier to explain than three, less noticeable."

I'm surprised she thought of that, and then a little annoyed at myself for being surprised. She's been resourceful enough to save our lives more than once—why shouldn't she be sharp now?

*Because you're not,* a voice in my head says. And it's right. I'm so hungry I can't think straight, and I'm scared I'm missing something.

"What shall I do if someone comes?" Keegan asks, looking around at the shadows with understandable concern.

Selly shrugs. "Say you're on the hunt for someone selling favors."

"I'd stay with you," I add, "but it would need to be a far better class of alley for anyone to believe good looks like these were on offer."

Keegan tugs his shirt straighter. "I would rather buy a book than a favor," he informs us. "And in either case, the contents would matter far more to me than the cover."

Selly snorts as I search for a reply, and before I find one, she turns to head back up the sludgy alley we came along. I hurry after her, catching at her arm before she reaches the doorway to the inn.

"Can I make a suggestion?"

"Let's have it," she replies, slowing her pace.

"I've had a few lessons on how to blend in—in case I ever found myself separated from the Queensguard, or in trouble."

"Or you decided to wander off and explore the Kirkpool docks, and annoy innocent girls trying to go about their business?"

"Hey, you're the one who leaped into *my* arms, *and* you were trying to illegally stow away on a boat, innocent girl. Anyway, the lessons were pretty inadequate, but I remember the best way to make sure people won't recall anything about you is to do nothing to draw their attention. But we can't do that, because we're going to be taking a room, paying, and someone at the inn will know about that. So the second-best option is to give them one big thing to notice, and they won't notice anything else. Have an outrageous accent, and they'll forget your hair color. Make sense?"

She looks back at me, considering this. "All right. I know how we can give them two people to remember who'll seem like anything but shipwrecked sailors." Her teeth glint as she grins, and for a moment I wonder if this is how other people feel when I tell them I have a plan.

"Do we need to worry about our Alinorish accents?"

"Look around you," she replies, one hand lifting to take in the chaos swirling past us. "You're in a port. Come on."

Before I have time to protest, she grabs hold of my hand, pulling me with her through the open door.

The front office for the inn is tiny, a woman with a friendly face and wiry gray hair crammed in behind the counter, rows of keys hanging on hooks behind her. A wooden staircase leads to the upper floors, and narrow hallways away to the rooms on this floor.

"Looking for rooms?" she asks, setting aside her newspaper to inspect the pair of us.

With a laugh and a quick tug on my hand, Selly brings me stumbling in to land against her. "One room," she says, practically waggling her eyebrows. "One *bed*, and a bath, please, ma'am. I heard you have them attached to the room, so we can have it *allll* to ourselves?"

I nearly choke on my own tongue, mostly because her acting is so over the top that there's no way this woman will buy it, and a little because it would have taken her ten seconds to bring me in on this plan, which means she didn't because she thought it was funnier not to. Still, here we are, so I sling my arm around her shoulder and let myself grin.

"It's extra for two people in it," the woman cautions, reaching behind her to snag a key without looking. "Twenty-five dollars a night. Running water, but it's cold. One night's coal up there, and a pot to heat the water if you want. Stay another night, it's another twenty-five dollars, plus two for more coal."

"No problem," Selly replies, leaning into me.

"And that's Mellacean dollars," the woman says firmly. "I don't take Alinorish crowns, or whatever else you picked up at your last port."

"Yes ma'am," Selly says, then squeaks loudly, as if my hands have just done something outrageous below the woman's eyeline, and somehow *I'm* the one who blushes when she looks across at me speculatively.

"Can you send up dinner for two?" Selly asks demurely.

"You want the two-dollar dinner or the five-dollar dinner?"

"Five." Selly digs in her pocket to produce some gold Mellacean dollars. "We're going to need our energy. And the bed's good? I'm *done* with hammocks for a night or two." She leans in to confide in the woman in a far-too-loud whisper: "No privacy. Very easy to fall out of, if you're not concentrating."

"So I'm told," the innkeeper replies blandly, clearly trying not to laugh at us. She takes the thirty dollars from Selly and hands over the key, gesturing toward the stairs. "Up one flight, second door to your right. Food'll be along soon."

"Thank you, ma'am," Selly chirps, and takes off trotting up the stairs.

"Better hurry," the woman says to me as I stare after her. "Might change her mind."

The tips of my ears are hot, and I mumble something that's not even words as I start up after her, tripping over the bottom step. What am I, twelve again, suffering through a first crush?

"Really?" I mutter to Selly as I catch up with her.

"What?" The look she shoots me is pure innocence. "I was doing my best impression of you. I thought you'd be a fan."

The hallway runs along the back of the building, with a door leading out to those metal ladders we saw in the alleyway. Selly trots ahead of me again and opens it, sticking out her head to whisper-shout to Keegan. "Up here, Scholar!"

I can't help grinning as I watch him climb up to join

us—Selly's already unlocking the door to our room, and when she holds it open, Keegan and I pile in through it.

Her mood is infectious, and it's like the turning of the tide. Just this small win—we've got a safe place in this big city—changes everything. And despite all we've left behind us, the realization that tomorrow morning I can hand this whole disaster off to a responsible adult is starting to catch up with me.

Our room is dark, but I can see it has a big bed, as promised, and a couple of chairs by a window that looks out on the square, with an awning beneath it.

"Where's the light switch?" Keegan asks softly in the dark, groping around near the door. The bright lights of the square below provide the only illumination in here.

"There's a fireplace opposite the foot of the bed," Selly replies. "Probably candles, too. Would you be so kind, L— uh, Maxim?"

There's barely room to squeeze past thc edges of the bed. I've complained plenty of times about the tiny country inns I've had to stay in when we were on the road, and I'm only now realizing how I might have sounded to the servants. This place makes those places look like palaces.

"I need something to give them," I mutter, patting my pockets.

"Tear a piece off your shirt," Selly replies. "We've got food coming up for dinner. Once it gets here, Keegan can eat that, and you and I can slip down the fire escape to the night market. We'll get more to eat and some fresh clothes. It's fine to walk around the docks in clothes so stiff with salt they could stand up on their own, but if we head out into the city to the embassy, we'll draw attention."

I hadn't even thought of that.

So I rip a section off my shirt and strike a match, and I reach out for the spirits that swirl around it on the warm air currents, encouraging them to creep across the rest of the coal. The section of my shirt vanishes as their energy pours through it, and they dance as light flares and the fire catches, and I get a glimpse of myself in the mirror by the window.

I look . . . well, I look like I've been dunked in the sea and sailed halfway from Alinor in an open boat. Selly, meanwhile, still has her hair in a neat braid and isn't even a shade pinker than usual beneath her freckles.

"Keep quiet," she cautions us. "The food will be here soon." She points at Keegan and beckons. "Come here and I'll show you how to heat water over the fire so you can wash while we're out. The bath'll be through that little door by the headboard."

"Should he go out into the city?" Keegan asks, tilting his head at me.

"Try to stop me," I reply. "I'm not missing out on this. Anyway, we're not sending Selly out there alone, are we?"

"Why not?" Keegan asks, brows lifting. "If it is too dangerous for her to go alone, it is surely too dangerous to risk you."

"He'll be all right," Selly replies. "This place is busier than Kirkpool, and he's not looking anything like his usual self. I'd rather have some company in a foreign port."

"Do you need more money?" Keegan asks, his hand going to his throat—after a moment, I realize he's pulling his shirt aside to show us the gold chain he was wearing when the ship went down. The twin to the one he gave the girl who sank it.

Selly's eyes widen as she studies him. Then she shakes her head. "I've still got twenty dollars," she says. "It's enough. When this is over, you still want to go to the Bibliotek, right? That's all you've got to do it. Hold on to it."

Keegan lets his shirt fall closed, his jaw squaring as he nods. I don't think he's used to that sort of kindness. He certainly never got it from me, back at school, and yet here he is, loyal anyway.

There's a sharp knock at the door, and Selly gestures at me vigorously—at first I'm baffled, and then I understand.

*Give them one big thing to notice, and they won't notice anything else.*

There's no way this woman's going to think of the lovers she gave a room to if anyone comes asking about princes or castaways.

I feel the tips of my ears turn red all over again, and my cheeks, too, I'm pretty sure. This *never* happens to me. But I follow Selly's mimed instructions and quickly unbutton my shirt, running a hand through my hair before I open the door a crack. I studiously ignore the way the woman shakes with silent laughter as she hands me the tray.

"Make sure she lets you get a little sleep," she cautions me, and I shut the door firmly behind her without a word.

Keegan's watching all this with interest, but asks no questions, though I almost wish he would.

Instead of trying to explain myself, I set the tray on the bed for him, maintaining what I'd like to believe is a dignified silence. My stomach is turning itself inside out at the scent rising from underneath the metal cover, my head spinning as my body takes this opportunity to point out it's starving. There's some kind of stew in there, and I could eat my way through the cover to get to it, then chomp on the tray for dessert.

"Ready to go, handsome?" Selly asks, tilting her head at the door.

"Oh, you finally noticed?"

She snorts. "I just wanted your attention. Let's get back down that fire escape. Time to hit the night market."

# SELLY

*The Night Market*
*Port Naranda, Mellacea*

A sailor out in the square gives me directions to the night market, which I've heard about the few times we came into port but never seen for myself. Rensa didn't want me going far from the ship.

"Back through there," he says, shifting whatever he's chewing on to one side of his mouth and storing it in his cheek, then pointing at the far corner of the square. "Then two blocks along, and you can't miss it."

He pauses, squinting at Leander, who's standing behind me, and my heart stutters. Surely nobody could recognize him here. I still shift my weight, preparing to move quickly, grab Leander's hand, and yank him away into the crowd. Then the sailor grins.

"Watch those accents when you get farther away from the docks," he warns us. "We saltbloods know folks come from everywhere, but not all of Port Naranda feels the same about Alinorish crews. And buy her something nice, son," he adds, shaking one finger at Leander in a fatherly fashion.

Leander's pulled himself together since I gave him a heart attack with the innkeeper, and he simply wraps one arm around my waist, tugging me in close, his body warm against mine. He smells like a sailor, like salt and sweat. "Yes, sir," he says before he pulls me away into the crowd.

He keeps his arm around me until we're halfway to the corner the sailor pointed out, and safely out of his sight, and I make no move to break away, far too aware of every place we press together, of the shift of his body against mine as we push our way through the crowd.

When he slides his arm free of my waist, I have only a moment to register the absence—to stifle my urge to reach for him—before he takes my hand, fingers sliding through mine.

"We should stay close," he murmurs when I glance across at him. I've never strolled along hand in hand with anyone before, so why not start with the prince of Alinor? I nod, swallowing hard.

The leather of my glove sits between our palms, and a part of my brain wants to dive into the dark waters of remembering why I wear those gloves, but our fingers are warm where they tangle together, and I focus on that instead.

Though darkness has fallen, electric lamps line the dockside square, and the bright lights on the signs flash in a rainbow of colors. Sailors and traders are here from all over the continent and probably beyond. Every language I know, every accent, all mingle together like the sound of seabirds. Like the fleet of ships moored out in the dark, skin tones range from the palest birch to the darkest mahogany, with every shade in between, with folks clad in the rough-spun or brightly colored clothes of their home ports, or the shirts and trousers of sailors.

Port Naranda is different from Kirkpool, but any port still feels like home. It seems as if Kyri and the crew should be pushing their way across the square to meet me, the *Lizabetta* waiting for us to hurry aboard so we can make the tide. My breath catches as I picture them emerging from the crowd— and then I pack that image away and seal it up for now. Later, I'll think of them. Later, I'll let myself ache. Now I have work to do, and I'm near enough to finished that I can't afford to stumble.

Leander pulls my attention back to the present, guiding me out of the way of an oncoming man hefting a huge barrel above his head, and we duck into the street the sailor pointed out. The crowd barely thins—there's a steady stream heading to and from the night market.

"Are you sure nobody's going to recognize your face?" I ask, keeping close to him as the crowd carries us along like a fast-running tide. Despite my reassurances at the inn, now that we're out in the open, it does feel like a risk.

"I'm sure," he replies, bending his head to speak in my ear, and I have to remind myself to get a grip and ignore his proximity. "Nobody here is expecting to see me. People rarely see things they don't expect."

"I hope you're right."

"It's like I said before: you give them one big thing—the title, the clothes, the Queensguard, the spectacle—and they don't register the specifics. Fewer of them could describe me than you'd think."

"Aren't you in official portraits, things like that?"

"Not where people really see them. I know it's impossible to imagine anyone could forget this face, but . . ." He shrugs. "They're not expecting me here. They'll think I'm staggeringly handsome, but they won't join the dots."

"You know, I'm not going to miss you even a little when I hand you over," I mutter. "There'll be so much more room to move, without your giant ego."

He doesn't reply—he just squeezes my hand instead. And I'm glad he doesn't call me on the fact that I'm holding his because I'm not sure why I still am. Or maybe he's holding on to me.

The truth is, there's a strange sensation in the pit of my stomach when I think about him making it back to Alinor without me, when I imagine him finally setting foot on the Isle of Barrica alone.

It feels like falling, and I don't want to look at it too closely.

There's no point wishing things were different. What use would I be if I stuck around?

The market turns out to be a whole street, closed off to wagons and autos at either end. Stalls line both edges and run down the middle as well, with racks of clothes, tables full of bits and pieces no longer needed by their owners, and plenty selling hot food. Performers roam the crowd with guitars, singing for their supper, and newsies shout the headlines.

Leander and I step into the lee of a building, getting a moment's shelter from the endless flow of people, and though my belly is begging me to follow the dizzying smell of food, he holds me by the arm, waiting for the girl with the stack of newspapers to cycle through her headlines.

*"First Councilor Tariden visits the House of Macean! Get the latest!"*

"I don't hear the words *war* or *assassination,* so I'm happy," he mutters.

"I'll be happier when we've eaten something," I reply, drawing a grin from him.

"I think I'm through hunger and out the other side. You're right, we should eat before we fall down."

We let the crowd carry us past the stalls, making our way along racks of clothes and tables of knickknacks and stopping when we reach the first food on offer.

This stall is run by a couple of women—married, I suspect, judging by the familiarity with which they push past each other in the tiny space. They have a huge shallow pan set up, and inside sizzles a mouthwatering mix of seafood, vegetables, and rice. One woman, green magician's marks snaking up her forearms, has an eye on the flame beneath the pan to be sure the spirits keep the heat even, and is busy taking money from those lined up for a meal.

Her wife constantly chops and stirs, throwing new ingredients into the pan to keep up with what's being taken out.

"Two please," I say as we come up to the front of the line.

"That's two dollars." As I dig for a couple of gold coins with my free hand, she continues conversationally, "Make it in all right, love, or were you searched?"

I have to blink at her a few times before I understand what she's saying. These last months, Alinor's ships have been subjected to extra searches and seizures, taxes and tariffs, every time they come into Mellacean ports. I saw it myself last time the *Lizabetta* was in port. Her question is a reminder that the man in the square was right—our accents give away where we're from.

She sees me hesitate, and shoots me a quick smile as she takes my money. "A sailor is a sailor as far as we're concerned," she says. "But stay close to the docks, you mind."

"Yes, ma'am," I reply promptly, and Leander echoes the words as we move along the line to where her wife is scooping up two generous helpings and dumping them onto tin plates.

"I can't believe you can get a meal for a dollar," Leander whispers, inspecting the pan as our turn approaches. "It smells all right. Will it be edible?"

I tilt a sideways glance at him. "Do you understand how much things cost at all?"

He shrugs. "Why would I?"

"You are . . ." I'm left searching for words. "Do you have any practical use?"

He just grins, watching the tin plates as we shuffle closer. "You're not supposed to ask. Why don't you treat me like everyone else?"

"Well, we're in disguise."

"Oh, because it started when we put on disguises."

It's my turn to shrug. "Then it must be because you annoy me more than you annoy everyone else."

"Funny," he muses. "You don't annoy me at all."

We're at the front of the line before I have a chance to reply, and the woman is handing us the two tin plates heaped with rice, a fork dug into the top of each serving.

Leander looks like he's not sure where to go next or how to eat the thing standing up, and I smother a smile as I tow him into the space between stalls, where plenty of others are wolfing down their meals. It's strange to pull my hand from his to eat—and strange that it's strange.

Silently we set to work, and for a couple of minutes all I can think about is the exquisite taste of the meal. I've never had rice this deliciously salty and good. I've never had vegetables that crunch in my mouth this way, exploding with flavor. The fish just melts, warming me from the inside out. Hunger makes a feast out of what was already a pretty good meal, but I'm still surprised when I look down and find I'm scraping my plate. After a moment's consideration, I decide I don't care what the prince thinks of my table manners, and lick it to get at the last of the sauce. With a wink, he does the same.

I like it when he's unprincely for me.

His smile fades, though, when a pair of green sisters make their way past our little alcove. It's not hard to see how the crowd moves out of their way. Not out of fear, but out of respect.

Many of the locals turn toward the two women, pressing their fingertips to their foreheads and covering their eyes. *Our god's mind awaits us, though his eyes are closed.* Da and Jonlon taught me what it meant the first time I came ashore in Port Naranda, when I was small.

The sisters nod and raise their own hands to convey blessings. I don't think I've ever seen a priest of Barrica treated this way in the streets of Alinor.

"What they say about Macean rising is true," I whisper. "We should find some clothes and get back. They'll be cheaper farther in. Everyone stops at the first few stalls."

We drop our plates and forks into a waiting crate, then join the crowd once more. Before we reach the clothing stalls, though, Leander catches my arm.

When I look back, he's ducking through the crowd toward a stall tucked between a fishmonger's and a spice merchant's with a flashing electric sign. When I realize what he's angling toward through the press of bodies, my gut clenches and drops.

Strings of spirit flags are strung across the back of the little tent, and great bins of brightly colored stones are carefully arranged behind the counter, where in an Alinorish stall there'd be candles poured in a temple to Barrica.

I've been steeling myself to walk up to stalls like this all my life, but now—the disaster of my attempt at magic on the *Little Lizabetta* flooding back through my body in a flush of shame—now I can barely bring myself to look at it.

I'd almost begun to forget, my mind determined to shove the whole experience—Leander's confidence, his confusion, that brief glimpse of the spirits who've eluded me all my life—down into a deep hole and ignore it. But the memory was just beneath the surface, waiting to make my insides lurch all over again, as if I'm back in our tiny, tipping boat.

What do I tell Da when I see him again? Is it worse to admit I finally saw the spirits and they wouldn't heed me? Or do I leave him in the quiet disappointment he's learned to live with?

I force those questions down too, and make myself keep my gaze on the prince. Of course he would want to visit this stall—he spent too much of himself to bring us here, and we can't be caught without a proper sacrifice for him again.

"Can't go past Audira," says a voice, and I blink, looking up to find a pink-cheeked woman pausing on her way past.

"Sorry, what?"

She nods at the stall, and I understand—she thinks I was considering a purchase. "They'll have whatever your ship's magician needs, mark my words."

"Thank you," I manage, with my best attempt at a polite smile, and she bustles on her way.

Leander's leaning in to talk to the attendant behind the counter—Audira, presumably—and it only takes a few words before their posture softens and they angle toward him in return, like he's about to tell them a secret. And just a beat after that they're both laughing, and he's practically batting his lashes as he asks them a question.

*Seriously, Leander? Of all the times, and all the places . . .*

Then he has the nerve to turn and flash a grin at me, waving me over. "Can I have a dollar, please?"

I dig in my pocket for a single coin, march through the crowd, and shove it into his palm, then turn away. How can he be— It's not fair that he and his effortless magic are what I want to rage *against,* but he and his crooked smile are the place I want to bring my complaints for comfort as well. It's not even like he'll say the right thing—he's hopeless.

When he finishes his purchase and steps up beside me, I head back into the crowd without a word.

"I got you these," he says, falling into step with me and holding out three brightly colored glass stones, green and blue and red gleaming up at me, the electric lights around us dancing across their rounded surfaces.

I pull my own hands in against my body, tucking them under my arms. "Put those away."

"You're a magician, Selly," he says, only just loud enough to be heard over the crowd. "You should always have something in your pocket."

"For what?" I snap, warning him with a glance to let it go.

He doesn't. "For when you need it," he replies. "We tried

once, that's all. I'm going to figure it out. We'll figure it out together. Now, put them in your pocket and know they're a promise."

I can't afford to stop in the middle of the night market and fight him on this, so I snatch them from his hand, curling them up out of sight in my fist. They're warm from his touch.

"They said there have been protests out the front of the Alinorish embassy every day for the last week," he tells me, switching topics now he's got what he wants.

"What?" I blink across at him.

"Audira," he says, jerking a thumb over one shoulder. "Who runs the magician's stall."

"Your new friend?" I mutter.

His face lights up. "Look at that scowl! You're jealous!"

"I will shout your identity at the top of my lungs and leave you to the mercy of the crowd if you don't shut up."

"Well, I love that you're possessive," he replies, "and I'd hold your hand again if I wasn't sure you're willing to bite if provoked. But I was talking to them because magicians tend to talk across a city in a way others don't—word often passes up and down the classes, between merchants and neighborhoods, in a way you don't see anywhere else."

My throat tightens as I absorb his words. *Magicians talk.*

I've been at those stalls all my life, picking up supplies for my own failed lessons or for Kyri, and never once have I been invited into that conversation. I didn't even know it was happening.

Leander's looking at me sidelong, pausing a beat. "You really thought I was just flirting, didn't you?"

I'm quiet because I have to either admit he's right or say nothing at all.

There's a dark twist to his smile that I wish away as soon as I see it. "Well, in fairness, I'm usually exactly as terrible as other people assume," he says.

"I've seen worse," I mutter.

He lifts one brow. "Really?"

"Probably not." I take his arm to guide him out of the way of an approaching wagon. "If there are protests outside the embassy, you can't go anywhere near it, though. If you were recognized *there* . . ."

He grimaces his agreement. "It would be better if you went ahead and delivered a message."

We make our way along to the clothes stalls, pushing past everything from secondhand books to thirdhand saucepans to a vat of frying dough that smells incredible but we can't afford. Plenty of the stalls have little statues of Macean perched somewhere, just as they would a statue of Barrica in Kirkpool, or any of the other gods in their home countries.

They have little medallions of the Mother, too, and I reach out to tap one with my finger. "She shows up everywhere," I murmur. "I guess she doesn't pick sides between her children."

"That's what they say," Leander agrees. "That all gods are present in the Temple of the Mother, and there they keep their peace, no matter what else is happening outside. I guess they're just like everyone else—forced to behave at their parents' table."

We find a likely stall, and it doesn't take us long to pick out two worn but respectable shirts and pairs of trousers. With any luck Keegan and Leander won't leave the inn again until the ambassador sends the Queensguard for them, but if they must, they'll blend into a crowd well enough. They'll still have to wear their own boots, stiff with salt as they are. I suppose we're lucky Keegan didn't know enough about surviving at sea to take them off.

"What do you think?" Leander asks, pulling on a newsie cap and striking a pose. "Does it hide my dashing good looks?"

It suits him. Of course it does.

"What?" he asks, adjusting the brim. "What's that look? Do I have dirt on my face? Do I *need* dirt on my face?"

"Just . . ." I refuse to give him the satisfaction of drawing anything more from me than he already has—and a part of me knows this has to be bravado. The relief of making it to land can only carry us so far. Like me, he must have a nervous twist in his gut that won't go away.

So instead I turn away to hunt through the racks of clothes, yanking the hangers along as I look for something in my size.

"Selly." He's right there in my ear, somehow close again. "I really don't want you to stomp on my foot, but I think you need to look at the dresses."

My hands go still. "Not my style, rich boy."

"Sure, but when you move away from the docks, do you want to look like a sailor? Everyone keeps warning us against that. The embassy is in a wealthy part of town, and the women around here are mostly wearing skirts, if they're dressed in clothes that are worth anything. We don't want you to draw attention. We want you to walk up to the front door without looking out of place."

He's right. I haven't worn a dress in years, though. Kyri

loves—*loved*—them, but they were never my style. She'd try to talk me into them, holding hers up to me and angling our grubby little looking glass to show me my reflection, and I'd bat her efforts away.

Now I'd dress head to toe in lace and frills if I could push away the ache in my chest and have her here with us.

The girl running the stall senses it's the perfect moment to pounce. "Looking for something special?" she asks, popping up beside me seemingly from nowhere. Her skin and hair are a rich mahogany, her intricate nest of braids coiled fashionably atop her head, her smile friendly.

Then, of all people, I hear Rensa in my head.

*Take some advice. Listen to someone who knows more than you for once.*

"I've got about eight dollars," I say. "I need the best kind of dress that can buy."

She looks me up and down, thoughtful. "And a pair of shoes?" she ventures.

I swallow. "And a pair of shoes."

She smiles. "I'm going to send you to my sister, Hallie. She's got a little place that does dresses you wouldn't believe." She produces a stub of a pencil and draws us a map on a scrap of paper as she speaks. "It's in an underground arcade with the most beautiful lights. There's a place that does cakes, a jeweler, the cutest little nightclub, and she's at the end. Tell her I sent you—she'll turn you into an eight-dollar dream."

She spins the map to show me—her sister's shop isn't far, but it's farther in from the docks.

"I'm taking you back to the inn," I tell Leander after we've thanked her and walked away.

"What?" he protests. "No, I'm coming dress shopping."

"We can't afford one for you, too," I reply, steering him through the market, toward the square.

He snorts. "Good as I would look, I want to help you—"

"I don't need witnesses, thank you."

"I should get a better look around the city," he tries.

"You should drop anchor at the inn and stay there. It's what I should have done with you in the first place. It's what I'm *going* to do with you now."

He huffs, but he lets me walk him back the way we came. We part with another twenty-five cents to pick up a paper from a newsie at the end of the night market, and Leander flips through it as we walk. He tears out a sheet that's nothing but an advertisement, then hands the rest to me to stuff into the bag of clothes I'm carrying.

"What are you doing?" I ask, pressing through the crowd and craning my neck to see.

His nimble fingers are folding it, turning it, folding it again. Then he offers it to me, taking the bag of shirts and trousers as he sets it on my palm.

It's a little paper boat, lines crisp, sails set.

"It's a promise," he says quietly. "You belong on the water. We'll get you back there."

Suddenly I can't speak.

The *Lizabetta* is gone, even the *Little Lizabetta*. My captain, my crew. Everything I own is gone.

And I'm not as sure as I used to be about where my course should take me next. Tomorrow the boys will be gone, and this little paper boat will be all I have.

"Thank you," I say after clearing my throat, and he offers me an almost wistful smile.

"My father used to make them," he says. "So I'm told. One of his friends showed me how, and as a boy I used to fold just about any piece of paper I came across. It felt like a link to him."

I know all too well what it means to want a link to someone who's gone, but I just swallow hard, glance at the boat, and nod.

"Haven't made one in years," he muses, and neither of us speaks again as we let the crowd carry us along to the inn.

There I make myself businesslike, firming my tone. "Now get inside, and stay there until I can hand you off to someone with more than a secondhand pair of trousers to hide you."

"My glory cannot be concealed, whether the clothing is secondhand or the finest in—"

"Go, you pain in my—"

"I'm going!" he laughs, and I watch until he disappears down the alley, to climb back up the fire escape once more. After all, our host is sure we never left. Then I turn away to follow the map a few blocks to the arcade, my stomach fluttering in a way I don't think has anything to do with the meal I just ate.

The entrance is down a set of stone steps that lead below street level, topped with a wrought-iron arch. As I descend into the passageway, I realize the shops and the nightclub must be in the basements of the office buildings up above us. They face onto a neatly cobbled underground arcade, the walls lit with golden lights on strings.

The lettering on each of the little shops is gold, the script curling, and this place feels like money. There are half a dozen people in the laneway, some looking at cakes and jewelry through the shop windows, and some lined up for the night-club inside a red velvet rope. The place doesn't seem to have a name, and on the bar where a sign swings for the shops, there's just a painting of a ruby, held in the palm of a woman's hand.

Music spills out as I walk past, wild and playful, and through the open door there are couples dancing and shimmying. I press on past it to the next little shop, whose window reads *Hallie's*.

The girl inside is a rounder, curvier version of her sister back at the market, with the same flawless brown skin and coil of braids atop her head. She's wearing a golden evening dress that shimmers as she moves around the shop. She has the same friendly smile as her sister, too, and when she spots me hovering in the doorway, she lifts a finger to beckon me in.

"You look like a girl in need of something special," she calls. So, swallowing hard, I step over the threshold.

It takes Hallie less than a quarter hour to shuffle through her tightly packed racks of clothing and transform me.

She's surprised by the thick, unformed stripe of my magician's marks, pausing to gently lift one of my hands in hers and take a closer look.

"That's a new one," she says in her lilting Mellacean accent, and I barely resist the urge to snatch my hand from hers.

"Alinorish," I mutter.

"You don't say." She's not disbelieving—just curious.

"Can we cover them up?" I ask quietly, my chest tight.

She searches my face, and whatever she sees there makes her nod, sympathetic.

Soon I'm standing in front of a mirror looking at a girl I hardly recognize. She's clad in a long-sleeved jade-green dress that reaches to her knees, sparkling beads creating a geometric pattern that starts at her waist and radiates out, up, and down. I can feel the beads clicking when I move.

The backs of my hands are covered too, with a piece of beaded lace Hallie quickly stitched onto each cuff and looped around my middle fingers, like an elegant version of my usual gloves. I curl my hands into fists, then flex my fingers, watching the green skin move beneath the lace, the anger and frustration bubbling up all over again. I was *so* close.

But I shove it inside the same box where it always lives and nail the lid shut. That's what I need to do.

"That dress had four owners before you," Hallie tells me with satisfaction. "Treat her right and I'll give you five dollars back."

There's quite a discussion over the shoes after that. I want them flat. She refuses. I end up with half the heel height she wanted, but still more than I'm confident in. There's a strap across the front, at least, so they won't fall off.

She watches me with a critical eye as I practice walking around her little shop, past the racks of clothes stuffed into every available corner, their colors bursting out at me like promises of a thousand lives I'll never lead and definitely don't want to try.

"You really like him, huh?" she asks.

"What makes you say that?" I ask, practicing turning a corner.

"Well, or her. Point is, a girl comes in and buys a dress when that's not her regular thing, there's a reason," she says. "Though for what it's worth, you're cute enough to wake Macean from his nap in your sailor clothes. Wear a killer dress if you like, but don't change what matters."

I knew I liked her. "Not a chance," I reply, pausing in front of the mirror to look at myself one more time.

Though I can't help picturing Leander's face when he sees me.

"Can I pack up my old clothes in a bag? I'll wear the dress out."

She chatters while I she puts my shirt, trousers, and boots into a bag, and I tuck Leander's little paper boat in among them between two layers of fabric so it won't get crushed. I leave the glass magician's stones Leander gave me in the pocket of my trousers.

Before Hallie lets me go, she shows me how to braid up my hair in a crown like the locals do, instead of letting it hang down my back. I like her—she's infectious, laughing and smiling, and soon I am too. It feels impossible that we could be enemies.

By the time she's dabbed a little pink stuff on my lips and cheeks, and dropped the jar into my bag for tomorrow, I'm more than ready for my mission. I look *good,* even if I mostly look like someone else.

Hallie whistles appreciatively when I turn to head out the door, and I toss her a wink over my shoulder—it's not just the new heels putting a little more swing in my hips as I walk, and I run a hand over the green beads down my front, smiling to myself as I feel them under my touch.

The music is still pouring out from the nameless nightclub, and I glance through the door again as I walk past, letting my gaze sweep over the dancers. They move as one, all a little different but all governed by the same beat.

Now I look like one of them. In a quarter hour I've transformed into a Mellacean, into the sort of girl who goes to clubs, into the sort of girl who'll walk straight up to an ambassador's door tomorrow.

Then my gaze snags on one figure in particular, and I stop so fast, I nearly trip over my new heels. He's in among the throng of dancers, a drink raised high in one hand, moving and laughing with everyone else.

Except he *can't* be, because I delivered him to the Salthouse Inn less than half an hour ago. But as I stand and stare, my mouth still open, I know in my gut there's no way I'm wrong. I could pick him out of any crowd.

Prince Leander of Alinor is drinking and dancing in a Mellacean club.

*Seven hells, I'm going to wring his neck.*

# LEANDER

*Ruby Red*
*Port Naranda, Mellacea*

We have nothing like this at home, and I wouldn't be allowed here if we did.

The music's playful and wild; the dance floor's crowded, everyone moving in time to the rhythm like a many-bodied beast. There's a ball hanging from the ceiling covered in shards of mirror, and tiny spots of white light whirl across us like a sky full of stars racing past, as if even the heavens are moved by the rhythm all around us.

They wear the most spectacular suits and dresses here, but I worked my way past the man on the door in my shirtsleeves and trousers, accessorized with a wink and a smile. Wherever in the world I am, a party's a party, and I'm right at home.

I down the drink a handsome boy in a very flattering waistcoat bought me as I rejoin the dancers, and it burns all the way to my gut, then tingles. I hand my glass off to a girl with a tray full of empties, and a laughing group welcomes me into their circle, showing me how to tap and hop along with the moves they all know.

Up the stairs from this underground club, this city is poised on the edge, with protests outside my country's embassy, a port full of ships being searched and taxed. All of it in preparation for a war I could have prevented.

Behind me is a string of deaths for which I can never atone, friends and sailors and innocents burned to death, shot, drowned.

I am irredeemable, and I've always known it. And now that we've slowed down, I've had time to come face to face with the knowledge all over again.

But this place is carefree, and I'm going to submerge myself in it until everything vanishes. I'm going to find a moment's relief, even if that's all I can get. I need it desparately.

If there's one thing I know how to do, it's hide from responsibility, and this is the perfect place to try.

Somcone lays a hand on my shoulder, and I swing around, ready to fall into a dance with them, and then . . . uh-oh.

It's Selly.

Uh . . . *oh.*

It's Selly, and she looks *spectacular.* She's in an incredible green dress covered in sparkling beads, every one of them afire as the mirrored stars whirl past. Her hair's coiled atop her head like a golden crown, and I've never seen anything like her.

Judging by the expression she's wearing, she might also be the *last* thing I see.

At least that much is the same—I'm not sure I would've recognized her if she wasn't scowling at me.

"What in seven hells are you doing?" she demands, grabbing for my arm and yanking me away from the circle of dancers to the edge of the crowd. The light glitters off her dress with every movement.

"Learning about Port Naranda's culture and traditions," I shout above the music. "Gathering intelligence."

"You wouldn't know intelligence if it marched up to you and tried to force its way in through your ears to the empty spot where your brain should be," she snaps, green eyes magnificently alight with her anger.

The snap of her voice, the snap of her eyes . . . something *snaps* in my heart, and suddenly I'm swept up by the insane urge to kiss her, to lose myself in *her*. I very nearly wrap my arms around her, but holding myself back with a kind of restraint I never knew I possessed—I'm not *that* much of an idiot—I manage instead to reach for her hand.

"Dance with me?" I ask her. I *beg* her. "I'll be gone tomorrow."

"Only if I'm lucky," she shoots back, snatching her fingers away, cheeks pink with fury. At least I assume it's fury.

*Goddess, what if it* isn't *fury making her blush?*

I should let it go, but the drink's warming my veins, and I've had too little sleep and far too much pain, and it's pushing up inside my chest, making me reckless. "Don't you care that we'll never see each other again?" I ask, before I can think better of it.

Her face goes still, and a little of the anger bleeds away, but she doesn't answer me.

"*I* care. It's one more thing than I can take right now. Dance with me?" I hold out my hand. "Consider it a last request."

She looks at it like it might grow teeth and bite her. "I don't know how." Suddenly, like the focus on a camera snapping into some other setting, I see the irritation in her features change.

*She's afraid.*

*Selly?* My *Selly, afraid of a dance floor?*

My heart aches to simply snatch up her hand, but I just leave mine extended, waiting. Hoping. "I can show you."

"Le— *Maxim,* what are you *doing?*" she replies, back to frustration again just a beat too late—I saw the way she gazed at me for a moment. Like she was realizing something, trying to figure it out. As soon as it's there, it's gone, but I'm *sure* I saw it.

I try a couple of the tapping, swinging steps my new friends showed me, shooting her a grin. "This."

Her hands curl to fists, and she takes a step in closer so she can speak without shouting. "Can't you— Don't you know what's relying on you? How can you be in a *nightclub?*"

Our eyes meet, and the music flows around us, and the lights gleam off her dress, and the burn in my gut settles back in like it was never gone. With it comes my own flare of anger, rising in a wave to take the place of that sudden, unbearable urge to feel her in my arms. "Don't I know what's relying on me? How do you think I could forget? I see them every time I close my eyes, Selly!"

"And yet here you are, dancing. I was just starting to appreciate you as a deeper human being."

It kills me that after everything we've been through together, she's falling back into seeing me just the way my sisters always have—a waste of space and privilege. It kills me that she's probably right.

I make myself shrug, keep my mask in place, and though my throat tightens, the thumping music is enough to disguise the change in my voice. "Well, that was your first mistake."

She draws a breath, her spine straightening, and I brace. "You wanted to get to know your father? What would he think if he could see you now?"

I take a step back, the air leaving my lungs. The thudding of the music fades. The whirling lights from the mirror ball overhead vanish at the edges of my vision.

"I think he would be very disappointed indeed," I whisper, half relying on the din to cover it, half too shaken to care.

But she hears it. She's frozen in place. She looks like she's just shot me, but didn't know she was going to pull the trigger. Her lips part, her eyes widen. "No, I'm—"

"Don't be," I cut her off. "Don't be sorry. You're right. And it's my fault, all of it. I'm the reason they're all dead. I'm the reason this war is . . . I'm the reason. It's my fault."

And that's what I was running from tonight. That, and the knowledge that soon I'd be leaving behind the only thing that's helped me survive it—this girl who sees through me, understands who I am. I've been so focused on our struggle that I only realized tonight: soon we'll part ways, and I'll never see her again.

I made her a little paper boat just an hour ago, to remind myself of the inevitability of our separation, but I want to cling to her, hold her hand, enjoy her insults, know she'll be there to lean on.

But she doesn't want that. How could she, after I cost her everything she ever knew and loved? If I were her, I'd want me gone.

"I'm the reason they're all dead," I say again, softer.

And I don't know what I was doing, trying to run from that, except it's all I've ever known how to do.

And it would have been so nice, to dance with her tonight.

Our eyes are still locked, and I can still barely hear the music, barely see the lights. I can't look away from her, and so I see the exact moment she crumbles, my words echoing between us.

*They're all dead.*

For an instant, everything she's been keeping packed tight inside is there in her eyes, and then she's in my arms. I don't know if I reached for her or she came to me, but we're together, clinging to each other like we did to the *Little Lizabetta*.

I'm her lifeboat, and she's mine. Sobs shake her body, and I hold her tight, tucking her in against me.

*This* is what I've been running from. Not just what I did, but what it cost her.

Neither of us speaks, and the band switches to a new song, and the crowd on the dance floor moves into a new pattern. The boy in the waistcoat who bought my drink salutes me over Selly's shoulder, raising his glass in a wry toast. He thinks he lost out on my company for the evening. He's right, just not in the way he thinks.

I can't let go of her, and I don't want to. So I hold her, and she sobs into my shoulder, and running here tonight seems just as foolish, just as hopeless as she said it was. Because there's nowhere I can go that will let me hide from what I've done.

And tomorrow I'll be on the ambassador's ship, and she'll be gone.

A couple of songs go by before she lifts her head, and now the glimmering lights catch the tears on her cheeks, and they sparkle like the beads on her dress, like the lights from the mirror ball. Gently I run my thumb across her cheekbone, across her freckles, chasing away the tears.

"I'm sorry," she says with a sniff, unwilling to look up and meet my eyes.

"The apologies are all mine." I bow my head until our foreheads press together, keeping my voice low. "There'll never be enough of them." The truth of that sits hollowly inside me.

I see her pull herself together—I see her deciding to take hold of herself once more and tuck it all away. She's so strong. I only have a second before she'll be back behind her shields. And I want, so badly—

"Can I kiss you?" I whisper before I can think the better of it.

Her breath catches, gaze flying back up to meet mine, and she goes still in my arms. The moment stretches forever as the lights play across her face.

"Leander," she murmurs. "I can't."

The knot in my gut tightens to a physical pain, and I know my mask can't possibly be good enough right now. "Of course. I shouldn't— You don't want—"

"No," she says quickly—her hand, resting on my arm, tightens. Suddenly all my awareness pours down that arm and into the skin yielding to her fingertips under my sleeve. She swallows, hesitating, her cheeks darkening. Her eyes and lips darkening. "I do want."

Her voice, barely audible over the music, echoes in my ears. I can't move, a tangible shock coursing through me. Hope, longing, wanting—they tangle in my throat, like horses jostling at the start of a race. And then dismay catches up and overtakes them all. "If you do, then why can't we . . . ?"

"It'll only make it worse," she says quietly. "Tomorrow."

I want to argue, but there's a look on her face that reminds me of just how much she's already lost. A mother who gave her away at birth. A father who sailed up north and left her behind. The ship that was her home, and crew who were her people . . . all gone.

Everyone and everything she's ever tried to love has left, and in the morning I will too. When I made her that little paper boat, and promised her she'd have a real one soon, a part of me hoped she'd turn it down, say she wanted something else. That was a foolish idea, even for a daydream.

I've taken everything from her, and I don't have the right to ask anything more. All she has left is the sea, and I won't strip that from her too.

So I find the smile everyone knows so well and get it back where it belongs. "Well, you look stunning, and we shouldn't waste it. Let me teach you one dance, and then we'll go back to jail."

She smiles, keeping hold of my hands. The backs of mine are etched with the intricate designs that mark my magic, hers with the thick green stripes that mark her lack of it, hidden beneath green lace unless you know they're there. But she's looking down at her glittering dress, moving so the beads shimmer in the light. "I thought you'd like me better in this."

I ache to lean in and kiss her, to feel her lips on mine. But I settle for squeezing her hands instead. And for the truth. Because it's not about the dress. This version of her is beautiful, but it's not who she is or who she wants to be.

"Actually," I say, meeting her green eyes, "I like you best with salt on your skin."

# SELLY

*Ruby Red*
*Port Naranda, Mellacea*

The only thing I want in the world right now is to step forward, curl my hands into his shirt, and kiss him until he stops talking.

But that's not for me—*he's* not for me.

"All right, you smooth talker," I say, tearing my gaze away from him and taking in the bodies on the dance floor. "Come on—the music's changing. One dance, and you'll be sick of me stepping on your feet."

I let him lead me to the dance floor, our fingers twined together—just an hour ago at the night market this seemed so strange, but now it's as though we've left the confines of the port and we're out on open water, nothing in our way. It's simpler. Even if we won't act on it, we both know what we're feeling.

Leander stops so suddenly that I crash into him, wrapping one arm around him to keep my balance in these ridiculous shoes. "What is it? Is this song too . . ." My words die away at the look on his face.

He's staring straight at a boy standing near the bar—I think he just came through the back staff entrance, and he was talking to one of the bartenders, but he's stopped too, frozen in place. Leander looks like he's seen a ghost, and so does the other boy, his mouth open in shock.

He's slim, wirily built, with black hair cut short, tanned skin, dark eyes, full lips. Handsome, but wary. One moment he's staring at us, the next he's backing up toward the door, and when he crashes into it, he starts.

"Jude," Leander calls, hauling me with him as he pushes his way through the crowd at the edges of the dance floor.

The boy called Jude has nowhere to go unless he disappears through the door behind him, and something seems to stop him from opening it. He's not dressed like the fancy dancers in the club, but like the locals up on the street, in shirtsleeves and a flat cap, a pin with a small red jewel on it stuck through his lapel, like the one on the sign outside. I feel like I've seen one of those pins before, but I can't think where. He's staring at Leander with his mouth open, shaking his head slowly.

"Jude, where in the seven hells have you *been*?" Leander demands as we reach him.

"Here," the boy replies, breathless. "Where else?"

"What do you mean, *where else*?" Leander's still staring at him like he's trying to believe he's real, but however pleased—if that's the right word—he is to see this boy, the feeling clearly isn't mutual.

Jude shakes his head again, shoving his hands deep into his

pockets, but not before I see they're shaking. "I— What are *you* doing here?" He seems about to say *Your Highness,* but he bites down on the words. He looks like he wants to be sick.

"I'm not here," Leander replies. "Never was, won't be tomorrow. Jude, do you *know* what I did to try and find you? I went to your mother's house in Kirkpool, but she said you were moving, so I left letters with her."

"You what?" Jude asks slowly.

"She said she'd give them to you," Leander says, running one hand through his hair. "But when you didn't reply, I went back, and you'd both moved out. I had the captain of the Queensguard out looking for you. I went to see your father's *wife.* She'd have thrown me out if I wasn't who I am."

"You're lying," Jude says, looking sicker still. "None of you ever . . . No."

"Why would I— Look, you shouldn't be here," Leander says. "There'll be a war—you have to come home. We can arrange that, you—"

"I can't," Jude says flatly, pulling one hand from his pocket and reaching for the door handle. "Forget me. I sure as hells never saw you."

"Jude, I—"

"You have to go." Jude cuts him off, his voice low, intense. "You have to go *right now.* Get out of town." In one quick movement he pulls the door open, slipping out through it and slamming it shut.

Leander's after him in a second, but when he tries to turn the handle, it's already locked. "Jude!" he calls, hammering on it. "Jude, get back here!"

"Stop," I hiss, grabbing for his arm. "People will notice." Already the boy Jude was talking to at the bar is looking at us—I glare at him until he turns away and picks up a glass to polish.

Leander whirls around to face me. "Selly, I have to—"

"No, you don't! He said no."

"But he can't possibly . . ." He trails off, shaking his head, and his bewilderment makes my chest ache.

"Who is he?" I ask, gentler.

"We went to school together," he says slowly. "He's a friend. A friend I had no idea was in Port Naranda."

"For a friend, he didn't seem to like you much. Between him and Keegan, I'm beginning to wonder if anyone from your school did."

"Me too," he mutters, but he's only half listening to me.

"Will he tell anyone he saw you?"

Leander shakes his head. "Never," he replies, and then he pauses. "I'd have said he'd never believe I abandoned him either, though."

"Did you?"

"Of course not. He just vanished on me one day—hard to help somebody you can't find."

"There must be more to it than that," I press, keeping my voice gentle, trying to figure out just how much of a grudge Jude might carry.

Leander inclines his head, pressing his hand to the door as though he could reach through it. "Jude had his mother's name at school—he was Jude Kien. His father was Lord Anson, but Jude's mother wasn't Lord Anson's wife."

"Ah."

"Yes. When His Lordship died, he left Jude and his mother nothing. Whether it was on purpose or an accident I don't know, but Lady Anson wasn't in the mood to help—she'd never liked her husband paying for Jude's schooling."

"So Jude had to leave school?"

"They just disappeared one day," he replies, helpless. "I tried everything to find him. I gave his mother letters—why wouldn't she pass them on?"

"Families are complicated," I murmur, and it sounds like a weak excuse even as I offer it.

"I'd have made sure he stayed at school, that he had somewhere to go, if I'd known were to find him," Leander says miserably. "But he vanished."

He looks so lost, and I hurt for him. I can also imagine how angry Jude might be, if he does think Leander abandoned him just as he lost everything. "I'm sorry he ran. He was right about one thing, though. We should go—it's not safe here. You can leave word with the ambassador to try and find him, get him on a ship home, but . . ."

He closes his eyes. "You're right. I know you are. I haven't seen him in two years, though, Selly. I tried everywhere. I don't understand. Why did he lock the door?"

I slip my arm through his and get him moving. It's strange to touch him like this—like I have permission—and it's also not strange at all. It feels dangerously close to right, even though I know it never will be.

"One problem at a time," I say, making myself sound businesslike. "Let's get back to the inn."

We collect the bag of my old clothes from behind the bar

and make our way out past the man on the door and up the stairs to the street.

Leander's still lost in his thoughts, his arm linked through mine as we walk. But I can't help looking back over my shoulder as we turn for the docks once more.


Keegan's relief is written all over his face when we get back, and he's full of questions about Port Naranda: about what we saw at the market, about the word in the city. Leander tells him about Jude and hands him the newspaper, and I guess not reading any new words for the last couple of days has hurt, because Keegan flips it open to soak them up like he's parched and they're cool, fresh water.

We took enough twists and turns, and I glanced back before we slipped into the alley to climb the fire escape—I'm sure we weren't followed from the club. But with that immediate fear behind me, everything else is surfacing again. The ache of tiredness behind my eyes. The awareness I can't shake of where Leander is at any given moment, and whether he's looking my way.

"You should sleep," Keegan says without looking up. "I napped while you were gone, so the bed would be free."

Leander and I both glance at the bed at the same time, and even though we made a point of it when we rented the room, there's still a long, long pause as we think about those words. *The bed.* Just the one.

My gaze flicks up in time to meet his, and I feel my blush heating my cheeks.

"Please, please don't make me be all noble and offer to sleep on the floor," he says, and though he makes his tone comically pleading, there's something else in his dark eyes, and I'm not sure I understand what it is.

"Of course not," I say automatically. "You're far too spoiled. I'll do it."

"I—"

"I am going to wash my face," Keegan announces, folding the newspaper and taking it with him as he practically vanishes through the door into our little washroom. There's a strong but unspoken note of *sort yourselves out before I come back* in his tone.

"Selly," says Leander, trying for reasonable, and keeping his voice down in the faint hope of some privacy, though the washroom door is thin. "Let's just go to bed. I'll keep my hands to myself. You told me you want me to."

I huff a breath, because I told him I *didn't* want him to, but I'm not going to say it out loud. Instead I just nod. "Turn around."

"What?"

"I'm not sleeping in this dress. Turn around while I get changed."

He pivots obediently on his heel, and a part of me is somehow disappointed he didn't protest. *Can't have it both ways, girl.*

I wriggle carefully out of my dress and my new shoes, folding them over the back of a chair. I check again for the little paper boat and arrange it so it won't be crushed or crumpled.

Leander's dutifully staring at the wall, but I know he's as aware as I am of every little noise I make—every whisper of fabric, every shift of my balance from one foot to the other.

I pick up the pair of salt-encrusted trousers I wore off the

*Lizabetta* and turn them over in my hands. I can feel the weight of the glass stones in the pocket, a reminder of something I refuse to think about just now. I've done enough, faced enough, tonight. I can't sleep in these anyway, they're too stiff.

So instead I pull on my crumpled cream shirt and button it up, then slip in under the covers. I've never hidden my body before, but I've never had someone around me so interested in looking at it, either.

"You can turn around now."

Leander turns back and eases down to sit on the edge of the bed, bending to unlace his boots. He doesn't speak, and I can't think of anything to say, and it's not until he straightens up again that he looks back over his shoulder. "Over the covers or under?"

I soften. "Under," I murmur, confident I'm blushing again. The crown of braids Hallie put my hair into is still there, so I get busy unpicking it, and that gives me something to do as he climbs in beside me and gets settled.

And then we lie there, both gazing up at the water-stained ceiling, listening to each other breathe, and noticing how incredibly close we are. At least that's what I'm doing.

"Keegan's really taking his time," he observes after a couple of minutes.

I glance across, and his wry smile is waiting for me, and a little of the tension that's been building in my chest comes undone. It's just Leander. "Hard to blame him."

We lapse into silence, but I'm still so completely aware of how close he is, of all the tiny movements he makes and the way they tug the sheets against my body. It would take just the smallest shift to turn toward him, and he'd pick up that cue in an instant. I'd be in his arms a breath later. But I stay where I am, and he does too.

I thought I'd lie awake all night, knowing he was there, but tiredness begins to creep through me, as warm as the blanket we're curled up beneath, and it doesn't leave room for much else—not for the anger that heated my blood as I strode across the club toward him, not for the pain as I told him he couldn't kiss me, mustn't kiss me. It doesn't numb the knowledge that he'll be gone tomorrow, though, and I don't want this to be the way we spend our last time together, in silence, with everything unspoken. So without thinking about what I'll say, I speak— and a question shows up. A question to which I suddenly think I know the answer.

"Leander?"

"Mmm?"

"The day we met, at the docks. What were you doing, lurking behind a pile of crates?"

He's quiet for a little. "Escaping," he says eventually.

"Like you were tonight." It's a statement, not a question.

"I suppose so," he agrees. "Sometimes . . . it's a lot, is all."

"What is?"

"Don't get me wrong," he murmurs. "There are people worse off than me, I understand that. But having every eye in the room on you, every moment of your life . . . it's a cage. I have all the privileges of being a part of my family, but all the expectations as well. There's very little freedom, and as the third child I have very little chance to do anything real with my life."

I huff a soft, involuntary laugh. "Well, I bet you're sorry you wished for something to do."

"If only I'd known earlier I could make wishes come true," he replies, and though he's reaching for a joke, there's something wistful in his voice.

Without thinking, I slide my hand across to his beneath the covers. Our little fingers bump, and he holds still just long enough to be sure it wasn't an accident, I think. But I shift my hand a little farther, and he weaves his fingers through mine so quickly, so tightly, it's like he's holding on for his life.

"Good night," I whisper.

"Good night, Selly."

Tired as I am, I don't think I'll fall asleep. But in almost no time at all, I'm drifting away, my fingers still entwined with his.

# JUDE

*Handsome Jack's*
*Port Naranda, Mellacea*

I push my way in through the door of Handsome Jack's, hardly knowing how I got here, and the roar of the crowd rises up to embrace me.

"You're not on tonight," says the man on the door, looking me over, then studying a grubby list in one hand. He glances up and considers me again, taking in my expression. "Want to get in the ring?"

And then I understand—*this* is why my feet carried me to the tavern, to the boxing ring.

"Yes," I rasp, already unbuttoning my shirt.

I should have stayed. I should have talked to Leander.

I should have asked—begged—for help. If he was telling the truth about trying to find me when we left, he would have helped me now.

But all I could think was, *I helped her kill you. Why aren't you dead?*

And in my head a softer, more persistent voice said, *You could turn him in right now, and all your troubles would be over.* Because that's the sort of person I am, it turns out.

But with guilt burning me from the inside out, instead of asking for help, instead of warning him of the hounds on his trail, I ran.

And now, the crowd-monster already building to a bellow around me, I stride toward the ring, and the only way I know to stop thinking.

I don't deserve what he offered me.

But I can't bear to know I gave it up.

# KEEGAN

*The Salthouse Inn*
*Port Naranda, Mellacea*

T he dockside square in Port Naranda never sleeps, but it's
quieter now, its activity reduced to those whose errands
can't wait for morning.

A group of sailors carry their cargo toward the nearest
pier, no doubt intent on setting sail with the tide. A pair of
city guards walk a slow patrol around the edges of the space.
Sleepy sailors head out toward their ships—I notice they move
in groups. Perhaps they always did, or perhaps it's the tension in the air here that makes them do it.

The curtains in our room are drawn, my companions asleep
in the bed, boneless in their exhaustion. Slowly they've turned
in toward each other, and now they sleep with their heads close
together, as though they're whispering secrets.

I should be sleeping as well—I could make up a bed on
the floor—but though my head aches with tiredness, rest
eludes me.

So instead, I've ducked underneath the curtain to stand on the far side, resting our newspaper on the window ledge and reading by the lights of the square below. It's an old habit. I've read by moonlight all my life, whether in the dormitory at school or during my time at home. It settles me, and never fails to slow my head or my heart.

There's nothing in the newspaper Leander and Selly brought back with them that speaks of the progress fleet or of Alinor's lost prince, though there's plenty of mention of Alinor—talk of trade, of politics, reports on manufactured insults. My guess is that another day or two will pass before Leander's fleet is due to make a stop—it would make sense to give Leander as much of a head start as possible toward the sacrifice before his absence was revealed.

Nevertheless, it won't be long before the headlines both here and at home—indeed, all over the continent—scream that Prince Leander is dead.

Then two nations will ready themselves for war. Alinor in revenge for the attack on her fleet, for there can be only one suspect in such a crime.

Mellacea will muster her navy too—ostensibly in response to Alinor's threats, but in reality as the culmination of a buildup that's been under way now for more than a year.

The words on the front of the newspaper I'm holding confirm as much.

FIRST COUNCILOR TARIDEN VISITS HOUSE OF MACEAN

In Alinor, Queen Augusta leads the nation—she has a pack of ministers and advisers, elected officials whose advice she often takes, and priests who speak on behalf of the church. Ultimately, however, hers is the last word on any subject.

Here in Mellacea their leaders are elected, but the real power lies elsewhere. That's why the first councilor is making the trip to consult the green sisters, the leader of the people making the journey to the church.

In Alinor, at least the woman who rules the country is honest in admitting she does so. The first of the green sisters can't say the same.

I wonder if they stock international newspapers at the Bibliotek. There would be a delay in shipping them, of course, but it would be interesting to see the same events reported from varying perspectives. Perhaps I can import them myself, if not.

The idea of being there—of seeing the great library, of taking classes in the legendary lecture halls, of debating and learning among students from all over the world . . . it's a dream I've fought for, and one way or another, I'm going to see it through. I might be caught up in world politics now, but the Bibliotek itself is independent, untouchable—it's home to the largest Temple of the Mother in existence for a reason. Just as all her children are present in her temples, everyone at the Bibliotek is welcome, and leaves their conflict at the door.

Before I see any of it, I must give some thought to how I'll explain the lateness of my arrival, because I'll certainly miss the first part of the semester, and I can't tell them the truth.

I think it's reasonable to hope the ambassador might put me on a ship there, but if not, I have my necklace—though I'd prefer to use it for my expenses until I can secure a scholarship or tutoring work. With any luck Leander will remember to ask somebody about passage for me before we part ways.

As if my mention summons him, the curtain beside me shifts, and the prince appears.

"Fancy meeting you here," he murmurs, leaning against the windowsill beside me.

I don't respond right away. We've never been friends, Prince Leander of Alinor and I. He wasn't the worst of them at school, but he never went out of his way to help me, either.

I still remember the first time we met, in fact, although I doubt he does.

I was in the library, sitting against the wall between two high shelves, a book resting on my knees. I was twelve, so no doubt I was passing my lunch hour with a geographical treatise, most probably something by Freestone.

The prince was newly arrived and walking with a gaggle of other students, all of them fighting to show him around. They came by the end of the aisle where I was sitting, and one of them—a broad-shouldered boy called Hargrove—happened to glance my way. Our eyes met, and I mentally urged him to keep moving, holding myself still.

"Look out!" he called, and my heart dropped as every head turned my way. "A bookworm!"

"Steer clear," called someone from behind him. "You might catch something! You never know where he's been."

*Everywhere,* I wanted to say. *And anywhere. That's the point of books.*

Hargrove snapped his teeth at me from the end of the aisle, and I flinched. "Worms don't bite," he said, grinning. "No teeth."

I thought about advising him that a Petronian knifeworm had teeth sharp enough to eat its way right out of his gut, if he consumed a piece of fish or game with one inside. But I had already learned to keep my own counsel, rather than engage with my classmates.

"Be brave," drawled Leander from behind him. Even at that age, his tone was full of assurance—it always held a hint of a smile, as though he knew a joke, and you were supposed to be desperate to be in on it. At first I thought he was talking to me, but then he continued. "I'm sure you'll all survive the local wildlife."

And just like that, the prince's stamp of approval was on my exclusion.

I was aware I was gawky, too long of limb, too pale for lack of sun, too wary of the world already. In that moment, it was clear there would never be any place for me there.

Four years later, when we were sixteen, I gave up the unequal struggle, pressing the headmaster to suggest to my parents that I learn at home, with tutors. Although I was pleased he agreed, the haste with which he did so was somewhat dispiriting, and only confirmed my own concerns.

Now Leander recalls my attention with a whisper, joining me in looking down to the square below. "I always thought it would feel different, to be a part of history."

"You've been a part of history all your life," I point out. "Have you got something to write with?"

He doesn't reply, but ducks away to the other side of the curtain, returning with the satchel that holds his family journal. From this he retrieves a stub of a pencil and hands it over.

I smooth out a piece of the newspaper and draw a grid for

a game of Trallian Fates, then set out a few of the brightly colored glass stones he bought from the magician's stall tonight in lieu of the candles I'm sure he'd prefer.

"I'm not really a part of history," he says belatedly, returning to our previous conversation. "Augusta is; Coria even, because it'll be her children who inherit. Me? Not even the spare. Once I've made this sacrifice—which, I might add, isn't exactly a skilled endeavor: all I had to do was sit on a boat, visit the temple of a goddess I get along with very well, and draw a knife across my palm, not what you'd call demanding, even though I did find a way to fail—once I've done that, what is there for me to do? Wait a quarter century for the next one?"

I nudge the last of the stones into place on the grid and nod for him to take the first turn. He pushes one forward and speaks again, keeping his voice low in deference to Selly.

"This is different, is what I'm saying. If we do this right, history will pivot. The three of us will prevent a war."

"That's true," I agree. "The hard work is done, though. We survived the attack and made it to Port Naranda. Tomorrow only the last and smallest part of our journey remains."

"I'll relax when it's over," he murmurs.

"Fair. Selly's asleep?"

"Yes. She stole the pillow." He doesn't sound put out.

"It's strange to think we might never have gotten to know her aboard the ship," I say, pushing my own stone forward. "If all had gone well."

"I hadn't thought of that." He makes his move, and I make mine before I speak again.

"You care for her."

That surprises him, and he glances up at me, uncharacteristically caught off guard.

"I'm not romantically inclined," I say, in answer to his unspoken question. "That doesn't mean my powers of observation fail me."

We pause our game, quiet as we watch a pair of green sisters cross the square below and disappear into the shadows. I can see a group of the city guard watching them as well—more than I'd have thought necessary at this time of night, but with arguments constantly breaking out between captains and officials, perhaps not. The whole place is on edge.

The guards watch the green sisters make their way across the square, dipping their heads respectfully when one of the two women glances over. I cannot imagine what her business might be at this hour, which only serves to underscore how little I know about the religion of Mellacea, and indeed about its god, Macean.

"You know," I say, watching as the women disappear around a corner, "the priests and priestesses at home might wear military uniforms, but they're nowhere near as threatening as the green sisters."

"They answer to a hierarchy," Leander replies. "Which answers to a goddess—a goddess of order, the Warrior and then the Sentinel. Who do the green sisters answer to? Their god is sleeping, and even when he was awake, Macean was the Gambler, the god of risk. Who knows what he might tell them to do if he were here?"

"I sincerely hope we never find out," I reply, to cover my mild surprise at this sort of insight from Leander. I do keep underestimating him. Then again, I'm starting to see he's put a great deal of effort into ensuring everyone does.

"Do you think Jude will say something?" the prince asks, shifting the subject and returning to the game before us. He told me about his encounter with our old classmate when he returned, more rattled by it than I'd have expected.

"Who would he tell? I think it's reasonable to hope that even if he is hostile, he'll take the night to consider how best to use the information. And by morning we'll be safe with the ambassador."

"I suppose so." He doesn't look much comforted. "I wish he hadn't gotten away."

"I agree."

"Is this what it's like?" he asks then. "In your history books?"

"What do you mean?"

"In the stories, the heroes are always full of purpose, sure of what to do. I'm just tired, and worrying about seventeen things at once."

I consider his question. "When one reads first-person accounts by historical figures—the original sources, I mean, rather than the formally documented versions—for the most part they're much as we are. Tired, hungry, afraid. But determined."

"I suppose that's true of the journal," he agrees. "My grandmother sounds a lot less stately than she was as an old lady."

"There you are, then." I nudge another stone into place, hemming in his pieces.

"You could have left," he says quietly. "When we landed, you could have taken that necklace and been on a boat to the

Bibliotek by now—at the latest, one would be departing tomorrow morning."

"I know," I say quietly. "Though if a war begins, even the Bibliotek will be affected, neutral or not. And think where it is located—there is no greater reminder in the world of the stakes at play than the Barren Reaches. Than the ruins of the city on which the Bibliotek is built."

He looks sideways at me, assessing. "That's true," he agrees eventually.

I have never cared what the prince thinks of me, but I nevertheless feel compelled to clarify my position. "Beyond that," I say, "it would have been the wrong thing to do."

"By Alinor? I didn't think you were patriotic."

"By you," I reply, moving another piece.

"Huh." He frowns at the board. "I usually win at Fates."

"You mean everyone else lets you win," I correct him. "You should have played with me sooner."

He's still studying me, brow furrowed as if I'm an especially complex text. The scrutiny isn't particularly comfortable, and I search for a change of subject. Before I find anything useful, though, he speaks.

"You're right. I should have. Keegan, I owe you an apology. More than one. It's not very comfortable to be standing here just now, thinking about how little I deserve your loyalty. I'm sorry I wasn't better to you at school. I'm sorry I didn't treat you with the respect you deserve."

I have no idea what to say. I've lost count of the times I've composed speeches in my head, late at night. Of the times I've excoriated my fellow students, tearing them to shreds for the many humiliations they heaped upon me. For the way they isolated me. For the way they left me questioning everything I did, never knowing the right thing to do or say.

But of all the responses I imagined, when I gave those speeches in my head, none of them ever felt like this.

I say nothing for so long that he bites his lip, and I realize he believes his apology has been rejected.

I must say something, whether it's polished or not.

"The reason I was leaving home for the Bibliotek was that I saw a chance to *choose* who I would be," I try. "Rather than existing as the person others wished to make me. The person I would like to be has changed over the years, though. I can't deny you the same opportunity I wish for myself."

He greets me with a familiar expression—it usually means someone is unpicking my sentences to make sense of them. "That was a lot of words, Keegan," he says eventually.

I try again. "I mean to say I'm more interested in who you are now, and who you'd like to be, than who you were."

He nods, and then nods again. And we both fall silent for a time, watching the activity of the square below once more.

"And I agree," I add, after that pause. "It's strange indeed to imagine we're in the middle of making history." I see a way to lessen the tension and decide to risk a joke—it's probably the tiredness that makes me so foolish. "I hope that when our parts are entered into the annals, they at least spell my name correctly in the history textbooks. People often leave out the final *e* in Wollesley, and it is tiresome in the extreme."

I am rewarded with a soft huff of laughter as he shakes his head.

It feels surprisingly good to make someone smile.

# SELLY

*The Diplomatic District*
*Port Naranda, Mellacea*

Braiding my hair like this seemed a lot easier when Hallie showed me how it was done, and my arms are aching, but I've mostly got it up into one of the coiled crowns they like to wear here. I dab the pink goo onto my lips, rub the tiniest smear into my cheeks, and slither carefully into my dress.

I tuck my little paper boat in against my heart, though it's bittersweet. It's the only thing in the world that's really my own, but it was made for me by the boy I don't want to leave, as a promise that he'll make sure I can. Soon Leander will find me a real boat, and he'll set his own course in another direction.

The dock square was rowdy this morning. It started with an argument about a confiscation from an Alinorish ship, the crew following the harbormaster all the way along the wharf, shouting protests that drew in others, and from there it whipped up into a hurricane before our eyes.

By the time the city guard arrived and bundled the Alinorish captain away and out of sight, we were more sure than ever neither Leander nor Keegan could risk being recognized at the embassy, especially if what the girl at the magician's stall said about the protests was true. So it'll be me, all by myself.

I lift the little scrap of mirror off the wall, tilting it to study myself, and the effect isn't half bad. I'm not sure I could wake Macean up from his nap, like Hallie said—in fact, let's hope I can't—but I could probably make him turn over in his sleep, from the right angle.

I run my fingers over the sparkling green beads, painstakingly sewn into a starburst pattern that begins at my waist and radiates out, catching the light with every movement. I've never owned anything like this. I never will again.

I buckle on my shoes, then step back out into our room, where Leander's lazing on the bed and Keegan's sitting in one of the two chairs, still glued to the newspaper.

Slowly he lowers it, peering at me over the top of the pages, considering my appearance, and nodding his approval of the disguise. Leander stretches and rolls over to see what Keegan's looking at, and doesn't bother to hide the way his gaze flicks over me, wordlessly renewing his offer from last night.

I could lean in, rest one knee on the edge of the bed, push him onto his back, and brush my lips against his. He'd let me.

But in a few hours he'll be gone, so instead I shuffle around the edge of the bed to the door.

"Stay out of trouble," I manage, and then I bolt.

\* \* \*

The farther I get from the docks, the less sure of myself I am.

Port Naranda is different from the places I know, uncomfortable in ways I didn't realize a place could be. There are little things I thought were everywhere—the scent of salt on the breeze, the sight of the sun overhead. They've always been the background heartbeat of my life, and suddenly they're gone. I'm off balance, and as I move deeper into the city, they fade away completely, and everything is strange.

The buildings here are so tall they form canyons for me to walk along, always in shadow. Once I was on a ship that went through a series of locks, and this place is drawing that memory up to the surface.

The locks themselves were set in a narrow river, with raised walls on each side. We would enter each new section and a gate would come up, holding us in place as the giant machinery worked, and water poured in to lift us up to a new level. Then we'd move forward into the next section and repeat the exercise. It was like going up a flight of stairs, one at a time.

I felt closed in, the ship trapped in place in a way she never was when she was sailing.

I feel the same way now.

The city of Kirkpool is all golden stone, but though Port Naranda is the dark gray stone of their mountains, the place is still more colorful. Bright signs adorn the buildings, calling everyone who passes them to buy everything from shoeshines to new hats, but nobody breaks their stride.

The men are in trousers and shirts, the women mostly in dresses that fall to their knees. They're like beautiful, colorful birds wearing jewel tones—deep reds, rich greens, the blue of the ocean when she's in a playful mood—and the colors flash from beneath their bulky coats. I'm pretending to be one of them, but I'm sure everyone can tell I'm not.

I remember my father telling me once that Mellacea didn't have much farmland—though I didn't understand how little until Leander explained the place was carved from solid rock by a Messenger of old. Da said the Mellaceans' greatest asset was between their ears, which is how they became the city of invention.

I'm used to the wide-open sea, to places I can point to on a map and cargo I can touch. Here I can't even glimpse the sun between the buildings to check the time or set my course.

All I know is the hour is marching on, and we need to be out of the inn by noon, because we don't have another twenty-five dollars for a second night.

I shiver in a cold breeze as I walk past what must be the largest church in the whole city. The pillars out the front are painted black, but unlike the god it worships, this place isn't sleeping.

Green sisters, some of them magicians, are lighting the torches that line the stairs leading up to the temple's grand entrance. Others stand ready to provide blessings, and the same passersby who ignore the offers of shoeshines and new hats most definitely *do* stop for the green sisters and their blessings. I pause a minute to watch, and the great front doors open, releasing the congregation from the morning service. They pour out in their hundreds, and I hurry on, pressing my hand against my heart before I realize what I'm doing— touching the place where my little paper boat is hidden inside my dress.

I'll be back on a ship soon enough, and far from the boy who made it.

The diplomatic district is set up in a wealthy part of town, the embassies in a large circle surrounding a public garden with trees, displays of flowers, and even an ornamental lake. It's a lot of land for a place that doesn't have much of it. At the far end of the garden, a high fence has been set up around a group of tents, and people in brightly colored clothes are entering through a gate. I think it's some sort of party.

Autos and horse-drawn wagons work their way along the road that divides the embassies from the park at their center, and I don't have to follow it for long before I see Alinor's flag flying outside a nearby building: sapphire blue, with a white spear across it.

Beneath it two uniformed members of the Queensguard stand at attention. I can only see them because they're at the top of the steps, though—facing them at ground level are dozens of people spread out along the path outside the embassy. The protesters.

The Queensguard stare straight ahead, as if they're unaware of the milling bodies in front of them—dressed in a mix of the dark colors and flat caps of workers and the bright colors of the wealthy. They're not a crowd you usually see mingling so freely, but they're all facing the one way now, and their shouts are rising to a roar.

Two men dart up the stairs, and one of the Queensguard steps across smartly to bar the embassy door, his face a storm cloud. Almost quicker than my eye can follow, he throws up an arm to block them and ducks as one swings a punch, and then the men are back down again, swallowed up by the crowd, as the Queensguard exchanges a long look with his fellow and steps back into position.

I've seen riots in port before, and in taverns and custom-houses. This one isn't ready to kick off yet, but I can feel the potential in the air, like the static before a storm. All it will take is one spark.

*Thank Barrica the boys aren't here.* It would be one thing to slip them past observers in distant windows, spying on behalf of Mellacea. It's another to imagine walking them through an angry crowd.

I'll go in by myself. I have Leander's codes, a list of four words that will identify my message as having come from him. They belong exclusively to Leander and his two sisters, Queen Augusta and Princess Coria. Any message I deliver with those words in the right sequence will guarantee me a hearing. But how am I going to do it?

I can't exactly push through the crowd and demand to get inside so I can deliver a secret message only the ambassador will understand. The guards at the front won't know the code—if everyone did, what use would it be?

But I can't stay out here forever, either.

As I'm standing there, sizing up the protesters, the doors to the embassy open and several more Queensguard emerge in their sapphire-blue uniforms.

They're escorting a figure in their midst, and when the crowd sees her, their shouts rise. I nearly mistake her for another of the guard—she's in blue as well—but then I get a proper look at her.

She's not wearing a uniform, but a sparkling, shimmering, and utterly glamorous dress. Nice to look at, no good for fighting in. The Queensguard hustle her down the stairs, pushing aside the crowd, and into a waiting auto.

Wait, is that the ambassador? Oh, spirits save me, it must be, the way they're surrounding her.

The auto's door slams, and as the sleek black vehicle pulls out into traffic, before I can even think about it, I'm running.

*Seven hells. I should have stuck with my boots and trousers.*

But fear is pushing up in my chest now as the auto accelerates into traffic.

How far can I possibly follow them, and who's noticing me bolting after the ambassador? What am I going to do if she gets away from me?

My breath's coming hard in seconds—I'm still so tired—but as panic threatens to overtake me, the auto begins to slow about a third of the way around the circle.

When it stops, I halt at a distance, crossing the street to shelter in the mouth of an alleyway and watch. The ambassador emerges from the auto, sleek black hair gleaming in the sun, the beads on her dress catching the light, and joins the group streaming toward the temporary fencing and the tents I saw earlier. She was avoiding the protesters, that's all. She heads in through the gates, pausing to offer what I assume is an invitation for inspection.

Her auto peels away once she's safely inside the party, and I'm left staring after her.

The fate of the world is in my hands, and the ambassador I need to help me save it is at a *garden party* on the other side of a fence.

She might as well be in Holbard with my father, on the far side of the winter storms, for all the good this does me.

But I don't have time to think like that.

I slow my breathing and try to still my mind like Leander taught me during my catastrophic attempt to communicate with the spirits. I need to think.

*Give them one big thing to notice, and they won't notice anything else,* he said. I don't think that's the right advice here. I can make myself as distinctive as I like—if I don't have an invitation, I'm not getting inside.

What else did he say? I close my eyes and reach for his voice. *Nobody here is expecting to see me. People rarely see things they don't expect.*

My lashes lift, and I allow myself a very small smile.

*Got it.*

It takes only a couple of minutes to confirm I was right about the fence. It's more about keeping casual intruders out than stopping someone who's really determined.

I trace a path through the trees, looking for the least observed part of the barrier. It runs through the ornamental lake at one point, and if I could afford to pull this off while I was soaking wet, I'd swim underneath.

Eventually I find my spot, though, and pause to shimmy my dress up to mid-thigh so I can move more easily. I bend my knees and jump up to grab at the lowest branches of the tree that sits against the fence, hidden from inside view by the white tent they're keeping the food in.

I heave and pull myself up as easy as if I were climbing the rigging, the leaves shimmering around me. I wish I knew how to tell the spirits to hold them still, but I'm not volunteering for another disaster. Instead I edge out along the branch, telling myself it's just the crosstrees. It's not the distance to the ground that's making me so nervous, though. It's what I'll find when I get there.

I drop into the gap between the fence and the tent and pull my dress down into place, waiting for my heart to stop hammering. It doesn't, so I walk out anyway, like I own the place, and nearly collide with a waiter carrying a full tray of champagne. *Really, people? At this hour of the morning?*

I take one when he offers, though, and then a second. There's less chance someone will talk to me if I look like I'm on my way to deliver a drink to a friend. *Nobody has any reason to suspect you shouldn't be here,* I remind myself. *They won't see what they don't expect, and they don't expect a gatecrasher. This is what Leander would do. Hopefully. Or he'd be having a heart attack right now—who knows?*

The guests are milling around like seagulls looking for the best snack—for them I'm sure it's gossip, but for me it's the trays with little pieces of food I'm watching go past, regretting the glasses in my hands.

Everyone here is watching everyone else, trying to figure out who they are and what they're worth. I need to move quickly before I become someone's mystery.

There are two green sisters here too, and everyone swirls around them like water around rocks, giving way as they move through the party.

They're both dressed in the same simple green robes as the sisters at the temples, but I don't think they're here because they're regular sisters. The one I'm guessing is senior has sleek black hair and moves so smoothly, it's almost like she's on wheels. As I watch, she waves away the offer of a drink, and inclines her head in greeting to a group of women who have approached her.

The women are dressed like a jewelry box, all reds and blues and greens and golds, bangles jangling on their wrists, ribbons woven through their braids. But every one of them lifts her hands to press her fingertips to her forehead, covering her eyes as she greets the two sisters.

My heart skips when I spot the ambassador up ahead, talking to two fancy ladies. She looks relaxed, her head thrown back in an easy laugh. *How can she do that when we're nearly at war?*

She's a tall woman with an easy smile and long black hair braided up the same way as mine—I guess Hallie knows her fashion. I casually work my way in closer to the trio, debating the best way to get her attention. I'm not going to catch her by herself—that much is clear. There's an assistant standing nearby, a brunette with a friendly, open face and dimples when she smiles. Whenever one of the ambassador's companions leaves, the girl feeds in another to take their place, skillfully managing the flow of traffic.

The sun edges its way across the sky as I wait, and my champagne warms, and I know I'm on a countdown until someone notices me. I keep hoping I'll catch the ambassador's eye, though I don't think I know the facial expression for *I have a top-secret message to deliver, come this way.*

I can feel what time I have left slipping between my fingers, though, so when a man in a finely cut suit leaves her, and she's down to only one companion, I shove my way into the gap, doing my best imitation of a seagull.

"Excuse me," begins the assistant, starting forward. "I—"

"Ambassador, I brought you that drink," I say, ignoring the girl completely and pasting on a beaming smile I'm pretty sure looks more like I'm baring my teeth. I bare my teeth at the ambassador's one remaining companion for good measure. "Do let me steal her for a moment."

"I'm afraid—" begins the assistant again, but the ambassador holds up a hand to stay her.

My throat's tight, my heart's pounding, as she lets me shove a glass of champagne into her hand and take her by the elbow to half lead, half push her away.

She really is a diplomat—she barely even looks annoyed, and she doesn't throw her drink at me, which would be my move in her position. Instead, she puts on a polite expression.

"I'm afraid I don't—"

I cut her off. "My code words are *archer, eternity, diamond,* and *salt.*"

She freezes in place. But this woman is *good,* because it's only for a heartbeat, and then she lifts her glass to take a sip of warm champagne. "Those have been superseded," she says quietly.

"They've what now?"

One brow lifts. "Those words," she says, "are out of date."

I feel like the ground is giving way beneath me. *No.* I did not survive an attack, a shipwreck, and an impossible trip to an enemy port with no map, wrangle a spoiled prince, and deal with high fashion for it all to end in sight of help.

Meeting her eyes, I lean in close and lower my voice. "The person who gave them to me was supposed to be at sea for a while, Ambassador. *He* must have missed the update."

I see my words hit her, and she takes another swig of champagne. "Supposed to?" she repeats.

"That's right, ma'am. Now listen close."

She's quiet, and the noise around us fades away as she fixes her attention on me. "I'm listening."

"Good. Because I have had the worst few days of my *life,* and I know something that could start a war. So why don't you come over by the fence, where nobody can hear, and I'll tell you all about it."

# LEANDER

*The Salthouse Inn*
*Port Naranda, Mellacea*

I'm like an animal in a trap, about to gnaw my own leg off to escape our room and go after her.

I've been pacing the same path across the worn carpet, trailing one hand over faded wallpaper, in motion every second since Selly left. There's barely space to move past the end of the bed, but I've made it an art form by now.

Keegan's pulled the bedcovers neatly back into place and sits on top of them, reading my family journal. I saw no harm in letting him. After all, when I write my own entries, he'll be a part of them. He's been through the newspaper a dozen times, and he'll never have the chance to hold a historical document like this one again.

I pause by the window. We're keeping the curtains drawn, but I can see a sliver of the busy square below through the gap. It's strange watching sailors, traders, and city folk go about their day as the morning wears on, with no idea that in a room up-stairs, history is being made. The world is changing.

I should be writing in the journal—my ancestors used it to record their journeys to and from the Isles, and there's never been one like mine, so it feels like I should get something down. But where would I start?

With the boy who lies on the bed, reading the very journal that's troubling me? With a description of this room? A list of those who've died so far? My musings on Jude, somewhere out there in the city with my name on his lips, for reasons I don't understand?

With Selly?

I wouldn't know what to write about her, apart from that I'm way past ready for her to walk through the door.

Maybe that wrapping my arm around her as we checked in here felt different from the times I've done it before, with others.

Maybe that I didn't want to let go of her hand at the mar-ket, almost *couldn't*. Maybe that she looked spectacular on the dance floor, and even better on the deck of her ship.

Maybe that ever since she said *I don't know who you are, but I don't have time for you* at the docks in Kirkpool, and hid among the flowers with me on top of a stack of crates, I've been wait-ing to see what she'd do next?

I've always known love wasn't in the cards for me, and I've never minded—both my sisters are happily married to political matches. But it has meant I've never really wondered about anyone before. It was the safest way to avoid disappointment. And I'm not foolish enough to think I'm in love with a girl I've only known a few days.

But I am wondering if, when I let the current carry me along all these years, I was missing out on something.

And if it's too late now to find it.

"Half an hour," I say again, swinging around to face Keegan. "Half an hour to walk to the diplomatic district. Even if she got lost, half an hour is generous. She should have watched the front door for ten minutes, then presented herself. If she said she had an urgent message for the ambassador, she'd get in quick, so ten more minutes to talk, and then the walk back. She's way overdue."

Keegan doesn't look up from the journal as he replies, "I can think of several schoolmasters who would be deeply surprised to hear you have such a firm grasp of the passage of time, you know."

I snort, but he draws a tense smile from me, and I finally stop to lean against the wall and tip my head back to study the water-stained ceiling.

I stretch my awareness out to register the comforting presence of the nearby spirits. The needle-sharp fire spirits dance and zip around the flames that are consuming the last of our coal, moving with all the urgency of their kind. They're quick to appear when a flame is lit, and just as quick to vanish when it's doused. It's always seemed to me they want to make the most of the time in between.

The air spirits waft gently on the warm air, more sedate. I still remember what I told Selly when she reached out for them. *You ask. You don't tell.* But she told. In the few days I've known her, I've had time to figure out that at least when she's at sea, giving instructions comes easier to our sailor than taking them.

Why did they ignore her all these years, though? Why do they treat her differently?

The mystery fascinates me, nags at me, and I desperately want to solve it. How can I do that if she's gone?

*Perhaps,* says a little voice in the back of my mind, *it could be an excuse to ask her to stay.*

*Perhaps she'd say no,* I reply, wishing I was braver.

The spirits can't do much for either of us now, though, however nicely I ask. I've been praying to Barrica for guidance and aid all morning, but solid wisdom is yet to arrive. I don't know if she hears me at all—usually I have much more of a sense of her presence, but in Macean's lands she's quiet. Or perhaps my appeals are working in Selly's favor somewhere out there. You never know.

For now, I brush my mind against the spirits and draw them around me like the comfort of a blanket. Getting to know them is a habit, wherever I am. There's a ripple in the air spirits out in the hallway, but before I can speak, there's a knock at the door. Keegan and I both freeze in place.

Then Selly's voice rings out in the hallway, singsong and cheerful. "Handsome, I'm home!"

I shut my eyes, melting into relief. Keegan closes my family journal and sits up straight, slipping off the bed to open the door and admit her. She hurries in and closes the door behind her—she's carrying a paper bag, and it smells sugary and delicious.

I only realize I'm holding my breath when slowly her lips curve to a smile, and I let it out. "You saw her?"

"I saw her," she replies. "It worked. She'll be here in half an hour, ready to eyeball you herself to be sure I'm not telling her some wild tale from the deep. Then she'll take you to the embassy in an auto and keep you there until she's arranged a boat for tonight." Her grin broadens, and she holds up her bag. "And she gave me money for snacks. I got this fried dough covered in sugar, and you've *got* to try it. I'm going to get out of this dress and back into something comfortable, but make sure you leave me some."

Keegan reaches forward to take it from her, but I simply stare at her, held in place by the magnitude of what's just happened. And then I can't help it—I'm closing the gap between us in two quick steps and folding her up in my arms.

She doesn't fight it—she wraps hers around my waist, burrows in against me, squeezes with all the feeling she has no words for.

"Selly, thank you," I whisper. A weight lifts off my chest, and tears prick at the backs of my eyes. I'm so light, I could float up to the ceiling.

Half an hour more. The ambassador will come. And this will be over.

I'll find a way to see Selly again. I'll figure it out. I have to. But we're safe.

*We did it.*

# LASKIA

*Skyline Diner*
*Port Naranda, Mellacea*

I'm perched on a stool at one end of the diner's polished wooden counter, my shoulder up against the wall. I have my curls tucked under a newsie's flat cap and my head down, but with Dasriel on the stool beside me, I'm shielded from view anyway.

There's always an itch between my shoulder blades when I'm not on Ruby's turf, and every time the bell on the door jangles, so do my nerves.

"We're going to be late," I mutter, drumming my fingers on the countertop, my nails landing in quick succession.

*Tap-tap-tap-tap.*

*Tap-tap-tap-tap.*

Dasriel shrugs, working his way methodically through his third slice of pie. He gathers up the crumbs meticulously, with far more care than his huge frame suggests he could manage, the tendons on the back of his hand flexing under his green magician's marks.

"How can you just sit there?" I hiss, keeping my voice low.

He shrugs again. "Starving myself won't hurry her up. She's coming or she's not."

I clench my teeth so hard I feel it in my temples, but he's unaffected.

I know why he stays with me. Ruby assigned him as my muscle years ago, when I first started working jobs for her. Now everyone sees us as a pair. Dasriel doesn't particularly like me, but his reputation is linked to mine, and he knows it. He couldn't leave even if he wanted to.

I stop my foot from tapping against the stool's footrest and stare at my own untouched slice of pie, trying to tamp down the anger coursing through me.

How dare they. How *dare* they?

I brought them the idea. I got my hands dirty—no, not dirty, bloodied, *soaked* in blood—and then Ruby and Beris think they can dismiss me?

"She's not coming," I mutter, pushing my plate toward Dasriel, who stacks it atop his own empty one and starts in on my pie.

"Perhaps she is," he says, unhurried.

"She's not. I'm going to church."

I need to pray, let the familiar chants calm me enough that I can think clearly. Sister Beris might have betrayed me, but my god knows what it's like to be denied his due, and though he sleeps, I'll take my frustrations to him and—

I slide off the stool. "Let's go."

"Not yet," says Dasriel mildly, nodding at our reflections in the mirror behind the counter.

I follow his gaze and watch as his eyes flick across the room—and there she is, standing by the door, glancing around the diner with something wild in her eyes.

The ambassador's assistant.

She spots Dasriel and comes running toward us, pushing past a pair of diners on their way out, past a courting couple. She's in a pale blue dress with a hem that fishtails down her calves, her curls held back in a jeweled headband. She looks like she's come straight from a party.

I don't bother with small talk. "What is it? What do you have?"

She shakes her head, and I see she's panting—she's run here. And she looks like she wants to be sick. It's an expression I'm familiar with—she doesn't want to talk, but she got in too deep with me long ago, and so she simply spits it out.

"You won't believe," she says quietly, "what I just heard."

# KEEGAN

◆

*The Salthouse Inn*
*Port Naranda, Mellacea*

T he ambassador is punctual, which I suppose is to be expected.

A sleek, black, locally made auto edges its way into the square, slowly nudging past stacks of crates and through the milling crowd. There are more people than there were yesterday.

We can see one of the Queensguard behind the wheel, but the auto stops about halfway across the square, held up by a Kethosi captain who's in the middle of a vehement argument with a group of customs officials—they appear to be confiscating her cargo, which is stacked haphazardly behind her, protected by a ragtag crew who look ready to defend it with violence if necessary.

When it becomes clear the auto is going nowhere fast, another of the guard jumps out and opens the door for the ambassador, looking around at the crowd nervously.

The ambassador shows no such hesitation, and turns unerringly for our inn, walking toward it alone.

"I'll go," I say, and I hurry out the door and down the stairs, only just resisting the urge to break into a run.

I reach the ground-floor entrance as she does, and when she looks up, her gaze lingers on me. I didn't think she'd recognize me, but I do bear a close resemblance to my father, and I assume she registers it, because she nods a greeting and walks past the gaping innkeeper to join me.

Possibly the innkeeper is wondering who I am, as I just came down the stairs without ever having gone up them, but the ambassador is very imposing, and it's also possible our hostess hasn't noticed me at all.

The ambassador hasn't bothered changing since the party Selly described—she's in a sapphire-blue dress and one of the oversized coats that are in fashion here. It's all perfectly tailored, but nothing about her fits with our surroundings. It's like the moment in a dream when some strange detail tells you that you're dreaming. The sparkle of her dress against the rough timber of the walls, the jeweled pins in her hair—just one of them would cover a week's stay here.

For all her strangeness, though, she's here and she's real. When she reaches me, we turn wordlessly together to make our way up the stairs.

"You look like a Wollesley to me," she says quietly.

"Yes, my lady."

"You must have a story to tell," she murmurs.

"*Yes,* my lady."

"Well done," she says simply.

And I'd like to pretend the words mean nothing, but the

truth is, they ease something inside my chest. We've done the impossible. She must have believed Selly's story, or she wouldn't be here alone.

But she still stops short when she opens the door to our room to find Leander standing there by the window, as if some part of her didn't actually expect to see him here. Slowly she walks in with a polite nod for Selly, who's standing beside him, back in her shirt and trousers, those fingerless gloves of hers dry again and free of salt, once more hiding the backs of her hands. Her hair is braided up into a crown, but that's the only trace of her morning's adventure.

I close the door behind the two of us.

"Your Highness," the ambassador says quietly, staring at him.

"Lady Lanham," Leander says, and I suppose I've gotten to know him better than I thought over the last few days, because I see the flicker. For an instant his gaze locks onto her, as if in shock, and my whole body tenses—can we trust her? Then he's easing into one of his signature grins, like they've run into each other at a party. "I didn't know you'd been posted here."

Selly and I exchange a glance. Do we need to be ready for something?

But as if my mind has been running a quick and frantic search through my mental catalog, it suddenly tosses up the reference card I need, and my gut twists. We went to school with Penrie Lanham—I remember she won the athletics medal every year. She was tall and long-legged, with brown eyes and sleek black hair like the ambassador, always laughing about something.

And she was one of Leander's crowd—which means she was almost certainly on the progress fleet.

Judging by the resemblance that's now obvious to me, Lady Lanham must be a close relative. Leander says nothing, though. This isn't the place for her to learn that news. I glance back to Selly and shake my head a fraction, and she eases back from her readiness.

Lady Lanham doesn't seem to notice anything out of place, and she raises one brow, taking us in. "This is a story I am *very* much looking forward to hearing," she says.

"You'll barely believe it," Leander replies, "but I'm looking forward to convincing you it's true."

"I'm told," she says, with a nod to Selly, "that the Mellaceans believe they've killed you, Your Highness. That puts us in a very dangerous position. I told Her Majesty in my latest report that we're doing our best, but tensions run higher here in Port Naranda every day—since I sent my last report, the situation has become even more serious."

"We were warned more than once not to go too far from the docks," he agrees.

"It's more than that. I've already sent some of my junior staff home. The first councilor attended church yesterday, with most of Mellacea's leaders. The green sisters grow stronger every day, and they preach that Macean must be awakened from his slumber and strengthened by faith so he can claim what Mellacea is owed. By which they mean the territory of other countries."

"They've preached that for centuries," Leander points out.

"True. But now their congregation is listening. I cannot

stress enough the change in their position. The green sisters are to be taken *very* seriously, and their agenda influences—or dare I say, controls—that of the Mellacean government in most significant respects."

"And they want a war," he murmurs.

"Just so. If news of your death were to become public—with the implication that the sacrifice has not been made, and Barrica is vulnerable—I have no doubt the Mellaceans will be emboldened to the point of attack. They would see it as the final step in resuming the war they've been waiting on for so long."

A sick feeling takes root in my stomach. "And Her Majesty would respond to the insult of her brother's apparent murder, starting a war herself, if they didn't attack first. She will believe we have secretly strengthened Barrica by now."

Lady Lanham's gaze moves across to Leander. "I am told you have not yet made the sacrifice, Your Highness. Perhaps I should send you straight to the Isles."

"I've got a map," Leander says, glancing at the bag that contains his family journal. "Sort of, anyway."

"But the trip there would be a few days in a fast ship, and then longer to Alinor," I point out. "All with no way to prove Leander's alive if the news comes out."

"Agreed," she says, frowning.

"And," says Selly, "you could never get a ride out of Port Naranda for the Isles without it being noticed. There's nothing else in that direction, so you'd have to sail a decoy course until you were out of sight. That adds even more time."

The ambassador abandons the idea with a wave of her hand. "Does it have to be you making the sacrifice, Your

Highness? I could send word ahead of you, ask your sister to dispatch someone else."

Leander grimaces, shaking his head. "It doesn't *have* to be me. But if it's not an immediate member of the royal family, the sacrifice would have to be . . . much larger than the one I'll make."

"Why so?"

"Well, if it's me, the queen's own brother, and the strongest magician our family has to lose, that's a real risk. All I need do is make the trip, cut my palm, spill a little blood, and the work is done. If we pick a distant relation who didn't really have anything on that month, who it wouldn't inconvenience the kingdom to lose, it's not much of a sacrifice, is it? So they'd have to make up the balance by offering something far worse. I'm worth enough that I can do less, if you follow."

She nods, puffing out her cheeks, then releasing a breath slowly. "All right, does it have to be the temple at the Isles?"

"Yes," he replies firmly. "Nowhere else will do—that much we know. You've heard that prayers are amplified when they're made in temples? Well, this is the *first* temple. There's no more powerful place. When the gods were with us, when their Messengers walked among us, it was different. Now we need a way to make our voices louder."

"All right," she says. "In that case, our best move is to get you home as quickly as we can."

"Agreed," Leander replies. "Demonstrate to the world I'm alive, and give no sign I'm even considering the sacrifice. Then we can make a surreptitious trip to the Isles, well equipped and well guarded."

Except that surreptitious trip was more or less the plan the first time. Technically, though, it didn't fail. It was only our bad luck in being spotted that brought us undone. There's no reason to think it won't work next time.

Lady Lanham inclines her head, and surprises me with a small smile. "I admit, this warms my diplomatic heart," she says. "Can you imagine it? The headlines, the condolences, and then there you are, healthy as ever. They can hardly say, *But we thought we killed you.*"

That smile of hers is painful to see because the part of the story she doesn't know yet is what it cost us—cost *her*—to make it here safely.

"No doubt their intention was to deny all accusations of involvement," she says.

"And so they could," Leander replies. "It wasn't the Mellacean navy that tried to take us out. They were . . . private interests, I suppose."

Her brows lift. "Describe them?"

Leander nods. "Civilians, but tough. I wouldn't be surprised if plenty of them were ex-military, or career mercenaries. I saw a green sister on the boat that attacked us, but she didn't board ours. The boarding party was led by a girl, couldn't have been older than us. Slim build, skin a deeper brown than mine, dark curly hair cut short. She wore men's clothes like she was used to them. Sharp, confident, absolutely no hesitation about killing." He looks across to me. "You got the closest look at her—anything else?"

I consider the question. "Her clothes looked well made. And she was wearing a piece of—jewelry, I suppose you'd call it. A pin at her lapel, with a small red stone I took to be a ruby.

I remember noticing it because it was made of gold, and I thought it would match the chain she was taking from me."

Out the corner of my eye, I see Selly go very still, but the ambassador's the one who speaks, grimacing. "That's the marker of the most influential crime boss in the city," she replies. "Her name is Ruby, and the pins are worn by all her people. The girl you're describing is her sister, Laskia. She's been working her way up in the organization, but this represents a leap. I'm not surprised she was focused on success."

"And she clearly didn't expect to leave any survivors, if she wore something that marked her identity," Leander supposes.

Selly makes a sound, and when I look at her again, she's white underneath her freckles. "Leander," she murmurs. "The boy we met last night—Jude—he had one of those pins. I thought at the time it looked familiar, but I couldn't place it."

"When was this?" the ambassador asks, crisp. "Were you recognized?"

"I was," Leander says slowly. "But even if he works for them, he'd have to be in on the plan to have a reason to mention seeing me."

"Surely he'd report seeing someone so important," I say, willing it not to be true. "Before, we thought he was alone. But if there's a way he could win favor with his employers . . ."

"I don't know," Leander says slowly. "We were friends at school."

"I don't think you're friends now," Selly says quietly. "I'm sorry."

"Then our plan to get moving is still the best choice," Lady Lanham says. "I'll bring the auto across the square to the front door. We'll take you straight to the embassy. You'll be safe inside while I make preparations, and tonight the Queensguard will escort you to a diplomatic ship and straight home. Tensions may be high, but the Mellaceans won't attack a ship flying the embassy's flag. Maybe one day soon they'll be game, but not yet."

"Can you arrange passage for my friends as well?" Leander asks, nodding first to me, then to Selly—his gaze locks with hers, and neither of them seems willing to look away.

"Of course, Your Highness." The ambassador takes this in without even a flicker of reaction, though the way they're gazing at each other must present a number of questions for her. "Wherever they wish to go."

How strange to think that by evening I'll have left Port Naranda, a place I should never have been. It's peculiar, to step so abruptly out of the story I've been living, and to part ways before our task is complete.

Would it be odd to write to Leander later? After all this has been resolved?

I wonder where Selly will go—it makes sense for her to return to Alinor, the home of her father's fleet, to seek another of his ships.

Suddenly a roar rises from the square below, angry voices audible above the crowd—dozens of them, by the sound of it.

Selly's gaze snaps away from Leander's, and she grabs him by the arm, pulling him away from the window. He lets her move him but cranes his neck to see past her. I hurry around the foot of the bed to get a look outside.

There's a brawl erupting below, a new group of sailors surging toward an advancing wall of city guards, and though their shouts are unintelligible, several of them are pointing back toward a ship flying the Alinorish flag.

They swirl around the ambassador's auto, the blue-clad Queensguard pushing them away—two combatants sprawl across the hood of the auto and are quickly hauled off and shoved back into the fray.

"We should go," I say, looking back over my shoulder.

"Agreed," says the ambassador. "I'll have the auto brought close now. Be ready." She nods politely to Leander. "Your Highness."

She takes her leave, and I stay by the window, watching the square, watching the fight begin to break up. As quickly as it began—however it began—it's over.

"You know, Keegan," Leander says quietly, "I think you'll be at the Bibliotek in time for your first classes after all."

At his words, a light, giddy feeling starts to spread inside my chest. It moves slowly at first, and then it begins to curl out and unfurl, like sunshine chasing away the fog. It reminds me of the first day of the school holidays—all the worries and trials of the term suddenly gone, free time with nothing but long walks and my library stretching out before me. It's strange to step out of this story, yes, but I'm going to the one place I've always dreamed of. And I'm leaving the end of our tale in safe hands. Someone else is taking over—someone with the resources to keep the prince safe.

Below, the ambassador emerges from the inn and strides toward the auto, unbothered by the crowd.

"We should stay close to the prince, Selly," I say, a part of me noting I've stopped using his name—as though I'm already preparing for the distance that was once between us to return. "As soon as the auto's out in front, we should walk out together—I'll go first, then him, and you come after. The crowd is still tense, but the Queensguard will be watching us. Don't stop, and climb straight into the auto, then move across to make room for us."

Through the window, I see Lady Lanham reach the auto and climb into the front beside the surprised driver. After a moment it creeps toward the inn.

"I've never been in an auto," Selly says, her voice a little strained. "They're so—"

Her words are cut off as fire blossoms in the square below, a huge ball of it growing, rising up like a bright orange gash in the air.

An instant later, a *boom* rattles our windows, and the screaming begins.

I'm frozen, staring, trying to understand what I'm seeing.

And then I do.

The ambassador's auto just exploded into flames.

# LEANDER

◆

*The Salthouse Inn*
*Port Naranda, Mellacea*

I scramble across to stare out the window, and someone cries
out in horror—I think it's me. An explosion is ballooning
upward, and once the paralyzing shock begins to fade from
the surrounding crowds, the square empties as traders, sailors,
guards, and townsfolk run for safety.

Their shouts float up to us on the wind as autos are abandoned, a wagon overturns. The sailors run toward their boats
and the sea, everyone else for the shelter of buildings or the
streets leading away from the square. There's a dark smear of
blood across the cobblestones.

Selly's beside me, lips parted with horror. Then she snaps
into action. "Grab everything," she raps out, whirling away
from the window. "We're going."

"You think it was for us?" I ask, blinking at her. "But how
could anyone have known we were going to be in the auto?"

"She went back to the embassy. Who knows what she said, what was overheard."

I look down at the square once more, at the fireball that's turning into a bonfire—I can feel the spirits whirling around it, feel the intensity of the fire. I can sense the origin point through them, a point of heat so intense it must have been—

"It was a bomb," I gasp.

Did it go off early? Were we supposed to be inside?

Suddenly I'm struck by the image of those two brawlers rolling across the hood of the auto—perhaps they weren't fighting, but working together to get to their target.

The flames lick higher, and I know with a certainty like tight bands around my ribs that nobody's alive in there. Not the ambassador, not the Queensguard.

Selly's already grabbing at the clothes we have hanging up to dry, stuffing them into the bag we brought back from our shopping expedition.

"We have to go *right now*. Maybe we were supposed to be in the auto when it went off. Maybe they don't know about us yet. But she just walked in and out of this place in full sight of whoever set off that bomb. So this is where they're coming next."

Keegan and I are frozen in place, simply staring at her. Then we snap into action, grabbing for our meager belongings. I shove my hand into my pocket, checking for the glass tokens I bought from the magician's stall, sifting them through my fingers in readiness.

Selly edges the door ajar, peering out into the hallway. It must be empty, for she pushes it open, ushering us out urgently.

"Fire escape," she says quietly. "Go, go."

Keegan runs out, but Selly holds me in place with a hand on my chest as he throws open the door to the fire escape, looking down into the alleyway.

"Nobody's here," he calls back, scrambling over the guardrail and starting to climb.

"Now," Selly whispers, shoving me after him.

"Leave the door open," I tell her, and she nods, standing guard as I follow Keegan, readying myself to climb down the ladder.

As I get my foot onto the first rung, her head snaps up. Someone's running along the hallway toward her, and I catch a glimpse of the girl from the ship—Laskia—her lips drawn back in a snarl.

There's a huge man behind her, and I don't need to see his magician's marks to know what he is: the spirits are in a frenzy, whirling around him as he pulls a box of matches from his pocket.

I grab the glass pieces from my own pocket, flinging them into the hallway as my sacrifice, and they vanish as I reach for the spirits.

I find them, needle sharp in the embers of our fireplace, riding the whirling winds set in motion by our movements, and I pour my frustration, my anger, and my fear into my mental touch as I reach out to embrace them. *Help me.*

# SELLY

*The Salthouse Inn*
*Port Naranda, Mellacea*

A column of fire comes roaring out the open door of our room, arcing around the corner to hurtle down the hallway toward our pursuers.

I drop to a crouch as a wall of scorching hot air hits me, scrambling toward the fire escape, Leander beside me.

Behind Laskia, the huge magician lifts his hand and twists it in a grasping motion, making a fist. His face is like a storm front, and he's moving toward us with the same promise of destruction.

The fire begins to slow, to blossom outward, and to roll back toward us.

"Leander, go!" It's as though everything around me freezes, the flames suspended in the air, my breath caught in my throat.

And then I see them—the gleaming forms of the air spirits whirling around the flames, driving the hot wind that was buffeting me, shaping the fire itself as it turns inexorably toward us.

"Stop it!" someone screams, and it's me, *I'm* screaming, high and hoarse. "Get back!"

I dig frantically in my pocket, pull out the three glass magician's stones Leander gave me at the market, and hurl them into the hallway just as he did.

They bounce once, twice . . . and then they vanish as the spirits claim my sacrifice.

The column of flame twists, gouts splitting off in every direction as the air spirits wheel furiously around the flames, rebelling against my orders, sparks flying.

A fireball roars toward the huge magician, he screams— then the flame's coming for *us,* like an arm made of fire reaching down the hallway, ready to press us to the ground, to smother us and burn us alive, the air spirits freewheeling around it.

Leander shouts in alarm, throwing himself over the railing, and I'm a heartbeat behind him, vaulting over the rail and half falling to the ground.

Keegan's hands are waiting to steady us as we land, and we snap into motion, sprinting along the alley.

My vision's still filled with stars, with the afterimages of flames, and my heart's thumping with the sick memory of Leander throwing himself clear of that flame as it screamed toward him, driven by my furious air spirits.

I nearly did Laskia's work for her.

I nearly killed him.

# LEANDER

*The Docks District*
*Port Naranda, Mellacea*

I barely know who's leading and who's following as we pound around the first few corners—I'm reaching back toward the inn, trying to calm the spirits enough to stop them from burning the whole place down, but sensing them less and less as the distance between us grows.

There's a roar from the direction of the square, and those fleeing the action are pouring down the side streets—we're buffeted by the current of humanity pushing us along, and I grab desperately for Selly's hand as a burly trader barges past us, nearly sweeping her off her feet. Ahead, Keegan ducks under a sailor's arm and swings around toward an alleyway.

Selly and I push our way after him, and in the sudden silence we slow, to move more quietly, more cautiously. Now we're glancing behind, taking each turn carefully.

After a couple of minutes, Selly pulls me into a tiny enclosed courtyard at the back of a bar, the building silent at this time of day. The tight space is shadowed by taller buildings, the air crisp and cold, the cobblestones slimy beneath my feet. Crates of foul-smelling rubbish are stacked along the walls, but it has a gate, and there are no signs of life.

Keegan pulls the gate closed behind us, and the three of us crouch, our breath coming hard from the run—from the fear. We find ourselves staring at each other, trying to make ourselves believe this is really happening. That Laskia has found us again. That our safety has been snatched away.

Selly has tears running down her cheeks, and I reach for her hand, the leather of her glove rough against my skin. "Is it burning down?" she gasps—it's nearly a sob—and I have to scramble to understand what she means.

"The inn? I don't know. The fireball just exploded, I don't . . ." My voice fades away at the look on her face.

"I saw the air spirits," she whispers. "I tried to tell them to keep us safe, but they— I couldn't control them."

I can't help it—I glance at the backs of her hands, where her thick, unformed magician's marks are hidden beneath her gloves.

She follows my gaze, then squeezes her eyes tight shut.

"You did your best," I murmur. "We're alive."

"I should have run. I nearly killed you. I shouldn't have—" She breaks off, and I ache for a way to comfort her. I don't know what to say, though. We're both quiet, helpless.

"I nearly killed you," she whispers again.

"You didn't."

"Which is fortunate," Keegan says quietly. "But we must decide what to do next. We can't go to the embassy. There's too great a chance someone there leaked word of where we were hiding, and that bomb in the auto was intended for us. One of us in particular."

His words yank me back to the present—we have far, far bigger problems than a fire. "It was Laskia," Selly whispers. "You were already down in the alley, but it was Laskia, with a fire magician. And she won't stop hunting us. Think what she's done already."

"Keegan's right." I'm sick with the knowledge, but it's true—we can't trust the embassy. I speak slowly, as the reality of the situation sinks in. "Laskia assassinated our ambassador. That means every way forward, except for one, was just closed off."

"What do you mean?" Selly murmurs, rubbing her cheeks with her free hand, scrubbing the tears away. Packing her feelings away in a box, like she's so good at doing.

I let out a shaky breath, and when I speak, my voice is hoarse. "The only way this ends now is war. And soon."

Keegan's white as a ghost, eyes unseeing as he stares at the crates of rubbish hiding us. Trying, I'm sure, to find a way out of this, to find any answer other than the one I've given. And coming up with nothing.

Selly's clinging to my hand like it's a lifeline, and I'm trying to fight the drum beating inside my head, drowning out everything else. *This can't be happening. This can't be happening.*

We've failed. My friends from school are dead. Her crew is dead. The ambassador is dead. Soon enough the whole world will think *I'm* dead, and if we're found here, I will be.

I want to crawl in behind the stacks of crates, lie down on the cobblestones, and hide until someone comes to take care of this for us. Until someone shows up to say *I'll take it from here* and tell us exactly what to do.

Except that was the ambassador, and now she's gone.

I don't remember the last time I cried—I must have been very young—but when I think now of Lady Lanham's face, of her smile, of Penrie Lanham on the progress fleet . . .

I squeeze my eyes shut against the hot ache behind them. Guilt is roiling inside me, twisting my gut with the sick knowledge that if I'd made the sacrifice when I was supposed to—if I had strengthened Barrica as my family has always done— Mellacea would never have been willing to challenge us.

I can't even think what I was doing instead that was so important. Parties with friends who are dead now, because they boarded my decoy fleet thinking it was just another stop on our endless train of good times.

Putting off the journey my father made on time, because I wanted to keep a piece of him—keep his journal entries—to myself for a little longer. If I wanted to be close to him so badly, I should have done my duty like he did.

*But I didn't.*

*And now I don't know what to do.*

Selly squeezes my hand again, and when I open my eyes, her steady green gaze is waiting for me.

"We could sell Keegan's necklace," she murmurs. "Disguise you, get you onto a boat home as a passenger on the lower decks."

I shake my head. "What good am I on a slow boat home when a war's beginning?"

"What else can we do but get you out of the city?" Keegan asks quietly.

And suddenly I *do* know, but I have to make myself speak the words. "I do need a boat," I say slowly. "But not to head to Alinor."

Selly lifts her brows, and I can see she's grasped my meaning. "The map in your father's journal isn't exact, Leander. It's a sketch—it's not like the charts you gave to Rensa, and a trip at sea isn't like traveling on land. If our course is off by even a fraction, we'll miss the Isles altogether. And if that happens, we'll die out there."

"We won't miss them," I say, soft but certain. "The map will be enough. And everything we need is in the journal— descriptions of the harbor, the temple. I know what we're looking for, and Keegan's read it too."

Selly studies me, biting her lower lip. "So we sail there ourselves and make the sacrifice." Everything she's done so far has been to keep me alive—it's what her captain sacrificed her ship and her crew for. And rolling the dice like this is just the opposite.

Finally, Keegan speaks again, slow and deliberate as ever. "I doubt anything we do can prevent a war now," he muses. "But perhaps we can make it short and sharp. Reduce the number of people who are killed. The Mellaceans are far more likely to back down again if they realize Barrica has been strengthened."

Selly sucks in a breath. "The type of boat we can crew with three people, two of whom don't know what they're doing . . ." She shakes her head. "It's a long way to go. I'm not sure either of you is understanding what this would be like."

"I'm sure we're not," I agree. "But I do understand the alternative."

"The odds are we won't make it," she says. "We have a drawing, not a chart. Winter's starting, so the weather will be unpredictable, and even if we did pull it off, getting from the Isles to Alinor afterward . . . we'd be against the wind all the way."

We're silent, Keegan and I watching Selly as she closes her eyes, biting her lower lip again. I squeeze her hand, but I can't bring myself to ask her again, not out loud.

Everything depends on her willingness to risk her life for this. Her father's fleet might fly Alinor's flag, but she didn't grow up in Kirkpool—she didn't grow up with the politics, or the people.

She could walk away from us right now, and with what she knows, take a place on the crew of any ship out there in the harbor. She could find a way back to her father's fleet.

Her lashes lift, and she tips her head back, looking up at the only sliver of sky we can see. "We can't just go out there to the docks and buy a boat. It might not be safe, with Alinorish accents, by now. Word spreads *fast* among sailors. We'd leave a trail a mile wide for whoever comes asking questions after us."

I nod slowly, my gut dropping as I reach helplessly for another idea, another way to get a boat, and come up short.

She lowers her gaze, studying each of us in turn. "So we'll have to go south," she says. "We can head down the coast, find a boat at a smaller town."

"You mean you'll . . . ?"

"I've gone my whole life without ever looking beyond the deck of my own ship," she says quietly. "Rensa used to talk about it all the time. Used to say that I should. I guess I'm going to take her advice. I told you on the *Little Lizabetta* that I was getting you to the Isles, if I had to sail you there myself. So be it."

"You're . . ."

"I lost my crew for this, my ship. What's happening is bigger than them, bigger than us. If this is the start of a war, we have to keep the gods out of it, whatever it costs."

Keegan reaches inside his shirt to touch the gold necklace there, then curls his fingers around it, pulling it over his head.

"I'm going to be too late to start this semester anyway," he says.

"Keegan, I—"

"I was always more interested in our schoolwork than you were," he says, his tone thoughtful, continuing as if I hadn't spoken. "I knew it was important to study history. To learn from it."

Guilt lances through me. If I'd thought the same, we wouldn't be here.

He glances across, reads that on my face, and waves the thought away. "What I mean to say," he continues, "is that, like Selly, I am forced to reconsider my previous beliefs. Sometimes one must study history, Your Highness. But sometimes one must make it. Whatever it costs."

# PART THREE

## THE SHIP ON THE HORIZON

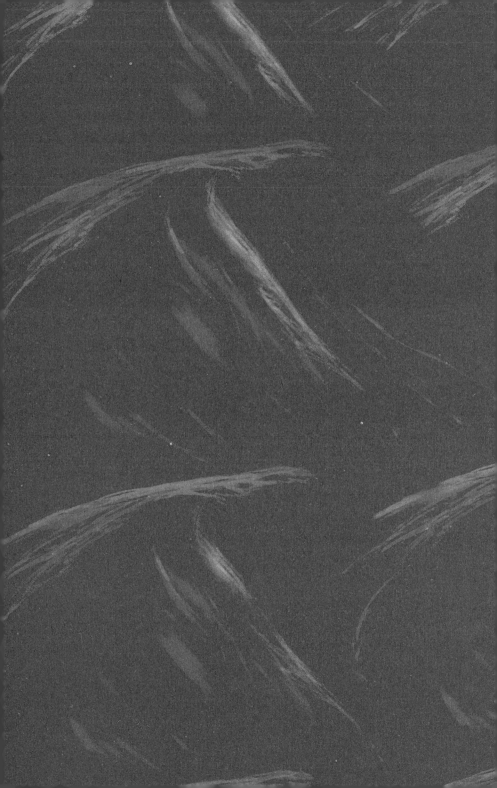

# JUDE

*The Tenements*
*Port Naranda, Mellacea*

I've been thinking about money all day.

Nothing in our apartment is worth very much on its own, but together, if I sell *all* of it and combine it with the bonus I've got coming from Ruby . . . perhaps that's enough to get Mum and me out of the city before this thing blows up. I've been running the numbers over and over in my head, trying to make them add up.

It's not about what I want, not anymore. It's not about what I could or what I should do.

It's just about finding a place to hide. There's no redemption waiting for me, I know that, and no way back to who I used to be.

I haven't wanted to look like I'm planning anything, so I've kept up my routine—I'm on my way back from training, muscles aching, sweat still drying, heart still beating faster. I'm covered in bruises from my last bout, but if I fight this weekend and pull in a decent purse, that'll make what's coming easier.

I have to get out of the city—that's what matters.

Before, I was just a boxer and an errand boy, and if one of those things was a relief and the other a necessary humiliation, they were both paths I could live with. But I stood by and watched Laskia kill and kill again, and I might as well have fired the bullets myself.

And then I ran from my friend—right after I thought about turning him in.

I looked at him, and I thought about betraying him.

I don't deserve Leander's help. That's the truth of it.

I reach the crossroads of New Street and Porter Lane and find myself stopping without thinking about it. I'm on the edge of the tenements, and I pause to look up Porter, toward the club where it happened. The place where everything that wasn't already unraveled began to come undone.

I was only there to see Tom, and even now I nearly let myself take a step in his direction. I can already see his easy smile lighting up as I make my way in through the door, feel how my heart will slow in his gentle presence.

He's a bartender at Ruby Red, and he's usually in before they open for the evening, polishing the glasses, cutting up garnishes. Sometimes I head there before the doors open, and we talk. Sometimes I pick him up after work, and we don't.

There's no arrangement between the two of us. Nothing agreed. We're really not anything. Sometimes I wonder what it would be like, but I could never drag him into my disaster of a life—even though I know he wishes I would. Despite his offers, I keep a distance between us.

I barely ever go in the evenings—I can't afford the drinks there—but everything's falling apart, and I wanted to see him, and I thought . . .

If only it hadn't been *his* club Leander walked into last night. It could have been worse—it could have been the Gem Cutter, the club Ruby uses as her personal headquarters—but if only he hadn't ended up at Ruby Red, where Tom was working, where I decided to head at a time when I so rarely do, because I wanted to see him. . . .

If only, if only, if only. Story of my life.

I'm still looking up Porter Lane when I turn toward home, and I take only a step before I run straight into the brick wall that is Dasriel.

Laskia's fire magician is huge, a full head taller than me, and when I crane my neck to look up, his hard eyes are staring down at me. His clothes are scorched, his skin reddened—and he looks like vengeance itself.

Something inside me curls up, an animal cringing toward the shadows. *Seven hells.*

He doesn't say a word, just lays a green-patterned hand on my shoulder and walks me into the tenements, silent at my back until he finds a quiet alley.

Then he turns me toward him, and without a word, drives a fist into my gut.

I double over, gasping for air as my lungs shudder, refusing to cooperate. I don't know if I could fight back, but I know better than to try.

His fist connects again, and I stagger back, crashing into the slimy brick wall behind me. Lights flash in my vision as my head knocks against the rough bricks.

He grabs me by the front of my shirt, drawing me forward, and I focus on the magician's marks winding their way up his forearms. Then he's slamming me back again, and this time my vision flashes to black.

When he releases me, I drop to my knees, seeing stars, pain lancing up to my hips, and I let myself fall forward, palms slipping on the filthy ground. I try to hold myself up, but my elbows sway and bend, and a kick under the ribs sends me sprawling onto my back.

I'm still fighting to breathe as he stares implacably down at me, digging into his pocket to produce a box of matches and a copper coin.

*No. Please, no.*

He flicks the copper up into the air for the spirits, and it vanishes silently. Then he strikes a match, turning his attention to the tiny flame as I desperately try to push myself up on my elbows.

I did everything they asked. I went on the boat with Laskia. I watched her kill and kill and kill, and I held my tongue. I don't want to die in fire.

The match's flame swells suddenly to half the size of my head, roiling and churning as the spirits gleefully bring it to life, and it hovers above the palm of his hand.

I stare up at him, wordless.

He gazes down without a hint of compassion. Without any sign that he cares whether—

"Stop that, Dasriel."

I turn my head, and Laskia stands at the mouth of the alley-way, her arms folded.

I don't know how long she's been here. I don't know if she was here all along. But with a low rumble, Dasriel steps back, keeping the flame dancing on one hand, to take her place and keep watch.

She walks forward to crouch beside me where I lie in the muck, her movements crisp and precise. There's fury in her gaze. And when she speaks, it's so soft I can barely hear it over my own labored breathing.

"You said he was dead."

*Oh no.*

Ten different things fight inside me at once—she knows Leander's alive, and from the sound of it, she knows he's in Port Naranda. Does she know I saw him? Does she think Tom had anything to do with it? Can I pretend surprise?

I want to protest, I want to tell her I *never* said he was dead—I said I didn't see him—but she's not asking a question, and I don't have enough breath for words. She's not looking for my opinion or my excuses. So I wait to see what she *does* want.

"The Alinorish ambassador," Laskia says softly, "just went to the docks to meet with the prince at an inn. I got it from one of her staff."

She pauses, but I say nothing, so she continues.

"We nearly had them, but this fool"—and she jerks a thumb over her shoulder at Dasriel—"blew up the auto before your royal friend was in it."

I blink up at her, fighting to keep my face straight. A part of me is desperately relieved she didn't kill Leander—kill him *again.* Another part of me is dully certain this is very bad news for me.

"He got away?" I whisper, between gasps for air.

"He's a powerful magician," she replies. "He almost burned me alive, but I caught a glimpse of him."

"How did he . . . ?"

"Survive? Excellent question, Jude. I sent my people out to search for the answer. And do you know what they found?"

Slowly, I shake my head. Perhaps she doesn't know about the club. She would have said something by now, wouldn't she?

"A boat, sold down at the docks last night. It's called the *Little Lizabetta*. You saw the name on the merchant we chased down, I'm sure. It can't be a coincidence."

My body turns cold as everything comes together. That ship was never sailing south just to escape us. It was sailing south *before it saw us*. On a course for the Isles of the Gods.

*And Leander was never on the progress fleet.*

I thought, for an instant, that I saw someone on the *Lizabetta* after we left. I saw someone scurry across the deck. And I said nothing.

It must have been him.

The ship's magician—the dead woman near the mast—was very, *very* good. Far too good for a regular merchant's magician. It would make much more sense if that wind, those waves, were Leander's doing.

This isn't going to play well with Ruby. And when Ruby's not happy, nobody else is either. I can't manage even an ounce of relief that Laskia doesn't know I've seen Leander too.

*All those deaths, and we didn't even get the one we were aiming for.*

"Did you recognize Lord Wollesley's son?" Laskia asks, soft and dangerous, and my breath stills. She wants to blame this on me.

"Yes," I wheeze. "But he and the prince hated each other at school. They'd never be on the same ship."

"They clearly *were*," she snaps, eyes flashing fury.

"Laskia, there's no way I could have—"

Dasriel abruptly shifts his weight at the mouth of the alley, and I fall silent.

"Now what?" I whisper instead, trying again to push up on my elbows, though everything hurts.

"Now," she says crisply, "we're going to finish the job."

"Ruby wants—"

"We'll talk to Ruby when it's over," she snaps. "Sister Beris can keep her company until then. They seem to be getting along well enough. That boy can't hide anywhere in this city I can't find him. And he can't get out of here without me knowing. I'm going to track him to whatever hole he tries to crawl into, and I'm going to bring her his head."

Her dark eyes are burning—something's snapped inside her.

And I can't run. Because she knows where to find my mother.

"Stand up," she snaps, rising to her feet. "And find something clean to wear. We're going to finish this."

Without another word, she turns on her heel, stalking past Dasriel and disappearing back out onto the street.

The big man turns to look at me and blink slowly. He doesn't move as I struggle to my feet, covered in muck, aching all over. He still doesn't say a word as he follows me silently to our apartment. And I still don't speak to him.

I take my time, my head spinning as I work furiously through every possibility, picking up ideas and discarding them in a frenzied rush.

But they all end in the same place: I need money to get Mum out of the city.

I don't have any.

And if I try to run, and fail, Laskia will kill us both.


My mother doesn't protest as I wipe myself clean and get changed. She doesn't even ask why Dasriel is standing in the doorway, watching me.

She just gazes at us both with dull eyes, accepting this latest blow as she's accepted every other. Eventually her gaze drifts to the window, to examine the passing clouds, and that's when the spark of frustration inside me springs to life, becoming a tiny lick of flame.

I've always saved my anger for my father, who left us with nothing. But why did she let him? Why didn't she make sure he provided for us? Force him to make arrangements?

She let him put her in a house in the city, away from her family, away from her friends. She let him choose my school and send me there, far from everything and everyone I knew, to live as a curiosity among the nobility.

And when he was gone, we lost everything anyway. My education. Our home. Our dignity.

For a moment she's not lying on her bed here in our apartment, but on her bunk in the third-class cabin we shared with a dozen others on our way to Port Naranda, crammed into the tiny space with the ship shuddering around us, a single lantern lighting the gloom.

A month before that trip, I was at school with the prince I'm now hunting, arguing with friends about nothing more important than whether we should walk to the village on the weekend.

I thought not one of those friends tried to help when we fell from grace, and Mum just accepted the hard landing. But did she *create* it?

*A clean break will be better,* she kept telling me. *We must look forward, not back.*

To learn that my friends *did* look for me—that they tried to find me and couldn't—I don't know what to do with that information.

Can I even believe Leander? Or was it his guilt speaking, just excuses for what he should have done? For failing to show up when it mattered, like my father? He knew how much that galled me—he'd have hated to feel like he was doing the same.

But the answer churns in my gut, slow and painful.

I believe him.

I know him well enough to know when he's telling the truth.

Which means he gave my mother letters for me, and she didn't pass them on. In her heartbreak over losing my father, she wanted her clean break from our old lives, and she got it.

Perhaps *I* could have tried harder, written to him once we got here. Refused to leave Kirkpool in the first place.

Mum shifts in the bed, and I glance up at her as I crouch to tie my bootlaces. I can't talk to her about it now, not with Dasriel here. It will have to wait.

I reach out to take her hand, her skin too dry, too cool. I'm caught between her and Laskia, the two of them as different as it's possible to be.

Mum's still accepting it, no matter what they do to us. She

helped it happen, so sure was she that our end was coming. And now, even as she lies here, too sick to get out of bed, she simply resigns herself to whatever comes next without a flicker of fight.

Laskia, on the other hand, believes you get what you take, not what you're given. She might be insane, but at least she's trying to choose her own destiny.

I don't want to end up like her—but I don't want to end up like my mother, either.

I want to make my own path, but I can't see any way out of this tiny room and the leash Laskia's holding in her fist.

"Come on, Your Lordship," rumbles Dasriel as I finish tying my bootlaces and slowly rise to my feet. "Hunt won't wait."

# SELLY

*The Docks District*
*Port Naranda, Mellacea*

I've left the prince of Alinor hiding in a filthy courtyard behind a tavern, tucked in behind a huge crate of empty bottles left over from last night's revelry. He has Keegan to guard
him, the two of them crammed in side by side, faces grim.

I nearly killed Leander with my stupidity, and horror is still
trying to push its way up my throat and overwhelm me with guilt.

This is why magic isn't for me. This is why the spirits never
responded to me, not through all the dozens of teachers who
tried to help. It took a royal magician to force them to notice
me, and even then, they rebelled against who I am.

But I *can't* let myself dwell there. Not when I have work to
do. Work that might well save everyone left alive that I care
about. My father, the crews on all his remaining ships. The
friends and acquaintances in every port. Thousands, tens of
thousands of people I've never met.

When I think in those terms, though, my heart tries to stop inside my chest.

So I just think in these, instead: Leander and Keegan.

That's who I'll do it for.

These two boys, who are counting on me.

"Be careful," Keegan said softly before I left, and I bring my focus back to his words now, reciting them to myself. "Every person you speak to is one more person who remembers you were there. Every person you pass by, there's a chance they take note of you. We have to assume Laskia killed the ambassador, and she's looking for us next. And we have to assume she has eyes everywhere."

Strangely, even though there's a girl out there trying to murder us, there's still something simpler, calmer, about where we are now.

Everything has narrowed down to just the three of us, and one task.

There are no more calculations, no more angles, no more risks to take or measure. We just have to get ourselves a boat and sail for the Isles.

Everything else, we can leave behind. Because nothing else matters.

We have to make the sacrifice—whatever it takes, and whatever it costs.

I steal a sailor's cap off the clothesline at the back of an inn and tuck my hair underneath it, giving me one less feature for people to remember me by. If I stick to the docks district, with any luck I'll be just another saltblood.

I speak to as few people as possible. Watch for anyone

wearing a ruby pin at their lapel. I go as few places as necessary, do nothing to draw attention.

The problem is, I'm Alinorish—and just how big a problem that is becomes clear in minutes.

Down on the docks the mood is volatile. I do get a look at the Salthouse Inn, and though there are fire crews clustered around it, they're packing up—their work is done, and nobody's carting away bodies.

The innkeeper is out front in tears, another woman's arm around her shoulders, and guilt lances through me. I did that to her. If I'd just let Leander fight the fire magician, instead of panicking, instead of making demands of the spirits a second time . . .

I turn away and push through the crowd. Alinorish crews are packing up, hurrying aboard as they prepare to cast off, with or without their cargo. Big barges from Kethos are doing the same, and a Trallian captain's talking to one from Beinhof, debating whether it's safe for them to stay. As a squadron of the city guard marches out into the square, they silently part ways and hurry for their own boats.

Within minutes the city guard are arguing with captains about searching the ships, and it's clear nobody would be willing to risk taking passengers, let alone allow Leander to talk them into changing course and heading for the Isles. I was right to say we'd have to go south, down the coast.

I slip my hand into my pocket and brush my fingers against the paper boat hiding there, warm from the heat of my body. It was a promise from Leander I'd be back at sea soon enough, but neither of us thought it would be like this. Still, it sits there at my hip like a good-luck charm, a companion, as I hurry through the city.

I try to pull off a Petronian accent when I take Keegan's necklace into the pawnshop, but one raised brow from the skinny man behind the counter tells me it's not going to float.

"And where did *you* get a thing like this?" he asks, running the links between his fingers. "Brass?"

"You know it's not."

"I know an Alinorish girl should be on her ship by now, and on her way to somewhere else. Not trying to sell me stolen property. The money won't be much use to you if you're not here to spend it, sailor."

I'm about to reply when a squad of the city guard goes marching past his shop window, the panes rattling with the heavy tramp of their feet. They're heading for the docks.

Our eyes meet. He could call them in, tell them he's got an Alinorish girl with stolen property. I'd lose the necklace. I might lose my freedom.

"I'll give you a thousand dollars even," he says calmly.

"A thousand?" I can't keep the anger out of my voice. Keegan told me it's worth at least twice that, even at pawnshop prices.

"Take it or leave it." He curls his hand around the necklace, gaze unyielding. "It's a generous offer under the circumstances. We can call the guard, if you'd like to complain."

My fury is boiling up my throat, and I clench my teeth to keep it there, my jaw aching. Silently, I curl my fist around the bills as he places them on my palm.

"Come again anytime," he says, and I barely resist the urge to kick over his displays as I march out of the shop.

If I'm tight with our cash, and I bargain hard, perhaps it'll be enough to get us a boat down the coast. I don't know what they're worth here.

After that, I sell my dress. It takes an extra few minutes, but I take it back to Hallie, and she greets me with a quick, sympathetic smile.

"Didn't work out?" she asks.

A bitter laugh escapes me. "Turns out it didn't."

"I heard what happened at the docks," she says tentatively, slipping it onto a hanger and lifting it onto a rack. I feel a little pang as the green beads are hidden from sight. But I have no use for it where we're going. I have no use for it anyway—clothes like that belong in Leander's world, not mine. "You all right to get out of town?"

"I will be," I say, torn between gratitude she thought to ask and wariness at revealing too much of my thinking, even to her.

She grimaces, then digs in her till, pulling out a ten-dollar note. Leaning over, she presses it into my hands.

"You only owe me five," I say. That was what she promised—and I only paid her eight. I won't be the guy in the pawnshop. I won't be anything like him. "And that was if it was in good condition. I climbed a tree in it, to tell the truth."

Now it's her turn to laugh, and it's a musical sound, over too soon. "Take it," she says. "And good luck. Maybe one day you'll be back in town, you can come and buy another."

I gaze at her, then nod my thanks, a lump in my throat.

It just doesn't make sense that she's so kind, when a few days from now we'll all be trying to kill each other.

I use the money to buy warm hats and coats for us all—though the Isles will be hot, we won't make it there if we freeze in the big seas waiting in our way—then duck into an outfitters bustling with panicked sailors, working my way quickly along the shelves.

The only place I'd feel more at home than this little shop would be the deck of a ship itself, and still my nerves are singing.

I can smell tar and wax and wood polish, and the shelves are built from timbers I think might have been part of a ship once. They're stacked with all the everyday items that have always been a part of my life, from knives to splicing kits, to spirit flags to the little jars of spices so many sailors keep in their pockets to season boring meals on long trips.

I pick up a string of spirit flags, and leaf through the charts until I find one with the level of detail I'm after. Next I scoop up a neat little navigator's kit, the tools nestled inside blue-dyed leather, and lay down money I can ill afford to spend.

I have only one more stop—the harbormaster's office—and it's carnage inside. Not the usual friendly chaos of sailors logging arrivals and departures, bargaining with merchants, and catching up with friends.

Instead, there's a frenzied note of panic as voices rise; clerks hurriedly scribble out departure papers, some working quickly, others glancing at the door, fearful the guard will arrive at any moment. I can see captains abandoning the attempt, breaking into a jog as they turn for their ships without the proper paperwork, while others argue helplessly, pushing money across the counter to speed the process along.

I squeeze past an angry man with a sharp Alinorish accent, and between two Nusrayan women, their hair shaved to a soft fuzz. The crowd pushes me up against the wall when I finally reach it, and I brace with my forearms to stop myself from being crushed.

The train timetables I was hoping for are here, though—sometimes cargo that comes in on ships ends up on trains heading away from the port, and the tattered list of schedules is pinned up between information on grain prices and an ad for a ship's cook.

The timetable is in cramped print, with row after row of names and times. I squint to make out the tiny words, trying to remember what the boys told me about how to read one of these, running my gaze down one column, then another.

There's a line along the coast, down to the southern tip of Mellacea, where it meets up with ships heading out to Brend's Gate, the island below the continent. Ships pass between Mellacea and Brend's Gate before they turn up toward the North Passage and Holbard. It's the route my father took a year ago.

There's a handful of villages along the way, and the map I bought tells me at least a few of them should have fishing fleets. So that's where we'll stop and bargain for a boat.

The timetable says we can be on a train in forty-five minutes if we hurry, with only one more departing after it—less chance for anyone to follow us.

Head down, I push my way out of the harbormaster's office, and though I don't have much time to waste, I throw in a few loops and extra turns on my way back to the boys.

I breathe a sigh of relief when I return to the filthy little courtyard and catch sight of Leander's dark eyes peering out from behind the crates. I slip in beside him where the boys are crouched, my arms full of supplies, and he reaches over anyway to weave his fingers through mine.

"If we get moving now, we can be on a train south to Port Cathar in just over half an hour," I say by way of greeting, squeezing his fingers hard. It feels like anchoring myself against a current that wants to sweep me away.

"That's where we want to be?"

"Well, it's on the train line," I say. "The way it's positioned on the coast, I'd say their main income is fishing. That means we should be able to buy some kind of boat with the money we've got."

"If anyone comes asking after us, we'll be more memorable in a smaller port," Keegan says, "but the odds of anyone tracking us must surely be lower than they would be here."

Leander nods as he releases my hand, and I begin to pass out the clothes I bought for the boys.

"They'll be looking for us to catch a boat out of Port Naranda," Leander says, pulling a sailor's cap over his black hair. "And maybe they'll be looking at the trains, too. Depends how good they are. But sailors in the third-class carriage, heading for a fishing port, have to stand out a lot less than someone forking over ready cash for a boat in a hurry. Let's go."


By the time we reach Port Cathar, I'm exhausted. The fear that pumped through my veins earlier has given way now to a bone-deep tiredness.

The huge central station of Port Naranda was bigger than any cargo warehouse I've ever seen, the vaulted ceilings soaring above us, the roar of the locomotives echoing off the stone walls. The crowd jostled harder than in the harbormaster's office, too.

I don't think Leander has ever been anywhere people haven't yielded for him—he stumbled the first time a porter shoved him out of the way.

I caught a glimpse of the first-class carriage as we hurried along the train platform, all polished mahogany, brass fittings, and red velvet. It was a world away from the third-class carriage we crammed into, which was packed tighter than a cargo hold, with hard wooden benches and bodies lining every inch of them.

The flurry and panic of the docks hadn't made it to the station yet—I suppose most people who were leaving were trying to get out by sea.

We found a spot in our crowded carriage up against the wall, and I was pressed back against it as we got under way. The back-and-forth rattle of the train unnerved me—I thought it would be like the swaying of a ship, but it was too even, too rhythmic, too loud. After a little while, Leander wrapped an arm around my shoulders to steady me, and I dozed with my head on his shoulder.

I woke when one of our neighbors tried to ask him the time, and he opened his mouth, getting about two syllables of educated Alinorish accent out before Keegan stood on his foot, leaning in to give his reply in a perfect Port Narandan accent I'd never heard from him before.

As the woman turned away, I raised my eyebrows at him, and he simply shrugged.

"I thought all nobles were indoor pets," I murmured, leaning in close. "But look at you."

"I'm in familiar territory," he said, keeping his voice down. Then, in response to my questioning look: "Not Port Naranda. Running away. I've done it before, and quite successfully, I might add. Or at least, if the ship I took passage on had not been commandeered for other purposes, my plan would have been executed without flaw."

"I don't think we can blame you for failing to see that one on the horizon," I murmured, and he shrugged, in a *what can you do?* sort of way.

I still don't know what happens inside our scholar's head most of the time, but it's a lot more complicated in there than I realized, that's for sure.


Now, someone out on the platform is yelling that we've reached Port Cathar, and the three of us are pushing our way past our fellow passengers to spill out into the fresh evening air, Keegan clutching the bag that holds all our belongings.

The sun is just kissing the mountains to the west of us. The air is laced with salt and seaweed, and my heart sighs with relief as I look down the hill from the station to spot a cluster of buildings around what's clearly a fishing port.

This is the sort of place I know how to deal with—no more stone canyons between high-rise buildings, no more armies of people marching all kinds of places with a purpose I don't understand.

We're coming back to the sea, and it's time to find ourselves a boat.

# KEEGAN

◆

*Port Cathar, Mellacea*

M y nanny—or my keeper, as my sister, Marie, and I used to call her—took us to the seaside every year. My parents and older brother stayed at home, and we were dispatched to enjoy the benefits of fresh air, salt water, and too many ice creams.

I didn't much like the seaside back then—the sun was too hot, the sand got everywhere, and it was impossible to keep a book in good condition at the beach—and I don't much like it now.

Port Cathar is a fishing hamlet of no particular distinction, and I wouldn't have thought we could be sure a secondhand boat would be available in a market this size, but Selly's confident she can find something suitable.

The three of us are making our way down the winding road from the station, which is set—along with the railway line— into the side of the mountain. Below us lies a cluster of buildings around a small harbor.

"We'll be remembered here," Leander says, "and easily."

"That's the gamble we're taking," I reply. "If we're followed, no doubt we'll be easily tracked. But the odds of anyone knowing we boarded that train—you'd have to have eyes in every corner of the city."

"I know, I know," he agrees. "I'll still be nervous until we're miles out to sea with no one on our tail."

"There was only one more train today," I remind him. "That improves our odds." But the truth is, though I keep my tone even and calm, I'm as uncomfortable as he is.

"Our money will go a lot further here," Selly says, studying the cluster of boats below us. "Everything's less expensive outside the capital, and they won't have heard Alinorish sailors aren't welcome yet."

Leander says nothing as we continue down the hill.

"If we can't afford a boat, this place seems pretty sleepy," I say, thoughtful. "We should be able to steal one without much trouble."

Selly glances across at me, eyes widening in shock. "Are you serious?"

To her, a boat is—well, I suppose it's what a library is to me. That around which one's life is built.

"It would be better to buy one," I say. "But if we have to choose between the loss of one livelihood and the loss of ten thousand lives . . ."

Selly looks across to each of us in turn, her gaze flickering over us in that way it always does when she takes our measure. I'm never entirely sure whether she finds us wanting.

"Fair point," she says eventually. "But there are boats down there that could overtake us, that will be bigger than anything we could crew. So it would be smarter not to be on the run from the good people of Port Cathar. I'll find something to buy."

We elect to divide the tasks that lie before us. The sun is already touching the mountaintop to the west, the sea to the east descending into the gloom of the evening.

Selly departs for the tavern, tugging her sailor's cap down firmly before she opens the door, and light streams out to envelop her before she disappears.

The prince and I are bound for the township's one general store—we require provisions. I'm confident he's never been inside an ordinary shop before—Selly and I agreed on this with a wordless glance, and so I am going with him to secure our supplies.

But Leander pauses, looking back toward the tavern.

"She'll be safe enough," I say.

"Probably safer than us, in a town like this," Leander replies. "She knows it better than we do. I was just thinking—what have I done to her life, Keegan? Nothing I ever do will make it right, will it? And yet . . . how will I leave her when this is done? I could never keep her from what she loves."

"There's no easy answer," I reply. "With respect, I suggest we put the solving of that problem at the end of the very, very long list before us. Should we happen to reach it, in what I estimate to be position number four hundred and thirty-seven, we'll find a way to solve it then."

Leander's grin is warm and sudden, white teeth flashing as he turns it on me. I don't think I've ever made him grin like that before—certainly not in all our years together at school.

"Well, if she's four hundred and thirty-seven," he says as we turn together for the general store, "then you're four hundred and thirty-eight. What did you plan to study?"

Surprise at the change in direction slows my reply. "History. And now I'm determined to survive, so I can write detailed and useful firsthand accounts of this experience for future students. Having studied many that are wanting, I have firm views on the sort of information that ought to be included."

The prince sounds almost wistful as he gazes ahead down the nearly empty cobblestone street. "What will you say about me," he asks, "when you write the story?"

I pause to consider my reply. For years I'd have taken this chance to hurt him if I could. At best, I wouldn't have paused to think about his feelings at all.

Even now I won't lie to him—that's not who I am. But there's something I can say that's true.

"I'll say you won loyalty easily. Which is a rare and valuable gift. I'll say you're a powerful magician, and that— What was it Master Gardiner always used to bellow at you in mathematics? That you had plenty of brain, if only you were inclined to use it."

Leander bursts out laughing. "How can you possibly know he said that? You weren't even in that class."

"I was in the classroom next door," I reply gravely. "I assure you, we could hear his words quite clearly through the walls."

He laughs again, and the tension that's lived in my chest for the last few days eases just a fraction. I wish we'd talked like this at school. It only took a shipwreck to close the gap.

"You should study philosophy," he says. "When you get there."

"I'll make my choice in my second year." I pause. "I'll keep an open mind."

"You know I'll fund it," he says, softer. "Or Augusta will, I suppose."

My gaze snaps across to him, but his expression is serious. I've been relatively confident until now that he'd at least see me safely to the Bibliotek. It never occurred to me his family might assist my studies.

The truth is, it would be useful in more ways than one. It's not just the finances—I could, I think, find the money, with a combination of scholarships and tutoring work. It's that when my family eventually discovers where I went, having the queen's stamp of approval—openly or implied—would change everything.

It would also be the first time anyone—including my family—has thought it worth their while to help me learn.

When he speaks again, I'm jolted from that thought before I can follow it all the way to its conclusion. "If you don't mind my asking, who was she?"

"Sorry, who?" I stall automatically. I understand the question, because apart from Selly, there's only one *she* in my life he could mean.

"Your betrothed," he elaborates, unfortunately. "Something made you run instead of staying to argue with them about the Bibliotek. I assume they were going to marry you off."

I wince. "It was Lady Carrie Dastenholtz."

His eyes widen. "Kiki?" Then he grins again. "Keegan and Kiki. The names are a match, at least."

"We did hear that joke once or twice," I murmur.

"Mmm. I suppose with your father's import interests, that makes sense."

There it is again. *Plenty of brain, if only he was inclined to use it.*

"She was a logical choice," I say.

"She's a good sort," Leander says. "I'll admit I have a little trouble imagining the match."

"She's a very good sort," I agree. "But you're not alone in having trouble imagining the match. If I'm being completely honest, she helped me climb out the window."

Leander tries in vain to muffle his laughter, his eyes dancing, and we pause together outside the general store, with its displays of preserved food and fishing gear.

"One day," I say, "I'll tell you the story of how she and I acquired the gold necklaces. But for now we should attend to business."

"Keegan," says the prince of Alinor, shaking his head slowly. "You're a gem. And I'm a fool for not knowing that earlier."

It turns out the general store is attended by a young woman far from immune to our prince's charms, and I gather the items from Selly's list while Leander flirts effortlessly, mostly managing to conceal the fact that he has no real idea of the prices of any of the items we're purchasing. He's the one who negotiates a discount, though, and the girl even lends us a barrow to take our purchases to the docks. He promises to return it in person this evening.

Leander takes the first turn at pushing the load—not something I would have expected of him at school. "I'd like to get the spirit flags up into the rigging tonight," he says, "and I'd like to go over the sailing theory again with Selly before we set off in the morning. Dawn, I assume."

I'm studying the town idly as he speaks, letting the words flow by. The sense of company is nice, but I'm content to stay quiet. It's almost an hour since we arrived, and already the streets are much darker, the sun mostly behind the mountain now.

I'm learning the lay of the land, for no reason I can particularly name except it might be useful if something goes wrong. It's when my gaze traces a path up to the station that I stop suddenly.

Leander does as well, nearly overturning the barrow. "Keegan, what is it?"

My words stick in my throat, and I lift a finger to point.

The last train for the evening is pulling away from the station, and three figures are emerging from the building and turning purposefully down the hill.

One is much larger than the other two, and it's the slightest of the three who strides out in front.

Though I can see nothing more than their silhouettes against the dying light, a chill twitches between my shoulder blades and travels straight down my spine.

There's no doubt in my mind I'm looking at Laskia, Jude, and the huge magician who nearly burned us at the inn.

And they're on the hunt.

# LASKIA

*The Black Barnacle*
*Port Cathar, Mellacea*

Dasriel pushes open the door to a tavern called the Black Barnacle, holding it for me as I stride through.

He's so big he'll need to duck his head when he follows, and I can't deny there's a small shiver of something inside me, knowing all that strength is at my disposal. It's like having a lion on a leash.

It's evening, and most of the town is here. The woman behind the rough timber counter has a round face, her hair pulled up in a coiled crown of braids, her cheeks reddened by years in the wind.

The patrons look like sailors mostly, clad in rough trousers and shirts. A fire roars in the fireplace, half a dozen pairs of seaboots tipped over in front of it so their insides can dry.

The hubbub of conversation dies away as Jude and Dasriel take their places behind me, one at either shoulder. Dasriel looms silently, and Jude is inscrutable—reluctant, I know, but he'll do as he's told.

All around us drinks are set down, and every face turns toward us.

I couldn't be more out of place here, in my city suit and waistcoat, my hair neatly razored at the back of my neck. But after years of feeling uncomfortable, years of looking to Ruby to see what I should do, years of hoping I would be good enough, I'm done with that.

If Ruby would rather confide in Sister Beris, then I'll show *both* of them I'm worth listening to. Who better to understand a god who's been bound for so long, unable to reach for his power—unable to show the world his might?

Here and now I'm the most powerful person in this room, and the odds are good Dasriel is the only one with a gun. They *should* pay attention to me.

I wait until they're completely silent before I speak. "Someone just came in here and bought a boat."

My statement is greeted by a sea of blank faces.

Forcing myself to patience, I wait. Eventually, it's the woman behind the bar who speaks.

"Well, what I sell in here is food and drink. Can I get you some of either? We have lodgings as well."

Jude shifts his weight uncomfortably behind me, but I ignore him, holding out one hand—palm up—to Dasriel, without turning my head.

He puts a heavy leather bag into it, and I walk toward the nearest table, pulling the laces at the neck of the bag undone.

Slowly, deliberately, I open it, and a shower of golden dollars clatters onto the tabletop. Some ricochet to the floor, rolling away to hide in the shadows.

I let them go, as if I have so much money, so many more dollars, that it doesn't matter if I lose these ones. In among the hoard lies a pair of rubies my sister gave me as a gift when I turned sixteen, and they glitter as they catch the firelight.

This small bag holds everything I have left.

I lift my head and look around the room once more.

If Leander and his crew beat me to the Isles, well, I have a plan for that, set in motion before I left Port Naranda.

But I intend to hunt them down myself.

"Someone just came in here and bought a boat," I repeat. "Whoever crews the ship that helps me catch them can have all of this, and twice as much again when we return."

I drop the empty leather bag onto the top of the pile and look around the tavern, slowly taking in their faces.

Their expressions are very different now.

I smile.

"Who's ready to set sail?"

# SELLY

*The* Emma
*The Crescent Sea*

I t's dawn when we know for sure we're not alone.

We'd planned to spend the night in port, to give me a chance to familiarize myself with our new boat, to give Leander and me a chance to go over the map in the journal and our new charts properly, and to give all of us the chance to get some sleep.

That changed after we saw Laskia, Jude, and their huge magician making their way down from the station—we cast off in a flurry of activity, dumping our supplies below, pushing off as we hoisted the sails.

The sun slipped behind the mountains, and we were left to wonder if they'd managed to secure a boat of their own, if they'd managed to catch sight of our course before the light faded. Now we have the answer.

We've made it through the night, at least. We've each snatched an hour or two of sleep, and Keegan's in our one bunk right now, in the cabin below us.

The *Emma* is a neat little fishing boat that does everything I could ask of her. She still smells strongly of her last catch, but she has a sturdy hull and sails we can handle. She was more than a bargain, because she didn't have the modern touches of the newer, bigger boats in the harbor. The old man selling her took a shine to me—and nobody else was in the market.

We've got her old sails trimmed in fairly tight, the wind coming from our port side, and we're clipping along at a good pace. The breeze carries the scent of salt, and the waves *shush-shush* beneath us as we cut a line through them. With my hair whipping around my face, I've set my course and I'm where I belong. I can almost feel my father by my side, almost see Rensa or Kyri coming up the companionway to take a turn at the wheel.

It feels like a lifetime ago that I was raging at Leander for stranding me with Rensa, for keeping me away from Da. In reality it's been just days.

I've mostly stopped myself from thinking about the crew now.

When I let their faces swim up from where I've packed them away, or when I look out at the deck of the *Emma* and imagine Jonlon casting me a wry look as he retrims my sail, or Kyri kneeling by the mast to charm the spirits, the ache of loneliness flows through me like physical pain.

I'd give anything to have even one of them aboard with me, to have someone to help carry the responsibility of getting Leander to the Isles. But I'm alone, and for now I need the loss of my crew to feel a long time ago, a long way away.

I don't have what it would take to face up to the reality that they're gone, not yet. I need to save everything I have for what I'm doing here. Because what I'm doing here is nearly impossible.

I think of my father, too, sometimes. Up north, with no idea the *Lizabetta* is gone, his crew are dead. No idea I'm here, in the middle of the Crescent Sea in a fishing boat, trying to stop a war.

If I fail, he and all his fleet will be conscripted to fight, to fill their holds with soldiers instead of bales of wool, sacks of grain.

If I fail, he'll never know what happened to me. Or that I tried.

Keegan cautiously held the wheel last night as Leander and I hunched over the chart together, comparing it to the sketch in his journal.

"The Isles are below Loforta," he said, tracing a line down the journal's page with his finger. "And straight across from Brend's Gate, judging by this."

I know Brend's Gate well—I would have sailed right by it if I'd been aboard the *Freya,* on my way to join my father.

"And that's where it was on the chart you gave to Rensa?" I pressed. "*Directly* below Loforta? *Exactly* even with Brend's Gate? There's a world of difference between a sketch in a journal and an exact marking on a chart."

"I didn't look that closely," he admitted helplessly. "I wasn't planning on navigating us there myself. I remember it being the same. I think."

Everything will hang on that memory being true. The Isles are tiny specks in a huge ocean, and I've been helming an unfamiliar boat through the night, on very little sleep. I know

Leander's been praying, but Barrica is at the very depth of her weakness now, waiting on an overdue sacrifice. I have to trust his bond with her will mean enough.

There'll be more than a little luck involved in this, but all I can do is get us close enough that I can climb the mast with a telescope and look for hope on the horizon.

We'll sail all today, and through the night again. And when dawn comes tomorrow, we'll know whether we've done it or not.

Leander is up on deck with me, moving around whenever I need the sails trimmed, while I stand at the wheel. There's nothing we can do but sail the boat, and when I'm able to set my worries aside, I'm finding I like working her together.

He returns from catching a line that was trailing in the water and slips inside the blanket I have around my shoulders, huddling against me with a grin.

I push in closer, shamelessly stealing his warmth, and he wraps an arm around me, presses a cheek to mine. His skin is rough with stubble, and he smells like salt and canvas.

"The sky's beautiful," he says, nodding to the pink and orange painting the horizon ahead of us.

"Red sky in the morning, sailor's warning," I tell him.

"Come again?"

"You don't know that one? 'Red sky in the morning, sailor's warning. Red sky at night, sailor's delight.'"

He squints sidelong at me. "What's it warning us about?"

"A storm." When I look up, he follows my gaze—the clouds are ragged up high, ripped to pieces by the wind, and the pink and orange ahead of us mellow to a sickly gold up above. When I glance behind us, the sky is an ugly green. Our hastily hung spirit flags flutter and snap in the wind as I study the heavy clouds suspended over Mellacea, trying to guess whether that storm will reach us—though the wind is blowing from the east, that doesn't mean it will be chased away. Often, higher up, these things circle around.

And that's when I see something on the horizon, just for a moment. A shape that doesn't belong with the waves.

I go still, and Leander's alert immediately.

"What do you see?"

"Hold the wheel." I reach into the pouch hanging beside it, grabbing for the captain's eyeglass. Then I turn to face backward, wrapping an arm around his torso for stability, widening my stance, and lifting the glass to one eye.

He's quiet, concentrating on steering our nose through each wave as it comes, waiting for me to tell him what I see.

"There's a boat behind us," I say finally. "They're piling on every inch of sail they can find. That's not what fishing boats do."

"Could they be a messenger?" he asks. "Or a merchant in a hurry?"

I lower the eyeglass and turn my head, lifting my gaze to meet his.

His jaw squares as he reads the answer in my eyes. But I say it out loud anyway.

"No. There's nothing in this direction except the Isles . . . and us."

# JUDE

*The* Mermaid
*The Crescent Sea*

L askia is keeping me on deck with her.

I'd rather be at the other end of the boat, but whenever I drift away, she calls me back to join her, and I swallow another wave of seasickness to take my place at the railing once more. At least she let me sleep last night—I know she didn't rest herself.

Our ship, the *Mermaid,* is bigger than the one we're pursuing, but she's made for fishing and there aren't that many bunks. Dasriel took one and the first mate the other. I got a few hours in a hammock, and I didn't think I'd be able to sleep—the swinging motion churned my stomach, the ship creaking around us, stirring up every dark memory I have from the voyage to Mellacea—but in the end exhaustion won out.

This morning the ship's cook, who seems to hold several other roles aboard as well, made porridge in a pot suspended above the stove. It was on a gimbal, swaying back and forth with the movement of the ship so it was always upright.

I bolted at the smell—even if I hadn't already been sick enough to throw up the soles of my boots, it was far too close to the meal I saw Varon down, aboard the *Macean's Fist*.

Dasriel went back for seconds.

I wanted to say something. I wanted to warn the crew—as they picked up their breakfast, as they piled on more sail and debated ways to catch up with our quarry—I wanted to tell them their new employer has killed, and she'll kill again. That she'll kill *them*.

Perhaps that urge is why she's keeping me so close. But she has my mother, and I won't say anything. There's no point pretending I've got a backbone.

It's late morning now, and Laskia stands like a figurehead in the bow, gripping the railing with both hands, bracing herself against the choppy movement of the boat. Or perhaps she's like a hunting dog, pointing at its prey. She never takes her eyes off the tiny ship ahead of us, her lips moving as she whispers prayer after prayer.

The weather has been whipping itself up into a storm since dawn broke, and the sailors say it will be a bad one. I can see they already sense something's not right with Laskia. These people know the sea inside out, but they're more scared of her. I almost wish Sister Beris were with us. Or Ruby. Nobody else has a chance of reining Laskia in, not anymore, and the truth is, I'm not sure they would either.

"What if they get there first?" I ask, breaking the silence for the first time in hours. "What if we don't catch up in time?"

"I planned for that before we left Port Naranda," she says, without taking her gaze from the little boat on the horizon. "Don't worry, Your Lordship. One way or another, we'll catch up with your friend, or he'll find a welcoming committee waiting for him. I'm going to bring back his body this time. That way we can be sure."

My stomach churns all over again, as if I'm back in the hammock and it's lurching with the movement of the ship. I wasn't seasick on the way out to meet the progress fleet, before the killing started. I wasn't sick on the way over from Alinor, two years ago. It's only been since the killing that I can't take it.

I look down to where Laskia's hands grip the railing. For all the time I've spent in the boxing ring, I've never killed anyone. But if Dasriel weren't aboard, I'd think about doing it now. About killing *her*, just to end this.

And perhaps I should anyway, and pay the price. But I lack the courage to accept the cost.

I keep thinking about Leander's face at the club. About his absolute shock at seeing me—his mouth open, his eyes wide. I don't think I've ever seen him lose his composure, and I've known him since we were twelve.

Leander's many things, but he's not a liar—not like that.

If he says he tried to find me, then . . . And why would he lie? How could he even think of a lie so quickly, when he was so clearly surprised to see me?

He didn't know I was one of Ruby's—probably didn't even know Ruby existed. He had no reason to protect himself from me.

I'm left with one conclusion: He really did come to our house, really did write. Really did search for me. And Mum, with her talk of how it's better to make a clean break—to look forward, not back—she never gave me his letters.

I'll ask her why when I get home. *If* I get home. Not that it will change what happened.

For now, I'd pray, but I don't know where to aim my prayers anymore. The temples of all seven gods and the Mother lie ahead of us, and if he makes it in time, it's Leander's prayer that will matter most.

For a long time I thought Alinor had done nothing for me, given me nothing but pain. But now I find myself closing my eyes against the wind and the salt spray and reaching silently for Barrica. Telling her to look for him, to wait for him.

Because if Laskia stops him from making this sacrifice, and Barrica's strength declines—and if the green sisters have their way, pulling the people of Mellacea into church until Macean's strength is so great that he can shake off his sleep—then I truly don't know what will happen next.

It won't just be a war between Alinor and Mellacea, or even just a war that drags in every other country and principality on the continent.

It will be something we haven't seen in five hundred years.

It will be a war between the gods.

# SELLY

*The* Emma
*The Crescent Sea*

The whole world has narrowed to us and the ship on the horizon.

Sometimes they draw nearer, their sails growing large enough that I can make out more detail. Sometimes they seem to fall back, but distances are hard to judge at sea.

The roiling gray storm has nearly overtaken both our ships. The wind has whipped up into a frenzy, the rigging straining, and I'm not bothering to hide my worry from the boys anymore. They're quiet and focused, taking orders without question as I teach them how to reef the sail—our pursuers might be piling on canvas behind, but we'll never see the Isles if the storm rips us apart.

Leander is the quietest of us all. I know he blames himself, and though he tries to smile, there's a sadness in it that's like someone reaching into my chest and squeezing my heart.

Each time he hurries by, he rests a hand on top of mine,

just for a moment. I'd like to turn my palm over and clasp his hand in return, but my wrists and knuckles are aching with the cold, and I don't think I can release the claw grip I have on the wheel.

Some part of me knows that a couple of days ago, a lifetime ago, I'd have resisted that touch. I don't remember why anymore. This connection is real, and it's comforting, and I'm beyond pretending anything else.

And I wish I'd let him kiss me when I had the chance.

I know what will happen when they catch us—and they will, when we reach the Isles and drop anchor. I've tried picturing what our bodies will look like, sprawled as bonelessly as Rensa's and Kyri's were. But that only makes me start cataloging all the ways they might kill us, so each time my mind tries to set course for that particular port, I spin the wheel and change tack.

My only job is to stop it from happening for as long as possible. The world has narrowed to this one task: to get Leander to the temple.

I glance automatically to where the little figurine of Barrica would be, on the starboard side of the wheel, if this were the *Lizabetta*. Countless times I've touched her when I had the helm, rubbed my fingers across her warm metal surface and asked her for luck, or guidance, or the patience to hold my tongue. She never really granted me that last. When we came aboard, there was a small statue of Macean there instead. I pried it free of its bolts and left it on the dock.

And though this is a Mellacean boat, and there's no hint of Barrica aboard, for the first time in a long time I'm praying to her properly—not making the desperate offers or exchanges

I've tried in the past, when things didn't go my way. This time my prayers are soft and simple, offered up from my heart.

We're doing all this for our goddess, and in her I need to place my trust.

*Help me helm this ship. Help me get him where he needs to go.*

I'm giving my life to this—and my future, and everything I might have done. Everything he and I might have been together.

I don't know how much more faith and sacrifice she can ask for.

A freezing cold spray showers me as a wave breaks across the boat, and I shake my head to clear it from my eyes.

Onward is all there is.


Night's coming on when we're hit by another squall.

The wall of wind travels toward us from our port side, and I see the waves shiver. The whitecaps break off their tops with renewed ferocity, and our valiant little ship heels hard to leeward.

· I lock my hands onto the wheel again, bracing my whole body, barely holding us on course. If an ill-timed gust pushes us over before I can bear away—I don't know if a fishing boat can come back from that.

"Leander!" I scream, the wind whipping his name from my lips as soon as it leaves them—but Keegan is nearest to the companionway, and I see him lean down to bellow the prince's name.

A minute later, as I wrestle with the wheel, Leander comes

scrambling up the stairs. We've been saving him for this moment.

Spray is smacking me in the face, my eyes stinging. The rigging is howling, the sails cracking above my head. I spit a mouthful of salt water to one side as the spirit flags flutter and shred up in the stays.

"I need help!" I scream.

Leander has what must be half our food in his arms—a sacrifice big enough for what he's about to ask. Unhesitatingly he throws it overboard, and it's already vanishing as it hits the water. Then he staggers across to take his place behind me, helping me brace the wheel. His arms bracket me, and his chest is warm against my back, and he lends me his strength to use as I need. When I turn my head, I see his features smooth out as he sinks into his link with the spirits.

"Don't drop the wind too much," I shout. "We still need speed."

The wind swings around us wildly, and I'm reminded of what he taught me on the *Little Lizabetta:* We don't tell the spirits what we want. We ask.

The whole boat shudders, and I wonder if he's asking in vain. If even the most powerful magician in Alinor can't control this storm.

I focus on helping us through the waves as we push our way up each one and crash into the troughs between them. Water washes across the deck in great sheets, foaming white swirling around the base of the mast.

I can't imagine what's happening on the boat behind us. They're bigger, but not big enough to ride out the storm like this, and whatever magician they've got aboard, they won't be Leander's equal—nobody is. If they've got any sense, they'll turn into the wind and heave to, wait for the weather to drop, and start again tomorrow. They might not have a chart showing the Isles, but they've got our bearing, so the reality is they can still follow us.

Another gust of wind hits us like a blow, and we crash off the top of the wave. I'm thrown forward against the wheel, one hand ripped free of it, pain shuddering through my ribs.

Then Leander's wrapping an arm around me, holding me until I can suck in a desperate breath, and we're wrestling the wheel under control together as Keegan scrambles across the deck, soaked to the skin, to haul in a madly flapping sail.

And we work that way together for hours.

As the last of the gloomy light dies behind us, and night falls, the stars and moons hidden by the dark gray clouds, Keegan risks a trip below, bringing us cheese and nuts that we can eat by the handful, and slices of sweet apple. Even as the spray hits them, they cleanse our mouths.

Leander manages to down a little, but he's swaying now, snatches of wind and troublesome waves getting away from him more often.

And as we sail through the night, I scream myself hoarse, sending Keegan scurrying this way and that—I don't know where he finds the strength in those gangly arms and legs of his as the hours wear on. I don't know where any of us do.

When he returns to me at the wheel at dawn, my voice cracks as I try to shout above the wind and waves, and he ducks his head so I can yell in his ear. "We need to get a look at the horizon."

Keegan looks up at the mast, then back at me. "Are you joking?" he shouts.

I shake my head. "We set our course based on Leander saying the Isles were directly below Loforta. We haven't seen the stars all night. I've been working off a compass in the middle of a storm. There's no way we've held our bearing—but now it's getting lighter. If I've done my job well enough, they'll be somewhere on the horizon, and I need to know where. You can't hold the wheel without me. You'll have to climb."

He's quiet for one heartbeat, then two, staring up at the tangle of lines and sails to the very top of the mast. I can see his dread stretching that moment out into an eternity. And then he nods. "I'll try."

"There'll be a harness below," I shout. "I can tell you how to clip yourself to the mast. You—"

A monstrous gust of wind tears through, cutting me off as I cling to the wheel with every last shred of my strength. Even with the scream of the gale, I hear the ripping noise above us—the mainsail is tearing, a great, ragged hole appearing as a seam gives way, growing larger every second.

The air spills through it, the fabric rippling and shivering, flapping and tearing at itself, and Leander cries out in alarm behind me as the spirits pour through the gaping wound in the sail.

The wind swings around every point of the compass as they react, swirling madly about each other, and then it drops to nothing for an instant, everything perfectly still and quiet, my own rasping breath suddenly audible, the press of his body, warm behind mine.

I turn my head, but before I can speak, beg him to charm

them again, the gale kicks back in with a vengeance, tearing my hair loose from its braid and whipping it around my face, setting the rigging shuddering and shrieking.

The *Emma* starts to heel, water washing across the deck, and she strains to leeward. I can barely control her now—we're going over, and there's nothing I can do to stop us.

Suddenly Leander's not behind me anymore—he's sliding across the deck, scrambling for purchase, and I catch a flash of his wide, terrified eyes.

Then he slams against the railing with a sound I hear even over the storm, and goes instantly still, facedown, water washing around him.

As the boat keeps tipping, he begins to roll, making no effort to stop himself, sprawling closer to the edge, closer to vanishing into the dark waves over the side.

"Go!" I scream as a wave crashes over him, and my heart clenches so hard I think it'll stop, shocking me with the depth of my panic. Keegan's already throwing himself across the deck. "Don't let him fall!"

Keegan half falls himself along the deck, slamming into the railing as he grabs the prince—when he rolls Leander over in his arms, his head lolls back horribly.

He's unconscious—or at least I pray that's all he is. He's utterly limp, and there's nothing of *him* in his body—the way he holds himself is gone, and he's a dead weight in Keegan's arms. I want to tear myself away from the wheel, slide across the deck myself, touch him, shake him, beg him to wake up.

But with his sudden disconnection from the spirits, they're going wild, whirling around us like a hurricane. The water spirits are panicking at his disappearance too, and below the ship the swirling sea starts to heave and twist, the very waves themselves churning into a rough whirlpool.

The *Emma* groans, a shudder running through her at the pressure on her timbers, traveling up through the wheel to my hands, like she's trying to buck free of my grip.

"Selly!" Keegan shouts. "Do something!"

"I can't . . . ," I begin, but the words die on my lips.

I can feel the *Little Lizabetta* tipping beneath me all over again.

The heat on my face as the hallway of the inn exploded into flames.

The sick horror of finding my magic after all these years—after every failure, every dark shadow of shame, every humiliation—only to have it turn on me.

I've reached for the spirits twice, and both times I've nearly killed us.

"Selly!" Keegan screams again, his face a white blur through the breaking waves, Leander still unmoving in his arms.

The *Emma* wrenches sideways, and something makes me look up as a pulley rips free of the mast and swings out at the end of its rope, slicing toward my head like a deadly weapon. I drop to my knees as it arcs just overhead, then around to tangle itself in the rigging. I brace myself against the wheel, using all my body weight to keep us from surrendering to the whirlpool forming around us.

*I have to try.*

Both times I've reached for the spirits, I tried to give them orders, tried to direct them to my will—it's what I've tried to do with everything, everyone, all my life.

I used to be so sure of everything I knew. But now all I

know is that the world is vast. And like this ship, I'm a tiny speck in it.

That's what Rensa was trying to show me—I'm just one part of something far larger, and there's no weakness in that. Only strength.

I dig in my pocket and pull out the little paper boat. This has to be a real sacrifice, and this little boat is the only thing I own that means enough to me.

It's a gift from a boy who could give me enough gold and jewels to fill my father's fleet, but gave me something priceless, instead—a piece of himself. It's a promise to send me back to the place I love most, even when he wanted to keep me by his side.

It's a gift that honors who I am, not who he wishes I could be. It's him believing in me, even when I haven't believed in myself.

At first I can't seem to make my freezing cold fingers let it go, and my hand trembles as I stare at it like it belongs to someone else.

Then suddenly my fingers open, and the fragile little boat is whipped away on the wind in an instant, vanishing into nothingness.

Vaguely I sense I'm still holding the wheel, but I'm already slipping into the headspace Leander showed me.

*Please,* I beg the spirits, asking now, not commanding. *Please.*

And then I see them. Panic rips through me—how *many* of them was he charming at once? I can't possibly—how do I—it's like ten thousand fireflies are whirling around me on the wind, angry, chaotic, their companion suddenly vanished.

I force myself to go slowly. I humble myself as the waves

crash over me. I show them how they can help us if they're willing—how to flow over the fabric of the sail and push the boat forward.

The mainsail splits further, the ragged edges immediately pulled to pieces, and the spirits dance in and around it, barely seeming to hear me.

In desperation, I throw myself so far into the connection, I don't know if there's a way back.

*Please,* I beg.

And then I do more than speak to them. I show them my heart. I show them my love of the sea and the wind. I show them they're a part of me, and that I need them. This is what Leander meant when he said the sea is where my magic belongs. He was right.

I show them how much I love to be here with them. How much I've always loved that. And I show them how much I love this little boat that's trying so valiantly to carry us. I show them I love the boys crewing her with me, brave and loyal and determined.

I show them the way my heart's tangled around Leander— that I'm just like them, drawn to him, and that I'm trying with everything I have to help him.

I show them that I understand now what Rensa meant when she said she'd die for her crew and they knew it.

And I show them that finally I understand what she wanted me to see—that the world is big, and so much more of it matters than me.

I try, not knowing if the spirits can possibly understand, to share the sacrifices each of us is making. And suddenly . . . something shifts.

The wind evens out as we leave the whirlpool behind, and the whole boat hums as we move away, as the air spirits begin to dance with me instead of whirling around me.

And it's glorious.

It's like sunshine on my skin, after I've been soaked in salt water and freezing cold for so long I've forgotten what warmth is. It's like that moment when you've been in harbor forever and suddenly your ship is nosing her way out into the open sea, picking up speed. It's that first hint of salt on the breeze, when you've been in a stuffy, stinking city all day.

The spirits dance with me and around me, and with a dizzying rush of bliss, I can't believe I've been missing this my whole life. All because I was too proud to *ask* for it.

I see the way they dance around Keegan and Leander— almost like they don't know Keegan's there, but swirling in wild eddies around my prince, tugging at his clothes and his hair, even as he lies unmoving. And I know—he's not stirring, but he's alive. They're still connected to him.

Exhilaration runs through me, and the spirits dance in response to it.

He's alive. He's *alive*.

Then something more occurs to me, and I reach out for them once more, trying to figure out how to show them my question.

The wind is whipping toward us across the sea from the northeast. There should be nothing between us and Kethos, but perhaps . . . Slowly, carefully, I ask if anything has interrupted that howling wind as it flies across the surface of the water.

At first they don't seem to understand what I'm asking, but

then the answer comes quickly and simply: a plume of spirits pushing in the direction I want, as sure as a compass needle.

There's something in the sea, almost dead ahead.

My eyes snap open, and I pull the wheel to port, correcting our course, baring my teeth in a ferocious grin.

The spirits have shown me exactly where to find the Isles of the Gods.

# PART FOUR

## THE ISLES OF THE GODS

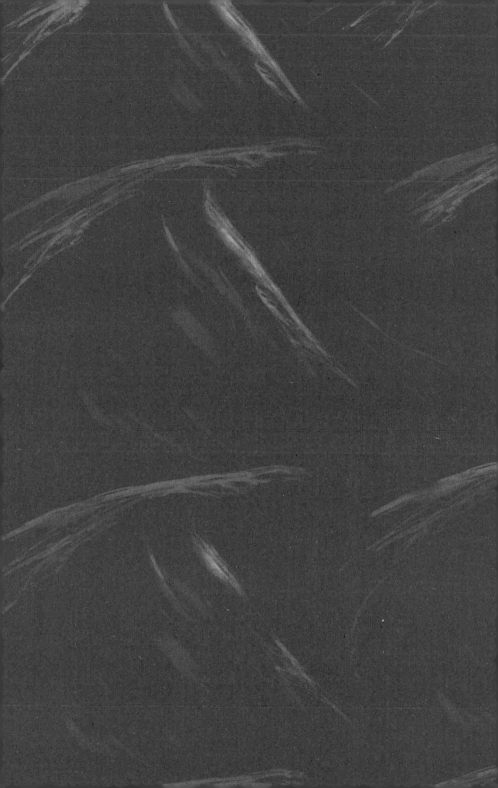

# LEANDER

◆

*The Isle of Barrica*
*The Isles of the Gods*

My head feels like someone's curled their fist around it and they're *squeezing*. When I risk opening my eyes, pale morning light stabs through them, and I wince. Then I blink, blink again, and the world above me swims into focus. Selly's leaning over me, her hair pulled free of her braid, eyes shadowed, and she's biting her lip, concern all over her features.

The spirits are dancing around her like a halo, framing her against the light behind her, setting strands of her hair wafting in the breeze they create for her. Something's different about the way they respond to her.

I reach up to trace a finger along her jawline, to tap it against her lips, to wordlessly tell her not to worry. I should probably wonder where we are, but I can't think why that would be important. With a soft breath out, she catches at my wrist and lifts my hand so I can cup her cheek. I like it.

"You," she says, "are an idiot."

"Hello yourself," I mumble.

She allows herself a small smile, and I study the way her lips curve. "Who doesn't hold on to something in a storm like that?" she whispers. "I thought you'd killed yourself."

"What happened?"

"You went flying, hit your head. The spirits . . . panicked."

My eyes widen as memory floods back and my heart tries to clamber up my throat. "They *what*? How are we still alive?"

"Well, I . . . had a conversation with them."

"You did?" I try to sit up, and she holds me down by the shoulders.

"Don't panic, Mister Magician. We figured it out between us. Had to, since you'd fallen down on the job."

"Sorry," I murmur, still gazing up at her as my heart begins to slow again. Her eyes are a mossy green, the closest I've ever seen to the shade of my magician's marks. I curl my fingers slowly, trailing my fingertips along her skin. I can feel where the salt's dried on it.

"Better not start apologizing now, my prince," she says. "You'll run out of time to cover it all."

I pause, halfway to a smile. "Wait. If you're here, who's steering the boat?"

"Keegan. Now sit up nice and slow, because you're going to want to see this."

She wraps an arm around me to help me to my feet and holds me steady as I check whether I can support myself.

"You all right?"

"Maybe hold on a little longer," I reply, sliding an arm around her waist and looking down at her. "Just to be extra sure."

Still smiling, she lets me get away with it, and together we make our way across to the port side of our little boat, to gaze out across the sea.

The wind is still whipping around us, the tops breaking off the waves into whitecaps, but up ahead of us it's like an invisible barrier slides through the air and the water—everything on the other side is different.

The change isn't gradual, the clouds lessening, the seas becoming softer. Instead, on one side of the boundary are our threatening skies and dangerous seas. On the other, the water is a calm and friendly sparkling blue.

As we pass through the divide, the *Emma*'s sails stop straining, and she settles from a canter to a stroll. The breeze is light and the air is warm, stroking my skin with velvety fingers, the air spirits almost playful. It's like we've sailed through an invisible dome, and inside lies a perfect summer day.

The sudden sunny atmosphere reminds me of Kethos. When I was young, we used to cruise down there on one of the family yachts in the summer. We'd anchor offshore and dive into the sea for hours, drying ourselves in the sun like a row of warm seals laid out on the deck.

But here I see not the Kethosi coast on the horizon, but all at once—though they must have been there before—eight islands rising before us. It's as if something stopped me from noticing them until this moment.

The largest is the Isle of the Mother, and her seven children are gathered before her in a circle. On the map, a lightly traced line joins the eight of them in a circle, and now I can see reefs beneath the water connecting them, dark shadows just close enough to the surface to cause little breaking waves. A crown of white, starred with the vivid green jewels of the islands.

The islands themselves are lush, crowded with impenetrable jungle, a hundred shades of green tangled together.

Selly shifts within the circle of my arm, peeling off her wet jacket and gloves without pulling away. She lets them fall to the deck, turning her face up to the sun and breathing out slowly. My gaze traces a path along her profile as the breeze teases her hair, strands of it drying in the sun and starting to curl.

Then, as she reaches out to rest her hands on the railing, I see something else, and a shock goes through my whole body. "Selly . . . your marks."

She glances down, then yanks up her shirtsleeves, gasping as she reveals her forearms. The thick, childlike magician's marks that were painted there before are gone.

In their place are finely wrought emerald lines, in geometric patterns I've never seen before. Like a kaleidoscope, squares and triangles and diamonds fit together in endless complexity.

"What are they?" she whispers.

"Nothing I've ever seen," I say slowly. The sight is electric, sending a shimmer through me I can't explain. An air magician's marks are all loops and swirls and curves, not . . . not this.

"What does it mean?"

"I don't know," I murmur. "These aren't even close to . . . Selly, I don't know."

She curls her hands around the railing, and we gaze at this new mystery. If she was unique before, now she's something I've never even imagined.

How did it happen?

And why?

"Selly!" Keegan calls from the wheel, and we both glance back together. "Do you want to take us in?"

She looks up at me, wonder still all over her face, though she doesn't slip from the circle of my arm just yet.

"Shall we go make this sacrifice?" she asks.

"All right." I sigh. "But we're not done figuring your marks out, not yet."

"I know," she agrees, her smile soft. "But we've beaten them here. If we're quick, maybe we can get back under way again before they arrive."

I can see it in her face, for the first time in a long time, and I'm feeling it spark inside my chest as well—hope.

We were prepared to give everything to this—to die in the effort to make this sacrifice.

But maybe . . . just maybe, we won't have to.

Perhaps we'll make it home—to Keegan's beloved libraries, which might explain her mysterious magician's marks. To my sisters, whom I'd happily invite to tell me everything I've ever done wrong, just for the joy of seeing them.

To . . . I can barely whisper it, even to myself, but somewhere within me is enough madness to imagine the idea.

To a future with this girl in my arms. Whatever it looks like.

All I know is I can't bear to part ways with her.

"Let's go," I say. "And Selly—I know you saved my life yet again. Thank you."

She gazes up at me, then smiles slowly, something softer, gentler than it's been before. I match it, my own lips curving in response. I can't help myself. I want so badly—if she just lifted her chin a fraction, gave me the smallest of signs—but then the boat hits an errant wave, and we grab at each other for balance, and she only laughs. "You're welcome."

She takes her place behind the wheel, and Keegan and I move without instruction to trim the sails for her. As I watch the spirits flow across the sails and loop around to play with her hair again, the realization hits me, an echo of that yearning moment just now when I wished I could kiss her.

They know I want to touch her. So they circle her instead—they tug at wisps of her hair, as fascinated as me.

As she guides us in toward the Isle of Barrica, I look up to study our destination—all black rock at the base, steep cliffs rising until they reach the island's crown of jungle.

I can't believe we've done it. We've made it here, and the temple is within our reach.

We're not far ahead of Laskia and her crew, but maybe, *maybe* we're far enough.

"I'll need directions, Your Highness," Selly calls, her tone light.

It's the first time someone's used that title in what seems like forever, but I don't feel the usual weight settling on me when I hear it. Not today.

I pull the journal from its waxed cotton bag and flip it open, leafing past pages covered in sketches and lines of scrawl—the handwriting of the generations of royals who came before me. I've read it enough times now that I know exactly what I'm looking for, and it doesn't take me long to find the description of our landing place in my great-grandfather's neat handwriting.

"You're looking for a cove," I call back. "The cliffs rise

higher on either side of the opening, but at the far end they drop to ground level. There's a strip of black sand, and we can drop anchor and get ashore there."

"Aye, aye," she calls cheerfully, and she bosses us around, calling out orders as she works the boat around the island in search of the little cove. We could almost be in Kethos, except the cliffs beneath the greenery are black stone, not white chalk.

Keegan ducks below, emerging with iced buns I'm glad I didn't see when I was throwing half our food overboard. They're sweet and sticky, the best thing I've ever eaten—my relief and the sunshine make them light and delicious.

I deliver one to Selly and stay with her as she rests one hand on the wheel and eats with the other. We lick our fingers clean, sugar and salt lingering, and she absolutely catches me watching her at work, her eyes dancing, though she says nothing.

The *Emma* cuts smoothly through the tropical blue waters around us, and as the sunshine warms us, it's hard to remember the desperation of last night.

"I see a break in the cliffs," Keegan calls from the bow, and Selly spins the wheel to turn us in toward it as I peel away to deal with the sails once more. But as our little boat noses around the bend to head inside the landing cove, Selly curses behind me, and I lift my gaze from the line I'm tying off.

*Please, no.*

The cove is already occupied by a sleek black boat. Its engines are silent, and it rests quietly at anchor. It's no larger than the *Emma,* but it's nothing like our faithful fishing boat. This one is made to cut through the water like a knife.

Selly drops her voice to a whisper, hands light on the wheel. "Seven hells. Should we find somewhere else to come ashore?"

I shake my head, eyes locked on the boat. "This is the only place. The journal's clear."

Keegan's studying it thoughtfully. "They don't have a lookout," he murmurs. "Perhaps there's nobody aboard. Or they're not hostile—maybe your sister heard the news, sent someone else to make the sacrifice?"

"Maybe," says Selly softly, not sounding like she believes it. "We should go now, go quickly, get ashore. We've got more room to move on land if somebody comes up on deck and sees us and doesn't like us."

Following her whispered instructions, we steer the *Emma* up into the wind, quickly furling her rustling sails, and drop her anchor—I'm dreading a noisy chain like the ones I've seen on my family's boats, but Selly produces something tied to a thick rope and casts it out into the water with a grunt of effort. It sinks silently, and the *Emma* swings out to the end of her line without anybody appearing on the deck of the other boat.

We'll have to swim ashore, so we sling fishing nets over the side to use as a ladder down to the water, the stink of the day before yesterday's catch enveloping us in a noxious cloud.

Selly spreads a waterproof fisherman's cape on the deck, and with a look that warns us against making any comment about it, strips to her underwear, laying her clothes on top of the cape, and knotting her shoelaces together so she can sling her boots around her neck for the swim.

I'm frozen in place. Then I realize Keegan's already following suit, and I fumble with my shirt buttons, struggling to think about anything other than the creamy skin of her long legs. I can practically hear Augusta: *Really, Leander? Thinking about that at a time like this?* But I can't stop thinking about Selly. And I don't want to.

*Just wait until you meet her, Augusta.*

Trying to recover my dignity, because I know at least Selly and probably Keegan saw me gawk at her—or maybe just trying to make her smile—I draw a breath for a whispered joke about my physique as we climb down the fishing net. And then I clamp my lips together, desperately holding in a choking cough as the smell of the fishing nets hits me all over again. Serves me right.

Keegan passes the parcel of our clothes and the journal, and I pass it on to Selly, who's the strongest swimmer by far.

She makes her way to shore on her back, keeping it out of the water, one eye on the silent boat keeping us company in this quiet little cove. There's still no sign of life from it as we reach the shore and find our feet to walk up the black sand.

The strangest feeling comes over me as I make contact with the island itself—it's like a sharpening of all my senses. The mysterious boat bobbing at anchor is forgotten—my companions are forgotten.

Birds scream in the trees, and the breeze plays through the branches. There are a thousand shades of lush green. I smell the clean, earthy scent of the undergrowth, the salt of the sea behind us.

I feel the island through the soles of my feet—but though everything around me is clearer, crisper, it's also more distant, because I can sense Barrica here, her presence pressing in around me. It's the same kind of closeness as when I pray at temple—her mind, for want of a better word, pressing in against mine. A familiarity, and at the same time a sense that she's so much more vast than I can properly understand. It's overwhelming, but comforting in its familiarity.

"Leander?" Selly asks quietly, her gaze on me as she picks up that something's changed.

"Can you feel it?" I manage.

"Feel what?" Keegan asks, turning toward me.

"She's here," I breathe.

Everyone goes still. "She's—" he begins, glancing around.

"No, not Laskia," I murmur, my lips curving to a smile. *"Her."*

Selly looks around at the jungle, then shakes her head, and so too does Keegan.

"Your family has a connection to her," he points out. "It's promising you can feel her presence, I suppose. Do you know the way from here?"

I do. There are still my father's pages of the journal I haven't read, but every member of my family before him left their account of the walk to the temple. And even if they hadn't, I'd know it instinctively.

We dress and lace up our boots, drying ourselves as best we can in the process.

And then we climb, leaving the boats behind.

We make our way through the greenery, undergrowth catching at our legs, leaf litter crunching beneath our feet. The warm, damp air embraces us as we follow the faintest of paths—they must have been created by animals, because I spot a broken stick every so often, a sign something has passed this way. Occasionally a breeze snakes through the crowded trees, sending them swaying.

There's a rhythm to this place that feels like my heartbeat.

The ground grows steeper, and my breath comes harder as we climb. I can see more daylight between the trees now—we're coming closer to the island's peak—and we pause to pull each other up the steepest parts, linking hands and heaving.

"How long do you think we've been climbing?" Selly huffs after a while, hauling on Keegan's arm as he scrambles up a slippery part of the path.

"Twenty minutes?" he guesses, producing a piece of cloth from a pocket—I can't call what he's holding a handkerchief, and I'm sure it never was. He uses it to mop his brow, mostly just spreading sweat and grime around.

"This is the path, right?" Selly asks, squinting suspiciously up what could only generously be described as a track.

"This is it," I say, holding out my hand for her to haul me up next. Her grip locks into mine, she heaves, I push off a tree, and somehow I clamber up beside her. We stand there, still holding hands, both panting for breath. "This is it," I say again. "Every account in the journal says the temple is at the summit, and if there's one thing we're doing, it's going uphill."

"Everything about you is uphill," she mutters, but the habitual jab feels like affection now, and she lets me twine my fingers through hers.

It's only a few minutes later that we find a clearing dead ahead. The trees stop abruptly, though there's no sign the clearing is man-made—no sign of stumps, or that new saplings want to impinge on this space.

At the center stands a temple of ancient stone. It's a low building, broad at the base, rising to a point at its peak. Vines creep up its dark sides, winding around the structure, tendrils tucked into every crack in the stone. Moss grows down the side nearest us, like green velvet pulled thin, giving the whole thing an emerald sheen.

I can feel the power of this place as I gaze up at it, but there's a strange thread of discomfort running through the sensation. Like I'm in the middle of a race I've trained to run, but suddenly there's a thorn in my shoe.

*Something's wrong.*

Does she find me wanting? Does she pay enough attention to the passage of time and the affairs of men to know I'm late?

"We're here in time." Selly's voice breaks into my thoughts, as if answering them somehow. But when I turn, she's looking through a gap in the trees to the cove far below.

I see the *Emma* anchored by the silent black boat, but there's still no sign of the pursuers we saw behind us on the horizon. My anticipation, though, my dreams of clambering back down the hill, of clearing the mouth of the cove before Laskia arrives—it's suddenly muted, half buried beneath this strange discomfort.

"Are you ready?" Keegan asks.

I nod, my mouth dry, and flex my hands, stretching my fingers and then balling them into fists. "I'm ready."

We walk toward the temple together.

I can feel the two of them behind me, but my attention is focused forward, and the world around me fades away as I let my senses range ahead toward the altar within the temple. I'm nearly at the entrance now.

Selly grabs my arm an instant before I stumble over the

bodies, yanking me back. For a moment I'm caught off balance, looking around at her with frustration that borders on anger. Then I follow her gaze, and Keegan's, and I see the four of them stretched out before us.

They're facedown, half in and half out of the temple's arched opening, one with an arm thrown out toward us as if in silent appeal.

They're aged and desiccated, hair stringy, skin stretched tight—but their clothes are still intact. And . . . the earth is disturbed around that outflung hand. There are scratch marks, as though the body tried to pull itself forward, and they're as fresh as if they were made only minutes ago.

"How could the clothes, the—" Selly grimaces and gestures to the scratch marks on the ground. "How could they have lasted all this time, while the bodies ended up like that? It must take a long time for someone to dry out. And why *did* they dry out instead of rotting, or whatever happens in a hot, wet climate like this?"

Keegan comes up beside us and drops into a crouch. He nods respectfully at the temple's opening, then gently turns over one of the bodies, easing it onto its back with a careful touch.

It was once a woman, I think, with long hair, clad in light cotton skirts, and at her collar is a ruby pin winking at us in the sunlight.

"They didn't come on behalf of Alinor, or Barrica's people," Keegan says quietly. "Behold the fate of those who do not come here to pray."

"Seven hells," I mutter.

"And he means that respectfully," Selly adds, nudging me with an elbow, glancing up pointedly at the temple, as if Barrica might overhear. In fairness, our goddess very well might.

Keegan points to the clawed marks in the ground, brushing at them with one finger. "I think these were made today," he says. "The marks seem fresh, and we don't know much about this place, but I imagine rain would have washed them away if they were older."

Selly nods, lifting a finger to point at another of the bodies without touching it. "Judging by his clothes, he was a sailor. I think this is the crew of the boat we saw anchored in the cove. The question is: What did Laskia send them to do? And did they succeed before they died?"

Now we turn to look at the temple.

The urgency of my own mission is beating like a drum in my chest now—I don't know what they wanted, but I know what *I* want.

I know my reason for coming here is pure—I'm here to worship. I'm here to make the same sacrifice my family has offered in Barrica's service for five hundred years, ever since one of us gave his own life. So the fate of this crew is not for me.

I rise to my feet, gazing at the entrance. Something touches my hand, and I see Selly holding out a box of matches, and her knife. I slip them into my pocket, step carefully past the bodies, and walk inside.

I thought it would be dark in the temple, but pinpricks of light stream down from the ceiling where stones are missing. They fall in patterns, a deliberate part of the design. The place is still dimly lit, though, and I walk forward slowly, shuffling my feet along the dusty ground.

As my eyes adjust to the gloom, I make out the faint shape of the altar ahead of me, strangely uneven. The journal says there should be a statue of Barrica behind the altar—perhaps that's what I'm seeing.

But as I draw closer, that clamoring sense of wrongness increases. I fumble in my pocket for the matches and strike one with shaking hands, a sick feeling burning in my gut.

I need more light, and I can't think what to sacrifice—with an urgency I can't explain flooding through me, I drop the rest of the matches to the floor, and grind them into the stone with the heel of my boot until they're unusable. An instant later they blink out of existence as the spirits accept them.

I can dimly hear Selly's voice from the entrance, only a handful of steps behind me, though it's like she's speaking from a distance.

"Leander, what is it?"

I reach out to the fire spirits dancing around the head of the match, and in response to my touch they joyfully flare higher, lighting up the scene around me before the flame burns out.

One glimpse is enough, though. One of the others gasps, and I finally understand what I'm seeing.

The altar and the statue of the goddess have been smashed beyond repair.

*This isn't possible.*

*This can't be happening.*

I stumble forward, nearly tripping over a sledgehammer lying on the ground at the base of the altar. I grab at the edges of the broken stones, every muscle in my body straining as I try to lift them back into place, but I can't budge them an inch.

I run my hands over the altar, over the piece of the statue

that's fallen into the middle of it—one of Barrica's great eyes stares up at me, carved into the stone.

I grab for Selly's knife, flicking out the blade, and slice it across my palm in one movement—I've dreamed of this moment, imagined what it might be like, all my life, but I don't even feel the cut. I tip my hand to let the blood drip onto the broken stone, my breath coming sharp and ragged as it patters down.

I close my eyes and reach for Barrica—reach for the prayer that's always allowed me to connect with her. But though she's here—though I felt her as soon as I set foot on the island—there's a gulf between us. A black chasm that swallows up my voice.

What was once a prickle of discomfort is now a screaming in my ears—or maybe *I'm* the one who's screaming.

I can feel Barrica all around me, but without her temple to amplify my sacrifice, I can't channel the strength of my faith into her. I grasp wildly for another idea—should I cut off a finger, my hand, should I give her more blood?

But deep in my gut, I know the answer.

Everything we've done, all this way we've come, everyone we've lost—all of it means nothing. We've come too late.

# SELLY

*The Temple of Barrica*
*The Isles of the Gods*

This cannot be happening.

    This *cannot* be happening.

Leander's on his knees before the smashed altar, a terrifying, broken sound coming from him, and he doesn't move when we call for him, doesn't give any sign he can even hear us.

I exchange a glance with Keegan, close my eyes to pray—*I'm trying to help, please spare me*—and step over the threshold. I take another step, and another, and then I'm running, crouching beside him to take him by the arm.

He lets me pull him upright—his hands are cold, his face blank of all expression—and he stumbles toward the entrance as I guide him. The sunlight is blinding as we step out into it, and my eyes sting and flood with tears. I only remember the dead bodies at the last moment, clearing them with a skip and dragging Leander to one side with me. Blood falls from the cut on his palm, hitting the freshly turned earth between us.

He wrenches free of me, stumbles to the edge of the trees, and bracing his hands against his knees, throws up.

I simply stand in the center of the clearing, staring at him, trying helplessly to force my brain into action.

I'm not royal—I'm just the girl who brought him here in a boat, and I have no idea what to do next.

I should try to get him to safety, I suppose, to the *Emma.* Get away from here, back across the sea to the queen. Should we run? Is there something more we can do here?

Keegan is clutching the journal, and he falls back on what he knows best, sinking down to sit on a rock and pulling it out to start turning the pages, looking for answers.

Finally our prince straightens and turns toward us, his brown skin pale.

"Leander," I try, aching for him, feeling his pain as though it's my own. "This isn't your fault. You couldn't have known—"

"Don't." His voice is a lead weight.

"But—"

"Do you want a list of everything that's my fault?" he snaps, anguished.

"That's—"

"The loss of the progress fleet, and the deaths of all my friends who were on it," he begins, stricken. "The sailors who were on it, people I never even *met,* dead because of me. The *Lizabetta,* your captain, and your crew. The ambassador, every ship that's had a cargo confiscated in the last year, every life that will be lost in this war. Whole *countries* will be lost—the Barren Reaches will be just the beginning."

"The war is more than—" But he's not finished.

"All this is happening because the green sisters sniffed an

opening. They've been working for generations to get their people back to church. It's not easy with a sleeping god, but they were finally starting to gather momentum. They looked at us and saw fewer people at temple every month, and they knew the day was finally coming when Macean could awaken. Barrica is the *Sentinel*—it's what she does—and my family are her servants. My sister chose *me* to send here. She chose *me* to strengthen my goddess.

"This war needn't have happened at all, but I put the sacrifice off. And now he's going to awaken—Barrica won't be strong enough to stop him—and we're going to find out what it's like when two *gods* go to war."

He lifts one hand, scrubbing at his wet eyes. I want to step forward, to go to him. To take his hands, to make him see that all this is too much for one boy to bear alone.

"They're going to catch up with us soon," he says quietly. "So my final act has to be taking responsibility. For the fact that I've killed all those people. I've killed Keegan, who's offered me nothing but undeserved loyalty. I've killed *you*, Selly. And I've dismantled your entire life first—yet you still saved mine, over and over."

I take a step toward him, and he lifts his bloodied hand as if to ward me off, his eyes wet.

"Leander, let me—"

"No!" His voice is a knife.

Wrapping my arms around myself, I turn away to stumble for the edge of the clearing, as if I can outrun this hurt. Pressing a hand over my mouth, I lean against one of the gnarled trees hemming us in, letting it take my weight as my knees threaten to give.

This can't be how it ends. With us giving up. With him pushing me away.

There's a parade of ants marching up the rough bark, and I want to tell them there's nothing at the top worth working for. I watch numbly as they laboriously work their way around a knot in the wood, and then I let my gaze range up until it finds a gap in the trees, and a slice of the cove where the *Emma* waits for us.

She bobs at anchor alongside the sleek, silent boat that brought the dead crew behind us to destroy this place.

I tilt my head, and it takes me far too long to understand what I'm seeing. Even when I do, I stare, blinking, my mouth dry, my tired head woolly, trying to form the words to describe it.

There's a third boat anchored in the cove.

I can't see anyone moving on it, which means they're probably climbing already.

"Leander." I whirl around, already moving toward him. "There's another boat down there—Laskia must be—"

But I'm cut off as Keegan comes abruptly to his feet, his eyes glued to the journal in his hands.

*"This is the sort of place I wish I could stay forever,"* he reads quietly, gazing intently at the words on the page as I fall silent. *"But the captain's calling me away. If only we could linger and explore. I wouldn't dare visit any of the other islands, where the other gods must be as strong as mine is here, but it would be fun to take a look from the boat.*

*"Most of all, a part of me dreams of visiting the Isle of the Mother. I pointed out to the captain that all her children are said to be present in the Mother's temple, so Barrica would keep us safe, but she's having*

*none of it. The stories say there's a temple on the Isle of the Mother, built before all the others. I wish we could see it, learn who built it, learn whether they knew their gods more intimately than we do today.*

*"What must it have been like for those early worshippers and temple builders to visit the Isle where they say the gods were born?"*

Keegan glances up, like we're in a classroom and he's waiting for us to catch up with him. But he loses patience in a heartbeat, lowering the book and looking to each of us in turn.

"Do you understand?" he asks.

"I don't recognize that. Who wrote it?" Leander asks, his voice a whisper.

"It's the most recent entry," Keegan replies. "It must have been your father."

"And you're saying . . ." Leander's words die out, desperate hope warring with the fear of being wrong on his expressive face.

"I am saying that judging by this journal, your father was at least as reckless as you, Your Highness. Imagine suggesting visiting the Isle of the Mother herself. No wonder the captain refused."

I could swear Keegan's smiling.

"And I am also saying that if he's right, we have one more card left to play. But only if we can live long enough to make it off this island."

# LASKIA

*The Temple of Barrica*
*The Isles of the Gods*

Jude stumbles out of Barrica's temple, dragging in a long breath of the humid jungle air. "They got to the altar before they . . . before *that* happened," he says, refusing to look at the dried-out bodies by my feet.

I'm leaning down to study the team I sent straight from Port Naranda, all of them dry as dust, while Dasriel explores the clearing.

They did their job and broke the altar, but they can't tell me where the prince is, and *that's* what I need. With a growl, I kick the nearest one in frustration—the bones fall apart inside the withered skin, but the clothes hold it all together. "Could you see any sign of where he went?"

Jude simply shakes his head, pressing his lips together as he swallows hard.

"The goddess, then. Do you think she's out of action now?"

Jude spreads his hands helplessly. "Not a priest, Laskia."

"Sure, but she didn't strike you down like she struck them down," I reply, and he shoots me a sharp look. I guess that's him figuring out why I sent *him* in to check on the altar, instead of braving the temple myself.

Perhaps the goddess is out of action—or he prayed while he was in there, to keep himself safe. I'd much rather we were on the Isle of Macean, where *I* could pray.

I want to tell my god what we've done—that the Sentinel, who's watched over him all these centuries, will lose her strength now, will loosen his bonds. I want to tell him *I've* done it. That I, Laskia, was the one brave enough, strong enough, to do what he's needed all these years.

I want to promise him I'll find the prince next, and I'll wipe out everything that stands between him and his return, but I daren't reach out to him—not here. If any part of Barrica is still present, a prayer to her brother must be the surest way to draw her attention.

"Any sign the prince has been inside?" I ask, grinding my teeth, casting about for something, *anything*. I can't go back to Ruby and Sister Beris with an *I don't know.*

Jude hesitates just a bit too long for my comfort before he shakes his head. "No way to know."

"Well, he's somewhere," Dasriel says, without looking up. The sailors stayed behind on the boat, and it's just the three of us up here, Dasriel roaming the edges of the clearing like some great hunting beast searching for a scent.

My anger bubbles up, bursting past the barriers that try to keep it in place. "How can they not be here?" I snap. "We followed the only path up from the cove. From their boat! It's the only way for them to get back to it, isn't it?"

"Should we . . ." Jude's voice trails off, and when I glance across, he's looking at the dead bodies.

"Should we what?" I grind out.

"I don't know. Bury them?"

I snort. "Wherever they're bound for, they're on their way already. Covering them in dirt won't make a difference. If you want to do something useful, Jude—" My voice rises, sharpens, and I ball my hands into fists. I have to stay focused. I can't afford to lose my temper. "If you want to do something useful," I try again, "then figure out where your prince went."

But before he gets a chance to reply, Dasriel drops to a crouch. "Here," he rumbles.

I'm across the clearing in a second, dropping to my knees on the damp earth beside him.

With one large finger, he taps the mossy ground—and then I see it. Two crimson drops of blood, fresh.

We might not know where they're going. But now we have their trail.

# KEEGAN

*The Still Waters*
*The Isles of the Gods*


I'm covered in dirt and sweat and scratches, half scrambling and half simply falling down the hill. But we're nearly at sea level—nearly at the reef.

Beside me Selly curses as she catches at a tree to slow herself, the rough bark cutting into her hand.

There's truly no way back now. We've left our boat on the far side of the island, anchored by the boats of the dead crew and the newcomers—we have to assume it's Laskia, Jude, and her magician. That it's the ship that followed us from Port Cathar.

And we have to assume that as soon as they work out which way we've gone, they'll be on our trail. But our goal is before us, and I can't make myself think a second past reaching it.

Leander shouts a warning as I push my way through a tangle of vines strung between two trees, and abruptly I burst from the edge of the jungle with too much momentum.

A cliff's edge looms ahead of me, and I throw myself to the ground in a desperate attempt to stop before I go over it, rolling, arms flung out to slow myself.

The world whirls by, and I come to rest flat on my back in the leaf litter, one leg hanging over the edge of the cliff, my breath loud in my own ears. I let it rasp in and out as I gaze up at the flawless blue sky.

This truly is the most beautiful place I've ever been. It's not a bad choice, if you need somewhere to spend your last day.

Selly crawls to the edge of the cliff, studying the reef below us. It's a dark mess topped with white foam, the rock just barely beneath the surface of the water, curving away like a seawall around the mirrorlike lagoon inside. The Still Waters, Leander said the journal called it, and I can see why.

The next island across from ours is the Isle of the Mother, larger than any of the seven islands dedicated to her children, rising steeply to a peak hidden in the jungle.

"The reef will be razor sharp," Selly warns us. "If it gets anywhere near your skin, it will shred you."

That means we can't jump off the cliff and then climb up onto the reef itself. We need to climb down instead, and hope it's shallow enough to wade the whole way along.

"This is a terrible plan," she mutters, peering over the edge of the cliff. "Completely terrible."

"It's also our only plan," Leander points out, glancing back over his shoulder.

So one by one, we climb down the cliff, muscles aching, cuts stinging, clinging to even the smallest of outcroppings.

When we reach the bottom, the water swirls around our ankles, soaking boots that had just begun to dry.

Selly and I exchange a look, and she takes the lead, gesturing for Leander to follow, while I bring up the rear. We both understand what we're doing—putting our sailor to the front, to plot the safest course, and putting me behind the prince, as a shield from his pursuers. He's so lost in his thoughts, I'm not sure he's realized. That's better—it would be a horrible thing to know.

The back of my neck prickles as we set out, and I'm not sure if it's sweat from the sun beating down on us, or my body's desperate attempt to warn me our hunters will soon have us within their sights. But after a couple of minutes, with the water washing across the reef ahead of me, the waves coming as regularly as a slowly ticking clock, I'm forced to concentrate on my foot placement. The rock and coral beneath my boots is uneven, pocketed with holes that are a broken ankle just waiting to happen.

Up ahead, Selly stumbles as she suddenly steps down to a knee-deep section, arms windmilling madly as she fights for balance.

Leander reaches out to steady her and snatches his hand back when she snaps at him: "No!"

And just like that, I'm yanked from the almost meditative state of concentration I've been lulled into as I pick my way along the stones.

She can afford to fall in. He can't.

The purpose of the next hour of her life is simply to find a safe path for him, and mine is to follow close, and stay between him and danger.

So I allow myself to sink into concentration once more, and focus on that lulling rhythm. Perhaps I should be spending this time detailing my regrets. Thinking about the things I'd like to have said to my parents, my brother, or my sister, thinking of the books I haven't read, the classes at the Bibliotek I'll never take.

Perhaps I should be mentally composing my firsthand account of this journey, even if no other scholar will ever read it, or composing a prayer to my goddess.

But it's a glorious day, in the most beautiful place I've ever been, and the Isle of the Mother is looming ahead of us. We might well be the first people to set foot on its soil in millennia.

So instead, I watch the waves break across the reef, and the waters swirl around my ankles. And I feel the sun on my back.

And I'm content to simply . . . be.

# LEANDER

◆

*The Isle of the Mother*
*The Isles of the Gods*

We're about two-thirds of the way along the reef when I see them behind us: three figures, one larger than the other two. Laskia, Jude, and their huge magician. The breeze is light enough, I can hear their voices when they raise them, though I can't make out the words.

I try to pick up the pace and stay on Selly's heels, but the truth is there's no fast way to do this. The only thing that might save us is that the same is true for them.

Suddenly there's a shout of warning from Keegan, and I turn, spreading my arms out for balance, already ducking as I see the big magician raising a hand.

At first I think he's pointing at me, and then, in horror, I realize he's holding a gun. There's nothing we can do but watch, trying to crouch, trying to make ourselves smaller. I can see Keegan shaking, and he's only half crouching, his hands braced against his knees.

"Keegan, get down," I hiss over the soft lapping of the waves. He doesn't move, doesn't look back. And then I understand. He's standing between me and the bullet.

Abruptly the water kicks up into a splash of spray just ahead of us, and an instant later a *bang* echoes across the lagoon.

Keegan's muttering something that might be a prayer, and Selly's calling out to me, urgency in her voice.

"Leander, we have to keep moving—we can't let them get closer!"

Jude's moving too, splashing up to the big man with the gun, calling something out to him. He gestures at the island ahead of us. Laskia snaps in what's clearly agreement, and something about his body language makes me think he's telling the man not to shoot.

He points at the island again: he thinks they'll have a better chance of hitting us with their limited ammunition at close quarters.

My heart lurches, and I turn to hurry after Selly once more—a glance back shows me Keegan's pinched white face, his gaze unfocused.

It seems unbelievable that Jude could be one of our pursuers—the same boy who sat around the dining table with us at school, who laughed with us, who was one of us.

I can see him now, sliding me a pencil in class, hiking out with me across the fields near school in pursuit of—I forget, a bull, I think?—on some prank or dare. I can see myself unpacking a box of treats from home and handing him the sticky toffee I asked for, just so I could give it to him. He didn't get boxes of his own, and I didn't want him to miss out.

But that was the thing, wasn't it? We all had boxes, and he had none, because however much I felt he was one of us, he wasn't. And in the end, that mattered.

I thought he was my friend, though. If you'd told me then that one day he'd hunt me to my death, I'd have thought you'd lost your mind.

When I next glance back, the trio are nearer than they were before—they're gaining ground, I'm sure of it.

They're closer still by the time we reach the steep cliffs of the Isle of the Mother—anytime Jude or Laskia is in danger of overbalancing, their giant simply takes hold of them and puts them back on their feet. And slowly that's let them close the distance.

My heart's thumping as I make a sling with my hands, sending Selly scrambling up the cliff, then—after a brief debate—Keegan, who weighs less than me. The two of them grab my hands, razor-sharp rocks cutting at my clothes as I plant my foot on a tiny ledge and boost myself up to clamber over the edge and onto the rotting leaf litter waiting for me, the rich, earthy smells filling my nose.

I'm an aching, sweaty mess, but we have to be close. I can't think properly anymore of the thousands—tens of thousands—of people who don't even know they're relying on us to prevent this war.

All I can think about are the two with me, and what we need to do to get to that altar.

I have this wild fantasy that somehow they'll get away—that Laskia will spare them, or they'll be able to hide. That she'll stop searching after she finds me.

I want Keegan to go to the Bibliotek, to learn, to share that brain of his with the world.

And Selly . . . oh, Selly. I want her to captain a ship. I want her to solve the mystery of her strange new magician's marks, and to learn to love the spirits as I do. I want her to see the world. I want her to think of me, sometimes.

And if we get none of that, then a small, selfish part of me wants them to shoot me first so I don't have to watch her die.

I grab at a tree trunk to stop myself from sliding back down the slope. "Which way?" I gasp, looking at Keegan, though I don't know why. There's nothing in the journal that reports anyone ever having come here—only that my father wished he could.

But he answers me with absolute certainty. "The temple will be at the island's peak. The Mother couldn't be anywhere else."

I stifle a groan. The ground is so steep, I don't think I can stand, so I don't try. With a glance back over my shoulder at the trio behind us, I get to my hands and knees, and together the three of us crawl and scramble on through the jungle.

Vines grab at our arms and legs, and bugs bite every inch of exposed skin as we force our way through, sweat soaking our clothes.

I spent all those years holding my father's journal, keeping back from reading the last few pages, because I wanted there to be some part of him still left to discover. That's who I am— always keeping something in reserve.

After all, if I don't give everything, if I don't travel to the end of the road, if I don't try as hard as I can, I'll never have to know if I'm enough. Or if I'm not.

But if Keegan hadn't picked the journal up, we would have

missed this temple, this one last chance. And I swear I'll learn, even if it's the last thing I do. Even though it will be.

There's nothing left to hold back now. I'm all in.

And we climb, and we crawl, pulling each other up through the undergrowth and the mud, as we head for the top.

# JUDE

*The Isle of the Mother*
*The Isles of the Gods*

This is a nightmare.

What is she even going to do when we reach the temple? Have Dasriel shoot them, and then—my mind keeps conjuring up darker and more outrageous pictures, hysterical laughter threatening to burst out of me—then am I supposed to help lug Leander's body down this impossible hill, hoping I don't let go and send his corpse rolling all the way to the sea, ricocheting off trees until it hits the water?

I'm assuming the Mother will strike us down before any of that happens, if Dasriel murders someone on sacred ground. And on this, the strangest and most terrible day of my life, that doesn't seem like all-bad news.

Laskia's lost her mind, of that I'm sure. And yet somehow I'm scrambling through the undergrowth after her, on my way to help start a war. If I refuse, she'll shoot me and do it anyway, so I'm holding on as best I can, in the hope that . . . the truth is, I don't know what I'm hoping for.

Ahead of me, Dasriel grunts as the ground levels out a little. We're filthy, soaked in sweat, scratched by branches as we force our way past.

"Maybe they didn't climb up," I pant, barely able to hear myself over the hammering of my heart.

"They're climbing," Laskia snaps, ragged. "The temple will be at the top. Where else, for the Mother?"

"Laskia, I—"

"No!" she shrieks, whipping around to stare at me, wild-eyed. Her shirt is filthy, the top button torn off her waistcoat. "Not a word, Jude! I have come too far, I have done too much—we will *not* stop now. We will climb, and we will catch him, and we will kill him."

Dasriel says nothing, but he takes hold of a tree with one hand and offers her his other, pulling her up a steeper section. He leaves me to struggle after, and with lungs burning, I do.

There's something in the air here—maybe it's the presence of the gods, or it's just humidity and I'm a fool, I don't know, but it presses in on me, forcing my thoughts faster and faster, like water speeding up as it heads toward a waterfall, then plummets to the ground.

What was it my mother said?

*Everyone tells the same story different ways. And the only version we're the hero of is our own.*

I wish I knew how to find the start of my story, how to untangle all the threads. How to trace them back past Port

Naranda to Kirkpool, past the death of my father, past school, back to the beginning.

I wish I could try it all again. I'd do it differently.

But I've always let others hold the pen—I've let them shuffle my pages with barely a protest, cross out what mattered most, scrawl all over the things I wanted to say and do.

I've never written my own words, but instead let others choose the twists and turns of my story for me.

I've let everything happen *to* me, compromising over and over again, until I've found myself here, finally desperate to act but completely out of options.

Ahead, Dasriel finds a rocky ledge, almost like a pathway leading around the outside of the mountain.

When I step out onto it, there's a sheer drop to my right— a death sentence if I slip. Far below lies the jungle, the sea, this impossibly bright part of the world, so different from the sedate green fields and sandstone of Alinor, the busy streets of Port Naranda.

To my left is a stone wall, trickles of water running down its grooves, moss clinging to its weatherworn surface. The path itself curls up and around the mountain and toward the peak.

If Leander and the others haven't found this path, then we're moving faster than them now. We might make up enough time to catch them.

It's not long before my world narrows to the path ahead of me, my whole body singing with tension as I place each foot, ready to scramble if it slips. The wet stone is treacherous, and time loses all meaning as I take one step, then another, then another. I'm truly not sure if minutes pass, or hours.

I'm pulled from my reverie when the air around me changes,

and a hint of a breeze hits my sweat-soaked skin. Up ahead there's a noise of surprise from Dasriel and a shout of triumph from Laskia—then I'm around the bend, and abruptly at the end of our rocky ledge.

Ahead of me, the path opens up into a clear space among the trees, and there's nothing but blue sky above us.

We've reached the peak of the mountain.

There's no temple here, just a set of stone stairs leading underground, and as the three of us fan out, I catch a flash of movement—someone's hurrying down the stairs, about to disappear out of view.

Dasriel has seen it too, and my excuses won't hold him now—he lifts his gun, closing one eye and spreading his stance as he takes aim with a steady hand.

I'm frozen, desperately wanting to move but pinned in place, bile rising in my throat.

But I still have a few more pages of my story left to write, and *I'm* the one who'll choose what they say. Even if I'm writing my own ending.

I raise my voice as I hear the click of the safety coming off.

"Leander, look out!"

# SELLY

*The Temple of the Mother*
*The Isles of the Gods*

Stone explodes above my head, and for an instant I glimpse a staircase leading deeper underground—then Leander crashes into me from behind.

He grunts as we fall together in a tangle of limbs—the stone walls and steps whirl past, and I throw my arms out desperately to try and stop my fall, but I can't even tell which way is up. I curl my head in and pray, and then abruptly I'm crashing into the smooth stone floor at the base of the steps. Leander lands on top of me with a thump, driving the breath from my lungs.

For a moment there's nothing but silence, the sting of cuts and grazes, and the sharp pain that tells me I'll be covered in bruises tomorrow. If there is a tomorrow.

"The gun," Keegan gasps from somewhere behind me, and I realize both the boys fell together, and we're still lying where we landed, stunned. "Quick, keep moving."

Leander rolls off me and onto his back with a groan, and I

scramble to my feet, grabbing his hand and hauling him upright. Still too winded to speak properly, he waves a hand toward the passage that lies ahead, stumbling desperately toward it.

Somehow, impossibly—because we're unquestionably underground—there's *daylight* ahead, just around the bend.

I push my aching body to a run, feet shuffling along the gritty floor of the passageway as I hurry past him to scout, straining my ears for footsteps behind us. Then, as I swing around the corner, I gasp as the temple opens up ahead of me.

The Temple of the Mother is *nothing* like the temple of her daughter Barrica—it's on a completely different scale.

I'm standing at the edge of a huge, semicircular cavern hewn from the black rock of the island itself. It's open to the sea on one side, the great mouth of the cave facing out toward the lagoon, guarded from entry below by jagged stones covered in razor-sharp shells and barnacles.

The passageway has led us onto a balcony high above the floor of the temple—as high as the *Lizabetta*'s mast—and it runs the entire half circle around the edge of the open cavern.

Far below lies a wide altar, and standing around it, facing out toward the sea, a statue of the Mother, flanked by her children on either side, their arms outstretched to the world beyond the temple.

Despite the dark volcanic stone, the temple is filled with light and with life, the opening in the side of the cavern framing the myriad blues of the sea and the sky and all of the Mother's creation.

I stare down at the altar, alone with all of it for a moment. Goosebumps prickle my skin—this isn't just *a* temple of the Mother.

This is *the* Temple of the Mother.

Leander and Keegan come hurrying in behind me, and I'm jerked out of my reverie. I grab our prince by the arm, pushing him along the little balcony, keeping myself between him and our pursuers. Keegan catches my meaning immediately, falling into place beside me.

Laskia and the others have to be close behind, but Jude has bought us a moment's reprieve, and if we can buy ourselves enough time to make the sacrifice . . .

Leander's voice distracts me from my thoughts, but he's speaking so softly I can't hear him over our footsteps.

"Leander, what is it?"

He stops short and turns to face me. "There's no way down," he says, breathing the words more than speaking them.

"What?"

*"There's no way down,"* he repeats, and as I swing around to run my gaze over the length of the balcony, my mouth goes dry, my gut dropping with a dizzying wave of horror.

He's right.

There are no stairs leading to the altar below. No ramp, not even a column we can shinny down. Just clear air.

"There must be something," I hear myself say, even as my eyes tell me there isn't. My voice rises, turning shrill. "How can there not be a way down?"

"Because nobody's meant to come here," my prince whispers, slowly shaking his head, as though he can deny his own words.

"Leander," Keegan murmurs beside me. "Watch out."

The huge man with magician's marks—the one who threw

fire at us back at the inn—is making his way through the archway and onto the balcony. He wears an expression like thunder, and holds the gun ready.

I lift one hand, as if that can fend him off—there's my arm, covered in the strange, geometric shapes my magician's marks have become. Did I really search for my magic all my life, only to die now, just as I'm on the verge of discovering why it's so different, what it means?

There's nothing I can do but stare at the huge man as he slowly lifts his gun and takes aim.

Was this how my crew felt, back on the *Lizabetta*?

There are no moves left to make, no cards left to play. I can't take my eyes off the barrel of the gun, but I don't want it to be the last thing I ever see, the last thought I have.

I wish I were out on the ocean instead.

I wish I were standing on the deck of a ship as she surged along atop the waves. I wish I could feel the air spirits playing with my hair, feel Leander at my back, helping me brace the wheel on a sunny day. I wish I could taste the salt on the breeze.

I see the tiniest of shifts as the man's finger begins to tighten on the trigger, and I wrench my gaze from the barrel so I don't have to look. I open my mouth, wish I had an instant to speak, to say something to Leander, to Keegan—

—and then the gun explodes with a muffled *bang*, and the man screams, falling to his knees as he clutches the ruins of his hand.

We're frozen in place, staring—but we're still alive. I take half a step forward, then stop myself, light-headed.

"What was . . . ?" I whisper, over the big man's gasping—he moans on each exhalation, curling over on himself as the color drains from his face.

"The Mother," Leander says softly. "She won't allow it. Not here."

I'm still staring at the magician hunched on the floor when Laskia appears in the passageway behind him. Jude's beside her—he has a bloodied nose now, and one eye swollen shut, panic all over his face.

He lifts a hand as Laskia stalks forward—she passes the kneeling magician without a downward glance—but there's nothing he can do to stop her as she draws a knife from her belt.

"Keegan," Leander murmurs from his place behind me, his voice distant. There's a strange, slow quality to it, as if he's thinking about something else. "You're sure I can make the sacrifice here?"

"As sure as I can be," Keegan replies, watching Laskia advance slowly, adjusting her grip on the hilt of the knife. "All the gods are present at the temple of their mother."

"Then I suppose this is where the faith comes in," Leander says softly.

Laskia stops just out of my reach, sizing me up—her gaze is wild now, eyes too wide, lips parted. Her perfectly tailored suit is filthy, her skin stained with dirt and sweat.

"Leander, cut your hand again." I don't dare take my eyes off Laskia. I won't be able to buy him more than a few moments. "If you can sort of *flick* the blood . . ." But I trail off before I finish. I can hear how it sounds.

"This is the Temple of the Mother," Leander says quietly,

echoing my thoughts. "Something far greater is called for here. No more holding back."

Laskia tilts her head—even through her madness, it's clear she heard the same strange note in his voice as I did.

"Leander?" I ask warily, not daring to turn my head, not daring to take my eyes off her.

"Give him to me," Laskia spits, losing patience.

Leander's hand closes on my shoulder and squeezes gently.

"You've both sacrificed so much to bring me here," he says, quiet and calm. There's a serenity in his voice I've never heard before, and it sets the hair on the back of my neck prickling. "I'm so sorry. You've given *so* much. Too much. Now it's my turn." And then, after a beat: "I wish we'd had more time, Selly. I wanted to teach you to dance."

"What?" Cold fingers wind their way around my heart, and I lift my hand to place it over his on my shoulder, weaving our fingers together. "Leander, what are you talking about?"

"Barrica," he calls, his voice rising, gaining certainty with every word. "I place my faith in you. I make my sacrifice to you. Grow strong, and stand strong in your role as Sentinel. Keep Macean bound in sleep, and let my people—let all our people—live in peace."

Keegan gives a strangled cry beside me, and as Leander pulls his hand from mine, I whirl around in time to see him rest it on the edge of the balcony.

In one quick movement he vaults up onto the railing, standing there, spreading his arms wide in supplication.

He's frozen in place for less than a heartbeat, but I lunge for him, already in motion before I have time to think.

My fingertips brush his leg, and I grab at thin air as Leander throws himself out into the empty space beyond the balcony.

My scream is ripped from somewhere inside my chest, and Keegan grabs for me, wrapping his arms around me in a bear hug as I scramble after Leander. I fight to throw him off as the moment between one heartbeat and the next stretches into forever.

But I know, even as my vision blurs, even before my scream has begun to echo, that it's too late, and instead I whirl around to bury my face in Keegan's chest.

I can't bear to watch Leander die.

# LASKIA

◆

*The Temple of the Mother*
*The Isles of the Gods*

 ime stands still.
 Between one heartbeat and the next, I see everything I
have done—every time I've proved myself, and Ruby changed
the rules. Every time I confided my fears, and Sister Beris nodded, and pretended to care.

I hear the whispers all over again, see the sidelong glances,
and rage washes through me, twists inside me like a fire taking hold.

I have come too far, done too much, to surrender now.

I will show them what I am worth.

I will show them I *do not lose.*

I drop my knife, scrambling up onto the balcony railing,
spreading my arms wide, just as the prince did. I teeter on the
edge as I instinctively try to steady myself—and then I remember, and I am utterly free.

Macean is the god of risk, and with my faith—with this

gamble of my life itself—I will fill him to the brim with power, and I will set him free.

He and I, we will set *each other* free. We have both been kept from all we deserve for far too long, he bound by Barrica and I by Ruby, by Beris.

He will see me, and know me, and reward me.

*He* will not let me down.

"Macean!" I scream, and everything is in my voice—my rage, my devotion, my conviction. "For you!"

In a single movement, I throw myself out toward the altar.

And I hear the waves beyond the temple's mouth, just for a moment, as I fall.

They're beautiful.

# SELLY

*The Temple of the Mother*
*The Isles of the Gods*

"Leander," I whisper, swaying on my feet. I can't make myself look at the altar—I don't want to see him lying there beside Laskia, both of them broken and bloodied. I'm outside myself, disconnected from my own body. I can't remember how to breathe, how to *think*.

But I can't leave him. I can't let him go.

"Keegan, we have to—"

He rests his hand on my shoulder, where Leander's was just a minute ago. I want to shake him off—I want to cling to him. "Selly, it's done."

"No, there must be something . . ."

I can see the air spirits whirling madly around the room, lifting up the sand and the dust and the dirt into wild eddies, as if they're picking up on my anger, my bewilderment.

But this was what we meant to do.

We knew Laskia would catch us, knew we would die when

she did. We only hoped to make the sacrifice first. To keep the gods from joining the war that was coming.

But now Leander's gone, and I'm realizing I never imagined I'd still be here, and he wouldn't. That there would be a moment *after* his death, and another, and I'd be supposed to survive all of them without him. Shakes run through my body. I'm cold, despite the warm air.

There are too many things I didn't say to him.

He wanted to teach me to dance.

It's as if that one thought unleashes a storm of memories—Leander letting me tuck a flower behind his ear the day we met, with that amused smile of his.

Leander marveling at the water spirits around the bow of the *Lizabetta* as they caught the rainbow spray and danced for him.

Leander with his jaw clenched, spent after urging our ship on for hours, giving of *himself* to pull Keegan along in our wake and save his life.

Leander at the market, posing in a newsie's cap to make me smile. Leander at the nightclub, desperately trying to leave behind the fear and guilt nobody imagined he carried. Leander asking to kiss me.

He shouldn't have died before the world really knew who he was.

"Barrica," I whisper, my fingers digging into the rock of the balcony railing, the pain an anchor.

I don't even know what my prayer will be, what I mean by it, but I throw my words out into the temple itself with everything I have. With a kind of surrender I've never known.

"Barrica, please, *please,* don't take him. It's too much. We need him." And then, my eyes shut tight, tearing down every wall I've ever built, leaving behind every time I've ever tried to prove I need nobody but myself: "*I* need him. . . ."

My prayer falls into absolute silence, broken only by my own ragged breath.

And then it's as if the temple itself responds, the air throbbing around me. Keegan gasps beside me, and I feel it too—it's like fire is crackling over my skin, the pressure around me setting my head pounding like the moment before a storm.

Though it's unspoken, I have the strongest sense of a question pushing at my mind, and I do my best to answer it.

"Please," I whisper again, opening up my thoughts and offering them to my goddess—opening up my heart, and for the first time I can remember, offering what's there without trying to protect it. "Please. I need him."

And then the feeling is gone, and there's nothing, just the waves outside, and the soft moans of Laskia's giant magician with the ruined hand. I'd forgotten he was there.

The loss of that overwhelming feeling is like having my legs knocked from under me, like losing something I loved without warning, and my knees shake—I think I cry out, but I can't tell if the noise comes from me.

And in the next instant, the temple is suddenly washed with a brilliant white light, blinding even when I close my eyes. Throwing up my forearm, I shrink in against Keegan as I turn away from it, and his body trembles against mine.

It's like being inside the sun, like the temple itself is aflame, and all I can think of is the need to protect my eyes, to try desperately to blink away the shapes branded on the insides of my eyelids.

Keegan makes a wordless sound, and when I lower my arm, the light is beginning to fade.

The first thing I see is Jude, standing farther along the balcony—our gazes lock, but his is impossible to read through the swelling and bruising blossoming all over his face.

And then he looks away, out toward the center of the cavern. To where Leander and Laskia fell.

Slowly, dreading what I'll see, I turn.

At the center of the fading light is a brilliantly glowing figure—it's rising up, its arms outstretched, the air shimmering around it.

My mind reaches wildly for the possibilities—is this the Mother, awakened somehow by the sacrifices? Is Barrica herself returning to take up arms?

But then the figure tilts its head a fraction, and the gesture is so achingly familiar that my heart stops.

It's Leander.

And he's *incandescent*.

He's suspended above the altar, held aloft by an army of air spirits. He throws his arms out wide, his head back, and he screams, and screams again, the raw sounds punctuated by soft, heartbreaking gasps.

"Leander!" I shout, finally wrestling free of Keegan's grasp. "Leander, here!"

His head turns, as if he hears me, and my heart leaps. Then a fierce wind whips up around us, stealing my voice away, ripping my words from my mouth and drowning them out.

That strange, dreadful pressure returns with the storm, my head throbbing in time with my heart. Voices whisper at the edge of my hearing. I can't think, can't focus. I only know one thing—one instinct drives me forward.

*I will not lose him.*

"Leander!" I scream again, holding out my hands to him. "Over here! Don't you dare leave me!"

Slowly, writhing in pain, he turns his head, lifts one hand in my direction.

I reach for him over the edge of the balcony, stretching out with every fiber, but he's too far away—I'm shaking with the effort, my body trembling, and still I can't get to him. He's suspended just out of reach, his back arching and his fingers curling as they grasp at nothing, his cries turning hoarse and jagged.

Then Keegan's hands are at my waist—he steadies me, grips me tightly, and with a grunt of effort, he lifts me, straining as he helps tip me just a *little* farther.

Leander's fingertips brush against mine, the lightest of contacts, and a bolt of pain shoots through me, every muscle contracting, every nerve on fire. With a shout, Keegan falls away from me as if he's been pushed.

All my instincts shriek at me to pull back from Leander, but as the fire threatens to consume me, I grab for his wrist.

*I will not lose him.*

I hold tight, pulling him closer as whatever raw magic is running through him begins to flow into me. Like lightning that needs to ground itself, the energy within him needs a way to escape, somewhere to go before it burns him up entirely.

And that somewhere is *me.*

*I will not let him go.*

We slam together, and his arms are around me, and beyond the discordant undertones of his unearthly screams, I can hear *him,* the boy I know, the boy who's laughed and teased and shown me his fears in the dark of the night.

He's still Leander, and I can't bear his pain.

My instincts drive me, and without thinking, I pull his head down, pressing my lips to his. I kiss him with all the desperation, all the fear in me, and with all the love as well. It's a plea, and an offering, and a surrender.

The world turns white around me, and I know nothing but pain. I can't feel the ground beneath my feet, can't see anything but brightness, can't hear anything but my own heart pounding—and a second *thump-thump* that runs right through me, which I know is Leander's heartbeat matching mine.

I cannot—I will not—let him go, and I hold fast as the raw power within him, the gift of the goddess herself, travels through me and out into the stone of the temple once more.

And then, in an instant, it's over.

The storm has passed, though the air is still heavy, pressing down on me like a weight. I pull back from the kiss, my arms still wrapped around the boy before me, panting for breath as though I've been running. My body aches, my very bones feel bruised, and I'm swaying on my feet—but I've practiced for that on stormy decks all my life, and I hold fast.

Leander's eyes are no longer brown—they're pure green, not a hint of white showing. They're glowing with magic, and tiny bolts of it leap between us, like sparks before a storm. And then I catch sight of my arms and the backs of my hands.

My new magician's marks—the ones he said he'd never

seen before—are glowing too, pulsing softly in time with my heartbeat.

*Were they made for this moment?*

"Leander?" I croak, but he doesn't reply. With his emerald-green eyes, I can't even tell if he's looking at me. If he can hear me at all. "Leander, are you there?"

"He's—" It's Keegan, barely whispering. "Selly, I think he's . . ."

"He's what? Quick, Keegan!"

"I think he's a Messenger," he manages. "Like King Anselm, the first king who sacrificed himself. Those stories about him becoming a warrior for the goddess, I think he's . . ."

He trails off, and when I glance back at him, he's looking down at the altar. At the girl, who lies there, perfectly still. Barrica reached out to touch Leander, but Macean didn't awaken for Laskia. And perhaps someone else would feel sorry for her, but with the trail of death she left—the progress fleet, the *Lizabetta,* Leander's friends and mine—I don't.

Keegan lifts his head, his gaze snapping across to me once more. "We should go. We should leave this place."

Leander doesn't seem to hear our conversation. He keeps one of my hands twined in his and turns away, as if he's going to walk all the way along the balcony to the end, near where the temple opens up to the perfectly flat lagoon—to the Still Waters.

I let him lead me, waiting to see what he'll do, and though he gives no sign of a command, or even of seeing his surroundings, the black stone around us starts to twist and melt.

I catch my breath as it forms into a set of rough stairs

leading down from where we stand to the altar where Laskia lies, and past her, along a smooth path and out toward the sea.

Without looking back at me again, Leander descends, still leading me by the hand, and he begins to half walk, half stumble along that path, moving toward the water.

When he reaches the edge of the sea, its surface smooth as glass, he simply steps out onto it, and it holds his weight like it's made of stone. I can hear Keegan hurrying after us, but he isn't the one who calls out as I'm about to follow Leander onto the surface of the Still Waters.

"Leander!"

Jude stands helplessly on the balcony, staring down at us.

I pause, and Leander stops with me, making a soft noise of pain, his grip on my hand tightening as he bows his head.

I hesitate, looking up at the boy on the balcony covered in blood and bruises. He's supposed to be our enemy. But he was Leander's friend—Leander wanted to help him back in Port Naranda. And Jude offered us something in return. He called out a warning, saved Leander from a bullet to the back.

"Jude, come with us," I call. "Quick."

His face is an agony of indecision. But just as it seems he might move, the big magician rises to his feet, cradling his bloodied hand, and shakes his head.

Jude's expression closes over, and he steps back into the shadows.

I gaze up at the empty balcony, willing him to come back, but he stays half-hidden. After a long moment I turn away to follow Leander out over the water, along the impossible path he's created.

He leads me straight out onto the surface of the Still Waters, and it's like I'm walking on glass—when I look down, I can see fish darting beneath my feet, but the water itself has no give at all. The islands form a ring before us, joined together by the reef to make a crown of jungled jewels. Behind me, Keegan whispers something to himself, and though I can't make out the words, there's awe in his tone.

Leander stumbles, and I keep hold of his hand, help him steady himself. My heart squeezes in my chest, and I twine my fingers through his.

I don't know what he's become, or where he's leading us, but I know I'll follow him.

*I will not lose him.*

*I will not let him go.*

# JUDE

*The Temple of the Mother*
*The Isles of the Gods*

I could still run after them. They'd hear me, if I called out.

But Dasriel's watching me, cradling his ruined hand, his breath rasping with pain.

And Laskia lies below us on the altar, finally still, her head turned to one side, her limbs splayed out carelessly.

Someone has to bring her home. *I* have to bring her home. Not because she's earned that sort of kindness or deserves some special dignity. She gave up the right to that long ago.

No. It's because my mother's still in Port Naranda, and if Dasriel brings her body home alone, my mother will never see another doctor, will never know what became of me. Will never know why I let her die alone.

More likely than not, Ruby will have me killed anyway, but there's at least a chance she'll let me leave. Let me disappear with Mum, if I do this one thing for Laskia.

So I will. I can't possibly go with Leander—not after everything I've done. I can never join with the three of them, because I can never be like them. Never again.

"Are you just going to stand there?" Dasriel finally manages. His hand—or what's left of it—has soaked blood through his shirt, and I think he's yanked his belt around his wrist to stop the bleeding. "Or are you planning on hauling her up here anytime soon?"

I make my way around the edge of the balcony and tentatively set one foot on the stone steps Leander—or whatever he became—left behind. Nothing happens, so I risk another step.

Slowly, heavily, I make my way down the stairs until I reach the bottom. Laskia's not bloodied, not as broken as she could have been. If anything, she looks like she's sleeping. I desperately don't want to touch her, let alone try to lift her.

But this is the road I've made for myself, and now I have to walk it.

I take a step forward.

A shift in the light makes me stop, wondering if what I see is just the sun coming out from behind the clouds outside. Some change in the light. Some . . . something.

But Dasriel curses softly on the balcony above me, and I know he can see it too.

Faintly at first, but more brightly every second, Laskia is starting to glow with a soft, white, pulsing light, just like Leander did.

And then, as I stand frozen in place at the bottom of the stairs, she begins to move. This is nothing like Leander's smooth, graceful rise—she's slow and jerky, like a puppet with too many people trying to yank at its strings, and she's making a *noise,* a moan that's ripped from her throat.

She pushes herself up to her knees, swaying, her head bowed.

Then she turns her gaze toward me, and her eyes are pure, glowing green.

# SELLY

*The* Emma
*Kirkpool, Alinor*

I can see the way the spirits swarm around Leander, fighting to be near him.

He's been touched by a goddess, and though he's slowly been coming back to himself aboard the *Emma,* the boy who stands beside me at the wheel now isn't the one I knew before.

His eyes have returned to normal—though they've shifted from brown to emerald green—but he winces away from the light, shudders at the slightest sound, the slightest movement. He's been rubbed raw, and every part of the world hurts him. Sometimes he barely seems to know where he is, or that I'm there at all. Unless I try to leave his side—then he grabs for my hand, stumbles after me, as though the distance between us causes him pain as well.

On the *Little Lizabetta,* on our way into Port Naranda, Keegan told me about Messengers. He told me they tend to disappear from the history books shortly after they arrive—that the here-and-gone-again of them is why most people doubt they existed. But now I think I can see what happens, and I refuse to let it happen to my prince.

Wherever I am, Leander is too now—even if he gazes straight through me half the time. The quick, easy smile that made me feel like I was standing in the sun has gone, but some part of him still seems to know me. He's calmer when he holds my hand, and I can sense the energy humming between us. It's not just magic. It's more.

I'm anchoring him in place, and both of us can feel it.

He hasn't eaten in the days since we boarded our little fishing boat. He hasn't slept either. I don't think he needs to anymore.

Keegan and I worked together as best we could to turn the *Emma* toward Alinor and set her course, but the wind and water spirits have carried us along so effortlessly that, in truth, we've barely needed to do more than trim our sails.

Mostly we stay on deck together, me at the wheel, Keegan nearby, and Leander always at my side. He doesn't even leave me when I sleep. He just lies there with me, crammed into the narrow bunk, his body curled around mine.

Sometimes I wake from strange, disjointed dreams, sure we spoke, but unable to remember our conversations. Other times I have nightmares, and see snatches of what torments him, though they're gone as soon as I open my eyes, drifting away like dust.

I want so badly to hear his voice. I want him to blink awake, to suddenly look across at me and laugh, himself again.

But though each day he seems a little more aware of his surroundings, and though he rarely lets go of my hand, the person I want to comfort me most in all the world simply isn't there.

We're a league from the harbor entrance at Kirkpool when we spot the flotilla on the horizon. The decks are crowded with bodies. Flags flutter from every mast.

A shiver of fear runs through me, but Keegan pulls the eyeglass from the bag beside the wheel, steadying himself effortlessly as he lifts it. He gazes through it, then wordlessly hands it across to me, his expression pensive.

This isn't an army coming to greet us. Every ship is packed with figures waving, many of them climbing up their masts to see us better. Every ship has an Alinorish flag hoisted high.

"Are they all for us?" I ask, my gut tightening with nerves.

"They seem to have known we were coming," Keegan replies, thoughtful. "Barrica is stronger than she has been in centuries. Perhaps she spoke to them, as she used to before the war, or sent them a sign."

"You think they know he's . . ." I can barely say it, glancing across to where Leander stands beside me, his eyes closed, his face turned into the wind.

*A Messenger.*

But he's more than that to me. More than the prince of Alinor. More than a Messenger of a goddess, a boy who survived death.

More than any of that, he's still just Leander.

I hope.

# LASKIA

*The* Mermaid
*The Crescent Sea*

I can feel Macean as he stirs in his slumber.

It's like a roll of thunder on the horizon, and the very fact that I can sense the storm so far away is a warning as to just how loud it will be when he finally turns his full attention my way.

For now, he knows I am here. Even in the deepest of sleeps, he felt my faith, he sensed my offering. It was enough to draw him back toward me, to empower him to reach out his hand toward me.

No other believed as I did, offered what I was willing to offer, and now I have my reward.

He is awakening, and together we will rise.

The green sisters will serve us—they will *worship* us.

Ruby will see me now, in all my glory.

But my body is burning from the inside out, and I cannot imagine how its fuel will last long enough for all I wish to do.

My muscles scream with every movement, but as tears roll down my cheeks, and my hands curl into claws, I make myself stand fast.

I need what he has—what the prince took from that girl. I need someone to ground me, someone into whom I can pour a part of this force that threatens to overwhelm me. I must find someone, and soon.

At the edges of my vision, the sailors around me scurry across the deck like ants, keeping as far from me as they can.

They are afraid.

They should be.

# ACKNOWLEDGMENTS

The sea is in my blood. Like Selly, my first steps were on a boat, steadier on the swaying deck than on land. I took my own daughter down to the sea when she was just two weeks old, to dab a little salt water on her. I'm glad that in writing this book I had the chance to take you—my reader—down to the sea as well.

My father taught me to sail. My mother strapped life jackets on me and set me free to fall in and fish myself out more times than any of us could count. My sister Flic was fearless, and made me want to be too. To all those I've sailed with, thank you. Being on the water made me who I am, and still does that today.

Back in 2013, Marie Lu read the first chapter of this book, and has asked every year since when the rest was coming. She believed it into existence. Meg Spooner has been my unfailing support, always there when I needed her most, to help or to cheer. Many friends improved these pages: thank you to C.S., Ellie, Lili, Alex, Nicole, Sooz, Liz, and Kate.

With Kate J. Armstrong, I host the podcast *Pub Dates,* which offers listeners a backstage pass to how books are made— including this one. If you've enjoyed reading *The Isles of the Gods,* take a listen! And if you'd like to stay up to date on what

I'm writing and my latest releases, you can sign up for my newsletter through my website.

But now, reader, a glimpse of how many people it takes to make a book—so many more than you think. I've always thought books should have rolling credits at the end, like movies. Let's give it a try.

I am deeply grateful for Melanie Nolan's editorial eye, her support, and her guidance. Thank you to all my editorial team: Gianna, Dana, and Rebecca.

A huge thank-you to my campaign team: Jules, Elizabeth, Erica, and Josh. Thank you to John, Dominique, and Adrienne.

To the bookmaking team—Alison, Artie, Tamar, Amy, Renée, Jake, Tim, Natalia, Ken, and Angela—thank you. Thanks as well to the publishing team: Gillian, Judith, Erica, Kortney, Joe, and Barbara Marcus. To the many, many folks in sales—too many to name—I'm so grateful for your work in getting my books into the hands of readers. To the Listening Library crew, including the legendary Nick—thank you for bringing my books to life! Thank you to Aykut Aydoğdu for the cover artwork of my dreams.

Internationally, my thanks to Team Allen & Unwin in Australia: Anna, Arundhati, Ginny, Nicola, Eva, Sandra, Simon, Deborah, Matt, Natalie, Alison, Kylie, Liz, and Sheralyn. In the UK, thank you to Team Rock the Boat: Katie, Shadi, Juliet, Kate, Lucy, Mark, Paul, Laura, Deontaye, Ben, and Hayley. Thank you as well to the scouts, agents, publishers, and translators who are bringing *Isles* to life around the world.

I am so grateful to the authors who took the time to read this book ahead of publication and offer blurbs and support: Stephanie Garber, Garth Nix, Brigid Kemmerer, Alexandra Bracken, C. S. Pacat, Kendare Blake, Lynette Noni, and Marie Lu.

I am endlessly grateful to my agent, Tracey Adams, for her patience, good humor, wisdom, and friendship, and to all the team at Adams Literary—Josh, Anna, and Stephen.

To my dad and my uncle Graeme, who answered my obscure sailing questions with patience, thank you! I also drew inspiration from the incredible photographs of Alan Villiers. And as always, I have been guided by a series of readers who offered me insight on experiences not my own—I'm grateful for your time and care.

My friends kept me afloat through the writing of this book, much of which took place during months of lockdown. I spoke every day to my wise council: Eliza, Ellie, Kate, Lili, Liz, Nicole, Pete, and Skye. Selly says to Leander that she'll get him to the Isles if she has to sail him there herself. Some days, they sailed me there themselves.

My love as well to my Roti crew—especially Emma, who made her way into this story to offer safe passage when needed most, and whom we miss every day. Allow me to add a few more names—I always think one should err on the side of saying thank you. So, to those I haven't mentioned yet, my love and my thanks: Kacey, Soraya, Nic, Leigh, Maz, Steve, Kiersten, Michelle, Cat, Jay, Johnathan, Jack, Matt, Kat, and Gaz.

To the booksellers, librarians, reviewers, teachers, and readers who share my books—I'm so grateful for your support.

And finally, my family. My sweet Jack was nestled by my feet as I wrote. My husband, Brendan, is my rock, the place I always return to after exploring other worlds. I love you. Our daughter is the light of our lives—Pip, you are the best part of every day. You've grown up alongside this story, and I can't wait for all our adventures to come.